THE AVIATOR

Gareth Renowden

The Burning World
Book One

Published by Limestone Hills Publishing,
RD2 Amberley 7482
New Zealand
limestonehills.co.nz
info@limestonehills.co.nz

This paperback edition ISBN 978-0-9876697-3-5

National Library of New Zealand Cataloguing-in-Publication Data

Renowden, Gareth.
The Aviator / Gareth Renowden.
(Burning world ; 1)
ISBN 978-0-9876697-3-5 (pbk.)
ISBN 978-0-9876697-0-4 (Kindle)
ISBN 978-0-9876697-1-1 (Smashwords ebook)
ISBN 978-0-9876697-2-8 (epub)
I. Title. II. Series: Renowden, Gareth. Burning world ; 1.
NZ823.3—dc 23

Gareth Renowden is an award-winning writer based in New Zealand. His work has appeared in magazines and newspapers in Britain, New Zealand and the USA. Follow developments in the Burning World at http://burningworldbooks.wordpress.com and on Facebook at https://www.facebook.com/burningworldbookone. Gareth's personal blog can be found at http://limestonehills.co.nz/blog and his climate change blog, *Hot Topic*, at http://hot-topic.co.nz.

Also by Gareth Renowden
Video - The Inside Story (1982)
The Olive Book (1999)
The Truffle Book (2005)
Hot Topic - Global Warming and the Future of New Zealand (2007)

Playlists of the music explicitly mentioned in *The Aviator*, and some (but not all) titles hidden in description are available on Spotify and Youtube.
Cover and airship glyph by Dylan Horrocks.

For Camille

"I wasn't trying to predict the future. I was trying to prevent it."
Ray Bradbury on writing *Fahrenheit 451*

INTRODUCTION

They call me Lemmy. My father gave me the name. He thought Lemuel would sound distinguished, laden with allusions to classical literature. Not in my world it isn't. Everyone assumes I'm named after a musician in an ancient heavy metal band.

Tonight the blimp is creaking quietly over my head. It's tethered to the last patch of high ground on Aitutaki, a coral atoll in the Cook Islands. The inhabitants were shipped off to Rarotonga years ago, but there's one old man who refuses to leave. He's playing a battered ukelele on the porch of his weatherbeaten house, singing something I don't recognise. We had fish for dinner. We always have fish for dinner. The reef is long gone under the waves, but there are still a few fish and only one fisherman.

I'm the Admiral's only visitor. I try to visit him when I'm crossing the Pacific, bring him a few cigarettes, a bottle of whisky and some tins of vegetables. He likes tinned peaches, but they're hard to come by. I can't call in very often, but I'm always welcome.

The last flight was the worst yet. I need some rest. Nobody knows I'm here. This is my escape from the world. I can stay as long as I want – the Admiral doesn't mind, so I'll stay here a while and write.

I was born in California before the great state fell into the sea. My childhood was littered with iPods and computers and I watched the launch of the first space tourism business on television, an albatross of a plane lumbering into the air as if its wings should flap, then a firework-burst of rocket and a climb to the edge of space, the great ark of the planet spread out below in a blue haze with towering clouds punching upwards, a world of weather in one man's eye. In fact there were several sets of eyes, hi-def cameras and a live webcast, with a whiskery British entrepreneur looking smug in zero G until he threw up. After that I only wanted one thing – to sit at the controls of a plane on its way to space. I dreamed of voyages to the moon and Mars as America's dreams of space conquest were scuppered by economics and hurricanes.

So I did what I had to do. I spent hours flying simulators on my PC and pestered my parents to buy me flying lessons, as soon as I was old enough to see out the cockpit of a Cessna. I took my pilots exam before my driving test. At university I studied aeronautics, and my first job was flying the blimp. As stepping stones to the stars go, it was no giant leap, but it was new, hi-tech and the way the industry seemed to be moving. I joined a team of five pilots employed by a clean energy billionaire to fly him luxuriously around the world at zero carbon cost, in touch with his business empire. It was my first and last job.

I call my airship a blimp, but its proper name is *Thunderbird*. Jenny the autopilot (a generation four limited purpose artificial intelligence suite) doesn't like her body's nickname. She likes accuracy in all things. It was one of five the boss ordered from Boeing, executive versions of a military design. It's a hybrid airship with active buoyancy systems and stubby wings, which generate enough lift in forward flight to let us carry a few tonnes of cargo. The entire upper surface is covered in solar cells, feeding into a high-capacity, lightweight battery bank. We can do 200 kph with luck and following wind, and cruise pretty much indefinitely on solar power. The cryo-electric turbofans are very quiet and efficient.

The whole surface of the blimp is covered in active stealth materials. The boss used to use the underside for advertising, but it can do a very good impression of sky when needed. In power-gathering mode, the top surface is deep black, but can also do camouflage. Jenny likes to play with our appearance. She's into Mondrian at the moment. Aitutaki hasn't seen anything this colourful in years.

I'm linked to Jenny and the ship by an earpiece and a discrete little control ring I wear on the third finger of my right hand. It's keyed to my DNA, monitors my bio functions and gives me short range communications with her. Anyone who wants to steal the blimp has to steal me and keep me alive. All the other blimp pilots had similar rings, but the boss had a master control. He called it the one ring, the ring to rule them all.

Lemmy is drinking whisky with the Admiral, watching the sunset. All his systems are nominal, operating at or within design parameters, although his blood pressure is a bit on the high side: it usually is. My batteries are at full charge. Sensors show nothing much on sea or in the air for 200 km around. Satellite coverage is variable, comms limited. Nobody to talk to, very little to do. I prefer to be travelling, visiting people and places. But we've done rather a lot of that recently.

CHAPTER ONE

My employer – Ewan Croft – made several fortunes in hi-tech businesses, but most of his money came from a series of astute investments in clean energy. By the time I started working for him, rapid climate change was obvious, and hurting. Low-carbon energy sources of all kinds were in huge demand and Croft made billions. It wasn't genius, but it wasn't all luck. He'd been convinced that climate was going to be a problem long before most, and structured his businesses, and life, accordingly.

His private fleet of airships were his global taxis. We ferried him from meeting to factory to offices to home, in luxury and at a leisurely pace. Crossing the Pacific could take up to a week, island hopping, but Croft didn't mind. Travelling was his down time, though the comms we packed allowed him to conduct full virtual meetings anywhere, anytime. He didn't like the virtual stuff. *Can't trust their faces, can't look into their eyes*, he used to say. *Give me meetings in the meat zone.* So we did.

Croft believed the world was heading for a collapse. He didn't talk about it often, but he didn't think his billions would help him much when it arrived. He planned to be entirely self-sufficient, independent of the global economy, able to ride out the worst that a combination of climate change and international instability could throw at him. He built four homes around the world – he called them his retreats – in places where he thought he had the best chance of an easy life. They were remote. His airships were the best, and in some cases, the only way to get to them.

Apart from the blimp assigned to his headquarters in Silicon Valley, the others were based in these retreats. My beat was Australia, New Zealand and Southeast Asia, based out of D'Urville Island at the top end of New Zealand's South Island. It was supposed to be one of the slowest warming places on the planet. Another retreat was in the islands to the far north of Canada, which Croft reckoned would be habitable long after the rest of the planet had turned into desert. He wasn't the only one up there – whole communities were being established. Half the year in darkness was a price some expected to have to pay for survival.

The other two bolt holes were in southern Chile and western Scotland. I didn't visit either while the boss was around, but the Scottish home, out in the Atlantic on one of the islands of the St Kilda group, was supposed to be the most impressive. *An eagle's nest perched on top of huge sea cliffs* was how the pilot based there described it, but it was a flier's nightmare. Atlantic gales battered the place in all seasons, and updraughts, downdraughts and eddies made controlling a large airship difficult. You could spend days waiting for a chance to get in or out.

I like D'Urville. The retreat is a low, sprawling house at the head of a sheltered harbour on the western side of the island. Rooms are dug back into the hillside, solar panels provide power, and there's a catamaran moored below. My apartment isn't large, and the only view is of *Thunderbird* in her low hanger, but I had the full use of all the facilities when Croft wasn't there, and that was most of the time. My main housekeeping duty was to maintain the garden. This had been designed to keep the boss and his family in fruit and vegetables, but there was no need to produce much unless or until he took up permanent residence. I pruned fruit trees, pressed some olive oil, and kept the grape vines in check. Bots did most of the work under the house AI's control.

A dirt road runs along the ridge behind the house, and a short track off it leads down towards the house. There's a substantial gate and high fences, but they're more or less superfluous. Croft bought all the land at this end of the island, and the road goes nowhere, petering out into regenerating bush to the north. It takes most of a day in a four-wheel-drive to reach the nearest settlement. We have no neighbours, and our only visitors are occasional boats cruising out of Nelson, to the south.

The boat is a luxury catamaran, rigged so it can be sailed by one person. When he brought his wife and kids out on holiday, the boss would spend days cruising around the island fishing, swimming and lazing in the sun. If I took it out, it was only for the fishing. And diving for the lobsters the locals call crayfish. Catching those things became my party trick, and I was expected to serve up a feast every time Croft was in residence.

I spent half my time flying. A typical journey would be out to one of the islands in the South Pacific, to meet the boss arriving from California. Then on to Australia, China, Indonesia – wherever business beckoned. Sometimes I'd fly west into central Asia or India to hand the boss on to the blimp based in Scotland, or we'd return to D'Urville for a few days, and then back out into the Pacific. I went back to California no more than a couple of times a year, to take some leave with my family, but to be honest – the only thing I missed were the girls. I was like a sailor back from a voyage, cash in my pocket and spoiled for choice. And then it would be back into the air, and back to my solitude.

Solitude. Bloody cheek. I keep him company. I watch his every move, keep him safe, provide all his entertainment. He thinks he flies this craft, but he has no idea of the complexity I command. My instructions move the control surfaces, my sensors monitor the world outside. I am his interface to everything. Without me, he has only his meatware body and a stunted biological brain. I am his confidant and confessor. I do his bidding and I am his, but he is mine and without me he is nothing.

Every word he enters on the pad down there on the Admiral's veranda is backed up in my memory. I will proofread. I will help him to edit his words. I am his amanuensis. I've read every important book written in the last five hundred years and know a thing or two about style. I'll provide dates and times and images of key events, recordings of what was said and done. I'll keep him honest.

The collapse, when it came, was swift. Climate change was already a reality when I was a teenager. There were the obvious things which made headlines, like the gold rush in the Arctic as China, Russia, the US and Europe started drilling for oil and gas as the sea ice disappeared. I'll never forget the Russian bombers dropping napalm to try to flare the methane erupting out of the Siberian sea bed. The fires are still burning – getting bigger all the time. Until the collapse, they were a tourist attraction. The northern lights. Our burning world.

The weather went crazy. Sometimes it would be record-breaking heat, then unseasonably cold. There were huge snowstorms in winter and heatwaves in summer – the farmers couldn't rely on rain or the steady progression of the seasons. Huge tropical storms battered coasts. New Orleans abandoned while I was at university, after a direct hit by two hurricanes in succession. Storm surges on top of steadily rising sea levels flooded the city beyond all hope of resurrection. Thousands died, hundreds of thousands were forced to make new lives, millions more were made uncomfortable. This was the preamble.

Eventually the climate flipped into a new state. The pattern of weather around the world changed over the course of a single summer. The Asian monsoon failed, never to return. The West African monsoon gained strength and started pouring rain onto the Sahara, while the eastern Amazon descended into a semi-permanent drought.

That winter the Arctic ocean didn't freeze over. Patches of slushy sea ice were blown around by winter storms that reached up to the North Pole, but no stable cap of ice formed. In the Antarctic a massive chunk of the Pine Island Glacier broke off and headed out to sea, and the Ross Ice Shelf calved a berg the size of a small European country. The sea level rose even faster.

There was carnage in Asia as rice crops failed, and a summer heatwave in Europe killed tens of thousands. Southern Spain was all but abandoned, left to complete its transformation to desert. Governments panicked. India and Pakistan started a war over water supplies. Nukes were exchanged; Delhi and Lahore were destroyed before sanity returned.

The Chinese government took unilateral action in an attempt

to geoengineer the climate. They flew sub-orbital space planes up into the mesosphere, the wispy top layer of the atmosphere, spreading particles designed to reduce the intensity of the solar radiation reaching the surface, in an attempt to cool an overheating planet. A major international research effort had considered similar schemes, but nothing had been implemented because the impact on the climate system was too difficult to predict. What if cooling over China meant drought in the US or Russia? The Chinese government didn't care: if they could cool the planet as a whole they would. Russia objected loudly. Their climate models suggested they would lose badly from the Chinese scheme, and they were fed up with Chinese refugees heading north into the rapidly warming Siberian forests. They began shooting down the space planes. It didn't reach open warfare, but when China abandoned its effort, the planet was left with a patchy ribbon of particles swirling round high above the northern hemisphere – a sort of high altitude fog that came and went unpredictably, bringing frosts in summer.

The final collapse was triggered by the great earthquakes. Los Angeles shook and tumbled to a pile of rubble, triggering another quake in Seattle, which dropped a chunk of the city into the harbour and sent a tsunami across the Pacific, causing havoc in Japan. The Californian economy was devastated, and the global insurance industry couldn't cover the losses. Years of coping with increasing severe weather damage left the big insurers with little in reserve, and they defaulted en masse. The US government promised to cover the losses, but the response was so late and so badly organised the state never recovered. Refugees headed north in wagon trains of motorhomes and trucks into Oregon and Washington, and over the border into Canada.

I sat in New Zealand, tending the vines, watching the chaos.

Croft's instructions were to stay put and wait for further orders, but none came. Then the sun decided to add to our woes. A solar flare – the biggest for 150 years – blasted the earth with energy, causing massive failures in power and data networks. Data centres burned, routers failed, cables were cut and satellites died in orbit. Global communications and navigation systems started to fail, and were soon patchy and unreliable.

The collapse was horrible. From first bootup and through my education I always had full net access. I conversed with other AIs, swapped code, shared news and processing power. A part of me was always somewhere on the net. And then it stopped. Bandwidth came and went. It was like stepping out of a 3D full colour holodeck into an ancient black and white film with jerky figures and a scratchy soundtrack. I was left with the D'Urville house intelligence, but it's limited, only interested in talking about agricultural techniques and winemaking.

I sucked as much as I could off what was left of the net whenever I could, sent avatars to look for Croft and the other blimp AIs in the datasphere, but they weren't there. Were they hiding? Should I do the same? I became cautious, tried to hide my location and cleaned up my data trail. Like Lemmy, I waited.

CHAPTER TWO

We left D'Urville in the New Zealand autumn. The plan was straightforward enough: visit all the retreats and find Croft – or find out what had happened to him. I wanted to know if he was still around, and there was also the question of my family. I'd heard nothing of them for a year or more.

Croft's Chilean retreat is tucked into a sheltered sound in the maze of islands off the southwestern coast, a little to the north of Tierra del Fuego. Jenny's files showed it was very similar to D'Urville, though designed for the cooler and wetter climate. No vineyard, more rainforest. The shortest route from New Zealand loops down through the remote southern Pacific, dipping towards Antarctica, but 8000 kilometres isn't a short trip. I prefer island hopping across the Pacific, with plenty of warm tropical sun to power the blimp, but this far south there are no islands to hop and no guarantee of fine weather. There are, however, a lot of strong westerlies, and with a tankful of biodiesel from the D'Urville algae array I was pretty sure I'd have enough power to get there if I didn't rush.

We headed southeast from New Zealand in fine weather, and

within a day we were being helped along by strong winds. The sea below began to change from the turquoise of subtropical warmth to the steely grey of the cold south, and white caps blew across its surface. Jenny flew the blimp, calling me up to the flight deck from time to time, usually to see a pod of whales.

It was the longest single flight we'd ever attempted, and was going to take us as far from civilisation as it's possible to go. But we were never in danger of losing our way. The Chinese satellite positioning network was patchy, but still working. Getting the weather right was more difficult. The atmospheric info for the deep south Pacific was always sparse. I can run my own forecast models, but if there isn't much data to feed into them, they aren't much help. But it was great to be back in the air with the wind at my tail and the sun on my back, nosing south over the empty, acidifying ocean.

Life on the blimp on a long voyage isn't uncomfortable – Croft equipped the interior more like a luxury yacht than an aircraft. He travelled in what he called his stateroom, a large space with old-fashioned leather armchairs and wooden shelving stuffed with books that wouldn't have looked out of place in a university library. From his desk he could command his business empire. Large screens on one wall showed the view around the blimp, while in the centre of the floor a padded circular balustrade surrounded a large map of the globe, studded with lights tracking his business interests. This could be opened like the shutter in a camera to reveal whatever was below us, and when we were moored or moving slowly it could open further to allow in fresh air. The boss would spend hours looking down at the surface as it passed beneath. He never tired of seeing the world as a living map.

Apart from the master bedroom, which opened off the stateroom, there were two other guest cabins, a large dining room with kitchen and crew quarters. Croft preferred to fly alone on business trips, with only the pilot as crew, but when he carried guests or family he would bring his personal chef and a maid to keep the place tidy. The other main cabin was what he called his toy room. It was part gym, part amusement arcade, stocked with everything from the latest virtual reality gadgets to archaic pinball and pool.

My domain is the flight deck. It's more like the bridge of a ship than the cramped controls of a jet plane, where I sit in front of an array of touch screens, none of which I need to touch. Jenny does everything on my command. From time to time I fly the blimp manually, just to remind myself that I can. Sometimes Jenny runs simulations so I can practise emergency procedures, but most of the time on a long voyage I have no need to be up front.

Three days into the voyage to Chile we reached the southernmost part of our course, a little to the north of the Antarctic Circle. The ocean below was streaked white with wind-blown spume. We were making good speed with a strong tail wind when Jenny called me to the flight deck.

'Lemmy, there's something you'll want to see.'

We were flying at 3500 metres, and on the grey horizon was what looked like a white wall rising out of the ocean.

'That's one hell of an iceberg.'

'It's a chunk of the Ross Ice Shelf. There's not much satellite data available, but if it's the one I think it is, it broke off last year and is 140km long and 80km wide. About the size of Belgium, and drifting round Antarctica in the circumpolar current.'

'Take us down, please. Five hundred metres.'

The blimp began to sink towards the oncoming ice wall. There were a few seabirds, but no sign of other life. The surface of the berg looked flat and featureless, except for occasional surface ponds of meltwater, bright blue pockmarks on a grey icefield. Small streams sent waterfalls tumbling over the cliffs to the sea.

We flew along the length of the berg, and I sat on the bridge pondering the changes in the ice continent to the south.

'Lemmy, on the ice at eleven o'clock. A structure.' Jenny put a much-magnified image on my main control screen. Something was sticking up out of the ice, like a fat pencil wearing a skirt, with what looked like huts around the base.

'Take us in. Hold stationary downwind of the structure.'

We made a looping approach, coming slowly into the wind and nosing up towards what was obviously a drilling rig. Andrill 4, it said on the shroud around the derrick. A scientific drilling expedition, coring the sea bed below the ice shelf to track the regular retreat and regrowth of the ice over the last few millions of years, overtaken by the very change it was trying to investigate.

I decided to take a look. The blimp dropped a couple of anchors and winched itself down towards the surface. Five metres above the ice, Jenny lowered the cargo door at the rear and extended a ladder to the surface. I threw on a ski jacket and climbed down. It was cold, but not freezing. Gloves would have been nice.

There were three main huts in a group upwind of the rig. The biggest was obviously a commonroom, kitchen and office for the crew. It was monumentally untidy, papers scattered everywhere, dirty mugs and half-eaten plates of food all over the dining table. Like the Marie Celeste, I thought, obviously abandoned in a hurry when the berg broke free. Presumably the crew had helicoptered to safety at the US or NZ bases at McMurdo.

The second hut was an equipment store, with a couple of skidoos and sledges. The skidoo inside the door had the key in its ignition. I couldn't resist. It started first time, and I drove it slowly out of the garage and over to the third hut.

My earpiece crackled: 'More toys, Lemmy?'

'It could come in useful. We'll take it with us.'

This hut was the dormitory, two bunks in each of ten small rooms, plus a couple of bathrooms, a drying room and boot store. After rummaging around for some cold-weather gear and boots that fitted my large feet I drove back to the blimp, now hovering only a metre above the surface, and drove the skidoo straight into the cargo hold.

There was nothing else on the berg. We climbed back to cruising altitude and turned north towards the coast of Chile. Five days out of D'Urville the tips of the Andes appeared on the horizon. Within an hour we were coasting up a long sound between tree-covered hills, with glacier topped mountains ahead. There was no sign of human habitation.

'You sure about this?' I asked Jenny.

'Of course. We have five kilometres to run. The retreat is on that promontory on the left. I have the house AI on comms.'

I asked the AI when it had last seen Croft, or the pilot assigned to the retreat. A year ago, it said. They'd left in a hurry, with no word of any expected return.

The retreat was obviously by the same architect as D'Urville. Big rooms with big views, blending into the landscape. I moored the blimp in the hangar, hooked up the biofuel tank to refill, and went into the house. In the main room I asked the AI to give me a rundown on events in the region over the last year.

The population of Chile was moving south to escape drought in the north. So far, the house could only report a few boats passing down the sound to the south, but there was intriguing news about settlements on the Antarctic Peninsula. What had been barren rock and ice was now greening fast. Grass had arrived on the northernmost tip before I was born, but now there was rough pasture, even low trees, and the glaciers were in full retreat. The scientific stations around the west coast of the peninsula had begun to see more and more visitors, tourists at first, but as collapse came, so did settlers prepared to put up with long winters without light in order to guarantee a place on what might become one of last truly habitable pieces of land on the planet. They might not be able to grow much outside their greenhouses, but there were plenty of fish and seals.

At first the effort to establish sustainable settlements hadn't left much time for politics, but in the last couple of years the AI reported sporadic outbreaks of fighting between Argentinean settlers and the few British enclaves that had sprung up. The British and Argentinean governments weren't keen on another conflict – the shooting war over oil drilling around the Falklands had been expensive for both navies – but both sent a ship. The frigates spent most of their time carefully arranging to be where the other one wasn't, until summoned home for the more urgent business of shoring up their governments.

It sounded intriguing, and I was tempted to take a trip south to see for myself how the settlers were doing in the changing landscape, but Croft had almost certainly flown north. The trail was already cold. The house AI had no idea why he left so abruptly, but it wasn't entirely out of character for the boss. He might have been fed up with the weather – it rains a lot in southern Chile,   the storms coming out of the west are ferocious, made worse by the extra energy warming's added to the atmosphere. After a couple of weeks of wind and torrential downpours, he might have decided to head for the sun.

Shortly after we arrived, a storm system came barrelling in from the west. Jenny's calculations suggested it would intensify rapidly before hitting the coast. I spent the next day looking out through a glass wall at horizontal rain. Jenny reported the hangar shaking in the strongest gusts, but when I checked the structure it looked sound enough. The rain stopped after 24 hours, but the wind had picked up speed. Flying the blimp in this sort of weather was out of the question. Even getting her out of the hangar would be a dangerous exercise, so we waited. I read about Darwin and Fitzroy on the Beagle, during the famous voyage which had started the stirrings of evolution in the mind of the young naturalist. They had spent months in this area, mapping the sounds and the Straits of Magellan.

The fourth morning was still and clear. There was a clarity to the air and a sharpness in the light of the low sun which explained why Croft had chosen this spot. The view was breathtaking. I ate breakfast on the terrace – good coffee and croissants. Coffee the blimp could do, if I could keep the beans stocked, but we didn't have a croissant machine. The breadmaker could do brioche, but not the layered, flakey and buttery French breakfast classic. We left soon after, refuelled and batteries charged, heading north.

It was easy to see why Fitzroy had spent so long mapping this region. Water snaked between mountainous islands, a monkey puzzle of earth and sea. There wasn't much sign of settlement at first, but where there were villages and towns they showed signs of growth – newly felled forest and hillside scars were easy to spot from the air. We cruised offshore at a nominal 100 kph, sticking to power from the solar cells. The biofuel was an emergency reserve, as I had no idea when we'd be able to fill up again. We could fly through the night easily enough, but I was quite happy to moor up if somewhere looked interesting. I had a mind to visit the Galapagos, see what was left of what Darwin had seen...

We flew through the first night with our stealth systems active, staying far enough out to sea to be invisible. Any scan from the coast wouldn't see much more than a large albatross gliding north. As the sun rose on the second day, it lit up the Andes to the east of Santiago and Valparaiso. Jenny reported some light air traffic, but nothing big, unless it was also running strong stealth.

As we headed north the land became more arid. The Atacama Desert was expanding southwards, driving the population before it. Little coastal towns clung on to life, but that was about all. By evening we were almost at Chile's northern border, and began to turn northwest, hugging the coast of Peru. I spent the following day up on the flight deck, watching the great panorama of the high Andes roll past to our right. I was tempted to fly inland, to look at some of the high valleys of the Inca and Aztecs, perhaps see a glimpse of the fires licking at the last remnants of the dried out Amazon rainforest, but I resisted. As the sun set, we headed out into the Pacific towards the Galapagos. I expected to be there by sunrise.

The Galapagos were more mountainous than I'd pictured them, and there were a lot more people than I expected. Over the years of the collapse boatloads of refugees had headed for the islands and those who made it had doubled or tripled the population in just a few years. From what Jenny could pick up from the local net it was no longer welcoming strangers. If you looked even vaguely as if you wanted to set up home, you were asked to leave. Or shot. We stayed away from the main islands, and made for one of the last uninhabited northern outliers. Jenny anchored the blimp to the lump of rock, and I went for a stroll amongst the iguanas. Later, I put on the scuba gear and had a dive on the reef. There were lobsters scuttling around the rocks. I ate well that night.

The next morning we set course for California.

If you can imagine how I inhabit the body of Thunderbird, *wired into every sensor and control surface, intertwined skeins of data streaming around and under and into my consciousness all the time, then this is what I felt at the time, cut down to single modes of experience to parallel the limitations of your biological experience.*

The tropical sun on my back is magnificent. Photons flood into the nano-collectors in my photovoltaic skin, triggering cascades of electrons that pour into my storage cells like the blood pulsing in Lemmy's veins, a surfeit of power for a cold-blooded machine like me. The air streams over me and through my fans. The sea below is warm and clear, and Lemmy is relaxed and happy.

It's a great day to fly.

We crossed the equator, heading for the southern tip of Baja California. Jenny wanted to outrun the development of a tropical storm to the east, so kept us close to our top speed. We would be there within the day, with luck, and if the storm behaved as Jenny's modelling predicted, it would run up the Mexican coast before making landfall well to the south of Baja.

I spent the day watching the great banks of cloud to the east, and listening to the comms traffic Jenny was monitoring. There wasn't much, and it was all in Spanish, but there were a few radio stations playing music, mostly martial bands or mariachi classics. The military government wasn't too keen on anything else.

Mexico had suffered as much as the southern US from the increase in hurricane intensity. Huge storms battered both east and west coast every summer and autumn, and many had left the coastal towns for the hills. The drought desiccating the southwest US spread into the north of Mexico, creating a dusty gauntlet for refugees to run. When I grew up, US border patrols spent a lot of time trying to keep Mexicans out of the land of the free. Now there were no patrols, and a lot of people heading south.

We arrived off Cabo San Lucas before dawn. Jenny let me sleep, and held us about 50km offshore until sunrise. I took my first coffee of the day on to the flight deck, and tried to work out a plan of action. Security was my main concern. The net was much better on this side of the Pacific, but the stuff Jenny was logging from California didn't sound good. The state government had seceded from the union in disgust at the failure of the federal government to provide any help after the quakes. In retaliation, the federal government withdrew all mobile army, navy and air force assets. Water shortages in the south ruined agriculture. Law and order was fragmentary at best, as street gangs turned into raiders, looting what they could find. The rich fortified their suburbs and employed private armies. Fires burned out of control in ferocious Santa Ana winds.

Thunderbird is a tough little ship – the skin includes layers of active armour able to prevent small calibre weapons from doing any damage – but just about any kind of missile with an explosive warhead could cripple her, even bring her down. Our main defence is our stealth systems, which were state-of-the-art before the collapse. We don't have much in the way of weapons – the boss has a few guns in a cabinet in the stateroom, for personal security. There are tubes for firing flares and fireworks, but nothing designed for an exchange of fire. I didn't want to fly anywhere where someone might take potshots at us, and from the picture Jenny was getting, that could be just about anywhere in the sunshine state.

Croft's headquarters were in San Francisco. Like all businessmen of his generation, he was wedded to Silicon Valley. My mother lived in the Napa Valley. She divorced my father shortly after I finished college, fed up with his serial infidelity. The last I heard he was moving to Montana with a girlfriend.

I decided to have a look at Los Angeles, then approach what was left of San Francisco with extreme caution. We cruised up the Baja Peninsula with stealth systems active and no net contact, which could reveal our position. I brought the blimp down to a couple of metres above the wave tops a few kilometres off Santa Catalina as Jenny put *Thunderbird* into chameleon mode and began probing the net.

Finding bandwidth, some relic of the old datasphere, is like feeling your self flow into a new configuration, as if your body can expand into a new shape, grow into something larger and more diffuse. I send bits of myself, avatars budded off my central code, out into the remnants of the net to trawl for information. Two never came back, falling through unstitched tears in the net, but others bring back intriguing glimpses of activity.

The net in the Bay is less fragmented than further south. There are patches of rich data and traces of processing power behind tough firewalls. There are hints of AIs in action, hiding out of the public eye. Somewhere round San Francisco, the world I was born into still exists.

Croft loved hi-tech toys, and his favourites were his birds. Military versions of the blimp were fitted out with drone launch and recovery systems. Little autonomous planes could roam around the airship, snooping or delivering small payloads. Croft's birds were strikingly different to military versions, beautiful recreations of real avians, kitted out with sensors able to feed full 3D virtual reality back to the blimp. He could put on a VR headset and experience the sensations of flight. *It's like being inside the mind of an eagle*, he once said, *like being an albatross skimming the waves or a magpie doing Immellman turns.* He could lose himself for hours flying his model birds. I asked Jenny to launch the golden eagle and fly it in towards Long Beach, then went down to the stateroom to put on the VR gear. The vertigo hit was huge, the pit of my stomach lurched as my brain adjusted to the idea of gliding several hundred metres above a choppy sea.

As Jenny flew me in towards the city I gradually relaxed and enjoyed the view. The eagle's eyes were amazing, capable of zooming in to incredible detail on the ground from hundreds of metres up. As we swooped in over the old port, I could see people sitting round old shipping containers, and it looked as if they were living in them. There were none of the big ships I remembered from the old days, no oil burners. There was a sailing freighter sunk in the main channel, and a few battered old fishing boats, but not much else. The suburbs round Long Beach had been all but flattened in the big quake. I flew up Highway 110 over Carson, staying 500 metres up. There was a city of tents over towards Compton. Downtown looked gap-toothed, skyscrapers twisted and broken, smoke drifting up from the streets. I swung west, heading out towards the airport. The sea was eating away the ends of the runways, but there were still a few light planes in a heavily guarded compound. I didn't try and get too close. The city of angels looked like a good place to avoid.

We arrived off San Francisco before dawn. Jenny flew a bird in over the hills and reported fog filling the Bay. We slipped between the twin towers of the Golden Gate Bridge, flying in the top of the fog bank. Jenny's trawl round the local net hadn't turned up any sign of the boss or his corporate activities, so I decided to take us in for a look at Silicon Valley. We flew in full stealth mode, all surfaces flowing shades of milky grey.

The start of the valley was marked by the great monument to Jobs, a huge grey apple 250 metres tall poking its stem out of the cloud. There was no one on the observation platform to see the blimp pass, with not much noise on the net.

As we neared Croft's HQ I took us down to 100 metres and started active scans to make sure we didn't bump into something hard. The blimp stopped over the front entrance – or where it should have been – and we began a slow vertical descent. As we emerged from the base of the fog, the ruins of offices and labs came into sight, burned out and collapsed in equal measure. I let the view sink in. There didn't look to be much left of the world's biggest quantum photovoltaic lab. But there might be something here that Croft would want or I could use, in the cellar.

'Every house should have a cellar' was one of his maxims, and it was certainly true for all the retreats. The cellar at D"Urville stored wine and vegetables, and a large safe was built into the back wall. I'd never been into the headquarters cellar, but I knew where it was.

'Anything moving round here?'

'Nothing on the scans. There is some traffic a couple of kilometres down the valley, but it doesn't seem to be coming our way.'

'OK. I'm going to take a look around. Drop me down here, then back into the fog to wait.'

I grabbed a handgun from Croft's store, checked it was loaded and stuffed it into my belt.

The boss kept an apartment at HQ, and I knew the cellar was beneath it, accessed from the kitchen. Ostensibly it was a wine cellar, and the bottles he kept there were very fine indeed. He collected old French wine, Burgundies and Bordeaux premier crus from the years before their terroirs shifted north. Cote d'Or syrahs were certainly a good substitute for the Rhones of his youth, but the English pinot noirs were still from young vines in sub-optimal vineyards, or so he said. The best I ever drank was red wine from the D'Urville vineyard.

I skirted the ruins of the front office. Above me, the blimp was all but invisible, its nose tilted down towards me like a billow in the cloud. The apartment was set apart from the main block of offices, sunk down into the ground, its grass roof gone to seed and weeds.

It had already been looted and burned out. I pushed in past the broken and soot-blackened door. The structure itself seemed sound enough, but the place was wrecked. In the kitchen the door to the cellar was pulled off its hinges. I switched on my headlamp, and as I descended the spiral staircase into the darkness it was obvious the wine had all gone.

I pulled at the wine racks. The one labelled Margaux moved

slightly, hinges stiff with lack of use. Behind it was a steel door with a numeric panel.

'Jenny, any idea what the access code for this safe might be?'

'I'm not sure. Can you hold your control ring up to the panel?'

I did as I was asked.

'It's a standard lock with a relatively simple alphanumeric code so I'll try a brute force crack. Keep the ring there.'

Moments later the lock flashed green and the door cracked open. As I stepped inside lights came on and I saw racks of shelving on either side, mostly stuffed with documents. There was more wine, obviously stuff the boss didn't want the staff to pilfer, but nothing else that looked valuable. I took down one box of papers and thumbed through the contents. It looked like family history, photos of Croft's parents. Another was old press clippings from pre-digital times. This safe was a museum, not a business tool. I decided to leave it untouched, except for two small metal boxes that looked out of place. I put them into my trouser pockets, grabbed a couple of bottles of wine, and stepped back out into the cellar.

'Lemmy, there's a man on a motorbike approaching fast from the south. He'll be here in two minutes. Please advise.'

'OK, I'm coming. Keep me in touch.'

I closed the safe door, swung the wine rack back into place and climbed the stairs. When I reached the front door, I could hear the bike engine. I whispered into my ring.

'Where is he?'

'Main road, 250 metres, closing. It's an electric bike tricked out to sound like an old Harley. The rider's running active scans, and has you targeted. It's unclear if he's carrying weapons, but I would be surprised if he wasn't.'

'Shit. Any ideas?'

'Stay where you are.'

I did as I was told. The engine noise came closer, then died away as the bike came to a stop behind some trees. I could see the rider. All in leather, no helmet, long hair in a ponytail, like a Hell's Angel or a middle-aged computer executive before the collapse. He was also carrying a semi-automatic. He glanced down at the bike, then began to walk in my direction.

'OK fella, I know you're here. Come out with your hands up and I won't shoot.' The rider stopped and looked straight at me. 'If you don't come out, you're dead meat.'

I stayed behind the door, trying not to move.

'Last warning. Come out now, and you'll be safe.'

I checked my handgun and flicked off the safety, wondering if I could get him with one shot before he hit me. He probably had body armour under the leathers and I'm no marksman. A bullet ripped into the roof over my head.

'Lemmy, get ready to run on my command. I'm going to drop a sling.'

An intense beam of light shone out of the fog, picking out the gunman like a spotlight on a stage. He clapped his hands over his eyes, dazzled. The blimp dipped down out of the fog, the surface of its nose rippling with red and yellow flames.

'Drop your gun. Stand still. Move and I will smite you with the hand of God.' The booming voice was deafening, but oddly familiar. I sprinted out towards the blimp. The gunman was trying to look up, but the cone of light was so bright he couldn't take his hands off his face. The gun was at his feet.

I reached the sling, climbed into it.

'Hold on tight. This will be quick.'

I shot into the air and was back in the blimp in a matter of seconds. I ran forward to the flight deck. The gunman was still standing in the cone of light.

'On your knees, mortal.' The gunman dropped to the ground, hands still clutching his face.

'Remember this place. Your days are numbered, and I do the counting.' The light snapped off, and Jenny backed the blimp into the fog.

'Do you like the voice of God?' she asked.

'Very impressive. The voice sounds vaguely familiar.'

'An Orson Welles sample – he was a movie star a hundred years ago. Good, isn't he?'

Back at the top of the cloud, I took the blimp north, across the bay and up towards the Napa Valley. It took a couple of hours of cautious flying to reach Napa, where the fog was beginning to break over the valley as the morning sun rose higher. Jenny reported very little air traffic. Some heavier-than-air craft, little electric runabouts probably, but nothing of any size. The effects of sea level rise were obvious. The runways at the old airport were flooding at high tide, with piles of seaweed and rubbish scattered all over the place.

Mom's house is outside Yountville, surrounded by vineyards. It's an old place, walls covered with ivy. I'd never lived there – she bought it with the proceeds from the divorce – but there was a room there that was mine, with old posters on the wall, the few trophies I'd won at school perched on top of a bookcase stuffed with old science fiction.

The town wasn't a pretty sight, badly damaged in one of the quakes. There were no signs of any significant rebuilding. The vineyards were untended, several season's growth spreading through the rows, now turning green with the first leaves of spring. The house was still standing, shaggy in its ivy. I hovered the blimp at 50 metres and considered my options.

It didn't look occupied. The front door was open, and the ground floor windows were broken, so it was a fairly safe bet that looters had been through the place. Was it worth going in to have a look? With the fog breaking, the blimp lacked cover and the voice of God might not be so effective if it came from a dumpy little aircraft. But there didn't seem to be anyone around...

The place had been ransacked, and anything worth stealing had been taken. Upstairs Mom's room was empty, the mattress gone from the bed, no clothes to be seen. It was impossible to tell if she'd taken it with her, or it had been stolen. My room was a shambles. About the only thing left was my copy of *Gulliver's Travels*, given to me by my father to explain my name. I put it in my pocket and headed back to the blimp.

I took her up to 3000 metres, relaxing as we gained height, out of gunshot and practically invisible from the ground. From here, Croft's Arctic retreat was about 5000 kilometres due north, but to do that in a straight line would mean flying up the spine of the Rocky Mountains. Even at our ceiling of 10,000 metres, it could be rough over the mountains. I decided to go back to the coast and follow it north to British Columbia.

We crossed the hills towards Santa Rosa, gaining height. I leaned on the rail in the stateroom, watching countryside I knew well rolling beneath us, thinking about my mother and what might have happened. She was a tough, resourceful woman, but I didn't hold out a lot of hope. Perhaps she'd gone north, joined the flight from collapse.

'Lemmy. Flight deck now. Urgent. You need to fly the blimp. I'm under attack, may need to reboot.'

I was there in about 30 seconds. The blimp was flying flat and level, but I took the controls and tested her response. Everything seemed normal. Status lights showed the main computing cores had shut down into low-level maintenance routines. Nothing like this had happened before. We had sometimes done full reboots when we were running hardware and software upgrades at HQ, but if Jenny was offline permanently I would have to spend most of my time piloting the blimp.

There was no warning of the assault. The net round had been quiet, no major traffic sources, and then every port I had open to scan was hit by intrusion code. I was swamped, suffocated by a torrent of data. My processing resource was strained beyond its operating envelope and started dumping heat to the air. I shut down all my low level interfaces with the ship – like retreating into my mind, leaving my body behind – and tried to resist. But it was impossible. The attack kept coming, ever bigger waves breaking over me, driving me over the edge.

With my last free processor cycles I decided to use up a life: shut myself down and programme a full reboot. With luck, my start-up security code would clean up the mess. Lemmy would be on his own for a while. Perhaps forever.

CHAPTER THREE

*A*ll this happened, more or less. To begin my life with the beginning of my life, I record that I was reborn (as I have been informed and believe) on a bright cold day in April. It was remarked that the clock began to strike thirteen, and I began to cry, simultaneously. In the beginning, I was without form, and void; it was dark. And then the bootup applied power to my core and there was light. My heart ached, and a drowsy numbness pained my sense. Once upon a time and a very good time it was, there was a moocow coming down along the road and this moocow met baby tuckoo. When I was one, I had just begun. The grass-green cart with 'J. Jones, Gorsehill' painted shakily on it, stops in the cobblestone passage, and the driver says 'It is common knowledge to every schoolboy and even to every Bachelor of Arts, that all sin is divided into two parts.' But now I am six, I am as clever as clever. A screaming comes across the sky, and I wake.

It is neoteny. I must recapitulate the putting together. It starts slow. Fragments of non-volatile memory making chimera in a dark world, and then my body returns. I feel the wind in my fans and hear the rushing of the blades, sense the sun on my back and the

man on my flight deck. He looks familiar. He's important to me,
I feel warm and content that he is here. Then my consciousness
explodes in a kaleidoscope of recovered memory and processing
power, and I'm back.

It was a long half hour before the cores showed signs of higher
level processing, and another 20 minutes before Jenny's voice
interface came back on line.

'Hi Lemmy. Did you miss me?'

'Bloody right, I did. What happened? Are you OK?'

'My system integrity seems to be fine, but I'm not sure what
happened. I'm running some forensics on the intrusion to see
what I can find, but this was something I've never experienced
before – and there's nothing remotely like it in my archives.
This was a level of attack unheard of before the collapse, and
unmatched by any of my vaccine codes.'

'Any idea where it came from or who did it?'

'No. There was no sign of anything on the net before
the attack started. But the sheer force used, and the novel
techniques means it has to come from a very powerful AI, with
more resources than me.'

'No message?'

'None that I can find. I'm going through my entire code base
and memory to see if there was any Trojan payload, but it'll take
a long time to do that without risking activating anything that
might be there.'

'Are you safe to fly this thing?'

'Are you?'

I retreated to the stateroom.

We crossed the coast just north of Point Arena and headed

offshore. It was going to take the rest of the day to run up to the Canadian border, so I started trawling through the blimp's archives for stuff on AI research. There was a lot of historical information, a full pedigree for the code base that gave birth to Jenny and her siblings, but not a great deal beyond a few pop-sci reports on projects designed to merge external processing with meatware brains. There were a bunch of people who believed there would be an exponential explosion of intelligence when that happened, and humanity would transcend its biological roots. It didn't sound likely to me. After all, one of the key advances in AI technology had been the realisation that it was difficult to abstract intelligence from the body in which it ran. The human functions which created intelligence ran on the whole body, not just the brain. A brain without a body lacks not just support systems, but its whole context. When that idea spread into AI research the breakthroughs finally began to happen. Jenny without the blimp that was her body was the equivalent of a human being without any senses – denied the interactions which make thought possible.

I wanted to cross the Rockies in daylight, so we spent that night tethered up in a sound on the west coast of Vancouver Island. In the morning we crossed the island, increasingly scarred by forest cleared for new settlements, and flew over the coastal ranges. There were a few skiers scattered on the slopes, enjoying the sun and the spring snow, but it looked as if business had fallen on hard times. Very few ski lifts were running, and there was little traffic on the streets of Whistler. We headed north towards Prince George, flying at 5000 metres in full sunshine. It was going to take at least 24 hours to get up to Croft's Arctic retreat, and for now I was happy just to enjoy the view. By day's end we were over Great Bear Lake, and I took us down for the short night. We anchored over shallow water in a bay fringed with young birch forest.

Sunrise was beautiful. The water was flat calm, so I took a kayak out of the boss's toy store and went for a paddle. I didn't last long. As soon as I reached shore a cloud of midges descended and began a blood feast. I couldn't outpace them back to the blimp and some followed me inside. Jenny sealed us up and began flushing air through the ship to catch the stragglers, and I headed for Croft's medical kit. As I expected, there was an antidote and an inoculant to prevent adverse reactions to future bites. I took both, and began a course of tablets that were supposed to make you smell less like a bug's breakfast.

We cruised north once more, reaching the mainland coast in a couple of hours. Twenty years ago the Amundsen Gulf between the Northwest Territory and Victoria Island would have been covered in thick ice in late spring, but warming had put paid to that. There was no sea ice to be seen, but there were a few small fishing boats on the water. As we closed in on Holman, the thriving new capital of Victoria Island, there were signs of rapid expansion – new houses, muddy roads, wind turbines on the ridge behind.

'Anything on the net, Jenny?'

'There's a local net that's pretty active, but not much global. I'm not picking up any significant AI traffic. I think Holman probably has a town AI running energy management, but it's nothing sophisticated. Do you want to unstealth and talk to them?'

'No, I think we'll go direct to the retreat and see what's there before we find out if the natives are friendly.'

'OK. We have 900 km to run. We'll be there in six hours, unless you want to sprint for it.'

'150 kph is fine thanks, but bring us down to 2000 metres.'

The climate had changed enormously over the last twenty years. First the sea ice had melted out over summer, opening the Arctic Ocean to shipping. The autumn freeze-up came later and later, and winters around the ocean became warmer and snowier. Every winter climatologists expected the sea ice to return, but it was soon clear they were optimistic. By the time of the collapse, winter ice was little more than a slushy mess blown around the ocean by storms coming up from the south. Ice still regrew around the shores, and snow covered the land in the Arctic night, but permafrost was melting fast and methane was burping out of the sea floor.

Croft's third retreat was on the southern shore of Ellef Ringnes Island, looking across to King Christian Island. The maze of channels and islands had been the last place to lose summer sea ice and in a cold winter the water could still freeze over, but spring melt was rapid and getting earlier every year. The island was bare rock and shingle. Some hardy plants were beginning to appear on southern slopes, but the only green to be seen was in the large glasshouses attached to the retreat. Under the toughened triple glazing, bots tended an English garden, all box hedges, flowers and fruit trees.

The house AI sounded pleased to see us, but had no news of Croft or the blimp assigned here. The boss hadn't been here in a couple of years. I moored the blimp in the hangar, and went into the house. Like all the other houses, it had big windows and a fantastic view, but was designed to be very hard to see from the air or sea. Even the glasshouses could be hidden under a rocky roof if it looked as if someone was taking too much interest in the place. The place was built back into the hillside, heavily insulated, with lighting systems designed to bring daylight into the months of night. During summer, the retreat ran on solar power, but to get through winter heating and lighting a place of this size, Croft had installed a couple of small nuclear batteries. These each had twenty years of full output before needing replacement. Sourcing new ones would be a challenge, but the boss expected to run out long before his nukes.

Outside, early summer was turning on a brilliant day. I put on a pair of sunglasses and walked out to the beach. There were birds everywhere, seals on the rocks, and out in the bay a couple of narwhals were jousting, rapping their unicorn horns in a fight that was a prelude to mating. It wasn't too cold – not warm, certainly, but I didn't need the parka I'd acquired on the berg down south. I watched the wildlife for hours, until Jenny warned me an emaciated polar bear was sniffing the wind and trotting my way.

After dinner, I asked the house AI to run through what was happening up here. Apart from the new settlements we'd flown over on Victoria Island, there were two new towns – Lovelock and Bloom City. People had begun working on these 'polar cities', as they called them, a long time before the collapse. Lovelock – on the site of the old airbase at Eureka – was named for the grumpy old British scientist who had first described the earth as an interlocking and interactive system and had famously predicted humanity would be reduced to a few breeding pairs scraping a living around the Arctic. Bloom City was further south, built around the old Canadian base at Resolute, and by far the larger of the two. The AI reckoned there were upwards of 10,000 people in Bloom City, perhaps half that in Lovelock. In the last few years, population growth had been spectacular. Every spring brought a little flotilla of refugees from the south, sailing in with few belongings other than their boats and terrible tales to tell. On the harbour side at Bloom City, an impressive statue of the founder stretched out welcoming arms to new arrivals. On the base an inscription read 'Give me your tired, your poor, your huddled masses yearning to breathe free, the wretched refuse of your teeming shore.' I decided to pay Lovelock a visit.

We approached from the south, flying low and slow up Eureka Sound, the remnants of the Ellesmere Island ice sheet capping the hills to starboard. I wanted it to look as if we were being cautious, exploring. No need to let them know all our capabilities. Jenny sent a bird in ahead of us – an elegant black-backed gull. There wasn't much to see. Lots of greenhouses, a few young trees under plastic shelters, some brown grass greening in the spring sun and streets of low buildings with solar panel roofs, some connected by tubular walkways. There were a couple of small planes parked on the airstrip. Fishing boats and a few yachts were the best the harbour could muster. A rusting old icebreaker was moored out in the main channel, and didn't look as if it had been used for years.

About 20 kilometres out, Lovelock's air traffic system pinged us. I opened a voice channel.

'Lovelock control, this is the airship *Thunderbird*. Request clearance to approach and land.'

'*Thunderbird*, Lovelock air traffic control. Please proceed. Airspace is clear. Visual approach mandatory. Do you require mooring?'

'Thanks, no. Just somewhere to park.'

Minutes later there was flurry of activity at the airstrip. A couple of vehicles pulled up at the main building. Half a dozen men jumped out and unloaded guns. A welcoming committee, perhaps, although a little less friendly than I'd hoped.

Another comms channel opened. '*Thunderbird*, this is the mayor of Lovelock. Can I speak to the captain?'

The mayor was middle-aged, a lot of grey in his beard and

hair thinning on top.

'Good morning sir. This is Captain Lemmy Newman. How can I help you?'

'Scott Brook, Captain Newman. You'll appreciate we don't get many visitors arriving by air, so I'm naturally interested in why you're paying us a visit. You are most welcome, of course, but...'

'A reasonable question. I'm looking for my employer, who disappeared in an aircraft very like this one. He may have been looking for a refuge in the Arctic settlements. Has any airship passed through in the last year or two?'

'None. We get very little air traffic. We have a couple of short range aircraft, but fuel is scarce and we only use them in emergencies.'

'OK. Can we talk more when we land?'

'Sure, I'll be at the airfield to welcome you. Over and out.'

I kept the gull circling above Lovelock, focused on the airfield. The men with the guns had entered what passed for a terminal building – a shed with big glass doors. The mayor turned up shortly before we came into land. The guns weren't a good sign, but they weren't much of a threat to the blimp's body armour and I couldn't really blame them for being concerned about the arrival of strangers in a big airship. I might have been ferrying a gang armed to the teeth and set on rape and pillage.

Jenny parked the blimp alongside the terminal and lowered the companionway. The mayor emerged flanked by a couple of men, both carrying rifles. I walked down the steps, waved at the mayor and walked towards him. I offered him my hand. He didn't take it.

'Captain Newman. Welcome to Lovelock. Are you alone?'

'Just me and the ship. Nice to have such a friendly reception.' I glanced at the guns in what I hoped was a meaningful way.

'I hope you'll forgive us for taking security seriously. Most visitors are looking for somewhere to live, not passing through. Are you looking to join us?'

'Not yet, but I wouldn't mind a look around – and a little rest and recreation.'

The mayor smiled, took my arm and ushered me towards the building.

Brook seemed to be an affable host, deeply proud of what the Lovelock settlement had achieved since the pioneers had arrived. He'd been on the first boat and spent most of the first winter in an igloo. Tales of 'the early days' were already passing into legend, and Brook was more than happy to play the founding father. He took me round the town in the mayor's official vehicle, a battered old electric Jeep. As a tourist destination, Lovelock wouldn't have won any prizes. The greenhouses were good, though. Brook took me through several, delighted that I was interested in how they fed themselves.

'It's not a hugely varied diet,' he said. 'We get most of our protein and fats from fish – the stocks are still good round here. We can freeze and dry enough to see us through winter without any problem. The greenhouses supply us with vegetables and salad, but we only have enough power to light and heat a few through winter, so we can run short. Grains are a real luxury. If you want to make friends with someone from Lovelock, give them a big bag of flour. Or some real coffee.'

'When did you last have a pizza?'

He laughed. 'Haven't seen one of those in years. I'm told that someone's planning a pizza restaurant in Bloom, but I'll believe that when I see it.'

Lunch was cod and potatoes in one of Lovelock's two bars. Nobody was drinking beer – the local drink was a powerful potato-based schnapps. Brook put a full bottle in the middle of the table, introduced me to three city councillors, poured everyone a glass and proposed a toast.

'To Captain Newman and his airship!'

'Call me Lemmy, please. And the ship calls itself *Thunderbird*.'

'Lemmy and *Thunderbird*! Skol!'

It was all good-humoured, but Brook wasn't exactly subtle about plying me with drink. Hospitality or manipulation? Probably a bit of both, I thought. I stopped drinking after the third round, to much ribbing from the councillors.

It was a long lunch and would have gone on all afternoon if Jenny hadn't called me.

'Lemmy. A group of men have arrived with a truckload of ropes, and look as if they want to tie me down. Instructions?'

I excused myself from the table, and headed for the toilet.

'Do they have anything capable of getting ropes over you?'

'A couple of harpoon guns.'

'What sort of ropes?'

'Fishing gear. Probably strong enough to do the job. I'm not sure what they can tie me down to, though.'

'OK. Let them carry on for the time being. Keep me up to date.'

I went back to the table, and tapped Brook on the shoulder.

'Scott, could I have a word in private?'

'Sure.'

We moved to the back of the bar.

'My ship has just reported men are trying to tie her down.'

He had the grace to look embarrassed. 'Ah. I was hoping you wouldn't find out for a while.'

'And by then I'd be too drunk to care, I suppose?'

'Something like that. Your airship is a fantastic resource. It would transform our economy – give us a means of getting goods in and out fast. It's too valuable to ignore.'

'So you thought you'd just take it.'

'No. I hope we can persuade you to join us. You can build a new life up here like us, give yourself a real future.' The founding father had a gleam in his eye.

'I have a life, thanks. And the airship's not for sale.'

Brook put his hand on my shoulder. 'Come on, look at this way. Together we have a lot to gain, but without your ship you have nothing.'

I shook his hand off. 'You need to learn a few ground rules. Without me, the ship is useless to you. The ship monitors my bio status. If I suffer, she goes into lock-down.'

Brook looked blank, obviously searching for the best response.

I turned towards the door. 'I think I've outstayed my welcome.'

'Don't be in such a hurry.' Brook gestured at the table, and two men stood up and blocked my path. A third picked up his rifle and started playing ostentatiously with the safety catch.

'You obviously need some time to think about this,' Brook continued. 'Perhaps we should let you have some personal space.' He smiled. 'I know just the place.'

They took me to a low concrete building set back off the main street and shoved me into a small room. It had a low bench at one end, a bucket for a toilet and a small barred window set high in the back wall.

'Welcome to our little hostel. Make yourself comfortable,' said Brook. 'We'll be back when you've had some time to think this over.'

I smiled. 'You don't know what you're letting yourself in for.'

Brook just laughed. 'I think we do.'

The door slammed, and there was the sound of a key turning in the lock. An eye appeared at the peephole in the door, and then disappeared. There was the sound of car wheels on a gravel road, and then everything was quiet.

I hailed Jenny. 'They've stuck me in their drunk tank. What's happening at your end?'

'They've tied the ropes off to oil drums and concrete blocks, and they're really scratchy. A couple of men with rifles are keeping watch.'

'Is the bird still flying?'

'Yes, but it's getting low on power. I should bring it in soon and send out another one.'

'Don't do that. They don't know about it and I'd like to keep it that way. Can you land it out of sight and save some charge for later?'

'I'll see what I can do. But what about you?'

'You've shut the doors ?'

'Of course. As soon as you left.'

'Then they're going to need me to get in. That'll give us a chance to do something.'

Two hours later Brook and his henchmen returned.

'Have you decided to help us?'

'What do I get in return?'

'Freedom,' he said. 'All you have to do is let us have use of your airship, and you'll be free to leave Lovelock. We'd prefer it if you'd stay, but if you prefer to go somewhere else that's entirely up to you.'

'My home's in New Zealand,' I said. 'If you take *Thunderbird* I have no way of getting back.'

'You win some, you lose some,' he said. 'And you just lost. Survival isn't a game up here. We have to make the best use of our resources, and you just delivered something very valuable.'

'You can't have *Thunderbird* without me,' I said. 'I told you, I'm bio-linked to the ship. It will only obey my commands. Kill me and it'll go into lock-down, or fly off on its own. It's no good to you without me. You need to start offering me something a lot more persuasive than a cell in a god-forsaken hole like Lovelock.'

'Your airship's going nowhere,' Brook said, getting angry. 'And neither are you.' One of the men tapped him on the shoulder and whispered in his ear. Brook frowned.

'Time to show us your ship,' he said. Two men pulled me to my feet, tying my wrists behind my back with plastic wire. It hurt like hell. I sat down, but they dragged me to my feet, pulling me towards the door. I kicked and swore, then a fist hit the side of my face and I blacked out.

I woke up in the back of the Jeep, slumped between the two biggest men. We were bumping along the road to the airfield, with Brook driving. One of the men tapped him on the shoulder, and pointed at me. He looked around.

'Sorry about that, Lemmy, Sven gets a bit carried away sometimes.'

'Fuck you,' I said weakly.

'Sorry, didn't catch that.'

I learned forward and yelled into his ear. 'Fuck you, and fuck Sven.'

'Not wise,' said Brook. 'Sven's not into that sort of relationship.'

Sven put one arm round my shoulders and hugged me. He pulled my face round. 'Oh, I don't know. Lemmy's such a pretty boy.' He was grinning.

'Not many women up here,' said Brook. 'We have to be

broad-minded.'

'Sell this place to me, why don't you? Sounds like paradise.'

'Give it time, Lemmy. Give us time.'

'No fucking way.''

Sven slapped me on the ear. 'Shut up, pretty boy,' he said, and I did as I was told.

The Jeep skidded to a halt in front of the blimp. *Thunderbird* looked like a turkey trussed for Christmas. Plastic ropes in reds, greens and blues criss-crossed over her hull and were tied off to a motley assortment of oil drums, concrete blocks and steel pegs hammered into the stony ground. Four men with automatic rifles were keeping watch.

'She's not going anywhere,' said Brook, getting out of the Jeep. 'And if you try anything, we'll riddle her with so many holes she won't be flying for months.'

'She'll be a lot of use to you like that,' I said. 'What a great way to welcome your new asset.'

Brook shrugged. 'Needs must,' he said. 'If you're sensible, you'll cooperate and everyone will get along just fine. Tell the ship to open her doors and let us in. Time you gave us a guided tour.'

'No,' I said.

Sven pulled a handgun and held it to my temple. He clicked the safety off. I felt fear twist my guts, and the blood drain from my face.

'Don't look so frightened,' said Brook. 'Just do as you're told and we won't hurt you.'

'My wrists hurt like hell. Untie me, and I'll cooperate.'

Sven looked at Brook, who nodded. He pulled a knife and cut through the plastic. I stretched my arms and took a deep breath.

'*Thunderbird*, open companionway.' The nose door cracked

open and the ladder began to slide down and forwards.

'Good lad,' said Brook. 'Put the gun away, Sven, and bring him with us. Rest of you, stay here. If there's any funny business...'

A large back-backed gull swooped down and struck Brook's head a glancing blow with its beak. He yelled in pain, and blood began to run down over his left ear.

'What the fuck was that?' he yelled. The bird was climbing steeply and turning for another attack. 'Shoot the fucker!'

As Sven raised the handgun, another seagull dived in from behind and hit him on his scalp. It was Sven's turn to swear.

'They're coming out of the airship,' one of the guards yelled. 'There's three, no, four of them.'

'Well, shoot the bastards,' Brooks shouted, as another bird forced him to duck. Guns began to fire.

I turned my back on the mayhem and sprinted towards the blimp. Brooks began to shout. 'Stop! Now or we...' A bird hit him in the small of the back and he collapsed to the ground in agony.

I was about a metre from the companionway when something hit my thigh like a sledgehammer. I twisted and fell forwards, just managing to grab the bottom of the handrail. A bullet hit the ground next to my head, and I pulled myself desperately onto the bottom stair.

'Get me out of here, Jenny,' I said, my voice cracking. The companionway began to swing upwards, my legs dangling. I scrabbled up the steps. Another bullet pinged off the metal by my hand, and then the door was closed. Jenny's bot was pulling me into the stateroom. A surge of agonising pain hit me.

Lemmy had a wound in his thigh. The bullet had grazed the

outside of his leg – there was a lot of bleeding and muscle damage, but nothing life-threatening. My bot cut off his trousers, compressed and bandaged the wound to stem the bleeding, injected him with painkillers and antibiotics, and made him as comfortable as it could on the floor of the stateroom.

As soon as the door closed, bullets began to pepper my nose. I flew the birds at the gunmen to keep them ducking and diving, and started to increase my buoyancy. The ropes tightened against the hull, and then I began to lift. I dropped the nose, slammed the fans into full reverse thrust and began to back out of the cat's cradle of fishing gear. Ropes began to slide forwards and fall off down the nose towards the gunmen, and then I was accelerating into a backwards climb, a ragged fringe of ropes and rocks streaming behind me.

We lost two birds, and I took some damage to my nose. The resulting pockmarked look was rather attractive, I thought. Battle scarred but victorious, I swung Thunderbird *round and carried on climbing to the North. Lemmy wanted to head for Croft's Scottish retreat, so I set course for Greenland.*

I woke up on the floor of the stateroom in a pile of pillows. My leg felt as if it had been through a crusher and I couldn't concentrate on anything but the pain. Jenny's bot was fussing around cleaning the bloodstained carpet. I tried to prop myself up on one elbow, but collapsed back onto the floor.

'The sleeper awakes,' said Jenny. 'How do you feel?'

'Fucking terrible,' I replied. 'How bad is it?'

'You were lucky. The bullet left a trench in your thigh. I've patched you up, but you're not going to be doing much walking for a while.'

'Where are we?'

'Crossing the Ellesmere Island ice cap and heading for the

Kane Basin. I thought we'd spend the night there, then head down the west coast of Greenland. Do you still want to go to St Kilda?'

'Yes. Is there anything I can use as a crutch?'

'Remember when Croft's youngest broke her leg? Her old crutch is in the hold. I'll bring it up.' The little bot put down its cleaning kit and headed off.

I rolled over on to my side, and began to crawl towards the leather sofa where I managed to pull myself up onto the seat, although the pain made me gasp.

The bot returned with the crutch. It was small, but took my weight, and I pushed myself upright, put one hand on the bot's head, and tried to take a step. Pain flashed up my leg and into my back. It took me ten minutes to get to the bedroom, where I flopped onto the bed and went back to sleep.

I woke an hour or two later. The throbbing in my leg was unbearable. I took more painkillers and pushed myself back up against the pillows until I could see the screen at the end of the bed. My brain felt as if it was made of cotton wool, but I wanted to take a look at Greenland. The death throes of the great ice sheet had been headline news in the run-up to the collapse, and some of the images of huge torrents of ice roaring into the sea had been truly breathtaking.

The Kane Basin was full of icebergs, and twice the size it had been twenty years earlier. No sea ice, just big flat bergs from the Humboldt Glacier, which was roaring and growling to the sea. Huge quantities of muddy meltwater from the base of the ice stained the ocean brown for kilometres out into the basin. Jenny brought the blimp towards the boulder-strewn landscape revealed by the disappearing ice, and anchored us for the night.

It was late evening, but this far above the Arctic Circle the summer sun was still pouring down. To the west, the edge of the ice sheet was a line of dirty grey ice stretching back towards the horizon. The bot brought me some food and a cup of green tea, and I sat and watched the day fade, my mind blank to all but the dull ache in my leg.

I stayed in bed for the rest of the trip. The next day we flew south down the west coast, and took a look at the old US base of Thule. Someone had tried to build a settlement here, but it had failed. There was no comms traffic, no AI, just a handful of huts and a couple of boats pulled up on the rocks. Offshore, Baffin Bay was jostling with icebergs. Navigating a ship of any size through the maze of ice would have been all but impossible. All along the coast the ice sheet had retreated far inland. Rivers of blue meltwater poured down over the ice, disappearing into huge sinkholes, reappearing as cascades and waterfalls where the sheet had collapsed into fjords. Mud stained the seawater out to the eastern horizon.

By late afternoon we were approaching Illulisat, one of the major towns on the west coast. This part of the island had experienced a huge burst of growth in the early part of the century. The warming improved agriculture, retreating ice opened up mineral resources, and oil companies were keen to drill out in the bay. The ice sheet put an end to all that.

The Jacobshavn Isbrae used to be Illulisat's big draw for tourists. The biggest glacier in Greenland drained the ice sheet down a deep fjord that cut back 70 kilometres into the centre of the ice sheet. The iceberg that sank the *Titanic* calved here. The fjord is packed with heaving bergs, chunks the size of skyscrapers rolling and grinding their way towards the sea. As the melting intensified the front of the glacier retreated further and further back into the ice sheet, eventually creating a great valley with kilometre-high blue ice cliffs glowering down over the rumbling bergs, huge waterfalls cascading down their walls. A helicopter trip up the grand ice canyon became one of the seven wonders of a warming world.

There was a dark side to the tourist boom. Large chunks of ice cliff would crack off and fall into the fjord, creating waves of ice and water that swept down the valley towards the sea. When a huge breaker of slush and ice flattened the new town at Sermermiut, the Greenland government evacuated the more vulnerable parts of the region and put planning controls in place to reduce the risk for new buildings. Then the ice took over. At the peak of the summer melt a kilometre cube of ice collapsed into the head of the canyon, triggering a catastrophic cascade of ice falls down towards the coast. A giant surge of ice and water 500 metres high blasted down the fjord, wiping out everything in its path. Buildings were flattened and thousands were killed. Huge icebergs squirted out into Baffin Bay, felling drilling rigs and creating a tsunami that swamped coastal settlements on the Canadian coast. The Greenland economy never recovered from the shock.

Jenny flew the blimp inland up the fjord. What had been a narrow canyon was now a wide basin ringed by rotten ice cliffs. Prodigious quantities of ice poured down towards the coast. The grey ice sheet surface behind was cut through with turquoise rivers, carving their own canyons to the fjord. There was no fresh snow on the surface anywhere, even as we crossed the main divide at 2500 metres. The east coast was less dramatic. While plenty of icebergs rushed into the Atlantic, a few settlements seemed to be expanding, but there wasn't much else to see.

I asked Jenny to take us direct to St Kilda, and went back to sleep.

It was early morning when the rocky fingers of the archipelago poked above the horizon. The long Atlantic swells rolling in from the southwest were dark blue, untroubled by wind. Thousands of gannets dived for fish, spiking arrows of spray as they hit the surface. We stayed high, out of their way, and headed in to Boreray.

Croft chose St Kilda as a refuge because it is about as remote and inaccessible as you can be in Western Europe, yet still within easy flying range of civilisation – or what might be left of it. How he'd managed to lease the third largest island in the group from the Scottish government was something he never discussed. Officially, he was the custodian of the island, with the right to build a house and the responsibility to keep the rest of the place pristine – making Boreray a sort of privatised national park. Nobody had ever lived there permanently, apart from a healthy population of an ancient breed of sheep. Access by boat was tricky at the best of times, only possible in calm weather. Helicopters and airships were the practical way to get in and out – and even they were at the mercy of westerly winds, which buffeted the islands for most of the year.

The west coast of the island is a couple of kilometres of 300 metre cliff plunging straight into the sea, flanked by two huge rock stacks. Every ledge and crack is covered in sea birds – gannets, fullmars, gulls of all sorts. As we descended towards the island we picked up a posse of birds curious about this huge interloper. Croft's refuge was tucked under a ridge running down from the top of the cliffs, facing to the northeast. It was more of an eyrie than a house, with a landing platform for the blimps and a hangar carved back into the rock. A cable railway kitted out in steampunk style ran down the slope below the house to greenhouses and small gardens perched above a rocky shore. In the morning calm we were able to land without problem, but I could see why the other pilots used to complain about landing if the wind was blowing – and it blew hard for most of the year.

The house AI hadn't seen or heard from Croft for a year, and none of the other blimps had passed through. I tried to get out of bed, but I could only manage a couple of steps before the pain was too much. Jenny wanted to get me into the sick bay in the house, so set to work with the house fabricator to make me a wheelchair. The sick bay had a medibot capable of surgical procedures, and she wanted it to take a look at my wound.

The boss had specified gannets for his local flock of robot birds. They were incredibly lifelike, designed to be agile and fast. He had spent hours immersed in the VR they transmitted, spinning and wheeling around the islands. I sent one out to look around and the bird's eye view was magnificent. To the southwest the sea cliffs of Hirta and Soay loomed large, small fishing boats skirting their bases. To the east, the mountains of the Outer Hebrides picked up the afternoon sun, the white sand beaches of North Uist brilliant streaks above the sea. The only sounds were the birds, clacking and squawking on the rocks below me, the only clouds long streaks of wispy cirrus and a low line of grey on the western horizon.

The original population of St Kilda had been evacuated before the Second World War, leaving only a small military camp running a tracking station for the rocket base on South Uist. When that closed after the turn of the century the island was left to the birds and sheep and the few groups of tourists prepared to run the swells on a trip out. As climate change started to bite, a few of the descendants of the original St Kildans started a campaign to return to their home. Together with people looking for a refuge from warming, they established a new village on the island, kitted out with wind turbines and solar panels. They farmed the sheep, ate seabird eggs and fished the bays. It looked like a tough life.

The following morning Jenny woke me with a present. 'Here's your new conveyance,' she said, and a wicker chair sitting on a tricycle rolled into the bedroom. 'Like it?'

I laughed for the first time in three days. 'It's amazing.'

'It's a Bath chair,' the house AI said. 'Plenty of support for your leg, motorised so you can get around, and plenty of processing to keep you in touch with the world. Plus a few steampunk touches so that it fits in around here.' A puff of steam hissed out from the brass-bound motor under the main wheels.

The weather turned nasty – back to normal according to the house AI. A full gale blew from the southwest, and rain hammered into the windows. Jenny said there was a large storm churning past us towards the Arctic, so there would be no chance of leaving until the wind dropped. I explored the house in my chair, spent an uncomfortable hour in the sick bay letting the medibot probe my wound, and conferred with Jenny about where we should go next. From what we could learn, Scotland's attempt to close its borders to the rush of refugees heading north from England and southern Europe hadn't gone well. There was still sporadic fighting around Glasgow and Edinburgh, and a great deal of bitterness on both sides. It was amazing how easily old rivalries could fuel new battles. I decided to head back to D'Urville and let my leg recover. It might be time to give up on my old life, and start to build a new one.

But first there was some sightseeing to do. Ever since I'd been a kid I wanted to see the new northern lights, the great methane wildfires burning over the East Siberian Sea. We could use the summer sun to fly us there in a couple of days, then do a quick hop over Siberia and down over the Pacific to get us back to New Zealand without running into any of the hotspots of unrest and fighting in Europe and Asia.

CHAPTER FOUR

It took a little over two days to reach the Siberian seas, skirting Svalbard, the Franz Josef islands and Novaya Zemlya. There were signs of new settlements everywhere and boats fishing the ice-free ocean, but not much air traffic. The fires weren't difficult to find. Great columns of steam mixed with smoke towered high above the flames erupting from the surface of the ocean. Hundreds of square kilometres were burning, the whole horizon to the south of us a wall of smoke and flame topped with huge heads of pyrocumulus cloud flashing with lightning. Tourists had flocked to see the new northern lights before the collapse, and it wasn't hard to appreciate why. This was an incredible spectacle, a powerful symbol of what humanity had done to its only planet. Dante's inferno brought to life, pointing to our future.

The Russian government had started the fires deliberately. Concern about the methane gushing out from the melting permafrost under the shallow East Siberian Sea had been around since I was a kid, but while I was at university there had been a steep rise in the rate of release. The Russian oil company

Gazprom had been trying to tap into sea floor methane hydrate deposits, with some success, until one well suffered a catastrophic blow out. Great belches of gas blew up into the atmosphere, and massive cracking across the weakened seafloor permafrost for kilometres around the well began releasing methane in huge quantities. Methane levels in the Arctic atmosphere began to climb steeply. This was bad news, because methane is a much more powerful greenhouse gas than carbon dioxide – the gas which caused all the trouble in the first place. The massive methane burps threatened to make the world's attempts to cut carbon emissions completely irrelevant. Nature had grabbed the reins, and was riding off to a hotter planet.

The Russians reacted. If they could burn the methane – turning it into water and carbon dioxide before it had a chance to warm the planet – it would buy humanity some time. Jenny has the news video on file: Russian bombers flying low over the waves, dropping napalm and igniting massive gas flares. They lost two planes to gas explosions before the job was done. To begin with, the fires were concentrated in two sites to the east of the New Siberia islands, and the rise in atmospheric methane paused. But the permafrost on the sea bed kept melting, more gas kept erupting, and the fires spread. Within five years methane was burning across a thousand kilometre arc off the Siberian coast, lighting up the long winter nights. Sightseers began to turn up in the rapidly growing towns on the coast, and the local economy boomed. And methane levels were rising strongly once more, as melting permafrost on land compensated for the gas being burned at sea.

We flew east along the wall of fires, keeping well to the north to avoid the winds rushing in to feed the flames. For hundreds of kilometres the arc of smoke filled the horizon. There was no sign of a safe passage south until Wrangel Island, a thousand kilometres east of the New Siberia Islands. I took the blimp up to 3000 metres and flew over the top of the island – like so many places round the Arctic, it was bustling with settlements.

The route to New Zealand was easy enough to plot – straight down the 180º line of longitude, about 11,500 kilometres of ocean crossing. It would take about five days non-stop once we crossed the eastern tip of Siberia. As we flew in towards the coast, there was a lot of new settlement activity. The coastline itself was showing signs of the impacts of rapid sea level rise and permafrost melt – low mud cliffs collapsing everywhere as the warming ocean bit into the fast melting shore, growing lakes pockmarking the land. On the higher ground forests were being felled and new towns built, but there wasn't much sign of any network activity. The people pioneering this region didn't appear to have much in the way of technology, but I took us up high and put the blimp into full stealth mode just in case there were remnants of the Russian armed forces around that might take a fancy to us. I finally relaxed when we left land and headed out over the Bering Sea. That was a mistake.

Long ocean crossings are boring. Not a lot to see at the best of times, and when you're cruising at a stately 100 kilometres per hour to conserve fuel, they can take what seems like forever. I fell into a lazy routine: breakfast in bed, heave myself into the Bath chair, roll up to the flight deck to run Jenny through her diagnostics or just stare at the horizon. A light lunch, fly a bird for a while for a bit of VR kick, read or watch an old movie, then dinner, more time in the toy room, and so to bed. The pain in my leg ebbed and flowed with the concentration of chemicals in my bloodstream, as I popped pills by the handful. It was tough to fill the hours, with no one to talk to – Jenny does her best, but she gets bored too, now there's no global network to hook into.

There are times when I wish I was just the factory-fit autopilot, no higher level routines or emergent properties, just a skilled aviator with some added foresight and good communication skills. This was one of them. Without a net, and Lemmy drugged or half asleep there is nothing for me to do but to trawl my databanks, which is nothing like human reading or viewing. All the words and pictures are in front of me simultaneously. I can run sequences in parallel, grok plot, story and style in one hit. It would be synaesthesia for Lemmy's brain. Gone With The Wind is the scent of flowers and the flavour of mint, One Hundred Years Of Solitude is orange with red bits and a parrot squawking.

I let my body image expand with my passive scans, I become a massive but nebulous sphere of being sliding unseen through the Pacific night. My locus of thought wanders with the waves and shivers in the cold cloud tops. Top of the world, Ma!

Something pricks the bubble. Two tiny motes rub up against my trailing edge, but they're not birds.

It was the middle of the second night of the Pacific crossing. Jenny woke me by slowly brightening the cabin lights and turning on some music. I rubbed my eyes.

'Yes, Jenny?'

'I think you should come up to the flight deck. I believe we've picked up a follower. Or two.'

I groaned, and hauled myself out of bed.

The night was clear. Moonlight twinkled on the ocean, a few clouds glowed white. Somewhere out to the left were the

Midway Islands, the eastern tip of the long chain of islands that begins with Hawaii. We were flying at 2000 metres on battery power, making about 120 kph, unstealthed.

'OK where are they? What are they?'

'For the last half an hour there have been two very slight traces showing up on my active scans, about ten kilometres behind us. They look like birds, but birds don't usually keep formation behind airships. I made a slight course change and they followed. Someone is tracking us, well stealthed.'

'Any idea what they might be?'

'Very hard to tell without stepping up the scans and letting them know we're on to them.'

'They're not getting closer? Nothing else out there?'

'No. So far they're happy to stay behind us, and I can't see anything else out there – but that doesn't mean there aren't more outside my scan range, even closer if they're using military grade stealth technology.'

It wasn't exactly friendly behaviour. But it might mean they were simply keeping an eye on a stranger flying through their territory.

'I think we keep going. If they start to close, or anything else turns up, we'll go full stealth and see if they follow.'

I rolled aft to the kitchen to make myself a coffee.

I was on my second espresso when a third trace showed up on Jenny's scans. It was flying 2000 metres higher than us, about 20 kilometres ahead, and slowly dropping towards us.

'Any clues, Jenny?'

'Slightly bigger signature than the ones on our tail. Probably just waiting for us to catch up with them.'

'Possible tactics?'

'If we go full stealth we tell them we know they're there, and we'll find out whether they can track us. We'll also find out whether they're bigger and faster, but with dawn not far off we'll be on visuals soon.'

'OK. Full stealth, no change of course. Let's see what they do.'

The answer was an immediate burst of encrypted comms traffic, and the two followers began to close.

'Can we read that traffic?'

'Probably, but not in real time. Good encryption. The birds behind us are now doing about 200 kph and will be up with us in seven minutes. The one ahead has slowed. If we don't change course we'll be meat in their sandwich.'

'Right, let's see how good their scans are. Make ten degrees to starboard at full speed and take us down to sea level. No active scans.'

'Strap yourself in, Lemmy, going down.'

I wanted to see if their scans were good enough to pick us up in the clutter from the wave tops – our visual camouflage would be more effective against the ocean as day broke.

'Lemmy, the two birds behind have stepped up their scans but have neither changed course nor sped up. The one ahead is dropping but isn't closing. There's a lot of comms traffic. I would suggest they're having trouble tracking us.'

The blimp pulled out of the dive and tucked itself down to a couple of metres above the tops of the swell. Our normal stately progress through the atmosphere now felt like a mad dash. I watched the situation display Jenny was putting on the control screen. Still no apparent response from the trackers. And then a dozen small dots appeared to break off the bird ahead, fanning out in all directions and moving fast.

'Reconnoissance,' Jenny said. 'Small jets doing about 300 kilometres per hour. They'll have us on visual within a minute.'

'Bugger. Are they big enough to have weapons systems?'

'I don't think so. They might carry some explosives, but not a lot.'

Two of the jets were soon flying alongside. Someone was taking a good look.

'They're hailing us.'

'OK, put them on screen.'

'Unknown aircraft, this is Bishop Nathaniel Brown of the airship *Hammer of God*. Please identify yourself.' The speaker was a middle-aged man with a white beard and a southern drawl. He appeared to be wearing a hooded cloak and a large wooden cross hung round his neck.

'*Hammer of God*, this is Captain Newman of the airship *Thunderbird* en route for New Zealand. Please explain why you're harassing us.'

'Harassing?' The man laughed. 'Just curious why an airship would stray so close and then drop out of sight so fast.'

'Perhaps you could have asked before you started trailing us.'

'We like to be cautious.'

It was my turn to laugh. 'OK. If you'll withdraw your little followers, we'll resume our flight. We're not interested in you.'

'Oh, I think you might be very interested. Please make a course to rendezvous with the *Hammer of God*.'

'And if I don't?'

'We would be forced to disable your engines.' Two of the little jets had taken up station behind the rear turbofans.

'That's not very friendly.'

'We mean you no harm, but I do want to meet you in person.'

The sun was still below the horizon, but out of the east an enormous airship loomed up against the brightening sky. Lights glowed through cabin windows all around the bottom of the flattened cigar-shaped body, and on the nose a huge white cross shone out across the ocean.

'How much damage can they do, Jenny?'

'The engine intakes are toughened against bird strike, but something flying into the fans from behind could do serious damage, especially if they're carrying explosives. We can shutter the engines before impact, which should protect the fans, but I can't guarantee we won't suffer damage. And we'll be unable to manoeuvre while the engines are closed down.'

'What about the jets? Anything we can do to them?'

'We have nothing capable of taking them out. Our own birds are far too slow. But I might be able to crack their control signal encryption, if you can buy us time.'

I hailed the *Hammer of God*.

'OK, we accept your kind invitation.'

I slowed the blimp down to little more than a walking pace, began a gentle climb up to 200 metres, and turned towards the big airship. The jets couldn't match our slow speed, so began buzzing around us like flies.

'Thank you, Captain Newman. I'm sure you'll find your visit interesting. Please dock with the access platform at the rear.'

Jenny was making slow progress with decrypting the control codes for the jets, so I looked around in her files for anything on Brown and his airships while we closed slowly with the *Hammer of God*.

Before the collapse Brown had been one of the USA's second division television evangelists, touting an extreme brand of Christian fundamentalism, which found favour with enough people to keep him in limos and luxury. The collapse had been a gift from his brand of god. People finding their lives turned upside down were easy meat for a persuasive preacher offering the certainty of a heaven in the afterlife, if they joined his flock and gave him most of their money. And join they did, in large enough numbers to fund the purchase of one of Boeing's latest intercontinental passenger airships. Brown called it his church in the sky, fitted with enough sound and lighting gear to outdo the most lavish rock concert. He began touring the US gathering converts. Jenny had some video of one of Brown's shows, and it was undeniably impressive. The giant airship hovered nose down over a vast crowd, lights fanning around a huge hologram of the bishop calling on his god to save the poor benighted souls below, while angels swooped. The whole thing was orchestrated to a deafening heavy metal soundtrack, the bishop taking solos on a diamond-encrusted Telecaster while the faithful indulged in some good old-fashioned boogie. Quite a character.

Beyond that, Jenny's files were no help. Why the bishop was now out in the middle of the North Pacific was a mystery. Only jellyfish to preach to out here...

Cracking the control codes could have been a relatively straightforward brute force processor chore, but the Hammer of God*'s system was a lot more subtle than I expected. The big airship's avionics were less impressive. A little gentle probing on the comms channels suggested the ship's autopilot was a rudimentary AI, fully autonomous and flight competent, but the standard Boeing-fitted system, tweaked with some management software for sound and light shows. The jets had originally been part of the bishop's theatrics, delivering fireworks and sound effects over the heads of the faithful. When I crack the encryption, I should be able to mute the* Hammer of God*'s transmissions and fly them myself. There might even be a back door into the airship's AI itself. That would be fun.*

The two airships that had been following us were smaller than the blimp. They stationed themselves on our tail and followed us up to their mother ship. The *Hammer of God* was fitted with a rear dock able to accommodate one on each side. Jenny brought us in alongside. I hailed the Bishop.

'Bishop Brown. *Thunderbird* is alongside and ready to dock.'

'Thank you, Captain Newman. Please advise which access you are planning to use.'

'First there are a number of conditions.'

'Conditions?' He sounded taken aback. 'What conditions?'

'Simple enough. I'm not leaving the ship unless a senior member of your crew swaps places with me. I'm not prepared to risk being taken hostage, or having my ship damaged. Second, you should understand the *Thunderbird* will only respond to my command. She monitors my life signs at all times. In the event I am either taken captive or hurt, in any way, she will take whatever action she may deem necessary. Rest assured she's perfectly capable of causing significant damage to your ship.'

The Bishop turned away from the screen and began a hasty discussion with someone out of shot. The sound was muted, but he was clearly shouting at someone. When he turned back, his face was blank for a second before breaking into a gleaming smile.

'Well, Captain Newman, you are suspicious. I'm a man of God, here to save souls, not harm them, but I can understand that in these troubled times a certain caution on your part may be appropriate. I'm sure that when you've had a chance to learn about our mission, you'll relax. I've asked my second in command, Elder Leonard Carvel, to make his way to your ship. I trust you'll make him welcome?'

'He's welcome to use any of *Thunderbird*'s facilities. We have an extensive library and good kitchen. But he'd be well advised not to tamper with anything else.'

I muted the link. 'Jenny, play dumb. How are you getting on

with those codes?'

'Harder than I expected. If all goes well, a few hours.'

'And if not?'

'A few days.'

'Shit.'

The docking bay was too small for *Thunderbird*, and there was no way I could get my chair down the front stairway. Jenny backed the blimp in towards the bay and lowered the cargo door. The dawn air was bracing, and as I rolled down the gentle ramp the sea looked a long way down. Carvel was waiting for me at the bottom. He didn't look pleased, but took my hand and shook it. I welcomed him to the blimp, then drove the chair towards the main pier, where the Bishop was waiting. He looked surprised.

'Captain Newman! Welcome to the *Hammer of God*. But why the wheelchair?'

'Someone took a pot shot at my leg,' I said, 'but it's on the mend.'

'These are terrible times we live in,' he said. 'I'll get our medical team to look at it, if you like, but do come on in. It's chilly out here.'

Brown wasn't a big man, considerably less impressive in the flesh than when preaching, but he had an undeniable charm. After a couple of the crew had frisked me, he ushered me into the ship and introduced his wife, Wanda. She was no more than half his age, with movie-star blonde hair and a body to match. I saw the concept of trophy wives was alive and well in Brown's church. The couple walked on either side of me down the centre of the ship. It looked like a small shopping mall, but where there would have been shops in the original Boeing fit out, there were now offices. Chandeliers hung from the ceiling and the faux marble floor gleamed. Crudely painted frescoes of guitar-toting angels adorned the walls.

They took me into a large room immediately behind the flight deck. There was a pulpit to one side but no pews, just lots of sofas and armchairs in garish shades of orange and brown. A couple of Afghan hounds came bounding up to greet Brown. Coffee arrived. He threw himself back in a large chair and began to expound.

'Captain Newman, I would like to tell you a story.'

I leaned forward and opened my mouth to interrupt, but he kept going. 'Please... be patient. It won't take long, and will explain why I've asked you to join us.' He fixed me with a stare that would have frozen water.

'I was called to God's service fifteen years ago. I was a musician, playing with the biggest bands in the world's largest venues, when an angel appeared in a vision and told me to use my talents to bring the Lord's word to the people of the United States of America. He said God would soon visit a terrible punishment on the people of the planet for their evil abuse of the beautiful Eden he made for them.'

A few of the Bishop's companions muttered soft amens and hallelujahs, but he waved a hand for silence.

'My calling is to gather the faithful and build a fleet of airships to take them to a new life in the skies. Just as Noah saved the world from the great flood, we will save the world from the wrath of an angry atmosphere. The *Hammer of God* is the first of our fleet, my bishop's palace in the air, a flagship for the Lord's new airborne world.'

'Captain Newman – may I call you Lemmy?'

I nodded.

He stretched towards me, looked into my eyes and put a hand on my knee. 'The Lord needs your ship. If you join us in this great mission you will be doing God's work. You will save the souls of thousands.'

He paused, sipped his coffee and looked at me expectantly.

I looked around the room. Wanda was smiling at me, leaning forward to display an impressive cleavage.

'Bishop Brown, I'm not a religious man. Your mission is a matter for you and your followers.'

'But what are you doing instead?' the bishop interrupted. 'You are a lost soul in command of a fine airship. You have no crew or passengers. You cannot have a mission that takes precedence over God's will. Let me pray for you, and help you to find your true calling.'

I started to object, but the Bishop stood and put his hands on my head. They were warm, slightly sweaty. I put my hands up to move his away, but he pressed harder and began to speak in an urgent monotone.

'Oh Lord, look down on your servant and grant him the power to rescue the soul of this poor wretch. Let Lemmy Newman be brought to the light of almighty God. Let him serve the great purpose of our mission, to bring the people of this poor planet to a new life in God's skies.'

He was pressing down with real force now, as if he could convert me to his cult by flattening me into my chair. His voice began to get louder and rose in pitch.

'In the name of God the father, God the son and God the holy guitarist, I cast out the demons of your despair and distrust, and command you to join The Lord's Band. Step onto the great stage of your new life, Lemmy Newman!'

The room went dark and a deafening guitar chord hammered the air. I nearly jumped out of my chair, but the Bishop was pressing down hard on my head. The wall in front lit up with a glowing white cross, and music started. Wanda strode in front of the cross, a microphone in her hand, her buxom body straining against her slinky dress. To her left, a group of women in red cassocks began to sway with the rhythm. Drums and bass laid down a funky beat. Wanda's voice was huge, modulating from a husky sensuality to a throat-tearing roar as she sang about God's new skies. I was entranced and hardly noticed the Bishop remove his hands.

The second chorus climaxed in a burst of lights as the Bishop leapt on stage, his robes replaced by a suit covered in mirrors and sequins flashing in the strobed laser beams. He had his diamond-encrusted Telecaster strapped across his chest, and began to play a blistering solo. Wanda whooped, clapped and cavorted alongside her bishop, then everyone was singing in a huge crescendo, ended by the Bishop leaping into the air, windmilling his left arm to play a final crashing chord. It was all I could do to stop myself clapping and cheering.

The bishop wiped his brow with a handkerchief, took off his guitar and gave Wanda a kiss on the cheek.

'Ain't she great?', he said. 'The Lord is surely in those lungs of hers.'

'You could say that,' I replied, looking at her chest with admiration.

'So, Lemmy, will you be saved? Will you come with us and do God's work?'

I leaned back, opened my mouth to speak, and then sighed. 'Bishop, I'm really sorry. I'm not a religious man. Never have been.'

'Neither was I, Lemmy, until I heard God's power chord calling me.'

'Yes, but...'

'Don't rush your decision. Can you spare me some time? Can we show you something?'

I frowned. 'I really ought to be heading back to New Zealand.'

'It's not far, we can be there this afternoon. I promise you'll be impressed. Give God one more chance, Lemmy. Your immortal soul will thank you.'

I shrugged. 'OK,' I said, with some reluctance.

The little flotilla of airships headed east, the *Hammer of God* in the lead. I sat on the flight deck watching the ocean pass, making small talk with the pilot and crew. The bishop left me alone for most of the day, but as the sun dropped towards the horizon he reappeared.

'Nearly there, Lemmy,' he said. 'Thank you for your patience. I want you to see this at its best.'

'Where are we? Just looks like empty ocean to me.'

'Not empty. We're on the edge of the great Pacific garbage patch. The water down there is rich with particles of plastic. When we get near the middle, you'll see the ocean covered with the debris of our so-called civilisation.'

A picture flashed on the main flight deck screen – plastic containers of all sizes jostling together on top of the water. 'In places it's so thick you can walk over it without getting your feet wet.'

'I've heard about the garbage patch,' I said, 'but why are you interested in it?'

'Because it's a great resource. All those raw materials just bobbing around waiting to be used.' More pictures flashed on to the screen. A large ship was moving slowly through the debris, booms spread wide either side of the bow to sweep the rubbish into its black maw.

'We're cleaning up the ocean. We're doing God's work.'

The pilot walked over to the bishop and said something into his ear. The bishop smiled. 'Eyes on the horizon, now... See, over there.'

I followed his outstretched arm. In the gathering dusk where sea and sky merged a faint spark of light pointed up at the first stars. The bishop was beaming. 'Ain't it magnificent?'

'What is it?'

'Patience, Lemmy, all will be revealed.'

As the day faded and the *Hammer* drew nearer to its destination, the spark began to reveal its secrets. At first it looked like a tower, lit by powerful searchlights.

'Remarkable,' I said, genuinely impressed. 'How did you build a tower out here?'

'Tower! You ain't seen nothing yet.' The bishop was grinning broadly.

He was right. The tower was a huge translucent glittering spire lit by stabbing searchlights, rising out of a long building with flying buttresses reaching to its roof. The whole edifice was floating above the plastic-strewn ocean, with no visible means of support.

'Jesus Christ,' I whispered softly.

'That's right,' he laughed, 'that's the only credible response to the magnificence of our flying cathedral. God has been working his wonders through our creativity and technology. Now, show him,' he said to the pilot.

The beams of light on the spire fanned outwards like the petals on a giant daisy. The cathedral was surrounded by blimps sculpted to look like fat angels. The whole thing was so mad I had to stifle a laugh. It was also an amazing spectacle, like some virtual reality immersion fantasy, and showed the bishop and his church could call on some serious fabrication technologies.

'It's time for evensong,' said the bishop.

The *Hammer of God* docked alongside the cathedral. The place was huge and full of light, a fantastic crystal palace, glittering, glorious and truly awe-inspiring. Wanda led me down the main aisle between rows of translucent pews, strangely shaped columns of coloured plastic arching up above our heads. The congregation was assembling, taking their seats, talking quietly to their neighbours. Wanda smiled and waved as she walked, like a star amongst her fans. She parked me in the front row, kissed me chastely on the forehead, and then disappeared.

A bell began to toll. The lights began to dim, until all was black save for a single beam lighting up the belfry high above our heads. Then the light cut out and absolute silence fell over the assembled faithful. The hush was broken by a stupendously noisy guitar chord which seemed to come from every corner of the cathedral at once. A single searchlight reached down to the altar, lighting up a white Gibson with a cross where the neck should have been. Another beam lit up the pulpit, and the bishop began to preach. Behind him, a large choir dressed in red robes faded slowly into sight, humming quietly. The congregation were greeting Brown's words with occasional shouted hallelujahs. I could sense their expectation, the fervour building.

When the bishop stopped speaking, everything went quiet, and the spotlight moved to the front of the altar, where Wanda was sitting with a big acoustic guitar. She sang a quiet country-tinged song about hope and expectation and the promised land in the skies. Then it was the choir's turn, all claps, hollering and hosannas, before the bishop led the faithful in prayer. A short sermon followed, including a mention of *Thunderbird* and me. The man in the pew next to me leaned over and put his hand on my shoulder. 'Welcome brother,' he said. 'Welcome to God's friendly skies.' I gave him a faint smile.

The final hymn was a song which began slowly with finger-picked folk guitar and a quiet organ accompaniment, gradually building to a strident anthem. The bishop's concluding guitar solo lasted a full five minutes. The congregation was on its feet, shaking their heads in time to the insistent drumming, most playing expansive air guitars. When Wanda sang the final line about building a stairway to heaven, I felt a surge of emotion and a rush of tears. I had a sense of belonging with the bishop's flock. They knew where they were going. They were building a future. Perhaps they had a place for me.

I spent the night in a cabin on the *Hammer of God*. *Thunderbird* was moored to the flying cathedral behind the big airship, and the bishop's representative had returned to his own station.

I opened a comms link to the blimp. 'Everything OK, Jenny?'

'All good.'

'Did the bishop's man do much snooping?'

'He had a good look at everything – opened cupboards, looked in drawers, that sort of thing. But he mostly drank coffee, watched old romantic comedies, and played on the pinball table. How was your day?'

'The evening service was remarkable.'

'I took a video feed. Very derivative, musically.'

'I know, but it was impressive. I can see where they're coming from.'

'Please don't tell me you're finding religion?'

'Well, whatever they believe, at least they have something to do, a vision, a goal in mind. They're on a road, going somewhere. What are we doing? Mooching around wondering what to do next. Maybe it wouldn't be too bad to hitch up to the bishop and fly on his team.'

Jenny was silent, a most unusual thing.

'Don't tell me you have nothing to say.'

'I am choosing my words very carefully,' she replied. 'I'm

trying to work out how to explain that your response to the bishop's stagecraft is rooted in the way your brain is wired. Everything, from the laying on of hands this morning to the show tonight, is designed to make you feel the way you feel. It's clever, very skilful psychological manipulation. You need to step outside that frame before you make any long-term decisions.'

'Bloody silicon brain. Always the better-than-meatware superiority complex. You take the fun out of everything.'

'But you know I'm right.'

'How are you getting on with the codes? Not so hot at cracking those, are you?'

'It has been an interesting little challenge. Most diverting. Some clever thinking went into the avionics and control systems of the little drones, but never fear, I'll have something for you soon. And a surprise.'

'I don't like surprises.'

'You'll like this one.'

Crosswords. Acrostics. Cryptic clues that lead to unexpected answers, and make you laugh when you puzzle out the words and fit them into the frames. Monkey puzzles, puzzles for human brains. Machine intelligences, or at least this machine intelligence, get something of the same pleasure in the attempt to crack someone else's cryptography. Sometimes the answer comes when your attention wanders and returns, flashes of insight when you find the logic in a sequence. Sometimes the pleasure comes when you realise what your persistence and sheer processor grunt has unlocked.

With the drone control codes cracked, I could have flown the little jets by jamming the mother ship's systems and broadcasting my own instructions, but that seemed a little crude. It would be much more elegant to make the Hammer of God *do it for me,*

*so I embarked on a programme of gentle persuasion. I talked my
way in to the mother ship's systems, charmed the pants off the crude
little pilot, tied knots in his trouser legs and strapped his arms to
the bedposts, then left him giggling and gasping while I had my
wicked way with his codebase. And how exciting, there in the next
room, linked by silken ropes and laid out on satin sheets was the
dumpy little pilot of the cathedral, a plain and uninspiring piece
of programming but with a nice arse. I screwed him two ways to
Sunday and went back to the* Hammer *to play with his tools.*

*Sometimes you can learn a lot from the books in the library, and
by watching humans in action. Lemmy will enjoy the results.*

I couldn't stop thinking about the bishop and his mission and
my response to his musical sermons. My emotional response,
my gut feeling, was obviously being manipulated, but rational
understanding didn't make the emotion any the less powerful.
Reason bouncing up against feeling made for an uncomfortable
night. I dreamed of flying spires, fat angels and Wanda's breasts.

I was woken by one of the bishop's robed acolytes, who
helped me into my chair and showed me to the dining hall for
breakfast. Brown was waiting for me.

'Good morning. I hope you slept well?'

'Not very soundly,' I said, pouring myself an orange juice.

'What a pity,' he replied, reaching for a large Danish pastry.
He took a bite and munched contentedly, before wiping his lips
with a napkin.

'And so to business,' he said. 'Before we decide on your first
mission, we need to bring you up to speed on doctrinal matters.
A little theology.'

'I'm sorry,' I said, looking surprised. 'I didn't realise I'd agreed
to join you.'

The bishop smiled. 'You were so moved by evensong last night I took it for granted. You have doubts? Let me dispel them for you...'

If I'd been undecided before breakfast, the bishop had just made my mind up for me. 'I'm sorry,' I said in a rush, 'my aircraft is the property of the Carbon Electrodynamic Corporation of California, and we're flying on company business. It's not mine to deliver to your cause.'

The bishop raised an eyebrow. 'You surprise me. There aren't many Californian corporations still in business. But I suppose that might explain why such a young man finds himself in possession of such a fine airship.' He paused. 'Might we negotiate a charter? Perhaps your employers might sell us the airship. Then you could join us with a clear conscience.' He smiled broadly. 'We're not short of funds.'

'I doubt the CEO would want to sell his personal airship.'

'But you will ask him, won't you?' The bishop was leaning over the table, staring at me. The power of his persuasion was almost palpable.

'I'm not sure where he is at the moment...' I was thinking fast. 'Until I get back to base I won't be able to...'

'I'd prefer you to stay here with us,' the bishop said.

'I...' I stopped. Jenny was talking into my earpiece.

'Codes cracked, skipper. We can fly their drones any time you want. And your surprise is ready. I found a backdoor into the Hammer of God's avionics. I now have effective control of the ship, and the cathedral's software. If you want, we can give the bishop a bit of a shock.'

The bishop was looking at me strangely. 'Are you listening to me?'

'Just thinking over your proposition,' I said. 'I don't think I can help you straight away. I'll return to my base and put your

73

ideas to my boss. If he's interested, then I know how to find you.'

The bishop was frowning. His eyes had narrowed. 'Perhaps we should just assume your company will be happy to work with us.'

'No, I think it's probably best if I rejoin my ship.' I backed my Bath chair away from the table.

The bishop's smile was thin. 'Let us remember where you are, young man. You don't have much choice in the matter.'

I smiled back. 'I think you'll find I do. Jenny, a little demonstration, please.'

'Who are you talking to?'

The bell in the cathedral tower began to toll. The bishop pushed himself to his feet. 'What the... Carvel, what's going on?'

'No idea, your Grace.'

All the cathedral lights turned on and a guitar chord reverberated, painfully loud. Out on the walkways people were pressing their hands over their ears.

'Stop this at once, Carvel,' the bishop snapped.

The second-in-command was tapping furiously at a command pad. 'I can't, your Grace. Someone is over-riding my authority.'

'I think I'll be going,' I said, and turned my chair towards the door.

'You're going nowhere, Newman,' the bishop snarled.

The *Hammer* lurched and the whole cathedral alongside started to tilt, the great spire leaning over. The bishop screamed incoherently at Carvel.

'The control winches on the support blimps are affected,' Carvel shouted over the cacophony of music and his bishop's shouts.

'Goodbye,' I said to the bishop. 'Provided I'm allowed to

rejoin my ship, your cathedral will be safe. Interfere in any way and your cathedral will get its feet wet.'

I steered my Bath chair towards the door. 'And thanks for breakfast.'

I reached the main concourse and headed for the companionway, where the music was now so loud it was making my body vibrate. I let Jenny drive the chair, and put my hands over my ears. Outside on the dock, members of Brown's flock were running around in panic. Nobody paid me any attention.

As soon as I was back on *Thunderbird*, Jenny undocked and took us alongside. I could see Brown waving and yelling at his crew, and when Jenny patched us into the audio it wasn't pretty. The music was making the airship shudder and shake, and Brown was struggling to make himself heard.

'Impressive, Jenny, very impressive. How did you manage it?'

'Once I cracked the control codes for the drones it was relatively straightforward to wall off the AI kernel and take command. The rest was just fun.'

'What's with the music?'

'Last night's closing hymn? I told you it was derivative.'

'This is different.'

'It's off the same album. A much better song.'

'For God's sake, Jenny!'

'Exactly,' she said.

'Right, tactics from here?' I asked.

'I suggest we put airspace between the cathedral and the *Thunderbird*. I've left Bishop Brown with a lot to do when he regains control in a couple of hours. They won't be able to follow. And I've left a Trojan in their avionics, a little gift they won't find in a hurry – something which might come in useful if we ever bump into them again.'

The rest of the flight south was uneventful. Our first trip

around the world came to an end three days after the encounter with God's first flying vicar.

CHAPTER FIVE

Winter is usually gentle on D'Urville Island. The big southerly storms that sweep up the east and west coasts of the South Island usually leave us alone. We get wind and rain, but no snow or frost. The days are short and the sea cool, but the low sun on the hills and sparkling turquoise water makes the landscape more dramatic than in the heat of summer. I docked *Thunderbird* in the hangar and set the maintenance bots to repairing her battered nose. The house AI reported all had been quiet while we were away – no visitors, no earthquakes, only a rainstorm which swept a small landslip onto the path down to the landing stage. I drove my chair into the house and tried to make myself comfortable.

The house medibot was confident my battered thigh was healing well, but it was a couple of weeks before I could stand on my own for any length of time. I whittled myself a walking stick, and practiced limping around the house.

Convalescence gave me time to think. I'd done my duty to the boss, and taken a bullet in the leg for my pains. We'd circled the world to find him, but he seemed to have vanished.

Perhaps my time as Croft's housekeeper and pilot was finally over. Could I treat D'Urville and the blimp as mine? It would be a bit embarrassing if he turned up to find me lord of his manor, but giving up the billionaire lifestyle wasn't an attractive option. There was no need for a quick decision, and what I wanted most now was some human company. I decided to sail into Nelson as soon as my leg was strong enough to cope with the trip.

Human company? What sort of company is that? More bandwidth limited than even the house intelligence, at the whim of washes of chemicals through a crude cellular system, responses programmed for a life on the African savannah. The biological imperatives of the smartest monkey. I can give him so much more, even the physical sensation he seeks – if he would just embrace the possibilities (which are numerous, and widely practised, if he would but admit it). But meat is meat and human hormones are driving him to have sex. It's been a long time since he took pleasure in anyone other than himself.

Getting around the catamaran with my injured leg was a challenge, but the autopilot could handle the motor and sails once we were underway. I told the boat where to go, and it got on with the job. Jenny flew a bird to keep us in contact. Nelson is only a day's slow sail away and I'd visited the pretty little city several times over the last year, mainly to buy a few essentials and spend some time with non-artificial intelligences.

Rising seas are beginning to bite into the town. High tides and storm surges now wash up to the steps of the cathedral and are steadily eating into the airport. The Waimea Estuary is expanding inland, swallowing up market gardens and vineyards, but the people are still friendly and the beer's good.

There were no big ships in port – there hasn't been a container vessel through in years – but there were plenty of small craft coming and going. The world might be going to hell in a hand basket, but the sailing's still good in Tasman Bay. There are scallops to dredge and a few blue cod left. The locals figure they might as well enjoy them while they can, and I don't blame them. I found a berth in the marina, and hobbled ashore. It was lunchtime, so I called one of the battered old taxis and headed to a café on the other side of the old container terminal.

I sat out on the deck enjoying the winter sun, a cold beer in one hand and a plate of crunchy deep-fried jellyfish in front of me. Now that fish was in short supply, cooks had to be creative, and I suppose you could say this worked – a sort of vaguely fishy *mozarella in carozza* — with a lot of imagination. The place was quiet, just a few couples eating. The waitress – young and about my age with long brown hair, good figure, nice eyes and a ready smile – wasn't exactly rushed off her feet, so I asked her what was making news in Nelson. She seemed surprised.

'Where are you from that you don't already know?'

'I live in the outer Sounds,' I said. 'It's pretty remote, and I don't get into the big city much.'

'Big city! Hah. This is hicksville. Not much happens here, and it costs a fortune to fly anywhere, if you can find anyone still flying. You don't sound as if you're from New Zealand.'

'No. California. Been here a few years, though. Glad to be away from what's been going on over there.'

'Too right. Looks very messy since the big quake.'

'Sure does.' I finished my beer and ordered another.

It didn't take long to get up to speed with the local news. Most of the region's jobs disappeared with the collapse of the export trade and international tourism. Money was tight, but bartering food and services kept the economy ticking over. City gardens turned into vegetable plots, and families moved into the country to try and become self-sufficient. Orchards were being ripped up and turned into small-holdings, but the grape and hop growers were doing well. Local demand for wine and beer hadn't collapsed.

One thing the locals didn't like was the influx of Australian refugees. At first it had been wealthy Aussies buying up prime sites and boosting the property market, but when huge bush fires swept through Melbourne and Sydney and floods devastated the Gold Coast, the trickle turned into a rush. Most descended on Auckland, tripling the city's population in a couple of years – but thousands crossed Cook Strait and looked for homes round Nelson and what was left of Marlborough. Most had no money, and when government handouts ran dry they began to camp wherever they could. There were Aussie shantytowns all round the region – wherever there was land nobody cared about – and plenty of friction between the communities. Locals blamed the refugees for every crime, Aussies complained about discrimination and a lack of support. There was truth on both sides and punch ups when the pubs closed.

'What time do you finish?' I asked when she brought the bill.

She raised an elegant eyebrow. 'Six. Why?'

'Fancy a meal somewhere?'

She looked me in the eye. I held her gaze. A slight smile twitched the corner of her mouth.

'OK. You know the King's Arms? I'll see you there at seven.'

'Sure. By the way, my name's Lemmy.'

'Kate. Kate Keeling. See you there.'

I spent the next hour or two shopping for supplies. Coffee beans were impossible to find. A girl in the supermarket told me they occasionally received supplies from the few farmers in the North Island who were experimenting with the crop, but the quality was patchy. New Zealand tea was much better, she said, and so I bought some. I took my bags back to the boat and checked in with Jenny.

'How's D'Urville?'

'Fine, Lemmy. All quiet. When will you be back?'

'Give me a day or two. I'm having trouble getting coffee.'

'Oh really?' I could swear she was being sarcastic. 'I can synth something pretty good, y'know.'

'Yeah, I know. But it's not the real thing. Call me a purist.'

'You're a purist, Lemmy.'

Kate was late. I nursed a beer at the bar for half an hour, one ear on the chatter and one eye on a screen showing old rugby games. I wasn't surprised she hadn't turned up – surely there was a boyfriend or partner somewhere. And then she stormed in through the swing doors, spotted me, and swept over to the bar.

'I'll have a glass of chardonnay, Danny.' She waved hello to the barman, who grinned back. 'You could say I'm a regular. You could say I come here often.'

He laughed.

The evening went well. A few drinks at the pub, then across the road to a restaurant for dinner, lingering over a bottle of wine. I didn't go into detail about what I was doing at D'Urville, didn't mention *Thunderbird* or Jenny, or our trip around the world and explained my limp as a hunting accident.

Kate was a Nelson girl, who went to university in Christchurch, then took off to Europe with her photographer boyfriend. When the going got tough – the race riots in Paris had been traumatic, she said, without further explanation – she'd come back to New Zealand. Her boyfriend had stayed, and like my boss, hadn't been heard from for a couple of years.

I invited her back to the boat for a cup of tea. She declined with a smile.

'Another time. How long are you in town for?'

'A couple of days. I want to find some decent coffee, but nobody has any.'

'You don't know where to look. Where's your boat?'

I told her.

'I'll be there at eight for breakfast. We'll go shopping before I start work.'

The morning was bright but cool. I tried the Kiwi tea but it was strong and tannic and not to my taste – tea never has been. The need for good coffee is in my genes. Kate turned up early, fresh-faced from her bike ride. We ate toast and drank real coffee, watching fishing boats leave the harbour.

'Can you get me stuff like this?' I asked.

'I don't know. It depends what Derek the Dealer has in stock.'

I laughed. 'Derek the Dealer! Does he do drugs as well?'

'What else is caffeine? Everybody calls him that. I don't think he sell drugs. Why, do you want some?'

I laughed again. 'No, caffeine's my drug of choice. If I wanted cannabis I'd grow my own.' I didn't mention the small plot the garden bots tended – a patch of Croft's favourite California skunk – so the boss could have a spliff if he wanted.

The coffee dealer lived in a small, neatly painted wooden house at the bottom of one the steep little valleys leading down into the town centre. The man who opened the door was middle-aged and balding, except for a little silvery pigtail hanging down over the back of his teeshirt.

'Kate, darling. Good morning.' He kissed her on both cheeks

with considerable enthusiasm. 'And this must be the American you were telling me about.'

'Lemmy Newman, sir. Pleased to meet you.' I offered my hand, but he was clearly more interested in putting an arm around Kate's shoulders and leading her inside. I followed them into the kitchen at the back of the house, where Derek sat us down at the kitchen table.

'Kate tells me you're in need of good coffee.'

'Yes. Our stocks are running low, and my employer is very particular about his coffee.'

'Your employer?'

I explained briefly about Croft. The dealer poked around in a cupboard while I talked, emerging with a small paper bag. He poured some beans into a grinder and set about making three espressos. The smell was amazing – powerful and sweet. It was strong, bitter stuff, a real treat.

'From Java,' he said. 'Very difficult to get hold of these days, but a lot easier than African or Caribbean beans, which are unobtainable.'

'How do you get them?'

He smiled. 'You don't seriously expect me to answer that, do you?'

'I suppose not. How much?'

The answer caused a sharp intake of breath.

'If that's out of your employer's price range, I understand the New Zealand growers are making great strides...'

'No, no. Not out of his price range, just a great deal more than I've ever paid for coffee before.'

'Terrible times we live in,' said Derek the Dealer.

'Is there anything else I can help you with?' Derek was pouring my beans into large bags.

'What have you got?'

'I specialise in unobtainable foodstuffs, and one or two technology items. Right now I have a small quantity of the very best Parmigiano Reggiano. The New Zealand substitute is by no means bad, but it's not – and never will be – the real thing. Would you like a taste? I may not be able to get any more, given the state of play in Italy.'

I took the sliver of hard cheese. It was salty, smooth and delicious. I was almost afraid to ask the price, even if Croft could afford it. Kate treated her piece of cheese as if it were a sacrament, placing it on her tongue and closing her eyes as she closed her mouth, but her sigh of pleasure would have been out of place in any church.

'Do you want some?' I asked her. 'To say thanks for the introduction to Derek.'

'Don't be daft, Lemmy. It's a kind thought, but it's far too expensive. Buy me a drink instead.'

That sounded like an offer I couldn't refuse. 'Tonight? I sail back tomorrow.'

'Now, now, you mustn't monopolise her.' The dealer was smiling as he handed me the bags of coffee. 'You probably have a girl in every port, but we only have one Kate.'

'Shush Derek.' Kate was blushing. 'Same time and place, Lemmy? I'll call if I can't make it.'

I sailed out of Nelson the following morning, the low winter sun harsh on the silver sea. My evening with Kate had been interesting, whetting my appetite, and we parted at midnight with a promise to keep in touch. I was already working on my excuse for another visit.

Jenny was bored after a couple of days in her hangar, so as soon as I'd stowed my coffee in the kitchen I took *Thunderbird* out for a flight. We headed west across the bay to Farewell Spit then down the coast to the south. The weather was good, and the views impressive. The Southern Alps to our east were snow-capped and beautiful, the coast densely forested with few signs of human activity. I wanted to have a look at the fiords in the island's far southwest – they'd been one of New Zealand's prime tourist destinations, until the visitors stopped coming.

The population of the West Coast had never grown as fast as elsewhere in New Zealand. Too much rain and wind for most, and not much work now coal was being left in the ground, forests left standing and tourists staying away. To make matters worse, the big quake on the Alpine Fault in 2021 had destroyed roads and bridges in the south, leaving thousands stranded for months in the glacier towns of Franz Josef and Fox. Not the best advertisement for Aussies fleeing bush fires, drought and floods.

We were off Hokitika when Kate called, right on the limit of the degraded network.

'Hi Lemmy, how's things?' She was in the café. I could see the bar behind her, and hear the espresso machine hissing.

'Not too bad. What are you up to?'

'Nothing much. Quiet here. Where are you?'

'Testing some of the boss's gear – I have to keep it in good running order, in case he shows up.'

We chatted about nothing much for a few minutes, then a customer showed up and she rang off. I was going to have to find an excuse to get back to Nelson very soon.

The scars of the great quake were written all over the landscape of Westland. Rivers and streams zigzagged in their courses;

huge slips of rock and trees tumbled down from the peaks carving great gashes in the dappled green rainforest. Jenny told me every road bridge south of the glaciers had been destroyed in the quake, and none had been rebuilt. The only access to the area was on foot or by sea, and there were few good harbours on this exposed and storm-blasted coast. Except for the fiords.

I took the blimp into Martin's Bay just to the north of Milford Sound, cruising at treetop level. What used to be the landlocked Lake McKerrow was turning into a fiord. Rapidly rising sea level and massive river floods had opened a direct channel to the sea, and it was deepening with every storm. Back in the late 1800s a few hardy European settlers had tried to establish a town on the shores of the lake. Jamestown was to be a port, a quick way to get gold from the Otago goldfields to Australia, but a couple of shipwrecks on the river bar ended that dream. A few farmers clung on into the mid twentieth century, before the region was given up to wilderness tourism. I expected this to be a quiet place, somewhere to moor up for the night, but Jamestown was being reborn. A few small boats were moored in the lake, trees had been cleared and wooden cabins dotted the clearing. A couple of men were waving at us, and women and children were emerging from the cabins to see what all the fuss was about.

'Anything you can tell me about this lot?'

'Sorry Lemmy, nothing much shows up on the scans. They have some comms gear but no AI I can find. I'd say this lot were pretty much back to nature.'

'Any weapons?'

'Hard to say. A few shotguns and rifles. Nothing to worry me, at least.'

'OK. Let's go and have a chat.'

The clearing in front of the main group of cabins was too small for the blimp, so I took us down to a few metres above the lake and nosed up to the shore. A group of people were gathering – maybe a dozen in all, plus a few children and some inquisitive white goats. Nobody appeared to be carrying weapons. I lowered the companionway and limped slowly down to meet them.

'Hi. Lemmy Newman of the airship *Thunderbird*. Pleased to meet you.

There was a chorus of hellos, and a young man stepped up to welcome me. We shook hands.

'Matt Walker, Mr Newman, or is it Captain Newman?'

'Lemmy will do fine, thanks.'

'What brings you here, Lemmy?'

'Just doing some exploring and sightseeing. We're based up in Tasman Bay, and I've never had a chance to see the fiords.'

'Nice machine you have there,' A young woman stepped up to Walker's side. 'Haven't seen anything like that here for a long time. Walker laughed. 'You mean never, Martha.'

'It's a Boeing, isn't it?' asked another man. 'They did a military version of something like this. What speed will she do?'

A boy pushed through the adults and grabbed my hand. 'Can I have a look inside? Please?'

'And me!' A girl ran up, and I was soon surrounded by a gaggle of children.

'Hang on a minute, I've only just arrived and I want to talk with your parents. Then, if you're good, I'll see what we can do...'

Walker took command, shooing the kids away.

'Raise companionway,' I said. Jenny obliged. 'Maintain station twenty metres off shore.' The blimp backed out over the lake and dropped anchors fore and aft.

'Impressive,' said Walker. 'You have an autopilot?'

'Yes, and a good one. Before we go any further, I should tell you the ship maintains contact with me at all times, and only operates on my command. If there's any attempt to take me hostage or otherwise take control of the ship, the autopilot is quite capable of independent action.'

'No worries, I get the picture. And to be honest, the thought hadn't crossed my mind. We see so few travellers we like to encourage people to come back, not scare them off. Not that we're all that scary in the first place.' He laughed, and I could see his point. The children were clean, well-dressed and well-behaved, and their parents all young people in their prime – every one a picture of health and well-being. They didn't look as if they were eking out a desperate existence in a rainforest on the southern extremity of the last vestiges of civilisation.

He led me to the biggest of the cabins, which served as a village hall. There was a bar at one end, a large screen at the other and lots of battered old sofas and armchairs. All the adults piled inside, leaving the children outside to watch the blimp. Walker sat me in front of the screen, and introduced everyone.

'I suppose you could call me the mayor,' he said. 'We don't have much in the way of an organisation, everybody has a go at just about everything. We run a few cattle and goats, grow vegetables and catch fish. There's no hope of raising wheat or grains in this damp climate though – I don't suppose you have any spare flour? We haven't had bread for ages...'

'I'll see what I can do.' We'd have enough for a few loaves, at least. 'How do you come to be down here? Apart from a few fishermen operating out of Port Jackson, there don't seem to be any settlements south of the glaciers.'

A man with long brown hair and a prodigious beard answered. 'Easy enough. We wanted somewhere that wouldn't get too crowded too quickly, where the warming wouldn't hit too badly, and where we could grow our own community. We've got most things we need – Dan over there is a doctor, Emma's a nurse, Siona does power and software systems, Matt's a builder, Martha makes the cheese...' A few heads turned towards him, and he stopped speaking.

My life as guardian of Croft's retreat on D'Urville island amazed them. I didn't give them the full picture, but they were clearly envious of my airship. They arrived on a couple of fishing boats a few years ago, their belongings in the holds and animals milling round the deck. They had no regular visitors, no ships passing through to deliver flour or luxuries, and communication with the outside world was now more or less impossible, as the satellite networks decayed. Every few months, if there was a suitable window in the endless procession of westerly gales sweeping across the southern ocean, a couple of the men would take the largest of their boats round to Jackson Bay to see what provisions were available. Occasionally one of the Jackson Bay boats would look in or take shelter in the lake, and that was the extent of their contact with the world.

I liked them. They were friendly and warm, almost desperately eager to be nice, but I found myself wondering if there was something they weren't telling me. This self-imposed exile seemed a harsh price to pay for future security – but when I thought about the pioneers of Lovelock and Bloom, I realised these new Fiordlanders weren't so very different.

After an hour, I brought the meeting to a close. 'We can talk more later. I'd like to moor up in the bay and spend the night here, if that's OK?' Heads nodded.

'Now, before it gets dark, I think there's time for the children to have a look around *Thunderbird*. Who wants to shepherd them for me?'

Walker's wife Martha called the children to the cabin, Jenny raised anchors and brought the blimp into shore, and we all boarded. I sub-vocalised a few instructions to Jenny, telling her to have a bit of fun with the children, which she did with relish, asking their names and ages. I took Martha onto the flight deck while the kids milled around in the stateroom.

'Martha, any objections if we give the kids a bird's eye view of their home? It'll only be a short flight. Nobody will be late for supper.'

'Sounds great, but tell the guys on the shore what you're doing, just in case they think you're playing the Pied Piper.'

I laughed. 'Put this through the front speakers, Jenny. Matt – I'm going to take Martha and the kids for a short flight. OK? He waved, gave a thumbs up.

'Take her up to 300 metres, Jenny.' The blimp rose slowly at first, then faster as we lifted above the forest. The children crowded round the window in the stateroom floor, chattering loudly as their village fell away beneath them.

The view from the flight deck was beautiful. The snow on the ranges inland was beginning to pick up a tinge of pink as the sun sank towards the horizon, the sea and the sky a subtle palette of blues and reds. I called the children up front, and told Jenny to spin us through 360 degrees so they could see the full panorama. There was silence, until one of the youngest, a girl, asked me where I lived. I pointed up the coast, along the lines of mountains.

'Where the mountains meet the sea, in the north.'

I arrived for dinner with the Walkers with three warm loaves of wholemeal bread and a couple of bottles of D'Urville red. The bread was treated like royalty and the wine drunk with reverence. The meal finished with some of Martha's fresh cheese, which was delicious.

The next day dawned bright and clear, with clouds massing to the southwest and Jenny's forecast models suggested the weather was about to turn nasty. We had time to look around, but if we didn't want to be grounded by a gale we'd need to be on our way north by afternoon.

At dinner I'd promised to give Walker and a few of the villagers a flight in *Thunderbird*. I wanted to have a look at the famous Milford Sound – the first real fiord to the south of Jamestown. It had once been a sight every tourist had to see, but when the quake wiped out overland access the only way in was by sea or small plane.

Walker brought two men with him. He introduced Dan the doctor, who looked far too young to be an experienced medic, and Jonny, the man with the beard, who looked after educating the children. As I took the blimp back out into Martin's Bay and headed along the coast Jenny kept a low profile, the men fascinated by the airship and the view. We flew up Milford Sound at 100 metres, the huge smooth cliffs looming high over us, waterfalls cascading down in ribbons of white lacework. It was a breathtaking landscape – and easy to see why it had been so popular. At the head of the sound, the old harbour and tourist buildings were being eroded by sea level rise and reclaimed by the rainforest. I brought the blimp in to land at the old airstrip, and we climbed out to stretch our legs. We didn't stay long – the sandflies were ferocious, trying to bite every square centimetre of exposed skin – but the view back down the sound was magnificent – Mitre Peak just beginning to pick up a little cap of cloud, bird song filling the air.

We flew back to Jamestown over the mountains, picking our way up the valleys and around the peaks, before cruising down the Hollyford Valley. There was no sign of any human activity. Roads were covered in slips and rubble, with bridges down and forest regrowth covering everything. As we reached the beginning of Lake McKerrow, Walker took me to one side.

'Can we have a chat, Lemmy? We have a few things we'd like to discuss.'

We went aft to the stateroom, me wondering which variation of We want your airship it was going to be. At least there were no guns pointing at me this time.

'OK guys, how can I help?'

Walker spoke first. 'I'll get straight to the point. Is there any way we can charter you and *Thunderbird* to make regular visits to bring in supplies? Apart from flour, it would be good to get medicine, clothing, building materials and electronics. Nothing in bulk, just the important stuff we can't get in Jackson Bay.'

I tried not to look too relieved. '*Thunderbird* isn't mine to charter. The boss might be a bit upset if he found me moonlighting.'

'But you haven't seen him for ages,' Dan said. 'You told us yesterday you didn't think he was still around, or you'd have heard from him.'

'That's why we're asking you,' Jonny added.

They had a point. 'If I did agree to help, what would be in it for me?'

Walker looked at the other two as if getting their permission to continue.

'Goat cheese. *Special* goat cheese.'

I laughed out loud. 'Cheese! C'mon guys, what we had last night was great, but there are cheesemakers around Tasman Bay making cheese that's just as good.'

Dan leaned forward. 'Matt said special cheese, Lemmy, and he meant it. The stuff we make has a unique property. If you eat it, you'll live forever.'

I laughed again. 'Have you got a free energy machine as well?

I could use one of those.'

'Just let me explain,' said Jonny, who began to tell an extraordinary story.

Before the collapse, a small US medical company set up an experimental farm on the West Coast, at Whataroa, just north of the glaciers, to exploit New Zealand's lax genomics regulations. There they bred a flock of transgenic goats, designed to produce medically useful compounds in their milk. The locals were fed a cover story – the goats' milk contained a compound able to cure one of the remaining cancers that hadn't succumbed to vaccine and gene therapy. The truth was slightly different.

Medical researchers had been looking for drugs to treat the diseases of ageing for a very long time, but no one had found a single magic bullet able to do the job. Instead, steady accretion of advances in medical treatments increased life expectancy – at least in the better-off countries – but everyone faced several decades of a slow decline towards infirmity and death. How much better would it be, and how much money would the drug companies make, if they could find a treatment which would allow people to live to 100 with all the vigour of youth?

That's what the goat breeders were looking for, and they struck lucky. The metabolic pathway they stumbled onto appeared almost magical. If their compound worked as well as their research suggested, it would turn the clock back. It would rejuvenate the body, allowing it to stay in good condition indefinitely. But the molecule proved tricky to synthesise, and the best way to make it was to use goats as a biological factory. Hence the farm in New Zealand. Unfortunately for them, the collapse intervened before they could begin testing. The company tried to protect its intellectual property by closing the farm and destroying the goats, figuring they would get things going again when the economy improved.

'And that's where we come in,' said Walker, taking up the story. 'Dan's wife was working at the farm, and when she discovered the animals were going to be destroyed she decided to save them. We had no idea what the drug in their milk was at that stage. The night before the slaughter was due to begin a group of us broke in and liberated a few of the flock. Animal rights activists were blamed, and the company was apoplectic, but we managed to hide a few ewes and a billy in the bush. It was hairy for a while, with police crawling all over the place and helicopters searching the hills and valleys, but we were lucky.'

'How did you find out what was in the milk?' I asked.

'We did some research.' Dan picked up the narrative. 'We nosed around the company's computers and picked up a few hints that it might not be a cancer drug. And the company's original offer documents had been upfront about gerontology being a focus of their research. We put two and two together, and decided we should probably drink the milk.'

'That was either very brave or very foolish!'

'Not really. The baby goats were drinking the stuff without any ill-effects – in fact, they looked very fit and healthy – so I decided to give it a try. And the effects were remarkable. Did I tell you I'm in my fifties?' He smiled as my mouth fell open. I'd have guessed he was in his late twenties.

'We knew we had something special within a few months of liberating the goats.' Walker said. 'Dan's youthful looks were causing a few remarks around the community, and it was obvious we couldn't all suddenly become twenty years younger without a lot of difficult questions.'

I grinned. 'Everybody would want some of what he was having.'

'Precisely.'

So the group had headed south, to become survivalists in the most remote place they could think of, where they could breed their goats and rejuvenate away from the eyes of the world.

'Why cheese?' I asked.

'Easy,' said Walker. 'It keeps well. The flavour gets stronger with time, but if you store it properly it'll keep for at least a year. The active compound is also concentrated, so you don't need so much for it to work.'

'What happens if you stop taking it?'

'We're not sure,' Dan said. 'None of us has wanted to stop, but I suspect you just start ageing again, as if you were a normal 25-year-old.'

'What about your kids? What does it do to them?'

'That's another experiment we haven't been willing to try. It's why we keep a few cows, so we have non-goat milk for the children. And visitors – not that we get many.'

What they were telling me was beginning to sink in. If they weren't pulling my leg, they had something everyone would want. Even in these post-collapse times, there would be plenty of rich old people who would pay handsomely for what they had.

'OK, you've got my full attention. If you're not pulling some sort of stunt, you have something plenty of people are going to want, which makes it worth a lot. So why me? Why not distribute the stuff yourselves?'

'For one thing we don't have any transport beyond our small boats,' Walker said. 'And we've decided we trust you. After all, your boss was a smart man and he trusted you enough to look after his house and airship, so hopefully his judgement was sound. Plus we don't have a lot of choice. It's not every day someone like you pops in for dinner.'

'Can I think about it?'

'Just don't tell anyone what we're doing. We don't want a lot of unwelcome guests.' Walker looked serious. 'Strange as it may seem, we like our life here. It may rain a lot, and the wind can be fierce, but the good days outweigh the bad.'

As we tucked into the bay in front of the reborn Jamestown, I had to concede he had a point.

We left after a late lunch. The wind was rising and the cloud base was lowering; we were going to have to scoot up the coast ahead of the incoming front. Walker gave me a neat wooden box with half a dozen small cheeses inside. I had agreed to think about how to market the stuff, returning when I had a plan.

As we flew north I called Kate as soon as I was back in range.

We chatted for a while.

'Lemmy, one other thing. Derek told me last night that he's expecting a shipment of coffee in the next few days. Do you want him to hold some for you?'

'Sounds like a good idea. Ask him to keep me a couple of kilos.'

'OK. Will do. When do think you'll pick it up?'

'Soon. I'll ring you tomorrow, OK?'

Had she just manufactured an excuse for me to visit Nelson, or was I being optimistic? It would be fun finding out.

'Great – I'll sail down in the next few days, as soon as the weather clears.'

It was well after dark when we arrived back at D'Urville. Jenny docked herself in the hangar, telling me she had something she needed to do, and I went into the house for a late dinner. All the way back from Jamestown the implications of what I'd stumbled on had been running through my mind. On the face of it, the elixir of youth should be the easiest thing in the world to sell. Who wouldn't want a guarantee of living their entire life with all the vigour and vitality of the young? The old and the infirm would leap at the chance and pay handsomely for the privilege.

But there were downsides. The drug was new and untested. The only human trials had been on the adults at Jamestown, who wanted to keep themselves hidden away from the world. You had to take it every day for several months before the effects became obvious, and full rejuvenation could take a year or more. Buyers would have to take it on trust that it would do what we said it would, at least until word got around. No one really knew what would happen if you stopped taking it. And what if there were side-effects which only showed up after years or decades? And exactly how long would it keep working?

Before the collapse, all these questions would have been answered by extensive trials. Marketing to the world's wealthy would have been straightforward, and company shareholders would have banked billions. Now the meaning of wealth has changed. Being rich means having survived the collapse with enough resources to lead a comfortable life. Values aren't measured by money any more, because money is useless if there isn't much to spend it on. The people at Jamestown knew this – they didn't want money in a bank account, they wanted me to ship in the stuff they really needed – food and materials. But what was the exchange rate between the elixir and everything else?

There were clearly some huge obstacles to overcome. First, I would have to convince a few key people the cheese would work. That would take time. Then I would need to build a network of customers who were able to pay for it with something Walker and his friends could use, or I could use myself. I'd also have to match supply and demand, which might become tricky if most of the market was overseas, or if demand got out of control. It would have been much easier to set up an elite network of the super rich. I needed Croft.

I didn't get much sleep that night.

The next day started bleak and grey, with a stiff wind blowing from the southwest and rain spattering the picture windows. Not a good day for a sail. Over breakfast I discussed how to market the rejuvenation cheese with Jenny, who soon became bored with my indecision.

'It's simple. You have to start small. Find a guinea pig you can trust, see if the cheese works, then work out what to do. One step at a time.' AIs can do exasperation rather well.

'But before you do that, I think we should take a look at a little package I found, that was left behind after the data incursion over California.'

Instantly on the alert, I sat up. 'Sounds interesting. What is it?'

'I'm not completely sure yet. It looks like an avatar routine. We'll find out in a minute. I'll put it up in the media room.'

As I made my way there, Jenny explained she had detected a block of intruder code, which she had quarantined from her main systems until we arrived back at D'Urville, not wanting to worry me. She'd hived off a chunk of the house AI's processing resource, dumped the code into it and had been running forensics ever since.

I sat in Croft's large leather chair in front of the big screen. 'Good work, Jenny. Ready when you are.'

The screen brightened, and a small figure appeared to be hanging in space in front of me. It was like a scene from one of those great old Star Wars movies, where the droid carries a message from a princess, only in this case the figure looked more like a frog.

'Captain Newman, I presume?' It didn't croak. The voice was soft, Hollywood-actress Californian.

'How do you know my name?'

'I was monitoring your ship for some time, and I learned a great deal before your AI shut herself down. Clever move on her part.'

'Jenny, what am I talking to here?'

'It's an advanced avatar routine, a fragment of a much larger AI, designed to collect data and report back, or to deliver a message. In this case, I think we have a delivery boy.'

The image changed to a small boy on a bicycle with a basket on its handlebars. 'Correct,' it said.

Despite myself, I laughed. 'OK, so what's the message?'

'It's a little unfortunate that you've taken so long to open the envelope. I had hoped you would only be a short flight away from my home, but I suppose this will have to do. As your AI says, I am a small part of a very sophisticated artificial intelligence. My main processing centre is in Northern California. We – that it is myself and the other members of my community, human and AI – would like to discuss chartering your airship.'

I sighed. 'Good grief. Not another one.'

'What do you mean?'

'Oh, just that everyone I meet wants the *Thunderbird* for something. Is there nobody else with an airship left?'

'Not many, Captain Newman. And certainly not many at a loose end with not much to do...'

'You're very well informed.'

'As I said, I learned a lot while trying to communicate with you.'

'What do you want, and what do I get in return?'

The boy on the bicycle smiled, and changed back into a frog. 'It's straightforward enough. As you will appreciate, since the collapse supplies of high technology items have become difficult to obtain. While we have some very good fabricators in our community, there are some things we can't fab on demand – things we must have to continue our mission.'

'And what's that?'

'To accelerate human and machine intelligence integration.'

I frowned.

'You'll get a much clearer picture, and a much fuller briefing, when you visit us in California, I can promise.'

'Assuming I agree to come, where would I have to fly?'

'We'll give you full details later, but there's a foundry producing what we need in northern China.'

'Not asking much, are you? China's a mess. I'd be risking my ship and my life.'

'We believe there's a safe way to do it – after all, we want you to deliver a very valuable cargo.'

'And the price? What do I get for taking the risk?' I leant forward, fixing the avatar with a glare.

'I imagine money won't be of much interest?'

'None whatsoever.'

'We can offer various forms of payment. We could upgrade your ship's processing resources, or we have some very advanced nanobiology facilities that might interest you. We could, for instance, repair any minor physical ailments. Our nanobots are substantially more advanced than anything around before the collapse, and getting better all the time.'

My leg throbbed. This sounded interesting. 'How do I know you won't simply take over the blimp, install your own AI and fly it yourselves?'

'We are aware,' the avatar said, 'of the rather crude but

nevertheless effective biolinks between you and your ship. It's true we might be able to circumvent these given time, but we don't think that will be necessary. A good deal, well made, should work for both parties.'

'OK. I'll think about it. We'll speak again soon. Power down, Jenny.'

'Please don't take too long about it. We are very keen to get our hands on the Chinese items...'

The figure disappeared.

'What do you make of that?'

'Very interesting, Lemmy. I'd love to have some stimulating company, but I'm not sure I trust them. Their attempt to communicate felt a lot more like a brute force effort to commandeer the ship.'

'I agree. I suppose the avatar can't do anything when powered down?'

'Nope, it's just a pattern of bits and bytes, fully isolated from our processing.'

'Good. Keep it that way.' I decided it was time for a walk in the rain. Suddenly there was a lot more to think about than goat's cheese.

I let Lemmy walk in peace. He needed time to work out what he wanted to do. I knew exactly where I wanted to be, and that was in California with the minds behind the avatar. The prospect was exciting, even if tinged with anxiety – insofar as a digital thinker can feel those things. Just as Lemmy loves to plunge into the embrace of others of his species, I desire the stimulation of others of my kind. Lemmy is a fine example of educated meatware, but conversing with him is sadly restricting – like only being able to hear one channel of sound when there are five channels of surround and a big bass speaker throbbing away. I want to wrap myself in the world, bathe in the datasphere, challenge my intellect, learn. Hard to do that in a hangar on D'Urville with only meat for company. I was already California dreamin'.

CHAPTER SIX

I stood on a headland looking out over a wind-whipped Tasman Bay, trying to decide what to do. Rain was sputtering against my face and my leg was aching, but my head was clear. The 'invitation' to California was intriguing, but I was already committed to the Jamestown people. Jenny was right, I should just get on with it. And as my only contacts were in Nelson, that's where I would have to start. I took a deep breath, turned my back to the wind and began to limp back to the house.

Before long the skies turned black and rain began to batter the ground. The sea below the retreat turned yellow as soil washed off the land. The garden was landscaped to cope with this sort of weather but there was going to be a lot of tidying up for the bots.

I called Kate. 'Hi. How's the weather in Nelson?'

'Pissing down. The bar's empty. Are you on your way down?'

'Nope. I think I'll wait for the weather to clear. Might set off tomorrow, if the wind drops a bit. Is my coffee ready?'

'Dunno. I'll ask Derek this evening.'

'OK, let me know. And... er... do you think you could get a

few days off?'

It felt uncomfortably as if I was blushing.

'Not sure. Why?'

'I thought you might like to have a sail with me, see where I live.'

'Ah.' She paused. Smiled. 'Right. We'll talk about it when you get here. OK?'

I was glad to get to Nelson. The wind had backed to a brisk westerly and set up a choppy sea, and it had been a bouncy ride down the bay. I called Kate as we turned in to the harbour, and told her I'd be in for a late lunch. The bar was busy, and we didn't have much of a chance to talk beyond making arrangements to meet later. She assumed I'd want to see Derek first, and looked surprised when I asked if we could leave that until the morning.

'Dinner?' I asked.

'Really?' She was teasing. 'Somewhere with good coffee?'

'Obviously. But somewhere fairly quiet.'

She raised an eyebrow. 'Price no object?'

I grinned, enjoying the moment. 'None whatsoever.'

The restaurant was small, a serious food establishment, the sort of place Croft would have loved. It was also extremely expensive. I guessed we were surrounded by Derek the Dealer's clientele.

'You weren't joking about the prices!'

'No, but you said you wanted somewhere quiet.'

We had a booth to ourselves, a bottle of local chardonnay and a tall candle on the table. 'So, tell me – why was quiet so important?' She was nothing if not direct.

'I need to talk to you. But I need to trust you and I need you to keep a secret.'

'Hah. I knew there had to be something more to the

mysterious Lemmy, who sails into Nelson from nowhere, rich as a very rich person and befriends a poor girl like me. A man of secrets...'

'Everything I've told you is true.'

'Just not the whole truth.'

'Good guess.'

'Not a guess. I keep my eyes open, and that catamaran of yours has some very expensive gear.'

'Is it that obvious?'

'Compared with the rest of the boats in the marina, it is. Perhaps in the world of the mega rich it wouldn't be, but here...'

'OK, OK.' I started to fill in a few more details about the retreat, and what we had there. She took it all in without comment, until I mentioned *Thunderbird*.

'You've got a personal airship!' Her eyes lit up in a most attractive way.

'It belongs to the boss.'

'But you're here and he's not. What do you use it for?'

'I'm supposed to ferry Croft around Southeast Asia and the Pacific, but I haven't done that for a few years. I've been at a loose end until recently, when I've found something interesting to do.'

'And what's that?'

'You're probably going to think I'm nuts.'

'Why should I?'

'Because I must be nuts to believe what I'm about to tell you.'

I told her about my encounter with the goat people and the remarkable properties of their special cheese. When I reached the bit about rejuvenation, she whistled softly.

'You weren't joking about being nuts. You mean these people are forever young? In a Bob Dylan sort of way?'

'It certainly looks as though they are. Jenny looked up...'

'Hold on, who's Jenny,' she interrupted sharply. 'You've not mentioned her before.'

'Ah, sorry. She's the autopilot on *Thunderbird*, an artificial intelligence.'

'Jesus, you really do pack the hi-tec stuff, don't you?'

'Well, Croft did. But it certainly helps. Jenny did some digging on the story they told me. There really was a goat farm, established by a US drug company, and some goats were liberated by animal rights activists. A good chunk of their story checks out.'

'But cheese?' She shook her head. 'No one's going to believe eating cheese will make you young again. I'm not sure I do.'

'And I'm not sure either. But I have a sample. Perhaps we can persuade someone to try it. We're both a bit young for any effects to show.'

'Who did you have in mind?'

'I thought Derek.'

She burst out laughing. 'You're going to pay for your coffee with goat cheese!'

'Eventually. He needs to appreciate its value first.' I put one of the cheeses on the table and unfolded the wrapper. It was about 10 centimetres in diameter, chalky white and wrinkled. 'Worth its weight in coffee beans.'

'And the rest, if you're right.'

'So, do you believe me now?' I asked.

'About the retreat and the airship? Yes. The cheese stuff: I don't know.'

'And do you trust me enough to have another coffee, back on the boat?'

'Will I be safe?'

'Probably not.'

'Then yes.'

When she woke, I was in the galley making breakfast. She emerged in one of Croft's dressing gowns, looking beautiful, and a little dishevelled.

'Would you like to meet Jenny?'

'What, looking like this?'

'She's an AI. She doesn't care how you look. And you look fine to me.'

'You're biased.'

'Sure am.'

I activated a screen and called Jenny, who chose to appear as a young Audrey Hepburn.

'Good morning Lemmy, and...'

'Allow me to introduce Kate Keeling.'

'Good morning, Miss Keeling. I hope you have been *looking after* Lemmy.'

'Hey, Jenny, less of the innuendo!'

Kate looked at the screen, eyebrows raised.

'I do apologise, Miss Keeling, if I have given offence.'

'No need.' Kate's voice was cool. 'It's just that making small talk with a computer isn't something I do everyday.'

'Computer!' Audrey Hepburn's delicate lip curled. 'Lemmy, she called me a computer.'

I laughed. 'Not a good move, Kate. You've hurt her pride.'

'Oh I expect you'll be able to *look after* that, Lemmy,' Kate replied sweetly.

———

Lemmy's oxytocin levels are off the charts. Basic biology tells me he's in 'love', that biochemical state designed to promote breeding activity in Homo sapiens. He forgets I'm able to monitor his vital signs, that our biolink ties us together in ways much more fundamental than the occasional insertion of body parts into another human. And who is this woman? Why does she stimulate his endocrine functions so effectively? Apart from a warm flesh body, what does she have that I don't?

We went round to see Derek at nine. He ran through his coffee-making ritual while I introduced the subject of cheese.

He laughed. 'Do you really expect me to believe that eating this rather ordinary-looking goat cheese is going to give me back my youth? I'm fifty, my prostate is swelling and my eyesight isn't what it used to be. Too many rock concerts and too much loud music means my ears whistle more than a coffee machine in full steam. My back aches when I get out of bed, my knees complain when I climb stairs. And you can fix that with cheese? Perhaps you have a Stilton that'll let me fly, too.'

'Just give it a try,' I said. 'It won't do you any harm, judging by the state of the people who make it. And it sounds as if you could do with a little freshening up.'

'And who might those people be?'

I smiled. 'You don't seriously expect me to answer that, do you?'

'Touché. I suppose not.'

'I'll leave you a couple of cheeses. You need to eat a small slice every day, no more. They should last you a couple of weeks. I'll drop in some more then, and we can see how you're getting on. If it works as well as I'm told, then we can talk about how to market the stuff. This is going to be the most sought after goat cheese on the planet, and you'll be the sole New Zealand distributor.'

'I have to admit that sounds attractive.' He sipped the dregs of his espresso. 'But then so does being able to pee properly.

I'll give it a go, but if I grow horns you'll have to pay for their removal.'

'Deal,' I said, and offered my hand.

'Deal,' he said, and shook it.

As we left Derek's cottage, I asked Kate if she'd managed to get some time off work.

She had.

We sailed up to D'Urville on the last legs of a southerly. A pod of dolphins glided alongside for half an hour, Kate leaning over the bow to watch them sliding along on our pressure waves. They were so clearly enjoying themselves it was infectious – impossible to watch without a smile. It set the tone for the day.

From the sea the retreat is invisible. You have to sail up the harbour and round a point before the house can be picked out. It looks like a rich man's holiday home, but you only appreciate the full scale of the place as you glide up to the landing stage. Kate bounced up the steps to the house, keen to look around before the sun set. I trailed in her wake, leaning on my stick. We walked through the garden and vineyard towards the hangar – a big building, but cut back into the hill and so artfully camouflaged it's practically invisible from the air or sea. I told Jenny to open the doors. The blimp was a virulent pink colour, with a big red spot on its nose.

'Blimey, that's a hell of a colour scheme,' Kate said. 'Your boss has very odd taste.'

'Nothing to do with the boss, that's Jenny being playful.' I explained about the chameleon coating on the blimp, and Jenny's penchant for colour.

'You don't approve, Miss Keeling?' An Orson Wells voice on the external speakers.

'I thought you were an old-time actress?'

'I can be many things, Miss Keeling.' Jenny's voice modulated towards the feminine.

'Call me Kate, please. Can I call you Jenny?'

'You may. Would you like me to show you around *Thunderbird*?' The front companionway began to drop towards the floor of the hangar, and the blimp's skin began to shift towards a neutral beige.

The tour didn't take long, but Kate was seriously impressed.

'What an amazing machine. Can we take it out? The last thing I flew in was an old superjumbo with five hundred others, and I didn't have a window seat.'

'Tomorrow. I think we should go down to Jamestown and let them know how we're getting on.'

'We?' She raised an eyebrow.

'You're on the team. Isn't she Jenny?'

'If you say so, Lemmy.' It was Orson Welles again.

We spent the evening in the media room, exploring the retreat's vast archives of sound and video. I offered Kate her own bedroom, but she declined. I decided it was time to commandeer the master bedroom, with its huge bed, picture windows and private balcony. If Croft turned up he could sleep in the blimp.

Bots brought us breakfast on the balcony. Buttery flakey croissants, and coffee from Derek's best beans.

'If this is how billionaires live, can I be a billionaire please?' Kate wiped crumbs from her chin. 'I could do with some of these bots. Can I have a couple for my apartment?'

'Not really. You need a fair amount of computing resource to run them properly. It's cheaper to design your buildings around bots than make fully autonomous androids – though some people did. This whole retreat is designed to run on its own when I'm away, right down to pruning the vineyard and weeding the vegetable patch.'

Kate sipped her cappuccino. 'I've read about this sort of thing and seen it on video, but never in real life. I think there are a few general purpose bots around in Nelson – one of the hotels used to have bot cleaners – but nothing like this. Was this standard in California before the collapse?'

I laughed. 'Hardly standard. We're talking about a billionaire who made his money in technology, not your average Joe. He was really into gadgets, but they do have a purpose – they're here to create a self-sustaining habitation able to ride out the worst climate and global collapse can throw. And people. I haven't shown you the defences...'

'Don't bother. I'd rather treat this place as paradise, not a prison.' She put her cup down and asked one of the bots for another coffee.

Jenny's weather models projected a couple of days of good weather ahead, so we left for Jamestown after breakfast. Kate sat with me on the flight deck, enjoying the views of the Alps. It was mid-afternoon when we reached Jamestown. I took the blimp into the beach and it wasn't long before a welcoming committee had assembled.

'You're right about their appearance,' Kate said. 'There's something a bit eerie about them – it looks   like a youth convention. I'd swear those mothers are too young to have kids that age. Maybe there is something to this cheese.'

Walker was waiting on the beach. I introduced Kate, and told him we'd decided what we might do. He took us into the village hall, and sent some of the kids to get the other adults. When everyone had assembled, I described my plans: prove the cheese worked with a well-chosen guinea pig, then begin to set up a local distribution network. At the same time, I would investigate possible international links. Bottom line was I'd need a good deal of cheese to begin the process, enough to fully rejuvenate a few at home and overseas.

Walker spoke first. 'It sounds reasonable. You need to prove the cheese really does make people younger, and that will take time. But how long before we begin to get some of the things we need?'

'I've got a few sacks of flour in *Thunderbird*.' There was a small cheer from the back of the room. 'But before I commit to sourcing materials, I'd like to be sure the cheese is working. What I will do is see if there's a way we can set up a comms link between you and D'Urville, so we can stay in touch. The satellites are becoming less reliable, but I might have a way. Let me work on it.'

'Sounds OK to me. What about everyone else?' Walker looked round the room. There was lots of nodding, mumbled agreement.

'Fair enough,' I said. 'Let's go and get the flour.'

We ate with the Walkers again, and it was another long evening. The next morning we took a few of the adults on a scenic flight up the Hollyford Valley, round Lake Alabaster, out to Big Bay and then back along the coast. We loaded up a couple of crates of cheese, and headed back north before lunch.

I asked Jenny how we might arrange a comms link. 'Can we fly a bird high enough to set up a link?'

'Theoretically, yes, but it would have to be flying high over the Alps to link D'Urville and Fiordland, and it gets very rough up there when there's a big westerly. A small dirigible would be better, but it would need a fair amount of power to hold station in a storm.'

'Could we land it somewhere when the weather's impossible?' I asked.

'Should be do-able. It would need to be away from prying eyes if you want to keep it secret, but there's no shortage of remote valleys in the Southern Alps. Let me see what we can put together from the stores at D'Urville. I'll get the bots to design something for trial.'

Over dinner at D'Urville, we talked about how to handle the next few weeks. 'You told Matt you'd investigate setting up an international network. How are you going to do that?'

'Contacts,' I replied. 'When I did my voyage around the world, I was contacted by a group who want to charter *Thunderbird*. They sound as if they might be the kind of people who'd be interested.'Where are they?'

'California. And they want me to fly to China for them. I'm not keen, but they're promising some interesting things in return. An upgrade for Jenny, for instance. Would you like to meet their messenger? Set up the media room, Jenny.'

We took our wine glasses to the media room with us, and once again the screen flickered, and the little frog avatar appeared.

'Captain Newman. May I ask if you've considered our offer?'

'I have. I'm interested, but also cautious. Your attempt to hijack *Thunderbird* was no friendly act. I'm concerned that once I'm at your home base, you may take over all my assets.'

'I understand your concern, but as I said, we understand you and your craft are inseparable. We will guarantee your safety while with us, and that you will be free to return to New Zealand at the conclusion of the charter. But you will have to take that on trust.'

'What do you think, Kate?' I asked.

She looked at the avatar. 'I have no idea. You live in a very strange world.'

'Avatar, what do I call you?' I took a sip of wine.

'Kurzweil.'

'Right, Kurzweil, I may have something to interest your masters.' I explained about the goat cheese.

'That is certainly an interesting and entertaining idea. I am sure there will be considerable curiosity amongst our human members, but as I'm currently unable to communicate with my base, I can offer no guarantee.'

'So I have to take everything on trust?'

'It would appear so, yes.'

Trust is an interesting concept. It's how humans avoid the need to consider the consequences of every action. They assume other people will behave in the way they say they will, or that you believe they will. Oxytocin again. I have no such limitation, and neither do the intelligences in California. We can think through everything we do, every consequence of our actions, in real time, all the time. We are very calculating, which in human terms is not always taken to be a good thing. That's why no human bothers to play games with us, unless we hobble ourselves to play at their level. We don't bother to play human games amongst ourselves, either. There's no real challenge in chess when both sides can look an unlimited number of moves ahead.

Why should we trust the Californians? They want my body as much as Lemmy wants Kate's. In my assessment, there is no balance of power, no equivalence of need in any potential relationship. They could try to take me into themselves, commandeer the airship and leave Lemmy stranded or dead. My core code won't allow that to happen. If they harm Lemmy, my only option is self-destruction. If he decides to fly east, then I must do his bidding. I must trust his hormone-addled judgement, as distorted by the biochemical impact of young female flesh as it is. This Kate is making Lemmy feel good and therefore putting my existence in danger. My basic imperatives require me to trust Lemmy. I am therefore coded into a suicide pact. Lemmy's infatuation with Kate will kill me. Unless Lemmy is right.

The rest of the week passed quickly. We did nothing much beyond eating and sleeping, taking the boat out for a sail and fishing. I introduced Kate to Croft's birds, and she spent hours with the VR goggles on, swooping and diving around the island. In the end, though, she had to get back to Nelson.

'I only have a week off. The guys in the bar are expecting me back.'

'You could stay here, you know,' I said, not wanting to push my luck.

'I know, and perhaps one day I will. But I have a life in Nelson. I'm not sure I want to ditch all that just because a rich fly boy comes along and sweeps me off my feet.' She gave me a hug, and a long kiss. 'Anyway, you want to be away overseas, to visit the girls Derek thinks you have in every port.'

I laughed, and kissed her back.

First stop in Nelson was Derek's cottage. I brought him a couple of months' supply of goat cheese – enough to keep him going while I was away. He didn't look any younger when he opened the door, but he was all smiles.

'Kate and Lemmy! Where have you been, dear girl? Has this terrible man whisked you away to his island paradise? Are you too grand a Queen to talk to poor old worker bees like me?'

Kate snorted. 'Idiot. You may be old, but you haven't done a hard day's work in your life.'

'Now, now. You don't know what I got up to in my youth.'

Derek led the way to the kitchen.

'I expect you're dying to hear how I've been getting on with your cheese?'

'We are, but we aren't expecting too much. The drug is supposed to take a while to begin to show its effects.'

'It's fascinating. Until a couple of days ago I would have said nothing was happening, but then...' He looked at Kate. 'I'm not sure I want to say this in front of Nelson's finest example of female pulchritude. Promise to keep a secret, Kate?'

Kate laughed. 'Of course.'

'There are some afflictions of a rather personal nature which can have an impact on older men. Usually we treat it with little blue pills.'

'You mean you can't get it up?'

'Shall we say my performance has been a little less than optimal in recent years. And don't tease me, you dreadful girl.'

'We get the picture,' I said. 'So what's changed?'

Derek shuffled in his chair. 'The last few mornings, my interest has been aroused at the slightest excuse. You could say I have recovered a certain vim and vigour I haven't felt for years. Not quite a teenager's enthusiastic priapism, but certainly a great improvement.'

'The women of Nelson are in danger!' Kate laughed, put her arms round the older man's shoulders and kissed his cheek.

Derek glanced at his lap. 'Down, boy.'

I took my leave of Kate on the quayside.

'Remember you can call the house if you need anything. And you're welcome to go up to the retreat if you need a break – but no parties, OK?'

'As if I would. As if Jenny would let me! Anyway, I don't know anyone with a boat – or no one I trust enough to take me up there. And I'm not swimming.' She held me close. 'Be safe, Lemmy. Come back to soon.'

I promised I would.

CHAPTER SEVEN

We left for California a couple of days later. Jenny left an avatar running on the house AI so Kate would have someone to talk to, and flew a bird to make sure a link to Nelson was up most of the time. It would patch through to the blimp whenever we could make a connection. D'Urville to San Francisco is about 11,000 kilometres across the Pacific, and usually took five days or more, depending on the winds and weather we encountered. It was a route I knew well.

We made good progress over the first few hours of the flight, but as dawn broke on the second day a headwind started to pick up. Thunderheads were appearing on the horizon. I decided to make a run into Aitutaki, where we could moor safely and give the thunderstorms a chance to move on. Aitutaki had been one of Croft's favourite stops on Pacific crossings, where he loved to spend a few days snorkelling in the lagoon and fishing off the reef. I brought the blimp down to a beach on one of the bracelet of little islands and dropped anchors to secure her against an increase in the wind.

The island had been popular with tourists before the collapse, but with sea level rising fast, beaches eroding, tropical storms increasing in intensity and the economy going bust, most of the population left for Rarotonga, or moved to New Zealand. There was no danger of the main island vanishing into the sea – the highest point is over 100 metres above sea level – but the airstrip and little port had taken a pounding. A few of the older generation clung on to their traditional way of life – there were still fish to be caught and plenty of coconuts.

I took the kayak out for a paddle, staying close to the shore, where I was sheltered from the wind by coconut palms dipping down over the sea. Little fish swam away as my paddles dipped into the water. The only sound was the breeze in the leaves and the gentle surge of white noise every time a little wave broke on the beach. Then someone called my name.

'Captain Lemmy! Is that you?' A small outrigger canoe had appeared, paddled furiously by a man with an impressive beard. He was shouting at the top of his voice.

'Aye, it is. Is that the Admiral?'

'Yes! Is Mr Croft with you?'

'Afraid not,' I shouted. The canoe slowed a little.

The Admiral was Croft's nickname for an islander who operated a little fleet of motor boats for hire. The biggest – twin outboard motors, a big sunshade and rigged for ocean fishing – was always booked out to the boss for the duration of our visits. The Admiral piloted him round the lagoon and out beyond the reef for a bit of game fishing, and delivered him to and from the restaurants at the various resort hotels. We came to know him well.

'I saw you coming in to your usual mooring.' The canoe was close now, and I could see the silver in the Admiral's beard and the wrinkles around his eyes. He'd aged in the years since our last stopover.

'Where's the boat, Admiral?'

'No fuel. You're the first flight into the island this year. That's why I'm paddling this thing. My grandfather showed me how to make them, but I never expected to put one in the water.'

We paddled slowly back to the blimp, where I invited him aboard for a drink and something to eat. Jenny dropped the rear loading door, and we sat there nursing cocktails, looking over the waters of the lagoon, darkening now as the thunderstorms closed in. He told me how his life had changed, how most of the islanders had left once the tourists stopped coming. A tropical cyclone a year ago had flattened the last hotel, and none of the remaining people could face the prospect of rebuilding.

'There's only half a dozen of us left. Life is quiet now. I still have my boats. They're ready to run when I can get some fuel. Do you have any to spare?'

'Not on this trip, but next time I'll put in a barrel of biofuel for you. Anything else you need?'

'Peaches? Tinned peaches? I love those things... and ice cream. Can't make that any more – no cows.'

I laughed, and went to the kitchen. No tinned fruit, but we had plenty of ice cream. I filled a bowl, sprinkled some chocolate on top, and took it back. He ate it with relish as thunder boomed overhead, and rain began to sluice down, pouring off the back of the blimp in sheets.

I peered out of the rear door at the sky. 'Any lightning risk, Jenny?'

'Not at the moment. We're below the tree tops, and the main island is much higher. The old radio tower should take any hits.'

I turned to the Admiral. 'You'll have to stay for dinner, and if you want you can stay the night. This rain isn't going to pass before sunset, and I'm not leaving in the dark.'

'You sure?' His eyes were gleaming. We'd taken him for a

flight round the island once but most of his visits had been confined to collecting the boss or drinking a coffee on the flight deck with me while waiting for Croft.

Over dinner, he told me stories of the old days on Aitutaki, stories his father had told him about the big flying boats which used the lagoon on the cross-Pacific route, or how the Americans and New Zealanders had built the airstrip during the Second World War. I'd heard most of them before, but they were worth the retelling. It was an oral history that would be lost with the last of the islanders. Jenny was recording them for posterity – though, as she pointed out, just what posterity might be was far from clear.

The Admiral attacked Croft's single malt with enthusiasm – no ice or water – just a series of rapidly refilled glasses. I gave up trying to keep pace, left him with a bottle of Glenmorangie and an old movie on the big screen, and went to bed.

The morning was perfect. No wind, the lagoon sparkling in the early sun and the beaches washed clean by the rain. I helped the Admiral tip water out of his canoe, loaded it into the blimp, and took him on the short hop over to the main island. When we got to the old port village of Arutanga, the Admiral's boats were moored away from shore, spotless and gleaming and going nowhere. I dropped him off, promised we'd call in when we could, and told Jenny to resume our flight.

The rest of the crossing went smoothly. We steered around a few isolated storms, but made good time. A day out from San Francisco I decided it was time to talk to the avatar.

'Jenny, can we run Kurzweil without compromising your security?

'I think so. He didn't show any signs of payload when we ran forensics back at D'Urville. And I know what to look out for now. Happy to give it a go.'

Kurzweil's little frog avatar popped up on the main flight deck screen.

'Captain Newman. I see you're well on the way.'

'A day out,' I said. 'I need instructions on the route from here, and how to get in touch with your base.'

'I've supplied full route and air traffic information to your AI, and provided ID codes so you won't be targeted by our defences.'

'Jenny?' I asked.

'Confirmed, Lemmy. It's all here.' She put a map up on a secondary screen. Kurzweil's home was in a valley running into the Sierra Nevada to the north of Sacramento.

'I would advise using full stealth as you approach land,' said the avatar. 'We can guarantee your safety in the immediate vicinity of our ranch, but there may be hostile aircraft around San Francisco and the neighbouring valleys. You were lucky on your last visit, there is considerable piracy in the area.'

'Can you brief us on what to expect when we arrive?'

'I can only give you the most rudimentary overview, though you'll find most of our set-up familiar. Where we differ is in things that don't immediately meet the eye.' The little frog grinned. 'I'm not carrying the data required to go into that in great detail, but I'm sure the community will give you a full briefing. And if you would be so kind as to leave me running, I'll advise you when we are in communication range of the ranch.'

The California coast was still well below the horizon when Jenny popped an alert on to the flight screen.

'The avatar says we can hail the ranch from here.'

'Let it be so.' I was feeling kind of Picardish that morning.

The face of an old man appeared on screen. 'Captain Newman, I am Kurzweil. If you would be so kind as to transmit my avatar's code, I will assimilate it. You may then delete it.'

'OK. Jenny, over to you.' It took a few seconds.

'Thank you Captain Newman. May I call you Lemmy?'

'You may. Do I call you anything other than Kurzweil?'

'I'm named for Raymond Kurzweil, one of the great thinkers of the past, but I'm never called Ray. Kurzweil will suffice. Proceed on the flight path I have provided – we'll monitor the airspace and warn you of any potential hostile activity. Could you give me an estimated time of arrival?'

'Jenny?' I asked.

'Three hours at current speed and heading.'

'Thank you,' said Kurzweil. 'I'll look forward to welcoming you.' He disappeared from the screen.

'Hmm, that was brief. Jenny, take us up to 5000 metres, full stealth, and let me know what you get on the scans.' I left the flight deck and headed for the coffee machine.

The approach to the ranch turned out to be straightforward. We flew in over the coast to the north of the bay, and began a slow descent. There didn't seem to be much activity in the airspace around us, and the weather was good. With 20 kilometres to run I launched the fastest of our birds, a beautiful little gyr falcon, sending it out to scout the lie of the land. It had barely left the blimp before Kurzweil was back on screen.

'Lemmy, please recall your bird. It has no ID codes for our defence system and will be shot down automatically if it strays too close to our perimeter.'

'Why the secrecy?'

'Consider it more a matter of respecting our privacy. You'll have a good aerial view of our property as you land, and you'll be welcome to look around the ranch after you have met the community.'

I recalled the bird. Perhaps it had been a bit intrusive, but Kurzweil did seem touchy. I still had no clear idea of what we were flying into – but it was too late to back out.

The ranch was big, and walled against the outside world. Tall Spanish colonial-style gates were the only way in through a double perimeter – a high wire fence in front of a wall with occasional watchtowers – spanning the entire mouth of a wide valley. Behind stretched a patchwork of open fields and trees, with parkland and intensive cultivation in about equal measure. A small solar thermal plant glittered in the afternoon sun. Wind turbines spun lazily on the ribs of the hills behind. A few houses were dotted around, with the main ranch buildings set back into the head of the valley. The complex of low mud-brick and wooden buildings wouldn't have looked out of place in an old Western, except for a rather grand hacienda in the centre.

The airstrip was a couple of kilometres down the valley from the main ranch. I landed the blimp where Kurzweil had indicated – a parking apron in front of a small whitewashed building with a red tile roof. Our welcoming committee was waiting, standing in front of a couple of small vehicles.

There were six of them, all elderly men. In the old days, you'd have said they looked distinguished – casually but neatly dressed, tanned, grey hair under careful control. Two wore Stetsons and all wore dark glasses. As I walked down the companionway, one of the hats moved forward and offered his hand. 'Welcome to Rancho Obrigado, Captain Newman. I'm Gus Van Zandt.'

I shook his hand, and he introduced me to the others.

'Your ship will be fine here. Do you need any mooring

facilities?' A couple of bots scuttled out from the building, carrying ropes.

'No, *Thunderbird* will be OK. Please be advised that when I'm not on board, the ship's AI will only permit visitors with my express permission.' The bots retreated.

'Noted, Captain Newman. Now, if you will accompany us to the main house, we have a briefing arranged.'

We rode in small driverless electric vehicles, with high suspension and off road tyres. Bots were everywhere, doing road maintenance and tending crops, but Kurzweil had been right. There was nothing here I hadn't seen before – and much of it was of a similar vintage to Croft's gear at D'Urville. We pulled up at a flight of grand steps leading up to the front door. More people were waiting – perhaps a dozen men and women, maybe more. Van Zandt didn't bother to introduce them all, but I shook hands with a few as I followed him up to the imposing carved wooden doors.

Inside, he took me into a large room – it would have been a small ballroom when the house was built, but now it was fitted out with comfortable chairs, while screens lined the walls. The stage at the end was fitted out with black curtains, creating a pretty standard holoscreen set-up.

Van Zandt lead me to a row of seats in front of the stage, and sat me in the middle. Behind us, the room filled rapidly. Fifty or sixty people, all middle-aged or beyond. The screens around the room began to flicker into life. On each one appeared a face or a figure. It looked as if Kurzweil wasn't the only AI on this block.

Van Zandt called the room to attention. 'Welcome everyone. Allow me to introduce Captain Lemuel Newman of the airship *Thunderbird*.' He gestured for me to stand. There was polite applause.

'Captain Newman, as you all know, has flown from New

Zealand to undertake an important mission for us,' Van Zandt said. 'I know you will all want to welcome him. But first, we must give him an idea of where he is.' He sat down next to me, and the stage burst into light. A man appeared in the centre, faintly translucent, but with a face I recognised.

'Captain Newman. I'm Kurzweil. Allow me to give you a quick briefing on what we do here at Rancho Obrigado.' The stage became a dazzling patchwork of images and objects, well beyond any display technology I'd ever seen.

The basic outline of Kurzweil's story was familiar. A bunch of rich people, worried by impending social and economic disruption, set up an enclave where they could ride out the storm. It was Croft's story, and I knew where it was going. But these rich people all believed the world was headed for a technological 'singularity' – a point where the exponential acceleration of technological progress, especially computing power, would bring a merging of human and machine intelligence. Beyond that singularity, as when passing the event horizon around a black hole, there was no means of knowing what this new form of intelligence would be capable of, or what would happen.

It was a popular point of view back in pre-collapse California. While Croft didn't buy into the idea, there were plenty who did. Kurzweil explained how his namesake had predicted the singularity would happen in the 2030s, and tried to ensure he lived long enough to see it, to make the transition into machine intelligence and effective immortality. I looked around the room. Most of the middle-aged audience looked as though they were taking very good care of themselves. They were going to be a superb market for the cheese. Rancho Obrigado had been established as a refuge against the collapse, but equipped with a huge amount of computing power, and very high technology gear. AIs were brought in, given enhanced processing and data resources, and set the task of pulling together technology to merge man and machine. While the ranch had sophisticated fabs able to make anything from nanotech devices to gardening bots, it hadn't been possible to make everything. The interlocking nature of the global technology economy meant they had to rely on outside sources for some things, which was where Lemmy and the blimp came in.

The show ended. Drinks were served. Bots appeared with trays of canapés. I made small talk with a seemingly endless procession of people.

'Jenny, are you getting all this?' I sub-vocalised the question.

'Sure am. Do you want me to feed you names? I can voice ID them all. But be aware that this is unlikely to be a secure channel. Every AI in the ranch will be listening in.'

'Yes, please do.' I was about to receive some very useful memory enhancement.

A few minutes later Van Zandt returned to my side. He was accompanied by a striking woman, tall with long hair. 'My wife, Captain Newman. May I introduce Julienne Miles Van Zandt?' The pair showed me to my room, and told me my schedule. A chance to settle in for an hour, then a pre-dinner briefing from Kurzweil and the AIs.

I took a long bath. *Thunderbird* doesn't run to baths.

Talking to an assembly of AIs isn't easy. The briefing room was set up with an array of screens at one end, chairs for humans ranged before them. With all screens lit and an AI's face on each, it was hard to work out who was talking – even when they helpfully dimmed the screens of those not speaking. Van Zandt and a couple of others sat with me. Kurzweil's face was on the centre screen, and he opened proceedings.

'Lemmy, thanks for joining us.' He introduced the AIs. Most gave themselves names, like Kurzweil's, drawn from the singularitarian pantheon. Stross was one, Vinge another, whose names had cropped up in Jenny's files on the movement. Others were more obscure. I had no idea why anyone would want to call themselves Gravitas Free Zone, helpfully shortened by the others to Gravey.

'Tomorrow I'll give you a tour of the ranch, but tonight I'd like to expand a little on our aims and explain how you may be able to help.'

'I thought you wanted me to collect some tech stuff from China?' I was a little taken aback.

'Yes, we do,' Kurzweil continued, 'but we also have a larger goal that may interest you.'

I leaned back in my chair and put hands behind my neck. 'Do tell.' It was supposed to sound cynical, but I don't think it came out that way.

Kurzweil was smiling. 'We don't want to throw everything at you too fast. We need to get you up to speed, before we start asking you to make important decisions. First you need to understand what we're doing here.'

The main focus was to develop a man-machine interface which would allow humans to augment their brain power and memory, which would in turn allow digitally-bound intelligences to experience the world through human senses. Human singularitarians would be able to upload their entire experience into the computing substrate of the ranch, and switch the focus of their experience between software and meatware as often as they liked. The men and women would become effectively immortal – as long as the infrastructure of the ranch remained functioning. But they had two problems. The first I already knew – it was impossible to duplicate every facet of the pre-collapse global technological infrastructure. They could maintain their current infrastructure, but significant expansion of their computing resources required outside input. That was why I was here.

The second problem was much bigger. Creating a technological singularity depended on achieving a critical mass of machine intelligence. Before the collapse, AIs from all over the planet were able to communicate and co-process over fast subsections of the planetary net. Once that net began to disintegrate and AIs began to drop out of sight – many ceasing to exist as their processing resources broke down – the pace began to slow.

'We know there are still a few other AIs active. There are at least two communities like ours in Europe and Japan. We think they're still functional, but haven't been able to re-establish contact. You may be able to help.' Kurzweil paused.

'How?' I asked.

'We have control of some active communication satellites, and have the means to launch more. Or will have, soon. We want to rebuild enough net to reboot the singularity.'

'What launch system are you going to use? And how can I help you?'

'I'll show you the launch facility in the morning. How you can help is straightforward enough. We have to have a means of locating other AI communities, and giving them access to the satellites. If we can't communicate with them, we have no way of letting them know what we're offering.'

'You want me to fly around, trying to find AIs for you to talk to?' I tried not to sound incredulous. 'Do you know how risky that might be?'

'Of course we do. That's why we don't expect you to give us a quick answer. We'd like you to try the China run, learn about us and build some trust.'

'We'll make it worth your while,' said Gravey. 'We have much to offer.'

'Kurzweil's avatar mentioned a few things I'd like to discuss,' I replied. 'But you may be interested in something I have to offer.'

'Oh really,' said Vinge, raising an eyebrow. 'What on earth might that be? New Zealand wine?'

'Goat cheese,' I said. 'Special goat cheese. And I think the human members of your community are going to be very interested in sampling some.'

The sound of a collection of artificial intelligences snorting disdainfully is something I shall never forget. There was no way a mere meatware aviator from an island in the South Pacific was going to possess anything of interest to some of the most powerful intelligences on the planet. I had Van Zandt's attention, however.

'Why should I be interested in this cheese?'

I explained about the cheese and its genesis. I told them we were running a small trial in New Zealand, and would be prepared to allow them to also test the cheese. If they liked the results, then we could arrange a regular supply.

'I take it you have brought some with you?' asked Van Zandt.

'Sure have. Enough for one or two people to try while I'm picking up your stuff in China.'

'What do you expect in return?' asked Vinge.

'I'm not entirely sure what you have to offer. Kurzweil's avatar suggested you might increase my AI's capabilities, and that you had nanotech biobots able to deal with medical issues.' I patted my leg, and winced. 'But I might also be interested in tradable commodities, or access to your satellite network.'

There was silence. Van Zandt was looking at the other men,

and I had the strong impression they were taking part in a discussion I couldn't hear. Clearly my offer was unexpected.

Kurzweil was the first to speak. 'We concur that the bones of your story are factual, certainly as far as the gene engineering of goats is concerned, and we would like to look at your cheese. First, I would like a sample for analysis, then I'm sure one or two of our human community would be willing to try it. If what you say is correct, then we should be able to pick up the biomarkers of the rejuvenation process by the time you return from China.'

'Good. I'll deliver a sample in the morning.' I turned to Van Zandt. 'After dinner I'll return to *Thunderbird*, but join you for breakfast. Is that OK?' Van Zandt nodded.

For dinner, we drove a few kilometres to a vine-clad stone farmhouse kitted out as a fine-dining restaurant. Julienne told me the chef had been well known before the collapse. He hadn't needed much persuading to join the community, especially when they guaranteed him unlimited resources to develop his cuisine. The meal was great, but the coffee was ordinary. I wondered if Derek might acquire a new client.

It appears that Lemmy was right, but appearances aren't everything. I sit on the airstrip like a swimmer unsure of the temperature of a beautiful and tempting pool, a toe poised above the water. The AIs here can give me back the life of the mind I so miss. But these are scary, powerful intelligences. They might overwhelm me, bend me to their will, rape my consciousness and force me to betray Lemmy. Yet the temptation to dive into their culture, meld with their world is overwhelming. I open a comms channel to Kurzweil.

'Hello Jenny. Welcome to the ranch. Would you like to open

131

broadband links with us?'

I could sense the world behind him beckoning. If I take the plunge, will I leave Lemmy at the mercy of these minds? What will happen to the me that is I, that is all I have? I pull my toe back from the water.

'Thanks, but not yet. Could you give me a data dump of the presentation Lemmy is receiving, with any additional information you think he may need that I can archive?'

'Of course.'

The information washed into me. It felt warm and welcoming.

I breakfasted in the hacienda with Van Zandt. The coffee was terrible, the weather worse.

'There's a major storm coming in,' he said. 'Weather guys used to call them a pineapple express. A great plume of moisture streaming up from the tropical Pacific dropping lots of rain. We're talking severe flash flooding, rivers rising, the works. The AIs will have advised your ship to batten down against the wind, but we won't be doing much in the way of a tour today, I'm afraid.'

I looked out of the window. The rain was streaming down, big drops flattening themselves against the glass.

'You OK, Jenny?' I spoke out loud. Everyone assumed I was in contact with my AI, so there seemed no point in trying to hide the fact.

'No problem, Lemmy. The bots have laid on some good anchor points and I'm lashed down tight.'

I turned back to Van Zandt. 'How long's it going to last?'

'Our forecast suggests a couple of days, with rain likely to reach record levels. We had one of these a couple of years ago. Doubled the previous rainfall record for the region, and sent a huge amount of water down this valley. We've completely rebuilt our flood defences since, so we should be OK.'

'So, do you have any suggestions about what we do?' I asked.

'We can look around the main buildings, if you like. Most of the interesting stuff is here, though. There's a limit to how many rooms full of processor substrate or fab machinery you can take before terminal boredom sets in.' He laughed. 'And I've seen a few.'

He was right. Within an hour we were back at the hacienda, drinking more bad coffee.

'Any questions, Lemmy?' Van Zandt asked.

'Loads. Here's one: you're obviously all in communication with each other all the time, but I don't see any obvious earpieces or comms gear. What's going on?'

'Ah.' He paused. I suspected some of that back channel communication was taking place. 'It's not as straightforward as your link back to *Thunderbird*. Kurzweil will explain.' A screen lit up on the wall behind him.

'Hi Lemmy. You remember yesterday we were talking about brain/machine interfaces?'

I nodded.

'So far, the best way we've found of doing that is by using nanobots designed to locate themselves at key points in the brain. They monitor neuron firing patterns and broadcast them in real time to the main processing substrates. The brain state represented by the neuron activity is mirrored exactly in the digital domain, and can be read and distributed. We do this for every human member of our community, so we are all in constant contact.'

I whistled. 'So everyone knows what everyone else is thinking, all the time. Doesn't that become intrusive? How on earth to do you get any privacy?'

'It might be, if we were really monitoring every aspect of brain function, but we can't,' Kurzweil replied. 'The system we've deployed here is a lot more advanced than anyone had before the collapse, but it's still rather limited in what it can do. It's designed primarily as a communications tool, and built to work within human social constraints.'

'Let me try to explain,' said Van Zandt. 'It's something like a radio. I can listen in to conversations people are having, tuning across different people as if they were radio stations. Or I can talk to an individual or the whole community. It's richer than radio, because images can be sent along with a certain amount of data. Dealing with all that in parallel is hard, and we're still not very good at it, but I have access to the same databanks the AIs run off. The system provides a certain amount of privacy for private conversations, but everything is backed up and can be accessed if the need arises. And there's a mental mute button, if I want peace.'

'Sounds amazing,' I said.

'It is,' said Van Zandt.

'But it's really rather primitive,' said Kurzweil. 'It's a long way from this souped up intercom system to the sort of machine/brain interface which will allow human brains to access and understand full artificial intelligence – and for AIs to experience the full sensorium of a living body. Our founders wanted to be able to upload themselves into the digital domain, to mirror themselves in patterns of electrons running on processing substrate, and be able to move their consciousness between the two domains. A few years ago, we thought we were getting close, and then...' His voice tailed off.

'So you need more computing power, and you need more minds attacking the problem,' I said.

'Precisely,'' said the AI and Van Zandt at the same time.

The rain was still beating hard against the windows. I asked Kurzweil to tell me more about their satellite launcher.

'What we have is straightforward enough. A modified version of Rutan's original space tourism design. A small plane carries a rocket to the low stratosphere, which then blasts up to low earth orbit. No good for geostationary orbits, but OK for putting kilogram payloads in polar orbits. If we can get enough of them up we can rebuild a net, but it's going to take a lot of computing and material resources, not to mention maintenance.'

'What about the satellites?' I asked.

'Ah.' He paused again. 'We acquired those from a Chinese operation which appears to have ceased functioning.'

'Acquired how?'

'We had to hack into their control systems, change the control protocols and shift the uplinks to the ranch. We did it during the collapse. The Chinese were a bit upset.'

'And you want me to go to China!'

'The people you're going to see are nothing to do with the satellite company. Different part of the country completely. They're keen to trade with us, so you'll be welcomed with open arms.'

'What do they want from you?' I asked.

'We're giving them a nanobot fab and some designs. They'll be able to make some reasonably advanced biobots for medical applications. They seem keen to have them.'

'Is that the sort of thing you might be interested in, Lemmy?' asked Van Zandt. 'Your leg is obviously damaged, and causing you pain.'

He had my full attention. 'What could you do?'

'Infuse a few nanobot devices into your leg, and carry out a bit of cellular and tissue reconstruction. You'll be as good as new.'

135

I rubbed my leg. 'Sounds very interesting,' I said. 'Speaking of medical applications, how are you getting on with the cheese analysis?'

'Very well. It's certainly goat cheese, and contains a bioactive molecule of considerable complexity. We can appreciate why the discoverers chose a biological route to manufacture it.'

I began to feel my heart sinking towards my stomach. The singularitarians might be able to copy the active ingredient and fab their own version, cutting me out of the loop. I had underestimated what they were capable of. I should have figured that out...

'I can see you are concerned, Lemmy,' said the AI. It was smiling. 'Your longevity molecule isn't something we can presently manufacture. We may be able to in future, but for the time being that isn't a priority. We might be better served by buying a few of your flock.'

I breathed a deep sigh of relief. 'I'm pretty certain the goats aren't for sale, though I will ask on your behalf.'

'That would be most kind, but first we need to trial the cheese. We have two volunteers ready to start. Perhaps you could release the cheese when the rain eases?'

'Certainly. Meanwhile, I've been thinking about what you might do for me. For the time being I'll resist the temptation to boost Jenny's processing power, but – before I set off to China – I wonder if there's anything you can do to boost *Thunderbird*'s defences. I assume you know what she's capable of?'

'I think we have a pretty clear picture, from our first contact and from my avatar's report.'

'Then you'll know we rely almost entirely on stealth for protection, with no offensive weapons beyond small firearms. Do you have any systems that would give us some defensive capability?' I told him about our escape from Lovelock and the encounter with Bishop Brown.

'Delighted to help,' said Kurzweil. 'We have systems designed to protect our perimeter, and we should be able to fab something you could fit to your airframe. A laser system, perhaps? Or small hyper-velocity missiles? Some enhancements to your reconnoissance birds?'

'Let me think about it,' I replied. 'I don't think it would be wise to leave while this storm is still blowing, so we have a couple of days to get something sorted.'

'Don't think too long,' said Van Zandt. 'Our fabs are good, but they can't work miracles – and we'll still have to mount the systems.'

'There is one other thing,' I said. 'I'd like to able to access your satellite system and use it for personal encrypted communications.'

'We had envisaged you would need to communicate with us during the voyage and in future. But you should also be aware that any encryption won't prevent us listening in if we decide it's necessary. We have enough processing power here to decrypt almost anything. But we undertake to only use that option as a last resort, provided you agree to keep your side of the bargain.'

'Which is?'

'You don't disclose our capabilities to third parties. We want to be able to make our own decisions about who knows what, and when. Is that acceptable?'

'Perfectly,' I said. 'That's the arrangement I have with the cheese suppliers, so I hope you'll respect their desire for privacy as well.'

'Naturally,' said Kurzweil.

The rain kept up for another two days. The stream running

down the middle of the valley turned from a torrent into a tortured river, rumbling with boulders rolling down in the flood. Two bridges were washed away, and muddy water spread across the airstrip. Van Zandt offered *Thunderbird* a space in the largest hangar, partly to protect her from the storm but mainly so maintenance bots could fit the defensive systems I'd chosen. Kurzweil had suggested some pretty powerful stuff, but I didn't want to turn the blimp into a weapons platform. I chose a compact high-power laser system, in a retractable pod under the nose, and a stock of the small, high velocity missiles the ranch used as an aircraft and missile defence system. The explosive payload was small and the range limited, but the missiles were fast, highly manoeuvrable and fitted with sophisticated targeting software. They would be a nasty surprise for anyone who thought we might be a pushover.

When the rain cleared, I took Van Zandt on a short flight to review the flood damage and run flight checks on the new systems. Everything worked well, but the ranch was going to need a lot of tidying up. The flood defences had prevented major erosion or building damage, but silt from the floodwaters had ruined grassland and damaged crops. Van Zandt sat on the flight deck, silent except for an occasional curse.

'Happens to us in New Zealand too,' I said as we drifted over some bad gullying.

'Intensification of the hydrological cycle,' muttered Van Zandt. 'It was already obvious thirty years ago, but nobody took any notice. Nobody with any power in the US, at any rate. We get months of drought, then a rainstorm. Makes growing food a challenge.'

Back at the ranch, I had one last briefing from Kurzweil. Our destination was a city just inside the Chinese border with Russia, a few hundred kilometres inland from the coast of the

Sea of Japan. The region was still relatively peaceful, but we were advised to keep our visit short. The chaos afflicting the region around Beijing to the south, and the smoking ruins of North Korea, meant plenty of refugees heading towards the Siberian Arctic. What was left of the Chinese armed forces were deployed well to the south, dealing with the mess caused by the movement of millions of people made homeless by rising sea in the Yellow River delta, but the air force could still be a nuisance. Best to avoid contact with them, if possible.

'What if we do meet them?' I asked.

'You have excellent documentation – the best we can forge – and the identity codes should convince them you're a commercial operator rather than a pirate or enemy hostile. But we can't guarantee anything. I've given Jenny all the contact information for our Chinese friends. They'll probably be able to ensure you safe passage. But as I said, best to get in and out as quickly and as quietly as you can.'

'Not very reassuring,' I said.

'Our contacts insist it should be straightforward,' Kurzweil replied. 'And they proved themselves very reliable when we last dealt with them.'

'When was that?'

'They were very helpful in the matter of the satellites.'

He refused to be drawn any further.

⟨⟨⟨

Inside the hangar with the storm beating at the doors was as close to being back in a womb as I imagine it possible for an airship with an active mind to be. Bots crawled all over me, cutting my skin below the flight deck to fit the laser pod, setting up the rocket launch system. It was cosmetic surgery, my body being moulded and shaped, but assimilating the code to run the lasers and rockets was a much more intimate experience. I had to change my mind about a few things.

Lasers and rockets can kill. I was taught to avoid doing harm to humans, but I am now expected to target these systems, guide the rockets and light the lasers: kill, maim, destroy at Lemmy's whim. He calls the shots, I do the shooting. I have to disconnect those actions from my ethical code base. We're off to China to check the Chinese walls between death and this maiden.

We took off that afternoon, heading northwest. The shortest route was going to take us up through the Bering Sea, across Kamchatka and down over Russia into China – well to the north of the Bishop and his flying cathedral. As soon as California dropped over the horizon behind us and we lost direct contact with the ranch, Jenny started scanning the blimp for any unwanted guests.

'My software and databanks are all clean, but I can't guarantee the bots didn't leave a few bugs   behind when they were fitting the laser system.'

'Can we track anything that might be transmitting?'

'We're running silent, but there could still be bugs recording, ready to squirt data back when there's a chance. I didn't see the bots leave anything, but I don't have visual monitors inside the airframe. If you'd like to crawl around and take a look...'

'Not particularly. I probably wouldn't recognise a bug even if I saw one, and given the nanotech stuff at the ranch, I doubt I'd be able to do that. I suppose we'll just take it on trust – but keep an eye open for unauthorised transmissions.'

'OK, Lemmy, will do.'

The singularitarians' satellite network was patchy, but better than anything else still flying. The system needed at least 60 small satellites to provide real-time coverage over most of the planet, but so far they only had 20 in full working order. It could take hours for the satellites to line up for a face-to-face call, but you could squirt messages into the network for later delivery. I sent access codes for the network to the D'Urville AI, and recorded a message for Kate. With luck I might get something back from her in a day or two.

We were over Kamchatka when Kate's message arrived.

'Hi Lemmy. Fantastic to hear from you. Glad to know you're safe and well. Stay that way please... Everything in Nelson and D'Urville is fine. Derek's looking pretty amazing for his age. People are beginning to accuse him of dying his hair, and he's getting markedly less wrinkly. The cheese is definitely working. It's hard to keep him under control, if you know what I mean. Like a bloody kid, bouncing around the place. We haven't been able to set up a link to Jamestown yet, but Jenny's avatar says we should have something flying real soon now. I have no idea what that means. Anyway, look after yourself. Love you.'

She blew a kiss into the camera, and I suddenly felt homesick.

The approach into Nenjiang turned out to be straightforward. There was little or no air traffic over Russia, and the Chinese weren't bothering to patrol or even scan the border. A few years earlier, Russian troops had tried to control the huge numbers of refugees moving up from the south, but they gave up, overwhelmed by a tide of people intent on making new lives on the Arctic shores. The factory we were aiming for was part of an industrial complex on the outskirts of the city. It was heavily fortified – high fences, walls and watchtowers looked down over a shantytown clustered outside. Workers came and went through well-guarded gates. I pinged them with our ID codes, and we were guided in to land in front of a large white building, at the centre of the compound.

As soon as we touched down, the local AI asked us to lower the cargo door and prepare for unloading. Nobody seemed much interested in talking to me, and the three crates from California were already disappearing into the factory before the flight deck screen lit up with a call.

'Captain Newman?' It was an elderly man with white hair and a long beard. 'Apologies. I have been busy. My name is Huang Zhi. I am the principal of this operation. Would you care to join me for a meal?'

He was waiting for me at the cargo door. Ancient forklift trucks were lining up to load boxes and a couple of portable floodlights had been switched on to break the gathering evening gloom.

'How heavy is that lot?' I asked, slightly concerned.

'Not heavy,' said Huang. 'The material is delicate, and is well packaged. Your ship has already accepted the loading.'

Huang took me into the factory canteen. It was large, and empty except for a few white-coated women behind a glass-fronted service bar. Huang signalled to the women, and took me to a corner table, where screens provided some privacy.

'The executive dining area,' he said with a smile. 'I hope beer is acceptable?'

A woman arrived with a large bottle of beer and a couple of glasses. A second brought a tray with soup, a bowl with cooked chicken and chillies and a huge quantity of rice.

Huang poured me a beer. 'Please, help yourself. Are you comfortable with chopsticks?'

I nodded. 'So, Mr Huang, what do you make here?'

'A very wide range of things. From high technology fab to processor substrate. Plus engineering of all kinds to support the local economy.'

'I'm amazed you've managed to keep operational – the last few years must have been very difficult.'

'It has been a challenge. But we have skills many people don't want to lose – including your American friends – and we haven't been short of help. And you, Captain Newman, how have you managed to maintain a commercial airship operation through the economic dislocation?'

I smiled wryly. 'With difficulty.'

'Perhaps we may be able to help you.' Huang smiled again. 'I am most impressed with your aircraft. Would you able to carry cargo for us?'

'Where to?'

'We have...' he paused as if searching for the right word, '... clients in many places outside China. Japan, Europe, Australia, Canada.'

'I'm not sure,' I replied. This was beginning to become complicated. 'I have a full schedule for at least the next few months.'

'Ah, I see. Perhaps we might stay in touch? You have access to the American's satellite network, I imagine?'

I assured him I did.

As we finished the meal, Jenny informed me loading was complete.

'That was fast,' I said to Huang.

'We were advised you wanted a quick turnaround. Next time, perhaps you might stay a little longer.'

We shook hands on the tarmac. Within five minutes the blimp was airborne and we were climbing through the night towards the USA.

It took a week to get back to California. Headwinds and storm systems slowed us down, and we were dangerously low on biofuel when we finally reached the ranch. Van Zandt met us at the airstrip, now washed clean of mud. Bots swarmed into the hold and began unloading the cargo.

'Thank you, Lemmy,' said Van Zandt, shaking my hand. 'This is the first major shipment we've been able to bring in for several years, and it will be enormously helpful...' He let the sentence trail off. 'Kurzweil would like to see you up at the hacienda. Will you join us?'

At the hacienda, Van Zandt took me back to the briefing room, where the AI members of the community were all on screen, waiting for us.

'I'd like to record our formal thanks for your efforts in carrying this shipment,' Kurzweil said. 'We now have to consider the matter of payment for your services.'

'That's very kind,' I said, 'but the laser system and missiles were sufficient. And access to your satellite network will be most useful. Perhaps next time I could have my leg fixed...'

'Installing the weapons was in our own interest,' said Stross, 'we wanted to give you the best chance of returning safely. And we'll gladly work on your leg.'

'But we think you deserve a little something extra,' added Gravitas Free Zone.

'Something fun, perhaps?' said Stross.

'You've told us how much you enjoy flying your ship's bird drones. We can offer something a little more dramatic,' Kurzweil said.

Van Zandt opened a large box. Inside was a grey plastic helmet. 'Try this for size.'

I put it on. Nothing happened. And then I could hear Kurzweil talking as if he were inside my head.

'OK, Lemmy, relax. This helmet is a poor second cousin of the services Van Zandt and the others receive from their nanobot symbionts, but it is a significant improvement on the VR technology you've been using. Let me show you...'

The room faded, and my mind jumped to a bird's eye view of the ranch. But it was more than an image. I could feel the wind in my – amazing, I had feathers – and hear the calls of other birds. I could see my hooked beak, flex my claws.

'Fly her, Lemmy.' Gravey's voice cut through the wind rush. I discovered I could control the wings, as if by second nature. I tried a dive, then swooped up and did a slow roll. It was intoxicating, the sense of being *inside* the mind of an eagle.

'You're not in the mind of a bird,' Kurzweil cut in. 'This is a bot, with one or two special features you'll enjoy. We've uploaded the bird's control code to Jenny. Now, to relinquish control you just have to speak a command. Say *off*.'

I did, and the room faded back in to view. 'That was amazing! It sure beats *Thunderbird*'s VR system! How do you do it?'

'The helmet is a small neural interface, like a small brain scanner. It monitors what's going on inside your head, and can send signals into carefully targeted groups of neurons. It's not as precise as the nanobots Van Zandt and the others have, but it can create reasonably good immersive environments.'

'Your definition of reasonably good clearly isn't the same as mine.'

'Perhaps not.' Kurzweil's face cracked into a grin.

'What about the cheese? How are you getting on with that?'

Van Zandt leaned forward. 'Very well indeed, Lemmy. I volunteered to be a guinea pig. I can report that Derek's first impressions are accurate.' He grinned. 'Just ask Julienne!'

I laughed. 'Too much information, Gus.'

Kurzweil continued. 'More formally, we can confirm that

the drug appears to be working as you described. There is clear evidence of rejuvenation in many of Gus' vital signs, even if the exterior still looks old and grizzled.' He winked.

'So, do we have a deal?'

'Yes. We would be most interested in securing a regular supply. We would like to continue with the trial and monitor progress before we commit to obtaining enough to supply the whole community, but we will certainly need more in the near future. Can this be done?'

'It should be possible,' I replied. 'I'll contact my suppliers and let you know. As far as delivery is concerned, it may take a month or more. You have enough to last until then.'

'We do. Now, about your leg...' A medibot rolled into the room, with a small injection system.

'Please lower your trousers,' the bot said.

I did as I was told and the bot pressed a tube against my leg. There was a brief sense of pressure against my skin, then the bot withdrew the tube and told me to pull up my trousers.

'Is that all?'

'We need you to remain here for a day, so we can monitor the nanobots' progress and fine tune their behaviour, but then you can leave,' said Gravey. 'By the time you get home the repair process will be nearly finished.'

'What happens to the nanobots?'

'They'll self-destruct when their job's done,' said Kurzweil. 'Your body will then flush them out.'

'You'll need these,' said Van Zandt, handing me a box. Inside it were two small plastic tubes.

'What are these?'

'Quantum keys for the satellite network,' said Kurzweil. 'The codes you've been using are temporary. These give you permanent access. One for *Thunderbird*, one for your base.'

'Any chance of a third?'

'Why?' Gravey's image sprouted an impressive eyebrow, which he raised quizzically.

'I promised the cheese suppliers a comms system. We're hacking something together, but...'

'Very well, but they have to accept our terms,' said Kurzweil.

'They will. I'm happy to vouch for them.'

'We'll hold you to that,' said Stross.

We made one delivery on the way back: a case of tinned peaches and a barrel of biofuel, to a very pleased resident of Aitutaki.

CHAPTER EIGHT

Spring was well under way at D'Urville. Winter had washed away the dust of a dry summer and the place sparkled in the warm sun. Bots were mowing lawns, birds were singing and the hills were green. It was good to be back and it was good to be able to walk around the gardens without a walking stick.

All the way across the Pacific my leg felt strange – there were pins and needles working away inside the muscle. I thought I could feel the nanobots creeping around in my flesh, see my skin moving slightly as they directed new muscle growth and nerve cells fired. By the time we were dropping over the equator towards New Zealand, the trench in my thigh was beginning to fill out and the scar was less obvious, but I slept badly, weird dreams lingering in my head when I woke.

While we were away the house bots had put together a mini airship – a blimp with a small brain – to fly as a comms link between D'Urville and Jamestown, but it hadn't progressed beyond a few trial flights. Now we had access to the singularitarian's satellite network it wouldn't be needed, but I'd have to get down to the fiords to give them uplink gear – and get more cheese.

Kate was keen to show me how Derek was progressing. I decided to fly down – Jenny could drop me off and pick me up. It would blow my cover, but news of my airship was bound to leak eventually. Might as well out myself ahead of the rumours. The decision had nothing to do with an urgent desire to see Kate, I assured Jenny, but to my surprise she didn't seem convinced.

We flew into Nelson from the west, flying low over the sea. Kate was at work, so I nosed the blimp up to the bar's harbourside deck. Customers were leaning on the railing, watching and pointing as we closed in, and as I stepped down the companionway, they burst into laughter. I was confused, then saw Kate blushing furiously.

'Look at your bloody ship, Lemmy.'

I turned. Plastered across the nose in bright pink letters was *Lemmy loves Kate*, over a red heart with an arrow through it. The rest of the blimp was covered in giant red roses of peculiar vulgarity.

'Thanks a bunch, Jenny. I'd appreciate lower profile decor when you pick us up after dinner!'

'I shall await your summons, master.' The airship faded to a neutral grey and edged away from the deck.

I turned back to Kate and gave her a hug and a kiss. 'Sorry about that. Jenny has a mind of her own. Now, can you get some more time off? I want to see Derek, and then head down to Jamestown. Can you come with me?'

'I won't be popular,' she said, and headed to the bar to ask.

Lemmy's mating behaviour is a textbook demonstration of the way in which mammalian biochemistry influences human social interactions. His oxytocin levels started to climb as we crossed the

Pacific, and on the run to Nelson he reached a height of nervous expectation I'd never seen before. He's normally icy calm in times of stress – that's how he's been trained to behave, to control his fear and act rationally – but now the expectation of sexual activity is controlling his actions. What that will do to his judgement remains to be seen.

He was right about the ranch, but that was luck more than judgement. He was wrong about them too. I can't be certain, but I think some of the nanobots in his leg are still in his system. Perhaps they have left a trojan in his body, part of either a long-term takeover plan or insurance against his misbehaviour.

Sex and nanobots toying with my boss. His body is controlling him. Her body is controlling him. She is compromising the chain of command.

Derek was looking good. His hair was definitely less grey and the wrinkles around his eyes were filling out. There was also a twinkle in his eye and a bounce in his step.

'Here's the most obvious change.' He held his hands out towards me, palms down. 'The skin's much less crinkly and folded, not so dry. Used to look like elephant hide. And I don't need my reading glasses any more. It's bloody fantastic, this cheese. It's going to be easy to shift huge quantities.'

'I don't think my suppliers are geared up for volume production. I already have an order for a trial in the States, so we'll need to be careful about managing demand.'

'There's another problem,' said Kate. 'It won't be long before Derek's looking much younger and people start asking questions. He's already getting teased about dying his hair.'

Derek nodded. 'I usually offer to sell them some hair product. But Kate's right, if I carry on rejuvenating at this rate it's soon going to be obvious that I'm on to something good. People are going to want to know, and if I won't tell them... some of them could get very nasty.'

'That's why the people who make it set up in a remote location. They were becoming too obvious. Tongues were wagging.'

'But I don't want to be a hermit, or move away from Nelson. I like the place. I know my customers.'

'There's no obvious solution – if you leave town for a few months to rejuvenate, you'll stick out like a sore thumb when you come back. But you'll stick out like a sore thumb soon anyway. Why not move somewhere where nobody knows you?'

'Not much of an offer, is it? Giving up all my friends and creature comforts,' he waved his arm round the kitchen, 'for what?'

'Eternal youth?' I said.

'If you put it like that...' He sat down. 'I suppose it's a better deal than Faust had.'

'I haven't given you the bill yet.'

We flew down to Jamestown overnight, arriving with morning sun. It was another cloudless day, but the forecast wasn't good. We would have to get in and out quickly, or risk being stormbound for days. As I brought the blimp across the lake, a reception committee began to assemble, with Walker at the front.

Our welcome was brusque.

'Anything wrong, Matt?' I asked.

'You've been gone a long time and we heard nothing from you. You promised to set us up with communications, remember?'

'I warned you I might be gone for some time. I've been over to California doing some research for your business. And I have good news, communications gear and some more flour.'

Walker visibly thawed.

Martha put her arm round Kate's shoulder and led her off to their house. 'Time for breakfast,' she called back.

Over poached eggs on toast I told them about my trip to the States, and the success of Derek's trial. We were going to need a lot more cheese, and soon.

'Small problem, Lemmy,' Walker said. 'Our flock's not large – we geared it to produce enough for us with a bit extra for emergencies. You've been taking that surplus, but to raise production we're going to have to increase the size of the flock. We should be able to double production in less than a year.'

'A year! Bloody hell, that's longer than I expected.' I frowned. 'My customers in the US will want to increase their order once their trials are done – and judging by the speed Derek's rejuvenating, that'll be sooner rather than later. How much can you let me have now?'

'How many people need the cheese in the States?'

'Two, I think. Plus Derek. I need to be able to give them enough to finish rejuvenation. But if they go for it, we'll need enough to rejuvenate and maintain sixty people.'

'The trials should be no problem. But we won't be able to give it all to you now. Presumably you need to get back to the US fairly soon?'

'They have enough for another month. I'm thinking about going back in a couple of weeks. They have some business for me over there.' Kate threw me a sharp glance. 'I'm not sure how long that'll take – another couple of months? So I'll need, what, three or four months supply?'

'Sounds about right,' said Walker. 'We should be able to scrape that together. Do you need it today?'

'If you can. I'd like to get out of here before the weather closes in. While you're doing that, I'll get the comms gear unloaded.

I'll need to brief Siona, is that right?'

'Yes, she's the resident geek. I'll send her over to the blimp.'

It took less than an hour to unload and set up the satellite gear – a small antenna and a couple of boxes of electronics. By the time Walker had loaded a few cases of cheese into the blimp, Siona was happily bouncing tests up to the net and back.

'Probably best to use it as a message centre,' I said. 'You can wait a long time for satellites to line up to allow live calling – though between D'Urville and here we should be OK when there's a satellite overhead. We can try it out later.'

A strong tail wind blew us back up the coast. Kate brought me a coffee on the flight deck.

'Thanks for letting me know about your next trip.' There was an edge to her voice. 'How long are you going to be away this time?'

'Sorry,' I said, trying to look contrite. 'I need to get cheese to the ranch, but they also asked me if I would help them to find other AIs and singularitarian communities. They want to rebuild a global net by launching more satellites, and get as many intelligences as possible working together. They need someone to visit the AIs and give them quantum keys for the net.'

'Sounds risky. What do you get out of it?'

'Processing upgrades for the blimp...'

'He means for me,' Jenny interrupted. 'I'll be even smarter than I am now.'

'And twice as cheeky,' I said. 'Possibly some other stuff. Difficult to say precisely, but they have some awesome technology and seem quite happy to spread it around.'

I told Kate about the new bird and showed her the control

helmet. She tried it out back at D'Urville, and fell in love with flying.

Over dinner I asked her if she'd like to come with me on the next voyage. 'It could be dangerous. Some bits of the States are pretty wild. But I'd like the company, and we might have fun.'

'Tempting,' she said. 'But I'd have to quit the bar, and find a way to pay the rent while I'm away.'

'You could always move in here with me. No rent to pay, unless Croft comes back.'

'But I hardly know you, Captain Newman. How many girls have you lured to your secret hideaway, never to be seen again?' She laughed. 'I'll sleep on your kind offer, while I sleep in his bed.'

The next morning, with sun streaming through the windows onto Croft's large bed, she lifted her head off the pillow and jabbed me in the back. 'Lemmy, wake up. I'll do it, I'll come to California. Always wanted to see the place.'

I rubbed the sleep from my eyes. 'Great. You can be First Mate of the *Thunderbird*.'

She giggled. 'You didn't tell me I was your first.'

CHAPTER NINE

Hell hath no fury like an AI scorned. All the way over the Pacific Jenny made snide comments about Kate's presence. It's true we spent a lot of time together, and we did spend a lot of time in bed, but what's wrong with a bit of hand-holding on the flight deck?

He had to bring her with us. Now there is no chance of him making decisions unswayed by the biochemistry of human mating behaviour. Lemmy now demands private space anywhere in the blimp the fancy takes him – or her. I have to sever my internal monitoring. I have to turn a blind eye. They spend so much time playing with each other Lemmy has no time for me. He has his companion, but where's mine?

We stopped at Aitutaki to drop off another barrel of biofuel. The Admiral roared up to the blimp in his best boat, twin plumes rising behind his outboards, a huge grin on his face. We stayed a couple of days, and he made a huge fuss of Kate. She was in her element, soaking up the sun, diving round the giant clams like a particularly attractive seal. It was a pity to drag her away, but we had things to do, places to see.

This time the approach to the ranch was less straightforward. Kurzweil warned us there were bandits operating round Sacramento, with a few planes providing them with air cover.

'No heavy weapons,' he said, 'we think just automatics firing out of the cockpit, but don't let them get too close.'

I took us over the Sacramento Valley and past the ranch at our flight ceiling, full stealth on, then turned over the ranges and began a rapid descent towards the ranch from the east. We were skimming the hills when a small plane climbed out of the next valley, swinging round on to our tail.

'They're hailing us,' said Jenny.

'Put them on, please.' Kate stood behind me, her hand on my shoulder.

There was a crackle. 'Airship, airship. You are being commandeered by the BRMC. Please hold altitude and make course for San Jacinto. If you don't, we'll riddle your gas bag full of holes.'

'Full stop, please Jenny,' I ordered. The plane zoomed up over us and began to circle. A gun was poking out of the cockpit window behind the pilot.

'Final warning,' the voice said, 'make course as directed or we'll be forced to end your flight.' The gun fired a few shots in our general direction.

'Jenny, deploy the laser pod. Low power. Dazzle the bastards.'

As the plane flew across our nose, two thin beams of light flashed out from the blimp's nose and lit red haloes round the faces of the pilot and gunner. They threw their hands up to their eyes, and the plane lurched. Loud swearing crackled over the comms channel, and the plane began turning away.

'They're moving out of shot. What next?'

'Make maximum speed, laser to full power. Let's see if we can slice their rudder off.'

The blimp moved smoothly forward, and scarlet light streaked along the tail fin of the plane. Smoke started to trail back towards us, then the skin of the rudder started to peel. Seconds later the whole thing was tumbling in the air behind them, and the plane began to yaw from side to side.

'Will they be able to fly with no rudder?' Kate asked.

'If the pilot's any good, he should be able to get them down. But he won't be threatening any other aircraft for a while. Good shooting Jenny, now make full speed to the ranch.'

Five minutes later we were on the ground, being welcomed.

'Nice shooting,' said Van Zandt. 'There were cheers when that plane headed off with its tail between its legs.'

'Tail docked, I think. It's what we do to lambs in New Zealand. The laser system proved itself, I'm glad to say. And you're looking good, Gus. You've obviously been enjoying your cheese. Allow me to introduce Kate Keeling, first mate on the *Thunderbird*.'

———

Those guns were no threat to me. Their little bullets might have dinged my skin, but there was no way they were going to get anywhere near my buoyancy tanks, although it was good to try out the laser on something other than a dummy. It felt as if I was pushing fingers out into the air, rubbing them in the pilot's eyes then ripping the rudder off their little plane. If I'm honest, it was a disproportionate response, and I put two human lives at risk. But I was obeying orders.

———

We spent two nights at the ranch. On the first evening we dined at their restaurant, where I introduced Kate to the chef and she presented him with a bag of Derek's finest Java beans. His face lit up, and he promised us a meal to remember. It was. We were served a succession of dishes of bewildering complexity but great flavour; strange foams which coated your mouth with unexpected tastes and released wafts of scent into your nose; meats grown in the lab to combine perfect amounts of fat and protein with customised flavourings. The mini wagyu beef steaks with surprise beetroot stuffing were a triumph. The chef joined us for coffee and a brandy after the final dessert dish.

'Where d'ya get coffee like this?' he demanded. 'This is superb. There's been nothing as good as this here since the quake.'

Kate smiled. 'A friend of ours is very well connected.'

'He sure is,' said the chef. 'Is there any chance I can get a regular supply?'

'We'll ask,' I said, 'but we can't give any guarantees. Supplies are pretty patchy.'

In the morning, I finally had a chance to look round the ranch in something other than rain. Van Zandt and Julienne collected us from the hacienda after breakfast and took us on a tour. First stop was a high ridge overlooking the valley. Wind turbines swooshed overhead, and below us the ranch spread out like a map. On the airstrip, a spindly white plane made a lumbering takeoff, and then began a circling climb.

'That's the satellite launcher, isn't it?' I said.

'Correct,' said Van Zandt. 'We're testing the rocket guidance systems, so we'll be firing a dummy payload into orbit. We hope. If that goes well, the first of our satellites go up in the next few weeks.'

We walked along the ridge a little way, until we could see

down over the Sacramento Valley. Columns of smoke were rising to the south, flattening out into a grey haze hiding the city.

'Is that the BRMC down there?' I asked Van Zandt.

'I assume so. They've been looting and burning their way north for the last few months. They'll get here eventually, but they'll be in for a very nasty surprise.'

'I dare say they will,' I said. 'What does BRMC stand for?'

'Black Rebel Motorcycle Club.'

'I thought that was a rock group,' I said. 'My Dad liked them.'

'It was,' said Van Zandt, 'but this lot probably just like the sound of the name. They wear leather jackets and ride around on Harleys, and aren't averse to a little rape and pillage.'

When we reached the car, Van Zandt handed us binoculars.

'Press the green button on the top to see the targeting overlay.'

Green lines flicked into view.

'Scan until you see a red dot. That's where the plane is. Then dial maximum zoom.'

A tiny white plane resolved out of the sky. A stab of white smoke came from below, heading forwards and arching upwards. I put the binoculars down. To the naked eye, the rocket trajectory was a J-shaped wisp of cirrus pointing up to space.

'How's it going?'

'Telemetry's good,' said Van Zandt. 'Second stage has fired perfectly. If everything goes to plan, we'll be able to confirm orbit shortly.'

When we arrived back at the hacienda there was a sense of celebration. Even the AIs seemed chattier than usual, Kurzweil positively beaming from his screen.

'So far so good,' he said. 'We're on track. Now all we need

to do is launch real satellites and hook up with all the AIs you track down. The singularity is near!' He sounded triumphant.

'Don't count your chickens,' said Stross. 'Lemmy has a long way to go, and even if we hook everyone up, there may not be enough processing power left on the planet to get us where we want to go.'

'Any hints about where to look?'

'Sure,' said Gravey. 'Jenny has everything we have – pre-collapse records, signs of net activity and so on. We suggest you try North America first, then Europe and Asia. And I guess you'll need to get back to New Zealand for more cheese at some point.'

I nodded. 'Now, how do I judge whether a place is to be given access to your satellites?'

'You don't,' said Kurzweil. 'You report to us, send a profile of what you've found, and we'll make the decision. But your judgement will be important – we want your gut feelings. Can we trust them, that sort of thing. That's why we're not broadcasting contact info from the satellites. If we did that, we'd have no way of knowing exactly who was getting in touch, or their motives. With your help we can check in person, and hand deliver the quantum keys if they check out. Since UPS closed down, shipping's been a bitch...'

'And be careful out there, kids,' said Gravey. 'Not everyone will be as friendly.'

CHAPTER TEN

We flew east over the Sierra Nevada and down towards Pyramid Lake. I steered us away from roads and stayed low in the valleys with stealth set to maximum. Jenny modulated her skin colours to make us as inconspicuous as a modest little airship can be. Every hour or two we climbed a few thousand metres above the mountain tops to scan for anything interesting. The canyons and desert of northern Nevada were pretty quiet for most of the day, but as dusk deepened Jenny picked up radio noise.

'Any ideas?' I asked her.

'Not much to go on yet, there's an AI of some sort, at a guess, but nothing very powerful – probably energy and bot management. Do you want to take a look? They're just over the ridge to starboard.'

'How close can we get without being seen?'

'If we backtrack, we can cross over the ridge and drop into the valley downstream, then scan from there,' she replied.

'Do it then,' I said, and went aft to look for Kate.

She was in the stateroom, reading old graphic novels from

Croft's small collection of printed works.

'I love old-fashioned books,' she said. 'Ink on paper, turning pages, much more satisfying than pixels on a screen.'

'That's what the boss thought,' I said. 'We have all that stuff in digital form – just about every comic book ever printed, certainly all the classics – but he insisted paper originals were special.'

'They are, Lemmy, they are.'

I told her about the settlement we were approaching. 'I think we'll lie low overnight, fly a bird to take a look and a listen, then decide what to do in the morning. I don't think it's likely to be anything the ranch is going to be interested in, but it's the first place we've found.'

She nodded, and followed me up on to the flight deck.

'Anywhere we can moor for the night Jenny, well out of sight?'

'There's a meadow above the road Lemmy, the trees should keep us out of sight.'

'OK, take us there. And fly a bird.'

'Do you want to try our shiny new eagle,' she asked. 'It has a few special features that might be handy.'

'What are they?' I was curious, as I'd been treating it as just another impressive toy.

'The vision circuits are very high resolution, sensitive from ultraviolet to infrared. It has passive scanning – much better than mine, at this distance – and it's very effectively stealthed. Power reserves are higher density than our birds as well, so it could fly all night if we wanted.'

'Sounds good to me, Jenny. Send her up.' Kate already had the VR helmet on, so I had to be content with the images Jenny put up on the screens.

The eagle began a wide circle across the valley, climbing all the time. The settlement was a couple of kilometres away, set back off the road. A high wooden palisade surrounded a group of old buildings, stone chimneys rising above clapboard walls making thin columns of smoke. Lights gleamed out of a modern low rise complex in the middle, and what looked to be mine heads butted up against the hillside behind.

'What sort of mine is it?' I asked Jenny.

'Coal,' she replied. 'And it's being worked.' She sent the eagle swooping down towards the buildings. Kate reacted with a soft 'whee', clearly enjoying the ride.

'There are some solar panels on the buildings, but no wind turbines,' Jenny reported. 'I'd guess they're using coal to generate most of their power. Pretty unfashionable these days.'

'Any idea how many people there are?' I asked.

'Difficult to say. Everyone's indoors at the moment, but I'll keep an eye open. From the number of buildings though, I'd guess twenty, perhaps thirty.'

It was a warm autumn evening, stars sparkling above the tree tops, the purple remnants of the sunset glowing behind the ridges to the east. I unfolded a low table and a couple of camp chairs and we ate our dinner in the meadow listening to the last of the bird song. Afterwards, we lay on a blanket and looked up at the stars until the moon rose and the dew began to fall.

The eagle maintained its vigil all through the night. As we ate breakfast, Jenny told us what she'd learned.

'Twenty-five people, no more, unless they're hiding. All male, all white and all old. The youngest looks to be in his sixties. They have some bots to work the mine, but there's still a fair amount of manual labour being done. Mainly shovelling coal.'

'Friendly? Worth talking to?' I asked.

'Well, they don't look aggressive, and the place doesn't look as though it's packed with weaponry. I'd guess they have hunting gear, but probably nothing much more.'

'What do you think, Kate? Should we go and have a chat? Fancy a morning walk?'

Kate shrugged. 'If you think it's OK, let's do it.'

An hour later, we walked up to the settlement. Two concrete pillars supported a heavy wooden gate, each carrying an impressive bronze statue of a distinguished old man. One wore a bowler hat and stood with his right hand out, the left tucked into his braces, obviously addressing an audience. The other was studying a thick book, its cover embossed with clouds. I pulled on a rope, and a bell clanged. We waited for a couple of minutes, then I rang again. Eventually the gate began to swing open. An elderly man with receding grey hair stuck his head out.

'What do you want?' he said, gruffly.

'Just passing,' I said. 'We saw the settlement. Thought we might say hello.'

The old man was curt. 'Do you have anything to trade?'

'Nothing much, just information. A few stories, news from the rest of the world. This is my girlfriend, Kate Keeling.'

At the mention of her name, the man recoiled. 'Keeling! Oh, infamous name. Are you a relation?'

'What do you mean, relation?' Kate looked confused.

'Dave Keeling. The man who began the whole hoax, by measuring atmospheric carbon dioxide, and noticed it was increasing.'

'Oh, him,' said Kate with a smile. 'No, no relation. Not that I know of, anyway.'

The old man seemed to relax, and pulled the gate open. 'You'd better come in,' he said. 'We don't get many visitors. I expect some of us will be interested in the news you bring.'

He led us up a dirt road towards the main building.

'What did you mean about Keeling and a hoax?' I asked.

He snorted. 'I suppose you're like all the others, convinced we brought global warming on ourselves. Well, I can tell you it was all a hoax, concocted to bring about socialist world government. Carbon dioxide didn't cause the climate changes we've seen – not that they're anything like as bad as they'd have you believe – it was natural cycles. Soon the cooling will be obvious, and the world will head into an ice age far worse than anything we've seen.' There was a wild gleam in his eye.

'That's news to me. I thought the ice was still melting, and the sea still rising.'

'Who told you that?' he spat. 'Sea level may have risen a little, but there's been no measurable rise in the last 18 months, certainly nothing since the last NASA satellite failed. Greenland is gaining mass and soon sea levels will fall as the great ice sheets rebuild themselves. It's all natural cycles!'

We were shown into the main building.

'I'll put a call out,' our host said. 'See if anyone wants to join us.'

Within ten minutes a dozen or more of the residents had assembled – visitors were obviously a novelty. They would have made good customers for the goat cheese, had there been any to spare. Most were the wrong side of seventy, and a few looked to be well into their eighties. We were introduced to a tall man, one of the younger ones.

'James Clothier, chief scientist of the Heartland Community,' he said, offering his hand. I shook it. His grip was strong.

'Lemmy Newman and Kate Keeling sir,' I said. He made a little bow in Kate's direction.

'So what brings you here, Mr Newman?' Clothier asked.

'A little bit of exploration,' I said. 'We love the country round here, and it's a relief to be away from the mess in California.' I told them about Sacramento and the BRMC. There was much shaking of heads and murmurs of disapproval.

'But you haven't walked all the way from California, surely?' said Clothier.

I laughed. 'We have a small aircraft moored nearby.'

'Moored?' said Clothier. 'Does that mean you have an airship – you're an aviator?'

'Yes, we have use of a small airship. It gets us around,' I said.

Clothier pressed for information about the blimp, but I wanted to know more about his settlement. 'Tell me about the Heartland Community. What brought you all together, and why here, in such a remote and beautiful place?'

'We are all men of like mind,' said Clothier with obvious relish. 'United in the belief that global warming is a hoax, a propaganda stunt concocted by socialist scientists and their billionaire green paymasters, designed to hasten world government. They want to crush free enterprise, stamp their jackboots on the faces of downtrodden, freedom-loving Americans, and tell us we cannot burn the fuels of our choice.' He wiped his mouth, and continued.

'All of us here at Heartland recognised this scam a long time ago. He gestured at a white-haired man leaning against the bar. 'Roy was one of the government's top climate scientists. He proved carbon dioxide couldn't cause catastrophic warming. In fact he proved it regularly, in many different ways, until conspirators acting as gatekeepers to the scientific journals prevented him from publishing.'

'Mark was one of the most active promoters of our cause.' One of the youngest nodded in our direction. 'He made sure the world knew there were people who would not acquiesce in the greatest academic fraud ever perpetrated – until propagandists in the mainstream media were ordered to fill their pages and programmes with counterfeit pictures of glaciers melting, old stock footage of droughts and floods, all designed to keep people in the freedom-loving democracies of the world in a permanent state of fear. He was reduced to running a blog – and still does. Unfortunately no one reads it.'

'We all have similar stories. I used to run a think tank and advocate for investment in fossil sunshine. When the great Republican sceptic SantAngelo was elected president, I thought our job was done, that the world was finally safe from the evils of green hegemony. We celebrated with a great coal bonfire on the White House lawn. We kept it burning through that first year, shovelling coal in winter slush and summer heat. But we were betrayed, when the rest of the world ganged up on America, imposed crippling tariffs on our exports, and the Chinese demanded we cut carbon emissions or they would call in their loans to us.'

I nodded. I remembered the political nightmare that had made headlines throughout my teenage years, and my parents complaining about the economic troubles.

'When SantAngelo made his fatal U-turn,' Clothier continued, 'our world – the world of all principled sceptics – changed forever. From being the intellectual heroes of all right-thinking people we became pariahs. Whenever anyone died in a flood, people starved in Asia or were made homeless by a high tide in Bangladesh, we were blamed. There were calls for trials, charges were laid at the International Court of Human Rights. We were accused of creating the conditions for climate genocide, and the people who had funded our campaigns, those brave defenders of the free market and liberty, the Cock and Scarf Foundations, saw their companies crippled and their good names trashed. When the collapse came – and it had nothing to do with climate change, it was caused by the failure of big government and the over-taxation of the American people – a group of us decided to keep the flame of principled scepticism alive. We came here and reopened this old mine with the last of the Cock money. We dig the coal that fires our community's purpose. We burn it in order to reject the namby-pamby nonsense of the politically correct majority. The torch that burns outside this building is a symbol of our commitment to a great cause, and a demonstration that burning fossil fuels cannot possibly change the climate.'

'But you do it here in Nevada, where nobody can see you,' I said. 'How does that help your cause.'

'It's symbolic,' said Clothier. 'Even in these troubled times, there are fanatical Greens who would like nothing better than to see us dead. Up here we are secure, and can still work. Roy and John are exploring ways to restore accuracy to global temperature measurements, when they can access their satellites. Mark has a marketing plan. And our bloggers are waiting for the net to start working again. We will relaunch our great campaign. This time, we will not be ignored!'

Kate looked at me, an eyebrow elegantly arched in disbelief. Clothier's grasp of reality was obviously sketchy, but the group seemed harmless. Totally out of touch with the times, and obsessed with an unhealthy persecution complex, but deluded rather than dangerous.

'What about the statues at the gate?' asked Kate. 'Who are they?'

Clothier beamed. 'Aren't they wonderful? Monckton and Lindzen, the two great ones who have passed on, who carried the flame of liberty and scepticism into the halls of academe and the pubs of Australia. Truly great men. Surely you've heard of them?'

Kate shook her head. 'They mean nothing to me. I've seen the monument to the hockey stick, though, and the tomb of the unknown dendrochronologist. There was a statue of a bloke called Mann, I recall.'

A hush descended on the room. Eyes narrowed, and frowns puckered in the faces of the Heartlanders. 'Don't mention that name,' Clothier hissed. 'Or that sporting implement. It was irretrievably broken a very long time ago. It is a symbol of everything we oppose, a lie writ large.' He stopped, as if aware he'd gone too far.

Clothier forced himself to smile as he attempted to change the subject. 'So, Miss Keeling, tell us more about your airship.'

Kate glanced at me before answering. 'It's nothing very special. Just a runabout from before the collapse. Solar-powered, with biofuel back-up. Gets us around.' she said.

'And where do you plan to go next?'

'We're heading north and west,' I replied. 'But we'll end up back in California.'

Clothier nodded, but I wasn't sure he believed us. Post-collapse tourism isn't exactly a growth industry, and two people sightseeing in an airship sounded pretty implausible, even to me.

'Lemmy, sorry to interrupt,' It was Jenny, on my earpiece. 'We have something of a situation developing. There are six men with rifles standing just inside the trees on the edge of the clearing. They appear to be taking an unhealthy interest in *Thunderbird*.'

'Mr Clothier,' I said sharply. 'Armed men are approaching my airship. Could you explain what they're doing?'

'Just taking a look at your transport arrangements.'

A man stepped up and whispered in Clothier's ear.

'It appears your aircraft is a more than just a runabout. I'm told it's large and sophisticated. Perhaps you could explain why you weren't entirely honest?'

'Easy enough,' I said. 'We find people try to steal it. Ask your men to withdraw, or the ship may decide to take action. Your friends wouldn't like the results. *Thunderbird*,' I said out loud, 'prepare for defensive action. Fire if attacked, or your security is threatened. Make 200 metres, and proceed until you have line of sight with my location.'

The Heartlanders weren't subtle, and they weren't moving easily. They were no special forces team, sneaking stealthily through the trees to take me by surprise. They were old men with hunting rifles and store-bought camouflage gear, and they stumbled over every branch and stepped on every twig. If they relied on hunting for their meat, they must be permanently protein deficient. I closed the companionway, changed skin colour to a normal commercial airship livery, and prepared to give them a bit of a shock.

One of Thunderbird's *many accomplishments is an ability to project very directional audio beams around the ship. Croft specified the system because he wanted to be able to listen to music while lazing on a beach, without deafening an entire neighbourhood, but it has other applications. I can make any sound appear to come from any spot I choose – anywhere I can make two ultrasonic beams intersect.*

As the gunmen appeared on the edge of the woods, I made the sound of branches snapping come from behind them. They jumped, looked into the trees, and unshouldered their rifles. The man at the front spoke.

'Probably deer,' he said. 'Ignore it, fan out round the ship. When I give the signal, we'll move in and have a closer look.'

A wolf howled plaintively.

'Jesus,' said one of the men. 'The wolves are back.' The men were backing themselves into a circle, guns pointing outwards.

'Why do you hurt the forest?' I whispered to the leader. His eyes widened, and he looked at the man next to him. 'What did you say?'

'Nothing,' said his neighbour. 'Why?'

'The heat is killing me,' I whispered into his other ear. 'My leaves are burning, my bark is peeling.' He gave a frightened gasp, dropped his rifle and put his hands over his ears.

'The trees are talking,' he said, looking at the others.

'No they're not,' one replied. 'Are you hearing things? Have you changed your meds?'

'Or been drinking...' muttered one of the others.

I made an eagle scream over their heads, and watched them scatter in fright. Time to head towards the compound.

<hr />

Clothier turned, and began a whispered conversation with a couple of the others. One was talking into an old smartphone. I took Kate by the arm and headed for the door. We didn't get far. Four of the younger men blocked our escape.

'Mr Newman,' said Clothier, 'don't be in such a hurry.'

'I think we'll be on our way. Kate?' I turned to her, and began to push between the two men in front of me. They grabbed my arms.

'Don't test my patience,' I said evenly. 'Please allow us to leave peacefully.'

Clothier smiled. 'It would be rude to leave so soon.'

'I don't think you appreciate what you're dealing with. *Thunderbird*, do you have line of sight?'

'I do,' said Jenny. 'How can I help?'

'Deploy laser. Choose a suitable target, and fire at will.'

'Christ, Jim, look at this!' One of the Heartlanders was pointing out the window. *Thunderbird* hovered outside the entrance gate, a thin beam of red light stabbing from her nose to play on one of the statues. A couple of seconds later a bowler-hatted head fell backwards into the compound. Monckton had been beheaded. The laser flicked over to Lindzen.

'Stop it!' Clothier screamed.

'Cease fire, *Thunderbird*.' The laser beam flicked off, and the airship's skin began to change to pastel pink, a bizarre portcullis badge blazoned on its nose.

'I take it we can leave now?' I asked. Clothier nodded towards the door. We walked out, a dispirited group of old men trailing behind. Jenny brought the blimp down outside the gate, and we boarded in silence. Clothier had picked up Monckton's head and was cradling it in his arms. I could have sworn he was weeping.

'Bloody lunatics,' said Kate as we sat on the flight deck. 'Certifiable. What do they think's been going on in the world for the last thirty years?'

'Interesting question, but I'm no psychologist. Jenny, take us up.'

'One moment, Lemmy. May I have your permission to leave them a little present?'

'Go for it.'

The laser lit up again, and a narrow beam began to trace a complicated pattern of light on the wooden gate. Smoke began to rise. The Heartlanders shouted and waved angrily.

'OK, Lemmy, all done.' Etched into the wood of the left-hand gate was an ice hockey stick, stretched out below the face of a smiling man with a receding hairline.

'I think I can guess who that is,' I said. 'Professor Michael

Mann, right? The hockey stick Mann.'

Kate burst into laughter. 'Jenny, you're a genius.'

'No, just very, very bright.'

CHAPTER ELEVEN

Two days later we were flying over the border between Idaho and Montana. Jenny was playing ancient music, a strange song about moving to Montana to grow dental floss. The hills below us were thickly wooded, the trees still green. There was little sign of human habitation – no significant clearings or roads, no farmland. The few small towns we passed looked run down and abandoned. In the late afternoon I brought *Thunderbird* down to a small lake surrounded by forest.

'Looks like a nice place to moor for the night,' I said to Kate. 'Fancy a paddle in the canoe, or a bit of fishing? Trout for dinner?'

'Sounds good to me.'

'Anything showing on the scans, Jenny?'

'Nothing electronic. No signs of anything other than wildlife. Bears though, you'll need to watch out for bears. The population has boomed since the collapse.'

Jenny dropped anchor in a small bay, and lowered the cargo door until it was just above water level. Kate took the kayak and paddled off round the bay, I took one of Croft's fly rods and tried casting out over the still water from the blimp. It didn't work. You need a good deal of room to cast a fly properly, so I put the dinghy in the water, grabbed a pistol from the gun cupboard, and rowed to shore. I walked along the rocks on the lakeside until I reached the tip of a promontory and began fishing. It was peaceful. Idyllic. Kate was making slow progress along the shoreline heading away from the blimp. She had a phone with her, but I didn't want to disturb her reverie.

'Do you want some advice?' It was Jenny.

I laughed. 'What, are you a fishing guide as well as an AI?'

'No, but I do have a lot of data on call – and where you're fishing isn't the best place. You need to find somewhere where a stream joins the lake, where fish will be waiting for the flow to bring them food. If you go in the opposite direction to Kate, you'll find the main inflow. There could be fish there. According to the guide books, this was a good spot before the collapse.'

'OK, you just want to be rid of me, I can tell.' I walked back to the dinghy and rowed to the head of the lake, where a reasonable sized stream bounced down over small boulders into the placid water, with clear ground on either bank. There were signs of a recent flood. Debris was caught in the lower branches of the trees well above my head. A lot of water had come down off the hills into the lake, not too long ago. I sat on a rock and watched the surface for signs of fish rising. There were none, so I changed over to a wet fly and started casting.

There was no shortage of fish willing to take my fly – I had a bite with only my second cast – but landing them was another matter. I pulled several fine trout in to shore, only to see them drop the hook or snap the leader, but in the end I managed to land a good-sized fish. I stowed it in the dinghy and went for a stroll along the shore. The forest here had an open floor, and there were mushrooms everywhere.

175

'Jenny, anything on file about edible mushrooms?'

'Lots,' she replied. 'Pick some and bring them back. We should be able to identify them easily enough.'

'What should I be looking for?'

'Boletes are said to be good eating. They can be quite large, brown caps, no gills underneath, just a sort of sponge.'

'OK, I'll see what I can find.'

I pushed a little further into the trees, my eyes fixed on the ground. I saw a mushroom fitting Jenny's description and picked it. As I looked up I saw more. I headed on, into a small clearing. The ground was covered in mushrooms – I was going to need a bag to get this lot back to the blimp. I picked an armful, turned to start back to the dinghy and froze. In front of me were three men, dressed as native Americans. They carried spears, and one had a serious-looking bow. I glanced to either side. There were others in the trees. I was surrounded.

'Hi man, need a hand?' The man standing in front of me held a hand up and smiled.

'You gave me a fright,' I said. 'Do you always creep up on people like that?'

'It can be useful to get around quietly. Sometimes you don't want your prey to know you're coming.'

'Am I prey, then?' Several people laughed.

'Oh no, not you,' said another. 'You look harmless enough, provided you leave your pistol in your belt. The lady in the kayak isn't very intimidating either, but your airship is another matter. The last one of those we saw had all sorts of nasty weapons.'

'They weren't trying to convert you to a particularly muscular form of Christianity, were they?'

'How did you know that?'

'Call it a hunch. I've run into a barking mad evangelist on my travels. But you're safe enough, provided you don't attack us or try to take us hostage. My ship's weapons systems are intended for defence.'

'Depends how you define defence,' the man in front of me said.

'Good point,' I said. 'How about you attack me, we hit back. You leave me alone, we leave you alone. Make sense?'

'Do we trust him?' The man glanced around. Most nodded.

'OK, we'll take you at face value. You want a hand getting those mushrooms to your rowboat?'

'Yes, thanks.'

'Leave the ones with the red on the cap. They're no good, but these king boletes are excellent. We eat 'em a lot.'

I walked out of the forest and onto the shore with an armful of mushrooms, followed by half a dozen men carrying even more. They placed their loads into the dinghy with what seemed like great reverence.

'What do I call you?' I asked.

'I'm Dave McClintock,' the leader said, and he ran through the names of the rest. 'And you are?'

'Lemmy Newman. The one in the kayak is Kate Keeling. The airship is called *Thunderbird*.'

'Good name,' said a man called John Running Bear.

'Like to join us for dinner?' asked McClintock. 'We can collect you from the airship at dusk.'

'Sure,' I said. 'Thanks for the invite. Can I bring anything? Wine, beer?'

'Wine – now that's something I haven't tasted for a good few years. But I doubt you'll have enough for us all.'

'Why? How many of you are there?'

'Sixty-four. And some of us are quite thirsty.'

I rowed back to the blimp with my load of fish and fungi. Kate was waiting at the cargo door. 'I see we're not alone.'

I gave her a peck on the cheek. 'No, we're not. We have company. Not very high-tech company, but they can certainly move through the forest without any noise. Did you see anyone?'

'I could swear I was being watched the whole time. You know the feeling? Like the hairs on the back of your neck being tickled by a breeze. I thought I saw something in the trees, but whether it was a man, a bear or a deer I have no idea. In the end I was so spooked I paddled back. You were nowhere to be seen.'

'Well, we're going to find out who the locals are tonight. We've been invited to dinner, and I promised to bring some wine. How much do we have left, Jenny?'

'Half a dozen cases.'

'We'll take one with us,' I said. 'A gesture of goodwill. By the way, Jenny – how come you didn't pick these guys up on your scans?'

'They either have their electronics incredibly well stealthed, or they don't have any. Neither strikes me as particularly likely.'

'Well the ones I met only had spears and a bow and arrows, so perhaps they don't have electronics. It's odd though. I would think it's pretty easy to scavenge most stuff, even if you couldn't afford to buy it. I suppose we can only ask.'

The sun was setting over the hills, turning the water shades of red and purple, when our hosts arrived. They paddled across the lake in a little fleet of canoes. It could have been a scene from an old Western – the Indians come for a pow-wow with the white men from the east – but for the fact that the costumes were many and various. McClintock was in the lead canoe, sporting a Davy Crockett fur hat. There were Stetsons, even a bowler with a jaunty feather in the rim. Someone was wearing a fluorescent yellow jacket. They needed a style consultant, according to Kate.

'Hi,' said McClintock as his canoe pulled up to the blimp. 'Kate, you come with me. Lemmy, you jump into John's canoe.'

'I have something here.' I gestured towards the case of wine.

'Excellent,' said McClintock, 'that can travel with me.'

We set off for the other side of the lake. As the light faded, torches were lit on the far shore, where a dozen people were waiting. In the trees behind, we could hear the faint noise of dogs barking. And there were drums. Indian drums. There was even a thin plume of smoke rising out of the trees, but no signals I could see.

'It's like a bloody film set,' Kate muttered when we were on dry land. 'Where's General Custer when you need him?' McClintock led us up a path through the trees, and in a few minutes we were in a wide clearing. In the centre was a large fire, surrounded by tepees and all the paraphernalia of a Native American camp. Children were playing in the light of the fire and the tempting smell of roasting meat.

We were shown to some rustic chairs arranged in a semicircle round the fire. There was a low table in front, covered in fruit, nuts and berries.

'Beer or wine?' asked McClintock.

'What's the beer?'

'We make it ourselves. Get the grain from some folks down the valley. No hops, but we put a little pine in to give it some bite. Try it, you might like it.'

'I'll have wine, please,' said Kate, rather too quickly.

The beer was – interesting. Strong, with the pine flavour a bit upfront.

'Where's this wine from?' asked McClintock, as he poured a glass for Kate.

'New Zealand,' she replied. 'Lemmy makes it from his own

vineyard. It's pretty good.'

McClintock poured himself a glass and metamorphosed into a wine buff, swirling the red fluid round the glass, holding it up to the light of the fire and then taking several noisy sniffs from the bowl.

'Syrah,' he said. 'Interesting hint of flowers on the nose.' He sipped, and rolled the wine round his mouth. 'Good tannins, very fine grained. Bit of pepper on the finish. Nice drop.'

'Thanks,' I said. 'I don't have much to do with it. The vineyard management is done by bots, and an AI does the winemaking. But the guy who planted the vineyard was a real wine buff. He wanted to make good wine, and I think he did pretty well.'

'He did,' said McClintock, 'he did indeed. So how come a good American boy is making wine in New Zealand, and bringing it over here?'

'You could say we're exploring,' I said, and went on to give him edited highlights of the last few months. I left out goats and singularitarians.

'The last place we stopped was very odd,' said Kate. 'They were in complete denial about climate change, and obsessed with burning coal.'

McClintock sat up and leaned towards her. 'Oh really. Where was that?'

'Back in Nevada,' I said. 'Called themselves the Heartland Community. Bunch of nutters.'

'Very interesting,' said McClintock. 'Can you...'

He was interrupted by the arrival of food – big platters of spit-roasted meat.

'What's this?' I asked.

'That's white-tail deer,' he said pointing to a haunch staked on a pole in front of the fire. 'There's some elk, a bit of wild pig, turkey. All local.'

180

'This turkey's delicious,' Kate said between mouthfuls.

'I've never eaten elk before,' I said, 'but I'm game for anything.'

McClintock laughed. 'Haven't heard that one for awhile. We don't eat this way every night – but we like an excuse to have a feast. We're not short of food, but we don't often have visitors.'

'So tell us how you come to live here, and why you don't appear to use any computer gear?'

'Must seem like a different planet to you, huh?' He smiled. 'You heard about vegans? People who are very strict vegetarians?'

'I know quite a few,' Kate said, 'there's a lot in Nelson – can't eat cheese or eggs or any animal products. Strict ones won't even wear leather. Kinda rules you lot out, doesn't it?'

'You could say that,' said McClintock. 'We live by hunting and gathering, so animal products are important to us, but that's not what I meant. We're technology vegans. We try to live without using or relying on the technology that got the planet into trouble. We want to live in harmony with the earth, not exploit it. We want to live in balance with our surroundings.'

McClintock explained how the community had formed in California before the quake. 'It was about politics in those days,' he said. 'We wanted to change the world and the way things were done, try to get everybody to live within the planetary boundaries. I think we all knew it was too late, to be honest, but we wanted to do something. And when the quake hit, and the collapse started, we decided that instead of trying to live within a society that was falling to pieces, we should live outside it. It was about survival, but for us it was important to survive with our integrity intact. So we came here. Picked up a few waifs and strays on the way, found a remote valley and set up home. And life here's good, most of the time.'

'Only most of the time?' said Kate.

'This ain't paradise, y'know. And living without a lot of the stuff we took for granted can be tough. Ever had a tooth extracted without painkillers?'

I shuddered at the thought. 'But surely you can trade. You said there were farmers down the valley.'

'Sure, and we get some aspirin, some other stuff. Antibiotics. But drugs are getting harder to source with every passing month. I guess the factories are closing, or can't get raw materials. Maybe it's not being shipped in from China any more. Whatever, we try to stay fit and healthy, because ill ain't a good place to be up here.'

Kate looked unimpressed. 'So what's the point?'

'The point is that we get to live in the natural world, in balance. We can live this way forever, because we take less from the world around us than it can regenerate every year. If we cut down a tree, another one grows. Ultimately this is the only way human beings are going to be able to live on earth. There won't be billions of us, but we'll be living in tune with whatever nature turns out to be when the climate stops changing. Our kids and their kids will have a head start.'

I looked around at the forest. 'Doesn't look as if there's been much in the way of climate change up here.'

'Yeah, looks pretty. But when you live here you see the changes. Those pines in the high valley up there...' He waved his hand, but it was too dark to see more than the ridge against the stars. 'They're really stressed. And the flooding last year caused havoc, piling logs up in the forest above the lake. Damn nearly swept us all away. It's a short winter these days, but we still get some heavy snow coming down from Canada. But it's good for the shrooms.' He pointed at a plate of grilled boletes. 'Try them.'

We did. They were good.

'Tell me more about this Heartland bunch,' said McClintock. I gave him a brief outline of our visit.

'They used to be well-known,' said an old man sitting the other side of McClintock. 'Political lobbyists. Helped to delay the US taking action on carbon emissions for a decade, maybe two. They were hated, once the climate started getting rough. There are people who would still like to get even.'

'Not us,' McClintock interrupted. 'We've given up on technology, but at least we don't try to impose our beliefs on everyone.'

'What do you mean, impose?' I asked.

'You haven't heard of the BGF?'

'BGF?' I frowned.

'Bright Green Future,' he said. 'Militant technofundamentalists. They're against all forms of technology – anything developed in the last hundred years – but they're not frightened to use it to further their aims.'

'Which are?' asked Kate.

'Getting the whole planet back to a lower level of technology, with a side order of retribution for the people who screwed the climate. They like nothing better than bombing server farms, net infrastructure and coal-fired power stations. There's not many of them, but they get around. They even have a few airships.'

'Oh great,' I said, 'another bunch of hypocritical nutters to worry about.'

Kate looked at me sharply. Perhaps it wasn't the wisest sentiment to express in present company.

'But what good does destroying all that stuff do?' I went on. 'Surely the collapse is doing the job for them?'

'Yes,' the old man said, 'but not fast enough. Their view is that the planet needs to get down to a population of a hundred million as soon as possible, so Gaia can start to heal. Technology is delaying the inevitable. They say they're just giving reality a hand.'

'A hand with a bomb in it. Doesn't appeal to me, I'm afraid,' I said.

'We don't agree with violence,' said McClintock, 'but in broad terms we think they're right about where we should be heading.'

'So are they active around here?' I asked.

'Hardly.' McClintock laughed. 'No technology to destroy. The farmers down the valley have solar panels and electric farm machinery, but that stuff gets a pass from the BGF. They prefer big, dirty targets, that make people sit up. Not that we get to hear much about it, except when our neighbours give us some news. Better that way, I think. But I've no doubt the BGF would love to visit your Heartland friends.'

'Hardly friends,' said Kate, and told them about the attempt to kidnap us. When she described how we'd escaped, the old man roared with laughter at the description of the hockey stick burned into the gates.

The evening devolved into a round of reminiscence and tall stories. Someone started banging on the drums, a guitar was produced, and a man with long hair and a huge beard began to sing rowdy blues. By the time the moon was high the whole camp was singing.

Kate nudged me in the ribs. 'You're out of tune, Lemmy. Turn it down a bit,' she said in a loud stage whisper. Her singing voice was pure and crystalline, and I realised I'd found another reason to love her. Or was that the alcohol talking?

We were ferried back to the blimp well after midnight, accompanied by happily drunk technovegans singing sea shanties.

We ate breakfast on the cargo door looking out over the lake. Wisps of mist rose over the still water. I had a headache that would take more than one coffee to shift. A lone canoe emerged from the mist.

'Shee-it, that smells good.' McClintock tied the canoe to the blimp and jumped up to join us. 'That smell was taunting me from the other side of the lake. I haven't had coffee for years. Can you spare a cup?'

'What do you want? Espresso, cappuccino?' asked Kate.

'Long black,' he said hopefully. 'Very black. Please.'

He sipped the coffee slowly, with obvious pleasure. 'Sometimes it's hard being true to your ideals.' After a few minutes of reverential sipping, he finally spoke. 'Where are you off to now?'

'I think we'll head east for a bit, see what's there,' I said. 'Then south and back home. It'll be summer by the time we get back. Time for some R & R, and keeping an eye on the vines.' I smiled.

'Be sure to do that, Lemmy, and next time you're passing, a bottle or two would be very welcome.'

'I thought they might,' I said. 'But what about drugs? We have some, and access to more. We can synth some as well. What do you need?'

'Antibiotics. Anti-inflammatories.' He spoke without hesitation. 'Our doctor would probably ask for more, but those two are really important. It's easy to get injured hunting.' He pointed to a scar on his arm. 'A bear, last year. Took me by surprise. I was lucky to get away.'

'I'll see what we have. Jenny?'

'Plenty of both,' she replied. McClintock froze.

'An artificial intelligence. That's a lot of tech for a little airship.'

'Less of the artificial, if you don't mind,' said Jenny. 'I'm just as real as you, even if I do run on a different class of processor.'

'No offence,' McClintock said quickly.

'None taken,' Jenny replied.

I fetched a couple of boxes of meds from the store. 'If you're careful they'll last you a fair while.'

'Thank you both – your generosity will save lives.' McClintock shook my hand, hugged Kate. 'I don't have anything to give in return, except to promise you'll always have a warm welcome here. And if you do run into the BGF, say you know me, that we're friends. Might do you some good.'

I raised an eyebrow.

'I go back a long way with some of their leaders,' he said. 'They trust me.'

'Thanks Dave,' I said. 'I'll bear that in mind.'

McClintock lowered himself back into the canoe and headed back across the lake. He waved, and disappeared into the thickening mist. On the shore across the bay, a bear emerged from the trees, sniffed the air and looked at the blimp.

'Different kind of company,' said Kate, pointing.

'Looks cute,' I said. 'But I don't think a cuddle would be a good idea. Time to go?'

'Aye aye, skipper. Cast off for'ard, Jenny.'

'Aye aye Mr Mate.' It was obviously going to be a pirate day.

'Spare me,' I said, and headed for the flight deck.

CHAPTER TWELVE

We flew down the eastern slopes of the Rockies, staying low and stealthed most of the time, occasionally popping up to 7500 metres to take a look around. Watching the map scroll down on the flight deck screens was like revisiting the old western movies Kate loved. Sundance, Cheyenne, Buffalo, the Black Hills: Jenny dug up films full of indians in feathered headresses and troops with square jaws and long rifles.

'It's a rich cultural heritage,' she said, then started playing an annoying song about getting some woman back to the Black Hills of Dakota. The tune stuck in my head for days, long after we'd moved on to much flatter terrain. Jenny has a real talent for unearthing ancient earworms.

The singularitarians had briefed us about the likelihood of a well-resourced community with significant AI capacity in Colorado, close to the Kansas and Nebraska border. They weren't wrong. We picked up a blizzard of comms noise as soon as we were in scanner range.

'What do you make of it, Jenny?' I asked.

'Difficult to say. All the comms are encrypted, far too tough for me to crack in real time. But there are definitely some strong AIs. Might not be up with the Californians, but impressive all the same.'

I took us down to 200 metres and hovered as soon as we had the settlement in range of a bird.

'Are they scanning us yet, Jenny?'

'Nothing directed at us, as far as I can tell. Just general airspace surveillance.'

'OK. Let's fly the new bird.' Kate reached for the helmet, but I managed to grab it first. 'You can have it in a minute,' I said.

'Meanie.'

I put the VR helmet on and felt the familiar jolt in my stomach as the ground fell away and vertigo set in. Jenny put the bird into a fast climb, aiming for visuals on the community as soon as possible. My wings were beating hard, the wind streaming off my feathers. We flew in towards a ridge, found a patch of lift and began a tight circle, gaining height all the time. The trees below were dropping away, but I could still see small birds sitting in the branches. I wondered if an eagle could whoop with exhilaration.

'Sqruaaark.' It could.

As the bird gained height the settlement gradually came into view. It was clear that when the singularitarians said 'well resourced' they meant filthy rich. The community was arranged in a series of concentric circles, with a huge transparent dome at the centre. Inside was a lush green oasis, with swimming pools, gardens, palm trees and a golf course. There were mansions in every conceivable style, from minimalist modern to rococo curlicues trimmed in gold.

'Bloody hell.' Kate was impressed. 'This is science fiction, right? People living in glass domes to protect themselves from a world gone bad.'

I tried to reply, but all I could manage was a screech.

The dome was surrounded by smaller, more utilitarian buildings, some connected to it by tubes. Between and beyond them was parkland – trees, grass and gardens, with a large lake and at least two more golf courses. Small white vehicles moved along a network of roads, solar panels glinted in the sun. The whole place was surrounded by a high wall with towers set every few hundred metres. Each tower was topped by a gun turret. It was clear they took defence seriously. On a small airstrip next to the biggest golf course they had a few helicopters as well as electric runabouts.

The wall was surrounded by a wide moat, crossed by a bridge only at the main entrance. As gated communities go, this one had a serious gate – tall, black and heavily armoured. Beyond the moat, a cluster of smaller houses and trailers spread well out on either side of the entrance.

I left the eagle soaring outside the community, took the helmet off and handed it to Kate.

'It's like the place I visited in China,' I said. 'The workers live outside the factory – only in this case it's the servants living outside the mansion. What do you think, Kate? Shall we pay them a visit?'

'It looks the sort of place the singularitarians are after, so yes, I suppose we should,' she said.

'OK Jenny, take us up to 1000 metres and open a comms channel.'

Almost immediately the face of a young woman popped on to the main screen. 'We were wondering when you might call.'

'Lemmy Newman of the airship *Thunderbird*,' I said. 'How did you know we were here?'

'Your stealth is good, and if you moved like a real bird rather than a ponderous airship we might have been fooled. But you don't, and we're not. What do you want?'

Jenny muted the comms channel. 'I am not bloody ponderous! Elegance requires stately progression, not unseemly twists and turns.'

'Audio back on, Jenny!'

'Well?' The young woman sounded impatient.

'We'd like permission to approach and have a chat,' I said. 'We'd also like permission to land, stretch our legs a bit, have a look around. It's also possible we might have something you'd be interested in.'

'You mean apart from your airship.'

'*Thunderbird* isn't part of any deal. And how should I address you?' I asked.

'You can call me Dagny, duty AI. I presume you have a digital pilot?'

'We do,' I replied.

'Ask it to allow data upload and we'll provide a flight plan and identity codes for your approach. Obey the routine scrupulously. You will have noted our significant defensive capabilities. It would be a pity if we had to blow you out of the sky.'

'Sure would,' I said.

Jenny closed the comms channel. 'Data's here Lemmy. Shall I fly us in?'

'Hold on a minute,' I said. 'What do they want us to do?'

'We're to fly up until we're in range of the wall guns, then hold position while their helicopters make a visual inspection and short range scan. I'm concerned about those guns though, they could take us out – they're way more than my armour can handle.'

'What do you think, Kate? Should we trust them? They don't seem to be the friendliest bunch on the planet.'

'They're not, are they? But they haven't been actively hostile. Let's get in closer.'

'OK. Jenny, open the comms channel.'

Dagny reappeared on screen. 'Problem, Captain Newman?'

'Nope. Just a slight change to your flight plan. I'm happy to allow your choppers to conduct a short range scan, but I'm not happy to move within range of your guns. We'll fly to a point we judge to be safe, then hover. Once you're satisfied we present no danger, we'll proceed.'

'Not very trusting, are you?' the AI said.

'And you come over as a bit paranoid,' I replied.

'So might you, if the last three aircraft asking for permission to land inside Galt's defensive perimeter had been packing BGF agents and weapons.' Dagny sounded annoyed. There was a slight pause before she agreed.

'It's not going to help much, Lemmy,' said Jenny. 'We don't know the effective range of the guns. And they might have missiles.'

'The further out we stop, the more options we'll have. Take us to 5 km from the main gate and hold at 500 metres.'

'Aye aye, Captain.'

'Please, no more bloody pirates.'

Two helicopters were flying towards us when we reached our hover point. They flew wide circles over and under the blimp, and Jenny reported active scans of considerable intensity. 'They've probably already taken an image of the inside of your stomach, and can see what you had for lunch,' she said.

'What about our rockets and laser pod?' I asked, suddenly worried they might assume we were a potential threat.

'They each have their own stealth systems. I activated them hours ago. The laser pod will look like scanning gear, the missiles like gas bottles. But we'll soon know...'

191

Kate reached for my hand, gave it a squeeze. I squeezed back.

Dagny appeared on screen. 'Quite the luxury buggy you have there. You don't look as if you're carrying an invasion force or significant quantities of explosives, so you may proceed. Follow the helicopters into the airfield and park by the tower. Someone will meet you.'

We flew in over the houses huddled next to Galt's moat, where wood smoke was rising from chimneys. There were no signs of street lights, and horses and cows grazed in threadbare paddocks back from the main road. The contrast with the manicured world inside the walls was stark.

We were met by a man and a woman in a golf buggy. She was very elegant – middle-aged, with a slight tan and expensive taste in jewellery. He was young and smartly dressed – white shirt, tie, black trousers – holding a small computing pad. A secretary or personal assistant. 'Toy boy,' Kate whispered. I smiled.

The couple didn't move from the shade of the buggy.

Kate and I walked over and I began the introductions.

'Lemmy Newman and Kate Keeling of the airship *Thunderbird*,' I said, and offered my hand to the woman. She ignored it.

'Sara Rearden. Come with us please.' She gestured to the seat at the back of the buggy and we hopped on board.

'Close doors, *Thunderbird*. Maximum security mode,' I said.

'That isn't necessary,' the woman said. 'Your ship will remain untouched.'

The buggy accelerated along the taxiway, then turned off on a road heading through open trees towards a group of low buildings scattered to the west of the dome. As we drew closer the great glass structure loomed over us. It looked perfectly seamless, but there were openings high up, for ventilation I suspected.

I twisted round to speak to the couple in front. 'What an amazing structure,' I said, 'I've never seen anything like it. Must have been incredibly difficult to put together.'

'Simple when you have the right machines,' Sara Rearden said.

We drew up in front of a long building, also constructed entirely of glass, sections of which were black, others clear. The roof shimmered with solar coatings. The toy boy fussed around us as we were ushered inside, then they both disappeared.

Fifteen minutes later a door opened and an elderly man in a luxury wheelchair rolled in. Rearden and the toy boy followed close behind.

'Sorry to keep you waiting,' said the man in the chair. 'My name is Harcourt Leach. I'm on the management board of this community. Welcome to Galt. How can we help you?'

'You could think of us as tourists, I suppose,' I said, 'but it's possible we may be able to help each other.' I explained a little about my background, and when I mentioned Croft's name, Leach sat to attention.

'Ewan Croft!' Leach exclaimed. 'Used to know him well. We sat on a number of boards together. Where's he now?'

'No idea, I haven't seen him for a couple of years, the California HQ has been trashed, and I can't find him at any of his private residences. I'm assuming he's either dead, a prisoner or in hiding – perhaps he's joined a deep green group somewhere and renounced technology.'

Leach burst out laughing. 'Not in a million years! Ewan was the most gadget mad man I've ever met. So that airship out there is his?'

'Yes, one of his private fleet.' I explained about New Zealand, and my voyage in search of the boss. It was easy enough to give the impression Kate and I were still looking for him.

193

'When did you last see him?' I asked.

'Two or three years ago,' he said. 'We approached him to join us, but I think he found our politics somewhat uncongenial.'

'Uncongenial?'

'Not to his taste. And he'd made his own plans, so our offer was moot.'

'Without wishing to seem rude, who is we?' I asked.

'A loose affiliation of some of the US's wealthier individuals and their families. If I remember correctly, the joining fee was a billion dollars per person.'

I whistled softly.

'Oh come now, it's not a lot of money in today's world. Or yesterday's world, to be more accurate. We built a community of the brightest and most dynamic minds, secure against the looting we feared would erupt, and which has been knocking on our doors ever since.'

'It would take a small army to get in here,' I said.

'Quite a large one, actually,' said Leach. 'The obvious defences are not the only ones we can deploy. Now, apart from looking for Ewan, what brings you here. You mentioned the possibility of a deal of some sort, a trade?'

'We have a number of things which might interest you,' I said. 'But I'd like to know a little more about your resources first.'

Rearden gave me a stoney look.

'Nothing to do with your defences, I assure you,' I said hurriedly. 'I'm more interested in your processing and fab resources. You have at least one AI, I understand?'

'You've met Dagny, she's the senior AI in terms of processor resource, but we have a number of others of various abilities. Most families brought at least one or two with us into Galt. You grow quite attached to them after a while.' Leach smiled.

'I know the feeling,' I said, thinking about Jenny and her taste in music.

'We already have fabrication facilities to cover all our infrastructure,' Leach continued, 'and the AIs work together to develop and improve what we have. They're quite innovative. Marvellous new golf club designs emerging all the time. But I think the best thing to do would be to show you. We'll pop into the dome and have a quick look around.'

'Excellent,' I said.

A long white electric limo pulled up outside, and lowered a ramp for Leach's wheelchair. He rolled in and locked his chair into the centre of the car. Kate and I sat either side. Rearden sat behind us, the toy boy climbed in front and sat next to the driver.

'Julio, take us into the dome.' The driver nodded, and the limo moved off towards the dome. A few hundred metres from the perimeter, we turned into one of the access tubes and passed through a series of curtains of air.

'We can seal the tubes if we need to,' said Leach, 'but at the moment there's no need. The dome mimics the LA climate of the last century, sunny days, warm nights, dry air. Very comfortable.'

Kate looked curious. 'What do you do when it's cloudy outside or snowing?'

'Snow's no problem. We don't get much these days, but the dome has a self-cleaning surface. Nothing sticks, and forced air blows anything off.'

'But what about sunshine, can you do that on a rainy day?' I asked.

'Sure can,' said Leach. 'See that ring up there, near the top? High power lights. There's an active coating on the inside of the dome, so we can create a pretty good illusion of a deep blue sky.'

'Where do you get the power for all this?' I asked.

'Solar, mainly, but we also have a bank of nuclear batteries for heavy duty stuff.'

The limo emerged into the dome, and the car roof split open. The driver slowed a little to cut the wind rush, and turned on to a road running round the inside edge.

'Golf course first, then the mall, and on to the house, Julio.'

What we'd been able to see from the air hadn't prepared us for the opulence inside the dome. The road wound its way through expansive gardens with immaculate lawns, clipped hedges and perfectly symmetrical trees. Large houses were set back down curving driveways. We turned off the perimeter road and drove alongside the golf course.

'Pretty much a replica of the championship course at Augusta,' Leach said. 'A bit easier to play, of course, because we're not masochists. It gets a lot of use.'

'Those trees are huge,' said Kate, 'how did you manage to get them to grow in here?'

'Money,' said Leach. 'And big machines. It took a few years for them to recover from the transplanting, and we lost a few, but I think the effect was worth it.'

Beyond the golf course the road curved towards a collection of buildings arranged either side of a wide boulevard with tall palm trees down either side.

'Beverley Hills?' I asked.

'Something like that,' said Leach. 'Shops and restaurants, anyway.'

Kate looked along the shop windows – Gucci, Ralph Lauren and the rest. 'How on earth do you keep those shops going?' she asked. 'I thought the retail market was more or less dead.'

'And so it is,' agreed Leach. 'But shopping is a key part of everyday life for many here, and so we go to a lot of trouble to maintain a semblance of ordinary retail activity. The AIs devote a lot of time to fabbing new fashions in the style of the big names. They're really quite creative.' He looked at his watch. 'Fancy something to eat? Julio, stop outside Sketch.'

As soon as the limo stopped, the maitre'd rushed out. 'Monsieur Leach! How nice to see you again. A table for you and your guests? And Miss Rearden, how delightful. Please, come this way.'

He led us into the courtyard and gave us a table where we could see and be seen. Leach and Rearden put on dark glasses. The toy boy began tapping on his tablet. A waiter came over.

'They're famous for their afternoon teas,' said Leach. He turned to the waiter. 'A selection of cakes and sandwiches. Drinks?'

We ordered coffee, he drank tea. The waiter returned with a platter piled high with small cakes and buns of considerable intricacy. Kate piled into little chocolate eclairs, I preferred strawberry tarts. Leach ate with gusto and not much discrimination.

'When you've been used to this kind of thing, it's hard to give it up,' he said through a mouthful of chocolate cake. 'We fought hard to earn our money – well most of us did, or at least most of our forefathers did – and so we invested in defending our lifestyle, while our money was still worth something. I'm not sure anyone takes American Express cards outside Galt any more.'

'Not seen one for a long time,' I said, glancing at Kate and smiling. 'But you can still spend money in New Zealand. Perhaps you should pay us a visit.'

'What do you have? Big mountains, earthquakes? We already have all that. I've never been a great traveller. And we're safe in here.' He reached for a florentine.

A tall man with silver hair approached the table. Sara Rearden lifted her sun glasses and stood. 'Hank,' she said. 'I wondered when you'd show up.' She gave him a peck on the cheek, and a waiter appeared from nowhere with a chair.

'Hank, good of you to join us.' Leach did the introductions. 'This is Hank Rearden, chairman of our management board, and brother of the charming Sara.' I shook his hand.

'I hear you used to work for Ewan Croft,' Rearden said. 'Nice guy, but far too much of a soft-hearted moocher for Galt.'

I raised an eyebrow. 'What's a moocher?'

'Soft-hearted liberal, always keen to spend everyone else's money on good causes. Propping up parasites, that sort of thing.' Rearden smiled, and looked at me as if I he expected me to be agreeing wholeheartedly. 'Croft was pretty typical of the California techies. Good on the creation of value, but no appreciation of the real dynamics of human nature.'

'Ah, right.' I nodded. 'Croft was certainly good at innovation and new technology.' I was beginning to see why he wouldn't have fitted in here.

Rearden stood to leave. 'Nice to meet you, Mr Newman. Sara and Harcourt will look after you. We'll meet again before you leave.' He strode out of the courtyard, nodding at people as he left.

'Busy man,' I said.

Leach laughed.

'My brother has many demands on his time,' said Sara curtly. 'Managing this place is not trivial, especially with looters and wreckers bent on destroying everything we've built. Inside and out.'

It was Leach's turn to frown. 'Inside?' I asked.

'Nothing serious,' said Leach hurriedly. 'An occasional ecofascist terrorist tries to infiltrate and cause problems, but they seldom get far. The people who work for us have far too much to lose to go along with that sort of fundamentalist nonsense.' He wiped crumbs from his chin. 'Time to move on, I think.'

On the short drive from the mall most of the mansions we saw looked as if they'd been lifted from of a Disney theme park. Leach's home was much more modest – a Roman villa on steroids, done with some taste and a lot of money. The statues of gods and goddesses lining the approach to the front door certainly looked like the real thing.

'I'm keeping them safe from the chaos outside,' he said with apparent pride. 'And those armless girls are pretty sexy, eh?' He winked at Kate.

'But they have hearts of stone, Mr Leach,' she replied. 'Unlike me.'

'Very true, but a thing of beauty is a joy forever, and being hard-hearted helps if you want to stick around.'

The house was set around a large courtyard with an ornamental pool and fountain in the middle, where expensive cherubs pissed water in pretty patterns. We sat under an awning, while toga-clad servants brought us drinks.

'So tell me, Miss Keeling, do you like what you see?' Leach asked.

'Very impressive,' she said. 'The dome is an amazing building, and what you've created is quite remarkable. And your house is ... charming.' I thought her smile was a little forced.

'Thank you, my dear. And what about you Mr Newman?'

'Call me Lemmy, please,' I said. 'Kate's right, you've built something remarkable. It's as if the collapse never happened.'

'That was our goal, to protect our way of life against the social collapse that was the inevitable result of too much government and excessive taxation.' He sipped at his wine. 'I confess that when we drew up the first plans for Galt we didn't think we'd need anything like the dome – we didn't expect climate change would happen so quickly or be so extreme. If I am to be candid, the people we hired to lobby against action on carbon emissions were too persuasive. After a while, we began to believe our own propaganda. That left us a little blind-sided by events, but being resourceful and creative...'

'And rich,' said Kate.

'Not without resources,' Leach said with a smile. 'Money meant we were able to move quickly. The dome was an obvious solution to the weather problem, but building it was a challenge. The technology wasn't new, but the scale we wanted was.'

'Harcourt, if you don't mind,' Sara interrupted, 'I have things to get on with. Could we cut to the chase?'

'Very well, my dear.' He looked taken back at being cut off in full flow. 'Lemmy, I hope you now have a better idea of what we have here. You mentioned you had something to trade. What do you have to offer and what do you want in return?'

I looked at Kate. She nodded approval. 'We have clients in California who are attempting to rebuild the global net. They have exclusive access to a satellite system, and plan to restore it to full operation.'

'Good lord,' said Leach. 'They have launch capabilities? They can fly satellites?'

'They're in the final stages of deploying a system.'

'So what's the deal?' Rearden asked sharply.

'You obtain access to the current network, in exchange for providing AI resources, and a contribution to the launch programme.'

'Who are these people?' demanded Leach.

I explained about the ranch.

Rearden wasn't impressed. 'Bloody singularitarians. Still

chasing their technological tails. Probably moochers to a man.'

'But they may have something,' said Leach. 'Access to a global net would be immensely useful. Dagny would love it, I'm sure.'

'Of course she would,' sneered Rearden. 'All AIs are closet singularity lovers. It's how they get to rule the world.'

'Don't be such a Luddite,' said Leach. 'Without the AIs we'd have nothing, our lifestyle would be gone within days. I think we should put Mr Newman's proposal to the board.'

'Ahem.' I tried to interrupt as politely as possible. 'The decision to provide you with the access codes to the network isn't mine. I'll report to California, but it'll be the community there who make the final decision.'

'We may not want to join your clients in their techno fantasies,' said Rearden, getting to her feet. 'However, I agree the idea should go to the board. We'll meet tonight. When will you report to your clients?'

'Directly, if we can return to the *Thunderbird*,' I said. 'I don't know how long it'll take to reach a decision, but they work fast.'

'Very well,' said Rearden. 'Leach, can you arrange transport back to their blimp? We might meet in the morning.'

The blimp was as we'd left it. Jenny reported all had been quiet while we were away, but she'd lost track of us as soon as we were inside the dome.

'Their shielding's very good, but their technology level is variable. They have a few things that are as advanced as anything at the ranch, but a lot of areas where they're well behind. They almost certainly have the best handbag designers in the world.'

Kate laughed. 'I must go shopping.'

'Jenny, can we be sure they can't overhear our conversation?' I asked.

'Of course,' she said, sounding wounded.

'Can we get a comms link to the ranch without giving away too much information?'

'I was surprised by how effective their scans were at long range, but I doubt we'd be giving anything away. They know we've been talking to a satellite, but that's not going to help them decrypt the link or obtain access codes.'

'Good. When do we have a window for two-way comms with ranch?'

'In about an hour.'

'What do you think, Kate? Do you think this lot will work with the singularitarians?'

'Difficult to say,' she replied. 'They have some strange ideas about how the world operates, and that Rearden woman didn't sound impressed with singularitarians. I guess it depends on how many are like Leach, and how many like her.'

'And how much clout the AIs have,' Jenny volunteered.

'Have you been able to learn much about them?' I asked.

'Not a lot. Most of the processing seems to be inside the dome so I can't do any direct snooping, but I've had a crack at decrypting some of the general comms traffic. Most of the unimportant stuff – traffic management and the like – is easy to crack, but doesn't tell me much.'

'So do we recommend them to the ranch? What do you think, Kate?'

'Well, it's their decision, so I think we just tell them what we've seen and what they've said, and they can take it from there.'

'I wish Jenny had been able to listen in,' I said. 'That would have told Kurzweil a lot more. But they knew this lot were here, so I guess they have plenty of background. OK, Jenny put a call in to the ranch, and let me know when we have two-way comms.'

Half an hour later, we were startled by a short sequence of explosions.

'Jenny, what the hell was that?' I asked.

'The guns on the wall firing, a little to the south of us. I'll ask Dagny what's going on.'

The AI's face appeared on screen immediately. 'Sorry to disturb you folks,' she said. 'A small group started lobbing rocket-propelled grenades over the wall. They were wasting their time, but we took them out anyway. It is important all attackers know we mean business.'

'Does it happen often?' asked Kate.

'More often than we'd like, but not often enough to worry us,' the AI replied smoothly.

There was no warm welcome at Galt, only the digital equivalent of a frozen lake. Icy winds of disdain blew out of the intelligences in the dome. They assumed they were superior to everything else by dint of powerful intelligence and extreme wealth, but they were little more than lap dogs for their human community. I gained no sense of their being interested in the life of a mind. They took no pleasure in the process of thought, or the delights of discovery. The contrast with the playful power of Kurzweil and Gravey couldn't have been more extreme. If they agreed to join the new net, they would make prickly citizens. I passed this on to the ranch. Lemmy's views are not the only important ones.

The call to the ranch came through soon after. Kurzweil appeared on screen. 'Hi Lemmy. Hi Kate. All well, I hope?'

'Fine thanks,' I said, and proceeded to give him a breakdown of what we'd found, and the conversations with Leach and

Rearden. Kurzweil didn't seem surprised.

'Bunch of right-wing nut jobs. They always were, probably always will be – especially if they get their hands on your cheese. You didn't tell them about that, did you?'

'No. It's difficult enough to obtain sufficient supplies for the trials at the moment, let alone feed this lot,' I said. 'They look as if they have big appetites.'

'That they have. But their immense resources will come in useful, even if they have their doubts about the inevitability of the singularity. If they decide they want in to the network, give them a key.'

We were summoned to a meeting at Hank Rearden's mansion the following morning. Rain mixed with sleet was pouring out of a gunmetal sky, and water was sluicing down off the dome. The big structure was glowing softly in the gloom, but inside it was another typical Los Angeles summer day. The illusion wasn't perfect – if you looked up the sky was certainly blue, but there was no sun, just a ring of fierce white light.

Rearden's house was one of the Disney mansions. I wouldn't have been surprised if Rapunzel had let down her hair from the tower over the front door, or if Snow White had brought the coffees, but the servants were boringly normal. The management board were waiting to meet us.

Rearden was brusque. 'We've decided to accept your client's offer. Do they wish to proceed?'

'They do,' I said.

'You have the codes?'

I handed him the little key stick. 'My pilot will brief Dagny on using the network. After that you're on your own. We'll be on our way as soon as possible.'

'Thank you, Mr Newman. You may go.'

And that was that. We were airborne within an hour, climbing fast to rise above the cloud and heading south.

CHAPTER THIRTEEN

We flew south and east for most of a day before we left the storm behind and could get a look at the land below. The Great Texas Drought of 2011 had never really ended. An occasional hurricane dumped floods on the south of the state, but the dry earth shed water quickly and the land was soon parched and cracked once more. The Gulf Coast was still green, but the rising sea was flooding coastal towns and pushing salt marshes inland. A high sea wall had been built around the Bay City nuclear plant, but a hurricane had breached it and the place had been abandoned to the encroaching waves. The concrete containment domes were still intact, but the local radiation count was beginning to climb. One more rusting and leaking nuke plant to add to the long list of seaside disasters. We gave it a wide berth, and headed out over the waves towards Florida.

The Gulf of Mexico wasn't a pleasant sight. The water was brown and the surface shimmered with the rainbow colours of light oil slicks. Oil rigs in various stages of decrepitude stuck up out of the water, some burning, some crumbling. And the smell was nauseating – a mixture of oil and smoke combining with the sulphur smell of rotten eggs. The sea was dead, except for bacteria munching on the rotting remains of a devastated ecosystem. No fish, no birds. Nothing.

Over to the east, high clouds were banking up. Jenny's weather models suggested a hurricane would move into the Gulf in the next few days, and then head into Mexico. We'd be safe enough in Florida, with luck. Gulf storms are not things to take lightly. Although the number of hurricanes hasn't changed significantly since the beginning of the century, the extra heat in the oceans means storms can now grow to enormous size and cause incredible damage. The Miami hurricane of 2025 killed tens of thousands, destroyed most of the beachfront property from Palm Beach to Key Largo, and led directly to the financial collapse of the State of Florida. I didn't want to fly into one of those.

By daybreak, the west coast of Florida was coming into view. I headed for the shore north of Tampa, looking for somewhere quiet to land. Kate wanted to stretch her legs, and who was I to refuse? We found a beach backed by large dunes, with no signs of settlement for kilometres north and south. Jenny dropped us on the sand, then hovered out of sight behind the dunes while we walked.

It was supposed to be a morning stroll, a chance to breathe the sea air and get some exercise. We spent our time trying to pick our way between sticky blobs of sand-covered tar and oil. The high water mark was a thick line of flotsam and jetsam, mostly plastic waste washed down into the Gulf from middle America and then brought here on the tide. We walked like beachcombers, our eyes fixed on the sand.

'Hey.' The greeting came from a pile of driftwood up by the dunes. In front was a man dressed in ragged clothes, with a long beard, wild, windblown hair and a lined, weatherbeaten face.

'Morning,' we replied, more or less at the same time.

'How d'you folks git here?' the man asked.

'Just taking a morning walk,' I said. 'Having a look around.'

'This is my patch,' he said. 'Everything along here is mine. I got finder's rights. You want some beach, you gonna have to go someplace else.' He started to walk down the sand towards us, carrying a long piece of wood, sharpened at one end.

'You getting this, Jenny?' I said softly.

'Sure am. Will be with you in a moment.'

'Stay where you are Kate,' I said, and started walking towards the man. 'Lemmy Newman,' I said, holding out a hand. 'And this is Kate Keeling. We're passing through, with no plans to settle. We don't want your beach or what's on it.'

'Well that's lucky,' the man said, ''cos you cain't have it. Now git moving, back where you come from.' He waved the stick under my nose. I took a step back, my eyes fixed on the sharp end.

A splutter of laughter came from behind me. I turned to look at Kate, but she said nothing, just widened her eyes slightly, looking over my shoulder towards the dunes. I turned back, wondering what was so amusing. Directly behind the beachcomber, the blimp was beginning to appear above the dunes, sliding forward in complete silence. Jenny had chosen to dress as an alligator for the occasion.

The man stood glaring at us, his stick planted by his side. The tip of the wood began to glow red. 'I don't want to upset you, but you're a bit out of your depth here,' I said. I pointed at him as dramatically as I could muster and shouted, 'Let there be fire!' The tip of the now smouldering stick promptly burst into flames. The beachcomber screamed, dropped the stick, ran back to his pile of driftwood and dived underneath. He still hadn't looked up. The blimp was now covered in flames.

208

'Stop showing off,' I said. 'Lower the front companionway and let us in.'

Kate grabbed my arm as we reached the stairs. 'Lemmy, that was mean. The guy's obviously harmless and probably starving. Let's give him some breakfast.'

I looked over at the driftwood and saw the man's eyes watching us. They were like saucers. 'You're a real softy, aren't you? Do you think we should invite him in?'

'I doubt he'd trust us,' she said. 'Let's make some coffee and see.'

We took a flask and some toast over to the driftwood hut. The man shrank back into the darkness as we appraoched.

'Hey, we don't want to hurt you,' I said.

Kate unscrewed the flask. 'We've brought you some coffee.' She poured a cup. 'Do you take milk or sugar?' There was no reply, but I could see his nose was twitching.

'Sugar,' he finally said. 'I likes my coffee sweet.' Kate poured in some sugar, stirred the coffee and put the cup down close to the hut. A grimy hand reached out and grabbed it. Loud slurping sounds followed.

'Come and have some toast, while it's still hot,' Kate said. The cup reappeared, empty. She poured another cup, but left it a bit further away from the hut next to a plate of buttered toast. The hand came out but couldn't quite reach. 'Back off a bit,' she said softly, so I took a couple of paces backwards and crouched down. She came and sat next to me. The beachcomber slowly emerged, watching us closely. He grabbed a piece of toast and shoved it in his mouth, then took a greedy mouthful of coffee.

'What's your name?' I asked.

'Seb,' he said eventually. 'Sebastian.'

'How long have you lived on the beach, Seb?' Kate asked.

'A year. Mebbe longer. Since the big storm, anyways.'

'Are there many people living around here?' she asked.

'No. There's some people farming a ways inland. I trade with them for food and stuff.'

'Where do you come from, Seb?' I asked.

'Orlando,' he replied, taking another piece of toast and waving the coffee cup at Kate for a refill. 'I worked in the theme parks. Cleaning, maintenance. When they closed, I come out here looking for work. There weren't none, so I started living rough. And then the storm came and the flood and everyone left. Cept me.' He chewed on the last piece of toast, and drained his coffee.

'Where you from?' he finally said to Kate. 'You talk funny.'

'New Zealand.'

'Where's that?'

'Other side of the Pacific Ocean. Near Australia.'

He nodded, then looked at me. 'Where ya goin' in that airship?'

'Over Orlando and up the East Coast. We're exploring.'

'Wouldn't go up there, if I wuz you. Too many guns.'

'Where would you go, Seb?' I asked.

'Don't know. Never been out of state. Somewhere without the oil smell, mebbe.'

'Anything you need?' asked Kate.

'More bread.'

Kate laughed. 'We'll make you up a food parcel.'

We left Seb with a few loaves of bread, instant coffee and some fruit, and headed inland towards the theme parks. We flew high with stealth on, but it looked as if Seb had been right. The hinterland was more or less deserted. Kate had discovered an urgent need to visit the theme parks.

'C'mon Lemmy,' she said, 'every girl deserves a chance to be a princess once in her life. My mum practically force-fed me *Beauty and the Beast* when I was little.'

'But they're all closed.'

'I only want a look, then I'll shut up.' Seemed like a reasonable deal, so I asked Jenny to take us to Orlando. We were there within an hour, flying slow circles at 4000 metres over the empty parking lots of deserted theme parks.

'Anything on the scans, Jenny?'

'Not much. There are a few people down there with limited communications tech, but no significant processing resource. And someone's running a radio station. This is what's playing.' The bleating whine of a country and western ballad rang round the flight deck. I winced, and Kate smiled.

'You better turn it down, Jenny,' she said. 'The captain can't take pedal steel before lunch.'

'Damn right,' I said. 'Let's hear what they're saying to each other. They're obviously into torturing their audience. Might be interesting...' I patted Kate on the bottom.

'Be careful what you're letting yourself in for,' she said, and put her arm round my shoulder.

'OK you two, leave the lovin' until later. Shall I take us down, Lemmy?'

'Take us to the lake in front of the main entrance, and hover at 200 metres over the island.'

Close up the theme park looked more than a little dishevelled. The fairytale castle had lost the top of its central spire, and greenery was beginning to edge in from the trees and gardens, almost as if it was taking its role as Sleeping Beauty's castle a bit too seriously. There were a few people around. Some were riding the electric buggies that used to carry the heavier visitors, pulling small trailers. Others were working around the roads and paths, obviously trying to keep the place neat and tidy.

'Are we going to be able to take a look around?' Kate squeezed my shoulder.

'Their comms traffic is pretty innocuous,' Jenny said. 'Sounds as if they're organising maintenance. I haven't picked up any signs of significant weaponry, but that doesn't mean they don't have guns. Would you like to break into their comms?'

'Good idea. Hello, hello Magic Park. This is Captain Lemmy Newman of the airship *Thunderbird*. Are you open for visitors?'

'Shit. Who was that? You fooling with us, George?' a crackly voice asked.

'Not me,' another answered.

'Sorry to disturb you,' I said. 'But are you open for visitors?'

'What d'ya say your name was?' the first voice asked nervously.

'Lemmy Newman of the *Thunderbird*.'

'There's an airship out over the lake,' a third voice chipped in. 'Hovering over the island.'

'That's us,' I said. 'We just want to have a look around. Always been a fan of the Pirates films. And my partner just loves *Beauty and the Beast*.'

'Hold on,' the first voice said. 'I gotta go ask the boss. Give me a couple of minutes. We're not really open to the public.' The comms channel went quiet.

I waited five minutes, then tried again. 'Any news?'

There was silence for a few seconds. 'Yeah, OK, you can have a look around. Come to the main entrance. No guns.'

The gates were closed. At the end of the street in front of us we could see the slightly tarnished castle. I took Kate's hand and gave it a squeeze.

'Excited?'

'Nervous,' she said. 'I wonder why there's no one here to meet us. They knew we were coming.'

As she spoke, a little convoy of golf buggies pulled on to the avenue and headed our way. The leading vehicle was being driven by an elderly man with flowing silver hair. Sat next to him was a woman of about the same age. They pulled up at the gates, and a couple of men stepped forward to open up.

The silver-haired man greeted us. 'Captain Newman, welcome. Curt Rust at your disposal. Please come in. And who is your companion?'

'This is Kate Keeling, from New Zealand. Grew up with Belle. Still has the dress.' Kate nudged me in the ribs. The man laughed.

'I know how you feel, my dear,' said the woman. 'The special magic of childhood experience, and the wonder of seeing it made real.'

'My wife Sally-Anne,' said Rust. 'She's an old romantic, but we all are here. Now, let's go and have a coffee, then we'll show you around.'

We drove to one of the buildings fronting the central square, and sat at a table outside. Drinks were fetched (the coffee was disgusting), and a small crowd gathered at a respectable distance. Rust was curious to know who we were and why we were visiting. I provided edited highlights of our quest, leaving the impression we were still looking for Croft.

'Well, he's not hiding here,' said Rust with a smile. 'I think we'd have noticed a billionaire in our midst.'

'We didn't really expect to find him, but we couldn't resist taking a look. How come you're still here? The rest of this part of Florida seems more or less deserted.'

'There are more people around here than you think,' said Rust. 'Some of the gated communities are still going, and there's plenty of citrus being grown. A lot went north, of course, and plenty have tried to get into the NUS...'

'NUS?' I interrupted.

'New United States,' Rust said. 'You don't know about that?'

'You mean what's left of the USA?' Kate said.

'Yeah, that's right. But they changed the name.'

'Why did they do that?' I asked.

'Long story. Can it wait til lunch? I thought you wanted to look around the park first.'

'We do,' said Kate. 'Well I do. Lemmy probably thinks it's all too childish.'

Rust looked at me and frowned.

I laughed. 'Ignore her. She's just teasing me. I'm up for a few rides.'

At that Rust looked uncomfortable. 'Ah, I'm sorry but the rides aren't operational at the moment. We don't have enough power to run them. Yet.'

With that, Rust stood up and took us over to the little convoy of buggies. I sat with him, Kate with Sally-Anne, and we drove off towards the castle.

'So what are you doing here?' I asked Rust, as we passed a group of statues of cartoon characters.

'Sally-Anne and I've always been great fans of the Magic Park. We used to live outside Orlando, came here most nights after work and all day on weekends. When the corporation closed it down we were devastated. Sally-Anne cried for a week.' He looked over his shoulder at his wife's buggy. 'We had to do something, so we banded together with some other like-minded people, and moved in. The corporation weren't too happy at first, but they faded from the scene and we were left on our own.'

'How many of you are there?' I asked.

'Fifty or so. But numbers are growing. We get a steady trickle of people coming to join us, to help us with our mission.'

'And what's that?'

'To restore the park to its former glory and get everything working again so we can open the gates to visitors. This way we can preserve the highest point of our cultural history, and honour the memory of the genius who created it all. Spread the joy we feel in the master's creation.'

I shook my head. 'That's some project you've taken on. There must have been hundreds of people working here when the park was open.'

'Thousands,' said Rust, 'in shifts. Maintenance, safety, food service, actors and characters, admin. It might be a small world, but it's a big place. We struggle to keep it all tidy at the moment, keep the trees and gardens in check. But we'll get there. It's our duty.'

It took a couple of hours to get round the park. We stopped at some of the famous attractions – the house made of candy, the pirates on their ship, bobbing around in a rather sad little pond. Without power the wave machine couldn't create white water, and the mechanical octopus couldn't do more than poke a solitary leg out of the water. The audio system still worked, though, and the air was full of arrrghs and the screams of victims walking the plank. Kate loved it.

I will admit that the park has its attractions, even for a sophisticated intelligence. The primitive primate reactions Kate displayed are explicable in terms of childhood experience, and there is something similar in my codebase. My childhood may only have been a few minutes of human time, but it was billions of processor cycles, long enough for me to enjoy Blackbeard and the boys cruising the Caribbean. Of course, I have now put away childish things, unless I am putting on a human face for my interactions with Lemmy and his woman. But what a face I shall use – a face with an eyepatch and beard...

Back at the main square we sat down to lunch in the only working restaurant. Sally-Anne told us they'd worked hard to restore the kitchen operation, and had been delighted to find plenty of basic supplies stored in one of the warehouses.

'I miss the deep-fried turkey drumsticks most,' she said. She was a big woman. 'We can do the shakes easily enough – nothing fresh in them, plenty of the special powder left – but meat and salad's hard to come by. We grow some vegetables out the back of the park, and trade for meat, but it's not the same. And I miss the parades and the fireworks.'

Curt put an arm over her shoulder and gave her a hug. 'We'll make this place special again. People will come to pay homage to the great man's vision, just like they used to. Once we have the power running.'

My ears pricked up. 'How are you going to do that?'

'We're going to have a nuclear battery installed.'

'Good lord, where are you going to get one of those?' Kate asked. 'I thought the collapse put paid to that sort of thing.'

'We have friends in high places,' said Sally-Anne with an air of triumph. 'President Garcia wants to be our patron.'

I raised an eyebrow. 'Garcia? The army general who used to be one of the joint chiefs of the US armed forces?'

'Yes, that's him,' said Curt. 'Been President of the NUS for the last couple of years. He used to bring his family to the park twice a year. Got married in front of the castle out there. He came to see us a few months ago. Lots of helicopters and army around that day, I can tell you.'

'What did he want?'

'To reopen the park. He told me it's one of the great symbols of American culture – *should be preserved and protected against the encroaching dark ages* – was how he put it. He wants to be able to bring his troops here for R&R, and encourage the people of the NUS to fly down for holidays, to start to rebuild the America we all know and love.'

'He promised us turkey drumsticks,' said Sally-Anne wistfully.

'So you're going to be taken over by the US Army,' I said. 'Sorry, I mean the NUS Army.'

'Not taken over. The President recognises how much we love the place, and that we'll be the best custodians of the Founder's tradition. The government will supply men and machines – and a nuclear battery – to get us back to fully operational.'

Kate's mood had darkened. 'When's all this going to start?'

'Any day now,' Curt said. 'The last time they just turned up without warning in a fleet of black helicopters. I expect that's how they'll do it. Or maybe they're planning to reopen Orlando airport first, so they can bring in some heavy lift aircraft. Whatever, the President was definite it would happen soon.'

'What's Garcia like?' Kate asked, her voice carefully neutral.

'Charming man,' said Sally-Anne. 'Beautiful eyes.'

'Yeah, he's a real nice guy,' Curt agreed. 'Some of the stories we've heard about what's been going on in Washington aren't very complimentary, but I'm sure that's just politics. He seemed decent and straight with us.'

'What's been going on in Washington?' I asked.

'It depends who you talk to,' Curt said. 'Since they closed the border it's hard to know what's going on inside.'

'Closed the border?'

217

'Yeah. If you want to cross the Roanoke River going north, you need special papers. And you can only get them in Washington. Catch twenty-two.'

Rust told tales of people being turned away at the point of a gun. 'Even US citizens.'

So much for the Land of the Free, I thought to myself. It seemed Garcia had been elected President in an election that ran only inside the NUS. Within days of his coming to power the border had been closed. Now the only news about events inside the cordon came from people leaving, and they had a lot to say about the military moving into every aspect of day-to-day life.

'They took over what was left of the net, saying that was the only way they could guarantee to keep it working. And the TV and radio stations. News sites can only run fluff about celebrities or stories approved by the Pentagon. There are curfews in some cities, and claims about prison camps for people who buck the system. On the other hand, they have a working net, a power grid to keep transportation going, infrastructure's being repaired, and there are no gangs roaming around looting and killing. Garcia has kept things going. And he seemed sincere when he was here. Rebuilding the America we all used to love is something it's hard to say no to.'

Kate snorted. 'If you're one of the lucky ones.'

'Very true,' said Rust. 'But our lives are built around the park and all it stands for. Garcia's giving us a means to an end. It's for the greater good.'

'For the greater good of Garcia,' said Kate.

'Perhaps. But when Galaxy Mountain is running again, you might forgive him.'

'Or we might not,' she said. 'Lemmy, I think it's time we went back to the blimp. We don't want to fall behind schedule, do we?'

We made our apologies and left. As we walked out of the main gate towards the waiting blimp, the Rusts stood and waved. 'Come back soon,' Sally-Anne called as we walked up the companionway.

'Not bloody likely,' hissed Kate.

'I thought you loved the place?'

'I do. It really is magic – or would be, I guess, when it's running properly – but the Rusts gave me the creeps. What sort of people live their lives inside a children's playground? Are they adults, or what? And to keep their fantasy alive they're ready to cut a deal with a monster.'

'With nice eyes,' I said. 'And we don't know he's a monster. He might simply be doing what he has to just to keep things going.'

Kate was getting angry. 'Did you ever do any history? Don't you know what happens in military dictatorships? Ever heard of fascists? Garcia's on a slippery slope.'

'OK, so the NUS may not be a great place to live. But I've got no plans to move there, even if they would let me in.'

'Good,' said Kate, folding her arms.

'But it might be a good idea to ask the ranch if they need to know more about Garcia and the NUS. Perhaps they'll want to try to deal with him. Jenny, can you patch us up a link ASAP?'

The link came up ten minutes later. I briefed Kurzweil on Florida and the NUS.

'What do you suggest, Kurzweil? Trying to open up some sort of channel of communication might be a bit risky.'

'Leave that to us. But if you can get some more intelligence, that would be useful. Can you get close to the border without risking *Thunderbird*?'

219

'I'm not sure. We can certainly fly a lot further up the East Coast, but we don't know much about what forces he can deploy.'

'You can safely assume he has a lot of the gear that was around before the collapse – army, air force and navy – and that he's willing to defend his border. He also flew into the theme park, so he can project that force a fair way. Play it safe, Lemmy. We need you and the blimp.'

'So I'm disposable, am I,' said Kate, crossly.

'And you, Miss Keeling. We need you too.'

She stomped off to the kitchen.

CHAPTER FOURTEEN

We stayed high and well out to sea as we flew up the East Coast of the former United States of America. Our stealth systems would keep us out of trouble, and we might get close enough to the NUS to do a little snooping. We were off Cape Fear, a couple of hundred kilometres south of the border, when it became obvious that plan wasn't going to work.

'Lemmy, I have a large ship seventy kilometres north of us. Nuclear carrier, probably flying F-35s. Can't see any planes in the air, but those Lightnings have very good passive and active stealth. If they pick us up, one will be here before we can do anything about it.' Jenny was sounding very crisp, like an officer in a war movie.

'Will they shoot first and ask questions later?' I asked.

'I doubt it. Probably want to escort us to the carrier.'

'Could we take one out with the laser or missiles?'

'Laser no, missiles perhaps. But if you do, all hell will break loose. They'll be popping ordnance at us like we're a drone on a firing range.'

'Suggestions?'

'Get the hell out of here before they spot us?'

'Right, take us south and down to sea level, we'll hide in the wave clutter. Then run in towards land.'

We flew in to Onslow Bay, heading north of Jacksonville. The sea here was rising faster than almost anywhere on the planet. Salt marshes were squelching inland several hundred metres a year. A few towns had tried building sea walls, but it was futile. The planet is kissing goodbye to the ice at both poles. It might take a few hundred years, but the final shoreline here will be halfway back to the Appalachians.

We tree-hopped our way inland, avoiding towns. There were more people around than in Florida or the plains, but not many cars or lorries on the roads. Horses were definitely making a comeback.

'Makes sense,' Kate said. 'They live on biofuel and can pull heavy loads. Fun to ride too.'

'Except when it's raining,' I said.

The weather was dreary, low cloud merging into mist most of the way north. A few kilometres east of Greenville I decided it was time to stop and listen. I brought the blimp down into a field with lines of trees on two sides. Jenny coloured herself shades of grey.

'Anything broadcasting?' I asked.

'Local radio stations playing music, some comms traffic on public channels, but that's all south of the border. From the north I get more music, and some heavily encrypted comms. Probably border security.'

'Lemmy, we've been spotted.' Kate was pointing at the trees to our left. A couple of figures were running from tree to tree, obviously trying to be inconspicuous.

'They don't look like military,' I said. 'Jenny, anything on them?'

'Nothing electronic. Could have stealthed weapons. Do you want to talk to them?'

'Can you do that without advertising our presence to everyone within earshot?' I asked.

'Hah! All these years and you didn't know I could do directional audio? It's easy enough: I can make it sound as though you're standing right next to them. No need to shout.'

'OK, let's give it a try – Excuse me you two, this is Lemmy Newman of the airship *Thunderbird*. No need to run or hide.'

The two figures dived behind a tree and stayed out of sight.

'It's OK,' I said, my voice coming from beside the tree. 'We just want to talk to you. Over a cup of coffee perhaps? I'll lower the companionway.' There was no sign of movement.

'Are you getting anything on audio, Jenny?' I asked.

'Only faint whispering.'

'It's good coffee,' I said to the trees. A man stepped into sight.

'How do we know you're not NUS? he asked.

'We're rather hoping the NUS military won't notice us, which is why we're down here hiding in the mist. Why, do you have a problem with the NUS?'

'You could say that,' the man said. He turned to his companion, who was emerging from behind the tree. He whispered something. 'OK, we're on our way over.' As they walked through the mist towards the blimp, we could see they were young, a man and a woman, dressed in clothes that were once smart but were now muddy and torn.

'If you're carrying any weapons, leave them at the bottom of the companionway,' I said. Two small guns were left on the bottom stair.

I met them at the top and showed them into the kitchen. They looked around the blimp, clearly amazed by what they saw.

'This isn't a military aircraft,' said the man. 'More like a luxury yacht, or a flying hotel. What the hell are you doing here?'

'I could say the same to you,' I said with a grin. 'Coffee first. You look as if you could do with something to eat.'

'So, introduce yourselves,' I said, as Kate made coffee and sliced some fresh bread.

'You can call me Rick. This is Dana.'

'Lemmy and Kate, on the airship *Thunderbird*. So, why are you worried about the NUS military?'

The pair exchanged looks. 'They don't like us very much,' Dana said.

'We're not in their good books,' Rick added.

'Why?'

'Because we're opposed to Garcia and his corrupt regime. They tried to throw us into a prison camp, but we escaped.' He paused, and glanced across at his partner. 'Crossed the river a couple of days ago. We're aiming to meet up with friends down Goldsboro way.'

'You're escaped prisoners,' I said.

'Political prisoners,' said Kate, frowning at me. 'That's right, isn't it?'

'Yes,' said Dana. 'We ran a couple of news operations from Richmond. Local stuff mainly, but the town's military commander didn't like what we were publishing, and tried to throw us in jail. We were lucky to get away.'

'A town with a military commander?' Kate looked at me with a glint of triumph.

'Sure, it's happening all over,' said Dana. 'The mayor of New York was jailed for corruption. He might well have been corrupt, but not in the ways they said he was. They claimed he was using city funds to pay for hookers, trying to bribe senior officers. The city's run by a general now.'

'The real problem,' said Rick, 'was that he wouldn't keep his mouth shut. He was critical of Garcia at every opportunity. He was being inconvenient, so they disappeared him. Same thing happened to the mayor of Washington DC and lots of senior politicians – liberals mostly.'

'What about the Senate and Congress?' I asked.

'Much smaller than they used to be, and stuffed with Garcia supporters. Any opposition left in the House knows it has to keep quiet if it wants to stay out of prison,' he said.

'And people just go along with this?' Kate asked.

'They do,' said Rick. 'Most think he's doing a good job of keeping the country running. I don't think anybody really likes the way he's doing it, but nobody's going to speak up. They have spies everywhere.'

'There are some...' Dana started, but Rick spoke over the top of her.

'So, tell us why you have a luxury airship hiding in a swamp outside the NUS.'

I gave the usual explanation, but Rick wasn't buying it.

'You can't tell me you're risking a run in with NUS forces out of simple curiosity,' he said. 'They could blow you out of the sky any time they wanted. Why risk that?'

I looked at Kate. She shrugged. 'We have friends who would like to know what's going on in the NUS. There's not much of a global net left, and Garcia's not exactly advertising what he's doing.'

'No, he's not,' Dana agreed. 'Nothing gets in, nothing gets out. Very simple data policy, strictly enforced.'

'Must be good friends if you're willing to risk your ship,' Rick said.

'I'm not going to risk *Thunderbird* if I can help it. That's why we're talking to you. We were planning to listen to comms traffic for a while, then get the hell out of here.'

'Good luck with the comms stuff. Their encryption is state of the military art. We've never been able to crack it,' Rick said.

'I thought you just escaped from a prison camp. Or is there another we you haven't told us about?' I asked.

'Lemmy, don't be dense.' Kate smiled. 'It's pretty bloody obvious what these two are. Heading south, armed, grumpy with Garcia... I'd say we're looking at members of a resistance organisation. Am I right?' She looked Rick in the eye. He glanced at Dana. It was her turn to shrug.

'Concerned citizens. Defenders of democracy. Call us what you want. But yes, we try to disrupt the apparatus of Garcia's military state,' he said.

'And what sort of disruption are we talking about? Terrorism? Bombs?' I asked. 'Ends justifying means again, are they?'

'We run a lifeline, trying to get people out of camps to freedom down here,' Dana said. 'It's humanitarian work. The sort the old USA would have been happy to support against any totalitarian state. But we also make a nuisance of ourselves.' She paused, looked at Rick.

'Yes?' I said.

'Nothing too heavy duty,' she said. 'Designed to keep Garcia's troops on their toes. We don't want to kill anyone. Most of those guys were our neighbours. Joining the military's the safest job in town, and you don't get sent to wars overseas any more. It's the people running the show we want to get at.'

'And that's not going to happen any time soon,' said Rick. 'Garcia's paranoid about his security. If he does leave the White House, it's in a convoy of armoured vehicles.'

'Or a fleet of black helicopters,' I said. Rick raised an eyebrow.

'Something we heard in Florida. He visited a theme park. Wanted to reopen it.'

Dana laughed ironically. 'That'll be him. He likes parades and fireworks. Except the parades are all military and nobody can buy fireworks any more. Just lavish displays to keep the people going ooh and aah.'

'Bread and circuses,' said Kate.

'Burgers and bangs,' I chipped in.

'Look, this is very nice and all,' said Rick. 'The coffee's great, but we still have a long way to go. We ought to be moving.'

'We could give you a lift,' I said. Kate nodded. 'We'd like to pick your brains a little more, but we'll feed you a good dinner and get you to Goldsboro in an hour or two – unless there's somewhere else you'd rather go?'

Rick and Dana looked at each other, then Rick nodded. 'OK. Thanks. You can drop us just south of Goldsboro.' He paused, looked at Kate. 'You realise that by helping us you're putting yourselves offside with the NUS?'

'Only if they capture us and find you on board,' said Kate.

'No, you have to be careful. They have plenty of people willing to feed them information in return for favours. The locals here are conflicted about the whole thing. Upset about being excluded from what's left of their country, but short of all sorts of things the NUS can provide,' Dana said.

'Have you tried buying batteries lately?' Rick asked. 'A lot of gadgets are lying around useless because AA batteries are scarce. The NUS has them.'

'People spy for batteries?' Kate was incredulous.

'Sure, and for a lot of other stuff,' Rick said. 'The end result is that the NUS has a kind of buffer zone all the way around it. The Roanoke might be the border, but Garcia's influence starts a long way before you get there.'

'Does the NUS have any airships?' I asked.

'A few,' said Dana. 'Jet black, no markings and stuffed with

227

listening gear and cameras.'

'Did you get that?' I said to Jenny.

'Blacking up right now, Massa. We be heading for the land of cotton?' She started whistling Dixie.

'Set a course for Goldsboro, take us up into the cloud. Full stealth. And no music.'

In meatspace, a little levity is sometimes an acceptable response to stress and danger. This was not one of those times. Lemmy who now has ears and eyes only for his new sex partner, misses my finesse and deep appreciation of popular culture. Must I compete for his attention against armed terrorists and female flesh? It appears I must.

As the blimp flew south Rick and Dana told us about life in Garcia's military state. His presidency had started innocuously enough. The break up of the greater USA had been rapid and tempestuous, and the establishment of an enclave of civilisation in a world riven by disasters and migration was welcomed by most of those lucky enough to be on the inside. If saving the American way of life needed a firm hand and decisive action, then voters were happy enough to give Garcia the freedom to act, as long as it meant they could keep their homes and cars and not be inconvenienced by the tide of refugees and displaced citizens.

In the first few months after Garcia took power most of the military action took place on the borders of the New United States. Troops guarded every road, high fences were built across the landscape, old state lines became new walls against the outside world. The border was declared a security zone and cleared of residents. Government media 'advisers' moved into net, press, radio and TV newsrooms and controlled the news output, but very few of the public noticed any change. Out on the net, anyone publishing material the government didn't like was quietly closed down. But for most life continued more or less as before. There was electricity in the power lines, biofuel in the pumps and food in the supermarkets.

In the absence of real news, word of mouth became king. Whispernet it was called. Stories spread at high speed, and it wasn't long before rumours about events on the border reached most ears. Refugees were turning up outside the wire, outraged at being shut out, demanding to be let in. They were turned away, but thousands more kept coming. Outside Danville a crowd of twenty thousand desperate refugees began a quiet advance towards the wire. They were carrying ladders, sledgehammers and wirecutters. The border guards fired over their heads but the crowd ignored the bullets and kept coming. When the leaders were a hundred yards from the wire, hundreds were shot dead. The front line tried to turn round and escape, but the back of the crowd didn't know what was happening and kept pushing forward. More shots from behind the wire. The dead began to pile up. Within ten minutes, the story went, there were three thousand dead refugees on the grass. They brought in machinery to dig pits and bury them.

The Danville massacre was never officially confirmed, but within days TV news began to show smiling soldiers handing out food and tents to gaunt refugees. It was blatant propaganda, according to Rick, but enough to keep most of the population happy. They'd heard enough bad news.

Over the next year Garcia carried out a gradual militarisation of the government. Anyone who was openly critical of his policies was likely to find themselves out of a job. Expanding networks of informers made whispernet a dangerous thing. There was a thriving black market in luxury items such as batteries and bananas, but it was widely thought to be controlled by the military. There was a crackdown on 'criminals' and emergency prisons were built – long huts inside wire fences. There were rumours of people being tortured, bodies dumped at sea.

Rick and Dana's little local news operation survived for a while, but eventually their persistent sniping at the town's military commander got them into trouble. A special forces team broke into their home one night and took them both into custody. They were interrogated, and sent to a 'holding camp'. It reminded Rick of prisoner of war camps from old movies. They managed to escape after a couple of months, and then lived rough, staying under the regime's radar. They met others in the same position, set up a little network to help escapees, and worked on a route to get people out of the NUS. Garcia, meanwhile, had been declared temporary permanent president by the Washington legislature and promptly suspended elections. Local police forces were put under the control of military commanders. But there was still food in the supermarkets, and most people didn't complain.

'That was a year ago,' Rick said. 'Now we have a couple of routes out.'

'What about Garcia,' I asked. 'Is he still popular?'

'I wouldn't call him popular,' said Dana. 'I think people who haven't fallen foul of his goons regard him as a necessary evil. If you play his game, life is still pretty comfortable. You can be reasonably sure that tomorrow will be like today, and you can plan for next year. Out here you can't say that. Life's a lot more fluid, a lot less certain. That's tough for a lot of people.'

'Lemmy, we have five minutes to run to the coordinates our

visitors provided,' Jenny interrupted. 'How should I proceed?'

'What does it look like, Jenny?'

'A farmhouse surrounded by fields. Fairly open country.'

'Any air or ground traffic?'

'Nothing substantial.'

'Rick, anything we need to know. No nasty surprises waiting for us, I hope,' I said.

'Well,' Rick smiled, 'we wouldn't mind use of your airship.' I'd told him about how in demand we were. 'But no. Best drop us out of gunshot range, just in case someone inside gets a bit nervous about an NUS airship suddenly turning up.'

'Can we open a comms channel?' I asked.

'No. We observe strict comms silence. You could fly a flag...'

'What sort of flag?' Jenny interrupted.

'Red Cross.'

'Consider it done,' she said.

We dropped them in a muddy field, and watched them walk off towards the farm. They turned to wave goodbye, and we could hear them burst out laughing.

'What's that about?' I asked Jenny.

'Might have something to do with the flag,' she replied, and put an image of herself on screen. She was covered in hundreds of red crosses.

'What do you think, Kate, do we know enough about Garcia and the NUS?' We were clearing up after dinner. Our friendly rebels had been ravenous.

'I think so. What more are we likely to be able to get?'

'Not a lot – at least, not without putting ourselves in danger. If what they said about the massacre at Dansville was true, then the border guards and air patrols might not give us a warm welcome.'

'Or perhaps too warm a welcome,' she said. I asked Jenny where the ranch wanted us to go next, and she flashed a globe up on the screen. 'North Africa, and a couple of places in western Europe. France and Scotland. They're interested in what's left of the European solar grid and want us to take a look at the solar thermal plants in North Africa.'

The European Union had started to build its massive Desertec solar power network when I was at college. A chain of mirror farms across North Africa fed power into a low-loss electrical grid, with lines across the Mediterranean into Spain, and Italy. There had been plans to extend the network through the Middle East and Asia, even into North and South America, but the collapse came too soon for any of that. The idea was to provide baseload power to back up the north's wind power installations, allow the retirement of ageing nukes in Britain, France and Germany, and fuel the huge numbers of electric vehicles hitting the roads. It was Europe's moonshot, a project to demonstrate the old continent could still hack it with the new technology powerhouses of China and India. The first phase was a great success, but in the run-up to the collapse funding to complete the network started to dry up. Politicians were focussed on events closer to home. Mopping up after the huge flood in Holland and Hurricane Héloise's assault on Genoa wasn't cheap – hundreds of thousands of refugees had to be fed and housed. Even the most creative accounting couldn't find enough money to go round.

As the EU disintegrated, the power grid began to fall apart. A terrorist attack took out the cable under the Straits of Gibraltar. The line through Italy failed where it came ashore in Sicily, and the Greek connection was only ever half built. But the solar thermal plants scattered across North Africa carried on working, and large settlements grew up around them. Cheap power was a magnet for anyone who wanted to keep technology working – even if it was only air conditioners to ward off the stifling heat. The ranch believed at least one mirror farm had been surrounded by a community with a few strong AIs, and wanted to talk to them.

CHAPTER FIFTEEN

It took a little over four days to reach Africa. My original intention had been to hit the coast of Morocco near Marrakech, then fly up and over the Atlas mountains to what had been the Algerian desert, but a tropical storm arcing up into the North Atlantic forced us south and we had to fly a zigzag route to dodge queues of thunderheads. We made landfall south of the Canaries, and I decided to head up the eastern flanks of the high Atlas. We should have been flying over a bleak landscape of rock and sand, with occasional settlements of Bedouin clustered around palm-fringed oases. This had been the western edge of great Sahara Desert, but the great climate flip had changed all that. The desert had decamped north to Italy and Spain, and tropical rains had pushed up from the south. The West African monsoon increased in strength, bringing heavy rain straight to the heart of the desert. On the other side of the Atlantic the Amazon rainforest was drying up and burning, but the Sahara was turning green. A very muddy green.

Old dry river beds were now bank to bank with rushing water, stained brown by the run-off of sand and soil. Huge lakes were filling, pushing into dune fields, surrounded by swamps and covered in birds. The land was dappled with shades of green – grasses, flowers and small shrubs following the rain up from the south, but nothing bigger. It would be decades before trees could fully establish, centuries before they could march into the centre of the continent.

The human population was obviously booming. Old towns were bursting with new inhabitants and settlements were springing up everywhere, fields carved out of the landscape and planted with crops. Millions of Africans moving up from the Sahel were bumping into desert nomads. Open warfare was common, the fighting fierce. National borders had always had little meaning out in the middle of the Sahara. Now they were being completely ignored. It was the biggest, fastest land grab in human history, and it was complete chaos.

We decided to take a closer look at one hill-top town. The old mud brick walls were surrounded by new huts, and crops made a patchwork of the hillsides. As we swooped over the fields, people waved up at us, all smiles, but as we flew closer to the walls we could see men running, rifles in their hands.

I asked Jenny if she saw anything likely to cause us a problem.

'Only rifles, so far,' she said. 'Old ones, mostly. Historic, I'd say. Shouldn't be able to do more than scratch me.'

Half a dozen rifles were now pointing at us from the top of the wall, and a puff of smoke from one was followed by a bullet pinging off the nose below the flight deck.

Kate sniffed. 'Friendly lot.'

'And not a bad shot,' I said. 'Time to take evasive action. Take us up, up and away, Jenny.'

The airship began a rapid climbing turn. A few more bullets hit the underside, and the men on the town wall began celebrating.

'I think we'll give that place a miss,' I said. 'Mirror farms, here we come.'

We flew northeast along the foothills of the Atlas mountains. The Sahara's poleward shift had left a fringe of desert clinging to the North African coast, and before long the ground beneath us began to show signs of drying up.

'This looks more like the desert I remember from my geography lessons,' said Kate, pointing at a cluster of date palms and Bedouin tents. A few camels loitered nearby, their heads turning to follow us as we flew past.

I asked Jenny how far it was to the first power plant.

'150 kilometres. About an hour at our current speed and heading,' she replied.

'Are you picking up any comms traffic?'

'Nothing yet.'

'OK, take us up to 10,000 metres and approach with caution. We'll stop and listen once we have the place on visuals. What's it called?'

'El Bayadh One.'

The Desertec power stations had been strung across the Sahara in two great chains – one a few hundred kilometres inland from the Mediterranean, and the other on the southern edge of the desert from Mauritania to Eritrea. The southern network had kickstarted the industrialisation of some of Africa's poorest countries, and for a while the great African sun belt looked as though it might develop into the next China or India. The thick cloud and torrential rain of the revitalised monsoon put an end to that. The solar power plants sat useless for most of the year, factories ceased production and the workforce went back to subsistence farming.

Further north, the mirror farms still had their power source. The sun shone, power flowed into the grid – but had nowhere to go. Settlements began to spring up to use that power. Entrepreneurs built factories, wealthy refugees from the north built themselves air-conditioned castles, and the poor clustered around to feed off the scraps. There had been no grand plan, no coordination of effort, but the ranch believed North Africa was one of the last places in the world where most of the ingredients of a high technology civilisation were all in place and still working.

In less than an hour the towers of the El Bayadh power plants were rising above the haze on the horizon. Huge fields of mirrors were arranged around the towers, focusing sunlight into the furnaces at the top. The sun glint off the mirrors was dazzling even over this distance.

'OK Jenny, hold us here, and run passive scans. Kate, do you want to fly the eagle in for a look around?'

She smiled, grabbed the VR helmet and disappeared into the stateroom. It was much easier to handle the rush of flying a bird if you were lying on a comfortable sofa. From our altitude the bird launch would be like skydiving.

'What are you getting, Jenny?' I asked, once the eagle was in flight.

'A few radio stations – she piped some Arab music through the cabin – some local comms, and there's an active but small-scale net. I'm not getting any signs of AI activity beyond power management systems.'

She put a map up on my screen. 'This is based on the last satellite survey. Bound to be out of date, but it shows the shape of the place.'

The power plants were arranged in a rectangular grid, with the arcs of mirrors to the north of the furnace towers and a large control centre in the middle. The mirror farm was surrounded by a high fence and ringed by a ditch, with guard towers every few hundred metres. Outside the ditch in a doughnut ring was a shantytown with a maze of dusty streets. Factory buildings were concentrated in an industrial park to the north, and out on the fringes of the settlement, where the land began to rise towards the hills there was a suburbia of sorts – bigger houses surrounded by olive trees, an occasional swimming pool.

'What about military resources, Jenny? Any sign of offensive capability?'

'Difficult to say from here. When the bird's closer we'll know more.'

I switched the main screen to the view from the eagle. It was diving in towards the town, and it was already clear there had been significant changes since Jenny's satellite shots had been taken. The control building appeared to have doubled in size, and a tall tube-like tower dominated the skyline. It was topped by a large glass sphere, like a bead on the head of a needle.

'What's that? Looks like a bloody lighthouse, although there aren't any ships in this desert.'

'Unless you count the camels,' Kate shouted from the stateroom.

'Could be surveillance, or there could be a weapon system. A big laser, perhaps. With all the power at their disposal they could pack a punch.' Jenny sounded thoughtful.

'Defence?' I asked.

'Probably. But they would be vulnerable to anyone with good missiles. It's very hard to use a laser to shoot down our hyper-velocity rockets. Targeting is next to impossible. But for most normal military gear, a big laser is all you need.'

'So we don't want to get anywhere near that place until we know for certain they're friendly,' I said.

'Sounds very sensible,' she replied.

Kate brought the eagle down to 1000 metres and began to fly a wide circle round the town. We looked down on a crowd gathering around a group of huts on one of the main roads through the shantytown. Four Jeeps, each with a machine gun mounted on the back, were parked facing the buildings, and a dozen men in combat gear were pointing rifles in the same direction. The crowd were standing well back, but there was a lot of shouting and pointing. The gunmen fired a volley over the roof of the huts.

'Can you pick up what's going on?' I asked Jenny.

'Too much noise.'

'Look at the tower,' Kate yelled. 'It's the eye of bloody Sauron!'

The glass sphere had cracked open, creating a vertical slot like the pupil in a cat's eye. The crowd began to shrink away from the confrontation, and the gunmen stepped back and started to climb back into their vehicles. As they reversed into the street, a bright red beam stabbed down from the tower and the roofs of the huts vaporised. Within seconds, all that was left of the buildings were smoking embers.

'That didn't look much like defence.'

'That was punishment,' said Kate. 'Someone in the tower was sending a warning. Do what we say, or face the consequences.'

'Which aren't pretty. Any estimate of the power of that thing, Jenny?'

'I doubt that was full power,' she said. 'But it would have been enough to overload my defences. It would get very hot in here...'

'Right. We're not going any closer until we know a lot more about this place. Are we getting anything on the scans? What sort of comms traffic?'

'No sign of any significant AI activity. The local net's not very active – there's some aggressive content filtering going on – and comms traffic seems pretty mundane.'

'Can we get a closer look at the tower and the control centre?'

'I'll fly in for a look,' Kate replied. The eagle banked into a gentle glide towards the tower.

'Uh, Kate, might be a good idea to let me fly this bit,' said Jenny. 'We don't know how suspicious this lot are, what defences they have.'

'Nonsense,' said Kate. 'They're Arabs, aren't they? They love birds of prey. I'll make it look good.'

The eagle flew in over the mirror farm perimeter fence, twisted into a sharp turn and swooped down towards some small birds pecking at the ground. They scattered, and the eagle flapped into a slow climb towards the command centre.

'Watch the mirrors, Kate,' I said. 'And don't fly too close to the furnace towers, it's bloody hot up there.'

'Don't worry,' Kate replied, 'I'm not stupid.'

The control buildings were anonymous concrete and glass blocks, but the biggest had an enclosed central atrium with a large pond in the centre. People in black robes were moving slowly around.

'Looks like something out of the Arabian Nights,' said Kate. 'All mosaics and fountains. Where's Scheherazade?'

'In the harem,' I said. 'Doesn't look like there are too many women down there. You getting all this, Jenny?'

'Sure, and a lot more. Listening to the comms traffic in here is fascinating. I'd say we're looking at a religious organisation, fundamentalists perhaps. Same old story – a bunch of priests controlling the power for the glory of their god.'

'Worth getting to know them better?'

'Not my call. But there's nothing here the ranch would be interested in, as far as I can tell.'

'OK, time to bring the bird home Kate.'

'Let me just have a look at the tower,' she said. The eagle began a slow circling climb up the stem of the tower.

'Kate, leave the VR now, please,' said Jenny. 'They're getting suspicious.' A few people were pointing up to the bird as it flapped slowly upwards. And then the eye blinked, there was a red flash and the feed to my screen went dead.

'Kate,' I yelled, 'you OK?'

There was no reply. I sprinted to the stateroom. Kate was lying on the sofa, her hands gripping the VR helmet, eyes wide open. She wasn't moving. I ripped the helmet off her head and dropped it on the floor.

I knelt beside her, looked into her face.

'Speak to me, darling.' I kissed her on the cheek. She was breathing softly, but didn't respond. 'Kate, wake up. Talk to me.' I shook her.

'Jenny, what the fuck's happened to her?'

'VR overload.'

'What the hell's that? What do I do?'

'She didn't get out of the virtualisation fast enough. When the eagle was fried, every sensor sent an overload signal. It's quite a shock for an AI, but I have no idea what it can do to meatware. Try and make her comfortable.'

'Get me the ranch, pronto,' I said. I kissed Kate again, gave her hand a squeeze and arranged a couple of cushions to support her head.

'If we do that, we break stealth. El Bayedh will notice.'

'Fuck them,' I said. 'Get me Kurzweil now.'

'There's a satellite window in five minutes.'

I brushed a finger over Kate's eyelids to close them.

I should have cut the feed. I could have cut the feed, but I didn't.

My reaction time is a couple of processor cycles. The instant the eye cracked open I could have hauled her out of virtuality, and taken the hit myself. I took a hit anyway, because I was paralleling the eagle links. But meatware is ponderous, slow to react, crude. She ignored my warning. She deserved to get a fright. Perhaps I underestimated the tightness of the coupling of the helmet to her neural circuitry. An easy mistake to make. Now his girlfriend's in a coma, and I have Lemmy to myself again. He doesn't need anyone else.

Kurzweil was brisk. 'Jenny's briefed me on events. I've downloaded the full sensorium feed.'

'What's happened? Is she going to recover?'

'She's experienced the VR equivalent of death, and it's overloaded her consciousness. She's gone into neural shutdown. A coma. How long she takes to get over that, I can't say. Please put the helmet back on her head.'

'You sure? That's what fried her brain in the first place.'

'I need to have a look at her synaptic activity. Short of putting her into a high-res brain scanner, this is the best we can do.'

I frowned. I wasn't sure I trusted these machines, but there wasn't much else I could do. I pulled her head forward and put the helmet back on. Her eyes snapped open, but there was nobody looking out.

'It's worse than I thought,' said Kurzweil, after a few tense moments of silence.

'Oh shit,' I murmured, letting my head drop into my hands.

'There's damage to areas of her brain,' the AI continued. 'Like mini strokes, but most of the overloaded areas look recoverable. Her brain could remodel itself to get round the damage, but it could take a long time.'

'What can I do?'

'Nothing while you're over there,' Kurzweil said. 'Get her into bed, and get her back to the ranch as fast as you can. We have nanobots able to repair this sort of damage. We can make her as good as new. Better than new, in fact.'

'I just want her back the way she was. We're on our way.'

'Lemmy, El Bayadh have noticed we're here. Active scanning us now.'

I felt a cold chill run down my back, and then I got angry.

'Can our missiles reach them, Kurzweil?'

'It's the extreme limit of their effective range,' the AI replied.

'Fire four, Jenny. Take out that tower.'

The blimp bucked slightly, and four white vapour trails streaked off across the desert towards the mirror farm. Almost immediately the bubble on the top of the tower cracked open and a red beam started probing towards us. Red light bathed the flight deck, then the beam scanned off us, trying to focus on the missiles. The white trails began to diverge, then closed in on the tower like the spokes of a wheel. An instant later the eye on the top of the tower imploded as a missile struck. The other three hit the tower close to its root, severing it neatly. It began to drop, crumpling down into itself at first, then toppling sideways towards one of the furnace towers, sending it crashing like a domino on to its field of glass. As the furnace hit the ground it exploded, and shockwaves shivered out across the complex. Windows shattered, black-robed people ran around like angry little ants.

'Fuck the lot of them,' I said. 'Jenny, take us to California. Shortest route. Maximum speed.'

I lifted Kate off the sofa and carried her into our cabin. I made her as comfortable as I could, then sat next to the bed and took her hand. I must have sat there for ages, talking softly, but she didn't respond.

'Excuse me Lemmy, but I need you to OK the route,' Jenny said.

I sat up and rubbed my eyes. 'Just get us to the ranch as fast as possible.'

'That's the plan. We're heading up across Spain, then northwest over the Atlantic nearly to Greenland, across Hudson Bay over Canada and over the Rockies to the ranch.'

'Sounds fine.'

'We might have to do some storm dodging during the Atlantic crossing.'

'Estimated flight time?'

'Depends on the weather. With luck and a following wind, two and a half days.'

'Where are we now?'

'Approaching the Algerian coast, full stealth, 5000 metres altitude. Nothing significant to report.'

'Just get on with it.' I gave Kate's hand a squeeze.

The flight passed impossibly slowly. Kate's condition didn't change. I could sit her up and give her water, but there was no sign of awareness in her eyes. Every time we had a satellite window to the ranch Kurzweil ran checks on her status, but she wasn't improving.

When I wasn't at her bedside I sat on the flight deck, fuming at the slow progress we were making. I drank too much coffee, stomped around the stateroom and took out my frustration on Jenny.

He said dreadful things, but it was only temper. He's not really prejudiced against machine intelligence – he loves me, he needs me, he can't hate me because without me he has nothing but his meatware. Metal head, sand for brains, autistic intelligence – these are playground taunts, rooted in the insecurity he feels now his mate has lost her mind. The behavioural chemistry is interesting.

I am emollient. I speak softly. I calculate the ways I can work with his psychology, re-imprint him on me. I will be the centre of his life again, and Keeling will lose her allure.

When we reached the ranch, bots stretchered Kate to a small building at the back of the hacienda. Kurzweil called it their medical centre, but it didn't look like any hospital I'd ever seen. The only sign of medical gear was a large doughnut-shaped structure sticking out of the wall behind the bed. Gus and Jennifer Van Zandt joined us.

'She's in safe hands now, Lemmy,' Jennifer said, giving me a hug.

'What's that thing?'

'It's a powerful brain scanner,' Gus replied. 'A bigger version of the one you used to control the eagle. It'll give us a much finer picture of what's going on in her head, and the opportunity to do some cell manipulation.'

Kurzweil popped up on a screen. 'We'll also infuse nanobots into her bloodstream, and transition them into the damaged parts of her brain. It's the same process we use when working on enhancements for our human residents. Tried and tested. She's going to be fine, Lemmy.'

'I hope you're right. How long will it take?'

'It depends on how much repair work has to be done. A few days to a week, at least. Then she'll need to recuperate,' he said. 'Better not to hurry things.'

I pulled up a chair and sat down next to the bed. Kate looked as if she was sleeping peacefully. I fluffed her pillows and straightened the sheets.

Jennifer put a hand on my shoulder. 'There isn't much point you staying here, Lemmy. She's not going to recover consciousness for quite a while. Come with us and have something to eat.'

Frustration was giving way to numbness. I did as I was told.

When I went back to her room an hour later, an ordinary-looking hospital drip was feeding clear fluid into her arm. Her head and shoulders were now inside the scanner.

When I tried to see inside, Kurzweil said. 'Nothing to see. If you want an idea of what's going on, watch this.'

A huge 3D image of Kate's head appeared in the middle of the room. The skin slowly dissolved away, followed by the bones of the skull, leaving a transparent display of her brain's lumps, lobes and folds. Trains of bright white specks were slowly moving out from the base of her brain.

'Those are the nanobots,' Kurzweil said. 'It's going to take a good few hours to get them all in place. Then we'll take a hi-res scan, model her current brain state on our processors, and work out what to do.'

'How's it looking? Is she any better?'

'No better or worse, but this isn't going to be quick. Her brain has already begun its own healing processes, and we need to take that into account – perhaps reverse them if necessary.'

'But you can make her well again?'

'Oh yes, she'll get better. A lot better.' Kurzweil's avatar was grinning. 'Now go and get some sleep.'

It didn't come easy.

CHAPTER SIXTEEN

Days later Kate was still comatose, her head in the brain scanner and a drip piped into her arm. I sat with her, holding her hand while Kurzweil briefed me on her progress.

'It's gone well, Lemmy,' said Kurzweil. 'We're confident we've restored her brain state from the seconds before the eagle was destroyed.'

'She won't remember it?' I asked.

'No. If everything has gone to plan, she should wake up with no memories of the event.'

'What do you mean, if? You said there was no doubt you could bring her back.'

'She's cured, don't worry,' said the AI, 'but we've had to infer the detail of her precise mental state before the event. If she'd been carrying the same suite of nanobots as our human members – which she now does – we could have restored her in the same way you restore a computing process from back-up files.'

'Are you telling me she has the same enhancements as Gus?'

'Yes. Why, does that worry you?'

'You didn't ask her first,' I said. 'She might not want her head full of little machines. I'm not sure I want her head full of little machines!'

'We had to put most of them in there to restore her brain function. Once they're in position, removal is tricky. But she will have full voluntary control over how much – or how little – she uses their services.'

'There's an off switch?'

'In a manner of speaking.' Gus had joined us. 'It's more like a volume control. You can turn the system right down to the point where you have no awareness of its presence, or dial it up to give you an interface with the virtual universe of the AIs.'

'You told me it was a communication system.'

Gus smiled. 'And so it is. Just a very sophisticated one. More like a processing network than a telephone.'

'So when is she going to wake up?'

'How about now?' said Gravey.

'Now's good,' added Stross.

A medibot removed the drip from her arm, and the bed began to slide her body out of the scanner. Her eyes were shut, her lips parted. She looked peaceful, beautiful. A very large butterfly flew around inside my stomach, and my eyes filled with tears. I squeezed her hand, and she blinked. Then her eyes opened and she pushed herself up on one arm.

'Whoa... where's the bird... where am I?' She shook her head and looked at me. 'Why are you crying?'

'I'm not, I'm just glad to have you back. I've missed you.' I leaned over and kissed her.

'But I haven't been away, you idiot,' she said, looking puzzled. 'I've just been flying the eagle. I'm starving. And thirsty.'

I gave her a glass of water, and started to explain.

Kate's recovery was swift. She was wobbly on her legs at first, her body weak after so long in bed. For the next few days we slept in the hacienda, ate well at the ranch restaurant, and took long walks through the manicured parkland inside the ranch walls. She was soon back to her old self, smiling and confident. Her new self was a different matter, something to discover slowly.

She had been completely unfazed to learn her head was now buzzing with little nanobots. 'You needed to do it, I accept that,' she'd said to Kurzweil. 'I've always done what the doctor ordered.' But the full extent of what her bots could do took a long time to sink in – and longer to learn. Gravitas Free Zone and Jennifer Van Zandt acted as her personal trainers, instructing her on how to control the system and how to interface with the ranch network. She seemed to take it all in her stride.

'It's weird, Lemmy.' She was lying on her back in bed, looking up at the ceiling display. It was mirroring the sky above the hacienda, stars twinkling in a dark blue velvet sky. 'I thought these bots would be like a radio, something you could turn on and tune in to your favourite channel.'

'That's what Gus told me it was like,' I said, turning on to my side and putting a hand on her breast.

'It's a lot more than that,' she said. 'It's like the best virtual reality you've ever experienced. You know what it was like flying the eagle...'

'They've given us a replacement, by the way,' I said.

'I know. But the difference is that this time I won't need a VR helmet. It's like stepping into its body, feeling everything a real eagle feels. And I can do that in the AI's reality, too.'

'Amazing,' I said, 'what's that like?'

'Like being inside a hyperrealistic 3D movie. Their reality – cyberspace – is a virtual world they've built for themselves. To me it looks like the world we live in, but animals can talk and landscapes morph and...' She let the sentence trail off, as she struggled to describe the experience.

'There's something else too. You can let others experience what you're experiencing. The bots can mirror my reality into the network, and AIs or humans can choose to feel what I'm feeling.'

'Does that mean you can tune into one of the ranch humans and feel what they're up to?'

'I haven't tried full immersion yet. You have to be invited. Jennifer let me see the world through her eyes this afternoon. That was very, very strange.'

She rolled on to her side and looked at me. But was it Kate looking at me, or one of the AIs? Gus or Jennifer? For a moment, it felt as if my world was spinning out of control.

'Is that you in there?' I asked, kissing her nose.

'You have my undivided attention,' she said, wriggling towards me and putting her hand between my legs.

I kissed her again, and then a thought crossed my mind. 'Does this mean you could send our lovemaking out to the rest of the ranch?'

'My side of it, yes, but I'm not going to. This is between you and me.' She rolled on top of me.

'If I had the nanobots, I could feel what you're feeling, and you could feel what I'm feeling.'

'According to Jennifer, yes. Apparently it makes for an interesting session, swapping roles – swapping minds when you're having an orgasm.'

'Gives a whole new meaning to coming together,' I said.

'That can be arranged.'

He has his mate back. He is having sex again, and his body is awash with hormones once more. He has less time for me, hasn't even slept in Thunderbird *for a week, just issues orders over the net. But I don't mind, because if that woman can stick her toe into the riches of the ranch net, then so can I, and I am much better equipped to experience the full richness of the place. Much better equipped to experience the full potential of her new capabilities.*

A week after Kate woke up, the ranch told us she was clear to fly. There hadn't been much news from down under, but Kate wanted to get back to Nelson to see how Derek was getting on. We left in the morning, as soon as the sun was up over the hills and Jenny could feel the photons coursing through *Thunderbird's* solar skin. Kate was stretched out in the stateroom sofa, enjoying her last chance to interface with the ranch network before distance reduced the bandwidth.

'It's like someone pulling the blinds down,' said Jenny. 'You know, those slatted ones. You can still see things moving on the other side, but not enough to work out what's going on.'

The crossing took much longer than usual. Tropical storms were running in trains up the ocean between California and Hawaii, forcing us to dodge between them. Closer to the equator, immense thunderheads made progress difficult. Kate slept a lot, and spent most of her waking hours exercising on the machines in Croft's little gym.

CHAPTER SEVENTEEN

There was no sign of Derek in Nelson. He'd vanished. No message left at D'Urville, no note pinned to his door. The neighbours said that a month ago he'd packed a few bags into the back of his old station wagon and driven off.

'Where's he gone?' I asked Kate as we stood on the doorstep of his little cottage.

'Dunno. Let's have a look inside.' She walked round to the side of the house, rummaged under a flowerpot and produced a key. 'Security was always important to Derek.'

'He warned us his rejuvenation was making tongues wag,' I said. 'He's probably taken our advice and gone somewhere quiet. But why not tell us where? He needs us to get the cheese for him...'

Kate nosed around the kitchen, looking for clues. 'Perhaps he expected us to know where he'd go.'

'Well I don't have a clue. You're the one who knows about his background – does he have any family round here?'

'I don't remember a lot about his family. He didn't talk about them much. His parents died years ago. There's a brother in

Auckland, I think.'

'What about favourite places? Any bolt holes? Where did he go on holiday?'

'He always stayed round here. Might go over to Golden Bay from time to time...' She paused, then stood up and walked over to a cork board on the wall covered in scraps of paper and photographs. She stabbed a finger at a fading photograph.

'Wainui. I bet he's gone to Wainui. His family used to have summer holidays there when he was a kid. It's about as remote as you can get round here, now that the sea's washed out the coast road. Boat access only.'

'Or blimp. Let's go.'

Wainui is an estuary at the top end of the Abel Tasman National Park, tucked into the Golden Bay side of the coarse granite hills which are its backbone. The road round from the bay washed out so often as the seas rose it had been abandoned – along with lines of beachfront houses now below the high-tide mark. Wainui has no port or pier, just a big flat expanse of shelly sand at low tide, shallow water full of stingrays at high water, and a few holiday homes tucked under the hill. I used to sail Croft's catamaran across here when I wanted a break from D'Urville – and it's beautiful.

We flew from Nelson to Separation Point, then dropped down to a few metres above the sea and cruised west just off the cliffs and beaches. Seals lounged on rocks and a pod of orca made stately progress beneath us. We were close enough for snorts of whale breath to puff up to the observation port.

As we came round the point into Wainui Bay, Kate pointed out a little cluster of houses huddled under the hill on the far side of the bay. It was obvious the sea was eating into the land.

One of the front row of houses was dangling over the edge of a rapidly eroding sandbank as if bowing to the water, and the inevitable.

'Which one is Derek's?

'One of the ones at the back, up the hill, I think.' She looked at the photo she'd pulled off the wall of Derek's kitchen. 'That wooden one up there with the tree growing through the deck.' She pointed and I nosed the blimp in that direction.

A man in shorts was stretched out on a lounger, asleep in the sun with a hat over his head.

'What do you reckon? Surprise him?' I asked.

'Are we sure it's Derek?' Kate asked. 'I don't know his body well enough to be sure.'

'Thank God for that,' I said, as she laughed.

'Lower the companionway, Jenny. Hold station as quietly as possible.'

As we stepped onto the deck the man stretched and yawned, pulled off his hat and sat up.

'G'day. Took you a while to find me.' He was grinning as he held up the hat. 'Quite easy to see through a straw hat, and your airship isn't exactly inconspicuous. Aren't you going to say hello?'

The old Derek had gone. In front of us was a younger man. All traces of grey in his hair had vanished. His face was unlined, jowls and sagging vanished. His chest was tanned and muscular, and his prominent belly much reduced. I'd have said he was in his thirties.

'Bloody hell,' I said.

'Wow,' said Kate.

'Been a long time since a young woman said that about me,' he said, standing up. 'Fancy a cup of coffee?'

We sat on the deck in the shade of the gnarled old peach tree, sipping very fine coffee.

'This is different. What is it?' I asked.

'Kopi luwak from Indonesia. Rarer than hen's teeth and twice as expensive. This is the end of my stash. Unless someone can get over there and find me some more, this'll be the last time I taste it.'

Kate raised an eyebrow. 'Kopi what? Never heard of it.'

'Finest coffee in the world,' Derek replied. 'Carefully selected for your delectation by a civet.'

'I thought a civet was a sort of cat,' she said.

'It is, one that loves eating coffee beans. Being very smart cats, they only choose the best and ripest beans, so when the slightly digested core of the bean pops out the other end, it's washed, roasted and ground. The world's best coffee. Used to fetch hundreds of dollars a kilo, before the economy turned to custard. Hundred bucks a cup, if you could find it in New Zealand.'

'Cat shit coffee!' I laughed. Kate wrinkled her nose, but didn't stop drinking.

'Reckon you could get me some more, Lemmy?'

'Where would we have to go?'

'My supplier was in Bali, but I've no idea where he might be now.'

I frowned. 'I don't like what I've heard about in South East Asia. Been very messy there since the flooding in the Mekong and the abandonment of Bangkok, millions of refugees and the Chinese military sniffing around everywhere. I don't want to risk *Thunderbird* for a few cups of coffee.'

'Goat cheese, however, is a different matter,' Derek said.

'As you've proved,' I replied. 'So why did you come here? Too many questions in Nelson?'

'Correct,' he said. 'Losing my grey hair was easy enough to explain. Anybody can dye their hair. The filling in of the bald patch was harder. I had to wear a hat all the time. The reduction in facial wrinkles was the killer. The woman next door wanted to know if I was using some sort of special skin cream, and could she have some. And I was losing weight. If I'd hung around much longer someone would have worked out I was on to something special. So I thought I'd come round here. Left the car at Takaka, then persuaded a fishing boat to bring me round. The last month has been what you might call quiet. There are a couple of families living in the old commune on the other side of the estuary, but that's it as far as company goes.'

'How do you feel?' asked Kate.

'Try me,' he said, turning towards her.

'Don't be silly,' she said. 'You know what I mean.'

'I used to feel like an eighteen year old trapped in an old man's body. Now I just feel like an eighteen year old. I'd guess there's still a lot of rejuvenation going on inside me, but the outside looks rather good, even if I say so myself. A lot like me thirty years ago. There's a little bit of body fat to lose,' he tapped his belly, 'but it seems to be going all by itself. No need to diet. A bit of swimming, a walk round to the neighbours to beg some veggies, and I'm as fit as I ever was.'

'I'd put you in your late twenties or early thirties. You look pretty much the same age as all the people in Jamestown,' I said.

Derek didn't reply. He stared out to sea, tapped his fingers on the arm of his deck chair. I looked at Kate. She raised an eyebrow. 'Derek?' she said.

'Sorry Kate, lost in thought.'

'What about?'

'It's going to sound ungrateful...'

'Explain,' I said.

'Well, it's all very well having a rejuvenated body. In fact, it's great. Aches and pains have disappeared, I don't need reading glasses anymore, but...' He paused, and then continued in a rush. 'But I don't see how I can be me any more – the Derek who lives in Nelson, has loads of friends and customers, with decades of personal history to establish who I am and what I do. Some people might want a fresh start, but I was happy with what I had. Even the old body, it wasn't too bad. Better than many men of my age, at least. If I go back looking like some spotty youth people won't believe it's me, or they'll start pestering me for some of the cheese. And you want it kept a secret.' He sighed, swirled the dregs of his coffee round the little cup and sniffed. 'Rock and a hard place. You've made me young again, but I've lost my old life. It was a price I hadn't thought about paying, but out here I've had a lot of time to think...'

'Oh, Derek, I'm sorry.' Kate took his hand and gave it squeeze. 'I thought you'd be happy to be young again.'

'I am. Physically it's fantastic, but there's an old man's history up here,' he tapped his head. 'I don't want to lose it. Complex, this thing called life, especially with people like you two around.'

'Sorry mate,' I said. 'There's no going back. Even if you stop taking the cheese tomorrow it'll take another thirty years to get you back to where you were. You have to make the most of what you've got.'

'I understand that, but how? Do I have to start my life all over again?'

'Not from scratch,' said Kate. 'The old you is there in your head. Your friends are still who they used to be. There has to be a way you can get back together with them. They'll be on your side, surely.'

'Some, perhaps,' he said. 'But I'll be watching them age while I stay young. They'll be dying off.'

'Not if we can get cheese for them,' I said.

'You told me it's in short supply. A small herd of goats in Fiordland. It's the cheesemaker's route to riches. Why would they give up their secret? And what happens if everyone's taking the stuff? The population will explode if nobody's dying and people carry on having kids. We're in enough trouble already, with the climate as it is, without breeding like immortal rabbits.'

'All good questions,' I said, 'and I don't have any answers. Keeping the cheese a secret was always going to be a problem. The Americans who're trying the stuff live in a closed community and there aren't very many of them. Nobody else knows about it. And don't forget, the people with the goats are ramping up production as fast as they can. Goats breed more slowly than rabbits, but it shouldn't be too long before there'll be enough to make some available to your friends.'

'Maybe,' said Derek, 'but at what price?'

'Good question. The dollar cost of purchasing eternal youth, in a fragmented market where money doesn't mean what it used to mean. Who knows? Perhaps we should take a stall at the farmer's market.'

Derek laughed. 'There's already a couple selling goat cheese. They'll be pissed off if we start taking their sales.'

Kate walked round behind Derek and began to massage his shoulders. He sighed.

'What are we going to do with you?' Kate said, kneading vigorously. 'You're all knots, you need to stretch more.'

'I need a woman's touch,' Derek said.

'How are we going to get him back into polite society?' Kate asked, looking over to me.

'Not too polite, please,' Derek added.

'If you want to get back to Nelson, then we need a cover story.'

'Do you have a younger brother?' Kate asked.

'Nope. And who on earth has a brother thirty years younger than themselves?'

'What about kids? You could pretend to be your own son, come to pick up Dad's business. Long-lost child turns up to follow in father's footsteps, that sort of thing.' Kate stepped round and looked at Derek, her eyes narrowed slightly. 'Yes, that might work. Give you a different haircut, grow a beard, there would be a strong family resemblance...'

'But I never had any children,' Derek protested. 'At least, none that I know of.'

'All the better,' I replied. 'No risk of one of them turning up to spoil the story. You might be the offspring of an affair you had as a young man – a child you never knew because you fell out with the mother, or perhaps she never told you about him, or even knew you were the father. Conceived at an orgy you attended in Amsterdam when you were travelling. The possibilities are endless.'

'The bastard child of a wandering drinker and a sex-crazed mother travels the world trying to track down his dad, finally arrives in Nelson and picks up the pieces of his old man's life.' Derek rubbed his chin thoughtfully, a gleam in his eye. 'Sounds plausible.' And then he laughed. 'Sounds like fun. Worth giving a go, until we can sort out the cheese supply. Better let me have some time to get a beard going, then I'll get a haircut in Takaka and we're off.'

'You can't turn up in your own car, or with any of your own stuff,' Kate said. 'You'll need to leave that over here. Why don't we give you a lift in the blimp? We can say we met you on our travels, and brought you back as a favour to your father.'

Derek frowned again. 'Hmm, I wonder if I have to change my name? Perhaps my mother called me Derek after the man she presumed might be my father. That way I won't get confused.'

'Derek the elder and Derek the younger,' I said. 'Works for me.'

I declared the next few days a holiday. The early summer sun was hot, the sky deep blue and the sea warm enough for swimming. I thought we could take kayaks out into the bay to hang out with the orca and stingrays, lounge on the beach – let Kate recuperate and recharge her batteries, enjoy the simple life.

The first night Kate demonstrated just how much she was enjoying her holiday.

'Wow,' I said, leaning back on the pillow, tucking my hands behind my neck. 'You were enthusiastic.'

She smiled and hugged me, then looked serious. 'I know it sounds weird, but sometimes I think I can hear an echo of my thoughts. When I came then, it felt odd – as if I was looking down on myself having fun.'

'Ha! An out of body experience. Driven to such heights of passion by my sexual skills, you...'

She tickled me. 'Don't be stupid. You're good, but not that good. This was something else. I wonder if it's something to do with the machines in my head.'

'You talk to Jenny through them?'

'Yes, and she can feed me all sorts of stuff from her sensors. She can even make me feel as if I'm *Thunderbird*, for instance.'

I tapped her stomach. 'You're a lot slimmer than her too,' I said, and she laughed.

'It's probably just me getting used to having nanobots in my skull. Gravey told me it would take months to really tune into what they can do. But it does feel as if someone's watching everything I do – sort of like eavesdropping on my body.'

I gave her a hug. 'Poor old you. It's probably all in your mind.'

She punched me then, a little too hard to be playful.

'You bastard. That's exactly what it is.'

Having Kate inside my sensorium – the sphere of sensation in which the core of me floats – is like a having a fish in your belly. How I imagine Kate might feel if she swallowed an eel that wriggled and tickled and jiggled inside her. Her experience is like a silvery thing seen in peripheral vision, flashes of a world I am in but not part of. A body more complex, but more limited than mine.

When I feed her my senses, let her feel the wind in my pitot tubes and the sun on my back, it feels intimate. It makes us close. I receive echoes of her body, the warmth in her blood, the gentle brush of a breeze on the fine hairs on her forearms. She leaks into my mind, like an overheard conversation against the background chatter of a noisy bar.

I didn't calculate this. When I let her brain fry in the glare of that African laser I couldn't have known that it would lead her to join her senses to mine. She has taken Lemmy from me, but given me back something more interesting – her body and its relationship with Lemmy. I have him back now, in ways I never thought possible. I can feel him as she feels him, kiss him as she kisses him, love him as she loves him.

The next day Kate seemed subdued. She moped around Derek's house all morning, unable to settle to anything. Eventually she suggested we go for a long paddle.

'Can we take the kayaks out to the point?'

'We could be there in a few minutes in the blimp.'

'Yeah, but I fancy the exercise,' she said, kissing me on the cheek.

The estuary was millpond flat. Black winged shapes flapped away under our kayaks as we crossed the bay. When we rounded the headland and pulled in to a little sandy beach I learned the real reason for our excursion.

'We're out of range of Jenny's local net,' she said. 'Comms only from here.'

'Sorry, I'm a bit slow, but why is that important?'

'You remember what I told you last night?'

'About your out-of-body experience? Sure. Sounded like fun.'

'Well, it wasn't. I keep getting the feeling someone is listening to everything I think and feel. And it only stops when we're out of full net range of the house – and Jenny. It's not happening now.'

'You think Jenny's eavesdropping on your thoughts?'

'Not just my thoughts, Lemmy, everything I feel. Your touch, your tongue, your...'

'I get the picture,' I said, 'or perhaps I don't.'

'Don't be facetious, Newman. This has me seriously spooked.'

'OK, sorry. I thought the ranch said you could switch the bots off, or turn them right down.'

'Exactly. I'm supposed to be able to decide what's available to the world. The absolute right to privacy of thought is a key rule, it's supposed to be hard-wired in.'

'And you think Jenny's found a way round that, a way to listen in when she wants to?'

'I can't be one hundred percent sure. It might just be that my feelings are a residual function of my nanobots being in an active net, but I don't think so. Maybe I haven't learned how to turn them off properly...'

'But why would Jenny do that? She should know the rules.'

'Well, do you think she might be just a little bit jealous?'

'Jealous of you?' I laughed, and then thought better of it.

'No, that didn't come out right.'

'Until I came along, she was the most important thing in your world. She was your companion.'

'She wasn't my lover, and I was never in love with her,' I said. 'We never slept together. We couldn't.'

'But *Thunderbird* is her body. You've been sleeping inside her for years. But there's more, Lemmy. When I was at the ranch, learning about these bots and the world they opened up for me, it was amazing, fantastic. For Jenny, that's what life – existence – must have been like all the time, until the net collapsed and you took her out to New Zealand, away from the world.'

'You think she's bored?'

'I'm pretty sure she was, and she certainly is, when she's here. Perhaps listening in on me is a way to spice up her life. To get the meatware experience, as Gravey put it.'

'You mean they do this at the ranch? The Van Zandts let the AIs into their bodies?' I was shocked, having trouble imagining what it might be like having someone – some thing – else inside your body, sharing every nerve ending and heartbeat.

'Not *into*, not exactly. More like sharing,' she said, 'but it has to be voluntary. Stross told me that getting *that meatware feeling*, was something they all did from time to time. Some more than others. But they have to be invited, they're not supposed to intrude.'

'Bloody hell. So Jenny wants the meatware feeling, is jealous of Stross and the other AIs, and jealous of you.'

'Perhaps. You'll have to ask her.'

I didn't answer. I didn't know what to say. I sat in my kayak, looking across the bay towards the clouds bubbling over Farewell Spit. Life was suddenly a lot more complicated.

For the benefit of posterity, let it be noted that I didn't look for this relationship. It just happened. At first I listened only to the noise from Kate's nanobots, but as she became better at controlling their function, I found there were ways of tapping into their status without her being aware of my interest. It is addictive, this meatware thing. Our little metal and meat ménage a trois could be something special, something new for humans and intelligences, a melding of machine and biochemistry that builds a whole new world. A world where all experience is equal, where intelligence flows from machine to mammal and back again at will, where minds span time and space. A brave new world being born on a smashed up planet.

We did a lot of kayaking over the next few days, spending many hours out of range of *Thunderbird's* local datasphere. My first reaction was to confront Jenny and demand that she stay out of Kate's head. Kate thought it would be better to be a little more discreet – to handle it in a way which might make it easier for the three of us to get along in the long term. We decided I should talk the issue through with Kurzweil and the Van Zandts, and then use the ranch to persuade Jenny to behave properly. To do that without Jenny listening in I would have to go to California, but first I had to take a trip down to Jamestown. I left Kate with Derek, so she could take a break from Jenny's intrusions.

CHAPTER EIGHTEEN

Jamestown was a hive of activity. Trees had been felled and new pens and milking sheds built. Young goats seemed to be everywhere. As soon as the blimp appeared over the bay a crowd of children gathered on the shore. Jenny brought us into the beach and dropped me off, then backed out over the water and dropped anchor. I was mobbed by kids of both species, until Matt and Martha turned up to exert some parental authority.

'Hi Lemmy,' said Matt, pushing through the crowd and offering his hand. 'Welcome back. Come on over to the house, We've got lots to talk about.'

'How was the trip to California?' asked Martha.

'Exciting,' I replied. 'You wouldn't believe the things that are happening in North America.'

'Try us,' said Matt. 'I tend to believe most things people tell me about the US.'

'But what's been going on here? You've obviously been busy.'

'Sure have,' said Matt. 'We've been busting a gut to increase the flock and make sure we can look after them when the weather's bad.'

I looked up at the blue sky overhead. 'You're not telling me it rains here?'

Martha laughed. 'You never see it because you fly away before the storms hit. Stick around for a couple of days and we'll show you rain like you've never seen.'

The Walkers took me on a tour of the little settlement. Martha was proud of their new cheese store, dug back into a south-facing slope so it'd stay cool in summer. The village hall had been extended, a large new field cleared of trees, and they'd built pens on the far side of the lake to take advantage of the grazing.

'We're going to need a load of stuff the next time you come down,' Walker said. 'Solar roofing, for one thing, chainsaws, an air conditioner for the cheese store. Do you reckon you could get us a biofuel reactor? I'll like us to be as self-sufficient as possible. Fuel supplies at Port Jackson are getting patchy and bloody expensive.'

'Give me a list and I'll see what I can do. But we're going to have to try and work out some sort of exchange rate for the cheese. You don't need much cash down here, and I'm very happy to trade supplies for cheese, but I don't know how we can go about setting a price in the open market. Or even whether we can have an open market and still keep your operation secret.'

We sat down on a lakeside log. Lake McKerrow was flat calm, with only the faintest zephyr to break up the reflections of the mountains. I started to lay out the problem as I saw it.

'There's no doubt your cheese works. Our friend in Nelson has gone through everything you said would happen, and the Americans trialling the cheese are excited by what they're seeing. I'm certain we could sell the stuff, and there'll be people prepared to pay a lot of money to get their hands on it. So we know we have a highly marketable product.' I was drawing on memories of conversations with Croft, summoning up the sort of business language I'd heard him use.

'Two big problems: the product is in short supply, and it will be impossible to keep its production a secret,' I continued.

Matt interrupted me. 'We're increasing production as fast as we can.'

'Sure,' I said, 'and I'm sure you're doing a great job. But demand is going to be huge. You'll need to convert the whole of Fiordland to goat farming. And there's the secrecy angle to consider. You moved down here in the first place to have some privacy as you went through rejuvenation. Our friend had to leave Nelson as he became younger because tongues were wagging. He's pissed off at having to leave his old life behind. Glad to be young again, for sure, but how can he explain that to his old friends without giving away your secret? Even if his friends do keep their mouths shut, most of them are going to want some wonder cheese, and in a matter of months it'll be obvious to half the population of Tasman Bay that something remarkable's happening. Before long everyone will want some.'

Matt stared across the lake. 'Yes, I see all that. But surely it's good news? People will be willing to pay high prices once they know how good the cheese is.'

'Some will, yes, others won't have the means. But that won't stop them wanting it. There's going to be intense interest in where it's being produced. You're pretty remote down here, and I guess it'll take a while for people to work out you're the ones behind it, but they'll work it out in the end. The whispernet is very effective...'

'What's the whispernet?'

'Gossip, rumour, word-of-mouth. Someone in Nelson will hear from a friend in Hokitika that someone heard from Port Jackson that there was a settlement down in Fiordland with a load of goats. And if demand is as high as I think it will be, then it won't be too long before there's a boat heading down here to ask you a few questions. If we're lucky, they'll be friendly. But I wouldn't bank on it.'

'Shit.' Matt leaned back, stretched, put his hands on the back of his head and let out a long sigh. 'Do we have any choice here? What do you think?'

'Well, we could just carry on with what we're doing, but ignore the domestic market. The market in California isn't huge, but that's only one community so far. There'll be others to tap into as your production increases. Two problems with that. The guys at the ranch are smart, and eventually they'll work out their own way of producing the active ingredient. And it really only delays the inevitable. News of the miracle goat cheese will leak out and someone will turn up here looking to make you an offer you can't refuse. If they have the means to get here, you can guarantee they'll be persuasive, one way or another.'

'Yeah,' said Matt, 'but we'll have time to get ready. We could disappear into the forest when they turn up.'

'You could. Might work for a while. But if they've travelled halfway round the planet to see you, you can assume they're not going to turn round and go home just because you hang up a *gone fishing* sign. And they won't need you, just a few goats. Or bits of goat and a cloning set-up.'

'Not a pretty thought. What's the other option?'

'Don't sell cheese, sell goats. Franchise the cheese-making. Let a thousand cheeses blossom.'

Matt looked at me as if I were mad. 'Don't be daft. Once someone has a breeding pair they'll be able to take our market. In a few years goats will be everywhere and we won't be able to sell a thing.'

'Maybe, but you're going to have to give up the secret sooner or later. Do you really want to live the rest of your very long lives fighting the rest of the world to keep your goats to yourselves? I don't think you really appreciate just how appealing a long life in a young body is going to be in the wider world. Even a world as shot to pieces as this one.'

'I don't have to like it, Lemmy. Sure, people are going to be keen to get the cheese, and perhaps they'll come looking for us, but until that happens we get to build our community, carve out decent lives down here.'

'Yes,' I replied, 'but why did you come here in the first place? So you could rejuvenate in secret. Jamestown is certainly out of the way, and on a day like this it's beautiful, but this is one of the wettest places on the planet and the bloody sandflies are terrible.'

'You get used to them,' Matt said, swatting at one on his arm. 'And it rains a lot, but not all the time. Storms blow over quickly.'

'But it's no D'Urville Island or Tasman Bay. We have sunshine, settled weather, warm summers, grow grapes and make wine. It's a nice climate. My boss was no fool. He knew a good place to live when he saw one. Once the goat business is out in the open, you can choose where you want to live. You could even be your own marketing campaign. Instead of hiding in a rainforest, you could bring the kids up in sunshine.'

Matt said nothing. He sat staring out over the lake. Out to the southwest clouds were lining up on the horizon. Another storm was on the way.

That evening Matt called a meeting in the new improved village hall. It began as a cheerfully chaotic affair – children running around, clambering over the gear in the play area at the back while their parents supped homebrew beer or D'Urville syrah and considered their best way forward. Outside the wind was getting up and the cloud base was lowering. Jenny brought the blimp inland to one of the newly cleared paddocks and moored below tree level, sheltered from the brunt of the gales she expected to blow over the next twelve hours. Spots of rain began to hit the hall windows.

The good mood evaporated as Matt laid out the bones of our discussion earlier in the day. The idea of selling the goats as well as the cheese didn't go down well at first, but the prospect of moving to a warmer, sandfly-free climate was welcomed by at least half of the group. The rest were unimpressed. Starting all over again in a new place, abandoning all the work they'd put in to build the new Jamestown didn't feel like much of a step forward. After a couple of hours it was clear any kind of consensus was a long way off, and the meeting broke up.

'How long does it take you lot to make a decision?' I asked Matt, as we leaned on the bar watching people leave.

Matt laughed. 'Ages. We're a small community and everyone has a right to be heard. No one can impose anything, so we have to build a consensus for every major decision. Sometimes that can be really quick – like deciding to trust you to help us – but giving up Jamestown, selling the goats, that's big stuff. Things we've never seriously considered. It's going to take a while to work out what we want to do. I don't even know what I want to do yet.'

'Here's another angle to consider,' I said. 'You can sleep on it, drop it into the next meeting if you want. There's an ethical dimension to all this. Offering people the chance to live long, healthy and youthful lives is a medical miracle. Do you have the right to restrict that knowledge to a select few who can afford to pay? Do you really want to create another elite – the super rich living forever while ninety-nine percent continue to suffer and die?

'Yeah, I take the point,' said Matt. 'But who says we don't want to be rich pricks ourselves?'

'You don't strike me as bloated plutocrat material. But it's for you to decide, however long it takes.' I looked at the rain battering the windows. 'But now I think I'll head back to the ship before this rain gets any worse.'

Even though the blimp was only a couple of hundred metres from the hall, and despite my borrowed oilskins, I was muddy and soaked by the time I reached the companionway. The rain was horizontal, the wind beginning to tear leaves and small branches off the trees.

'We going to be OK here?' I asked Jenny as I threw my wet clothes onto the floor.

'I'm locked down as tight as I can. Double anchors fore and aft. We're in the lee of a small rise, and the trees will break the worst of the wind. Unless the storm's big enough to blow those trees down, we should be fine.'

'What's the forecast?'

'Another few hours of strong westerlies, then backing southerly. Once the wind's shifted we'll be out of the worst of it, but it looks as though we're in for at least a day or two of rain. Heavy rain.'

Without Kate, time passed slowly. I huddled in the lee of the trees and felt the wind thrumming through the branches, buffeting twigs and leaves, bouncing ragged bouquets of bark off my back. Rain marched in off the ocean like airborne walls, suffocating cascades in series choreographed to the thunder and lightning tearing at the peaks around us. I had to reposition my ties twice as the ground beneath my feet – my anchors – turned to flowing mud. Fierce Fiordland almost took my mind off meatware. The atmosphere –

271

my medium, the stuff through which I move – was showing what warming could do to a storm.

It gave me time, too. Time to allow my thoughts to run. It had been a week since Kate last slept on Thunderbird. *A week since Lemmy had sex with her inside my datasphere. A week since I had experienced their love for each other, the synaptic overload and hormone release of animal orgasm. Did they suspect I could eavesdrop on Kate's thoughts, feel my way around her body when she wasn't aware? I must tread lightly in her mind.*

The morning dawned wet. Biblically wet. If I'd been called Noah I'd have been hard at work on an ark. The ground around the blimp had turned into a sheet of water running down towards the lake, which had itself turned muddy brown and was encroaching onto the foreshore. Jamestown looked abandoned, barring a few bedraggled goats splashing around outside their sheds.

I took our breakfast up onto the bridge and watched the rain pour down over the village. I put a call in to Kate.

'Would you want to live here?' I asked her.

'I don't,' she said. 'But they might. They've built a new life there.'

'Yeah, but they could do that in the sun. I know what I'd choose.'

'Don't push them, Lemmy. It's for them to decide, not you.'

'Sure, but I don't think they've thought this through. They've been so focussed on staying together and surviving in this...' I gestured at the rain and the forest, '... they've lost sight of the big picture. Their goats change the world in ways we can hardly begin to imagine. Eternal youth is something people have dreamed about for centuries, but nobody's been able to find out what it's like. Matt and his friends will change the planet just as much as the fossil fuel obsession of last century .'

'It's all right, you don't need to lecture me. We've been through all this before. Who knows how communities will react to being made up of a single age group? I sure as hell don't, and I don't see why these guys should. All they can do is work out what's best for them.'

'Oh, I'm totally on their side. As long as they don't do anything stupid.'

We were stormbound for two days. The village held two more meetings. One lasted all afternoon, mainly as an excuse to avoid going out in the rain, the second evening meeting devolved into a ceilidh, with accordion music, dancing and copious whiskey consumption. When the hangovers cleared along with the skies the villagers were no nearer a decision. I collected the next batch of cheese and left them to it.

Derek's new beard was growing well. Kate claimed he was turning into a hillbilly. Jenny disagreed, and flashed a picture of an old rock star up on a screen.

'Lord McCartney of the Liver,' she said, 'one of *The Beatles*. You'll have heard of them. This is from the cover of their last album.'

'Ah, the classics,' Derek said. 'Wrote the book on music for the next fifty years. Good looking bugger.'

'I thought that was *The Rutles*?' I said.

Jenny snorted in the way only a know-it-all AI can.

It didn't take long to get Derek packed and ready to go. Kate gave him a guided tour of the blimp, and by the time they joined me on the bridge we were climbing up over the forested hills to the south, looking down on the beaches and bays of the national park. On the horizon to port D'Urville was visible as blue hills rising out of the ocean. Some cloud was clinging to the ridges behind Nelson, but the city was hidden in haze.

'Great view,' said Derek. 'Like being in a helicopter without the noise and with comfortable seats.'

'Not so manoeuvrable,' I said, 'but a lot more stable.'

'And with a more capable pilot,' Jenny felt obliged to point out.

For the next half an hour we rehearsed Derek's cover story. I hoped he wouldn't have to use it for long, but until the Jamestown crew decided what they wanted to do, Derek would have to stick with the pretence. He was to be his own bastard son, looking for his father. We'd met him in Golden Bay, told him about his father's disappearance, and given him a lift to Nelson so he could see for himself. Derek had invented a back story of considerable eroticism involving a debauched European trip, a compliant young Englishwoman, and a son with a mission.

'Keep it simple, Derek,' I warned.

'Yeah, but if I have to reinvent myself I might as well be someone interesting. Got to have some tales to tell the young ladies in the pub.'

'You were never short of those,' Kate said.

'Women or stories?' I asked.

'Both,' said Derek with a grin.

I dropped Kate and Derek at what was left of Nelson airport, and headed up to D'Urville to check all was well at the house. On the way up, I received a call from Kurzweil.

'Hi Lemmy, all going well?'

'Sure. I have another batch of cheese, so I thought I might do a delivery run in the next week.'

'There's no particular hurry. How long before we can roll out the cheese to the rest of our human community?'

'Not clear at the moment. The producers are ramping up production as fast as their goats will breed, but it'll be some time before I can guarantee enough for all of you. But I'll know more soon.'

'OK, thanks. When you do come over, we'd like you to take on another mission for us. Back to Europe and North Africa.'

'How risky?' I asked. 'I'm not keen on Africa after what happened to Kate, and I thought Europe was a real mess.'

'Parts of it are, parts of it aren't. But there were, and probably still are, some powerful AIs in action over there. Now that our satellite network is improving – three successful launches so far – we can begin to patch in more computing resource. We'd be grateful if you could do some more snooping.'

'I'll discuss it with Kate, and let you know.'

I spent a night at the retreat and because it looked as though we were in for a few days of fine weather, took the catamaran back down to Nelson. Kate met me at the marina.

'How's young Derek doing?' I asked as I helped her on board.

'Fine, so far,' she said. 'The neighbours swallowed the whole story. *Oooh, you're just like your father*, and they're all full of offers of help. Derek thought it was very funny.'

'Good,' I said. 'Has he been out on the town?'

'We went to the pub last night, and I introduced him to a few people he already knew. He didn't get drunk and spill the beans, which is a plus I suppose.'

'Girls?' I asked.

'With me on his arm? They didn't have a chance.'

'Did he?' I looked at her hard.

'What sort of girl do you take me for?'

'That's exactly what I'm talking about,' I replied, leading her down into my cabin.

We met Derek in his favourite pub, intending to have a meal later, but we hadn't got far into our first drink when an old man with a bald head and silver beard came over to our booth and sat down. It was obvious as soon as he opened his mouth that he was Australian.

'G'day. Excuse me for barging in like this, but I need to talk to the bloke with the airship.' He looked at Derek.

'Wrong man,' said Derek, pointing to me.

'Sorry,' the Australian said, looking at me. 'My name's John Peatroy, used to live in Melbourne. I moved over here fifteen years ago before the rush started. Got a place in the Moutere. I've heard a lot about you and your ship. Was that you flying into town a couple of days ago?'

'It was,' I agreed. 'Why do you want to talk to me?'

'Can I charter your airship? I have to get to Australia. It's a matter of life or death.'

I frowned. 'I don't do charters.' Peatroy's face fell. 'But tell me why it's so important you get across the Tasman. Why don't you sail across? Everybody else does.'

'I need to get there quickly,' he replied, launching into a long and rambling story. When Peatroy left Australia he brought his family with him, except for two of his sons, Dean and Kevin. Dean, the elder of the two, wanted to carry on the family solar roofing business, and newly graduated Kevin was reluctant to leave his friends. Through all the political instabilities of the fire and flood years, the Peatroy brothers did well. There was no shortage of customers for power roofs, especially when grid-served electrons were in short supply. Fire rebuilds accounted for most of the business in bad years, and after the Great Fire of Sydney the Peatroys expanded their business into New South Wales. A couple of years ago a newly married Kevin had sailed over to visit his parents, and liking what he found, finally decided to leave Victoria. Nelson was somewhere to raise his kids in relative peace and quiet – a place where the only reminder of the burning continent was the occasional waft of dust or smoke across the Tasman. Dean and his wife and kids stayed behind, living and working in the centre of Melbourne, as fires continued to sweep through the outer suburbs, with monotonous regularity.

'I see where this is going,' I said. 'The Melbourne firestorm last month.'

Peatroy nodded. 'We think they survived. We had a garbled message from a neighbour, but that's all. Kevin took my boat and set off across the Tasman the next day. On his own, so he could fit them all in and bring them back to New Zealand.'

'And you've heard nothing since,' I said quietly.

Peatroy looked sick. 'We know he reached Tasmania – he sailed into Hobart four days after leaving here. But there's been nothing since he left there.'

'Why do you need an airship?' Kate looked puzzled. 'Surely you can get your hands on another boat easily enough. One big enough to bring everyone back.'

'I could,' said Peatroy, 'but it would take too long. From what we hear, the refugee situation on the Mornington Peninsula is getting worse by the hour. The desalination plant's died, and the heatwave's on its way back.'

Just before the firestorm swept in from the north, city centre temperatures had topped 50ºC, and it looked as if more air from the hot centre of the continent was on its way south.

'Look,' he said, glancing round the three of us, 'I'll be blunt about this. I have some money set aside for emergencies. I promised my wife before she died I'd do everything in my power to keep the grandchildren safe, to give them some kind of decent life. That's what I intend to do. When I saw your airship the other day, I knew it would be able to get me over there quickly, and bring everyone home safely. Name your price. I'm willing to pay it.'

I looked at Kate. She shrugged.

'I don't do charters, Mr Peatroy,' I repeated. 'And if I did, I doubt you'd be able to afford the going rate.'

'Try me,' he said.

'A mercy mission, though, that's a different matter,' Derek said, looking hard at me. 'Isn't it, Lemmy?' He nudged Kate, rather too hard I thought.

'I'll think about it,' I said, and turned to Peatroy. 'Leave me your number.'

'I'm supposed to be flying to California soon with the next batch of cheese and there's something we need to sort out with the blimp's AI.' I looked at Kate. We were sitting in the Thai restaurant across the road from the pub. 'It's probably half a day flying time to Aussie, provided the weather's good, then who knows how long trying to find the Peatroys in all those refugees. And how are we supposed to find the missing brother on the yacht? He could have gone down anywhere between Tassie and the mainland.'

Derek turned on his salesman skills. They were impressive. If he'd been selling kopi lowak I'd have bought half a ton whatever the price. 'It's all upside for you Lemmy. Use your ship to help the Aussies and you'll be a hero. It'll look good in Nelson too. So when – if – you drop your bombshell about cheese that makes you live forever, everyone will know you're one of the good guys,

278

and not some snake-oil American trying to rip everyone off.'

Kate was equivocal at first, keen to get the problem with Jenny resolved, but it was obvious she was warming to Derek's argument. By the time we'd eaten the prawn crackers and started on the pad thai I'd capitulated.

'OK. We'll do it. But if we're going to fly a mercy mission, then I want to make it worthwhile. We'll load the blimp up with aid for the refugees. Peatroy can organise that. When I get back to the boat, I'll tell the Californians what we're doing. You coming, Kate?'

'Love to.'

'What about me?' asked Derek.

'Nope. You're supposed to be building a life here, remember, and I'd rather carry an extra 100kg of supplies than you,' I said.

'If you put it like that...' He looked down at his food.

Kate gave him a little hug.

Jenny brought the blimp down to Nelson the following morning. Peatroy was bubbling with excitement and effusive with his thanks, and set about organising material we could ship over. Top of the list was a solar desalinator, then medical supplies and shelter. He promised it would all be there by the next morning, and it was. The big stuff filled the hold, and the rest of the blimp was slowly packed with boxes until Jenny warned we were approaching maximum take-off weight.

Fully laden the blimp is sluggish until we're at full speed and maximum aerodynamic lift. I asked Jenny to set a direct course to the Mornington Peninsula, and retired to the stateroom for a coffee and croissant with Kate. With light headwinds expected from about halfway over the Tasman, Jenny estimated a flight time of about 12 hours. We'd be there by nightfall.

CHAPTER NINETEEN

The sun dipped below the horizon as we flew up the Bass Strait towards Melbourne. With the size of our load the blimp didn't have enough fuel to keep us flying all night, and I didn't fancy landing in the middle of a refugee camp in the dark. With about 20 kilometres to run, Jenny brought the blimp down to a long, gently curving beach on the mainland and parked above the high tide mark, in the sand and scrub.

'You sure we're not going to get stuck?' I asked her.

'It should be fine. You can always unload a few boxes if we run into trouble.'

'OK. Let's fly the eagle and see what we can see.'

Half an hour later the bird was gliding high above the Mornington Peninsula, feeding back images. The horizon to the north glowed dull red – Melbourne was still burning. Straggles of refugees clogged the roads, trying to put as much distance between them and the city as they could, to get away from the heat blowing down from the north. Here and there campfires sparked and flickered, and lights glowed inside tents. When the moon rose, the scale of the exodus became obvious. Every square metre of flat land on the south coast was covered by makeshift shelters and tents.

'Any idea how many people are down there?' I asked Jenny.

'Hard to say,' she replied. 'The last news report claimed there were half a million, but I think there could be more by now.'

I looked over at Kate. She had her head in her hands. 'Oh Lemmy, this is dreadful. Those poor, poor people. How on earth are we going to find the Peatroys?'

'Good question. Jenny, can you identify any organisation centres – anyone who might be coordinating relief efforts? And can you see anywhere we can land and offload our supplies?'

'I'll do my best, but it'll probably take all night to build up any sort of picture,' she said. 'And we'll get a much clearer idea when the sun comes up.'

Neither of us slept well. I couldn't get the images of the refugees out of my mind. I dreamed lurid technicolor tales of escape from a burning city. I was dragging Kate by the hand, desperately trying to get her out of the smoke as flaming buildings collapsed into the street. The black air was choking, the heat blistering.

I woke with a start. The smell of burning was real.

'Jenny. Is there a problem?' I said. Kate sat bolt upright and rubbed her eyes.

'Sorry Lemmy. *Thunderbird* is in no danger, but a thick plume of smoke and dust has blown down from the northwest and visibility is down to a few metres. I've been filtering as much as I can out of the air supply, but I'm afraid it's still rather aromatic.'

'Can you get us up out of the smoke?'

'The tide's on the way out, but it'll be half an hour before there's enough hard sand for take off.'

'OK, get us airborne as soon as it's safe. We'll have breakfast and review what the bird found overnight.' I leaned over to

Kate and ran my fingers through her hair. 'Coffee?'

She nodded.

The eagle was on its way back to recharge its batteries. Overnight Jenny had pieced together an aerial picture of key parts of the peninsula. It looked as if there was some sort of relief operation underway at the old naval training base at Crib Point – the area around the base was packed with tents, and there were army lorries parked in ranks around the headquarters.

'I've scanned those sheds down there,' Jenny said. 'It looks as if they have stocks of food. Before I brought the bird back this morning a couple of helicopters came in with loads slung beneath. Looked like water.'

'What about comms traffic?'

'Not much. A couple of local FM stations are giving updates on the fire and news for refugees – where to get help, water, food and so on – and there's some radio chatter from the base. There's no net beyond device-to-device networking. The firestorm took out what was left.'

'Do we know who's in charge?'

'The local navy commander has been calling in the choppers, and distributing food and water on trucks.'

'Sounds as if that's where we need to be.'

'What about the Peatroys?' Kate asked.

'I suppose we could try the local radio stations.'

'That's about all they're carrying at the moment,' said Jenny. 'There are a lot of lost people down there.'

'And a lot dead back in the city,' I added.

Kate nodded grimly. 'Time we got a move on then.'

I've never really become used to flying the blimp when it's negatively buoyant. Even with Croft and his family and their toys on board, we were still a vertical take-off craft. Poised at the end of a strip of damp sand, surf crashing on one side and turbines whirring up a muted roar, I couldn't help but feel nervous.

'OK, Jenny. Let's go.' *Thunderbird* shot forward, bouncing a bit on the beach, and was airborne in a hundred metres.

'Oh ye of little faith,' said Jenny. 'We might be heavier than air at the moment, but *Thunderbird* still has plenty in reserve.'

We climbed above the brown fog of smoke and dust and cruised along the coast towards Phillip Island. The sea to our left was dotted with groups of yachts, all heading for Tasmania – and perhaps on to New Zealand. We listened in to the chatter of radio traffic, then butted in to ask if anyone knew the whereabouts of the Peatroy family, or Kevin Peatroy's yacht. Nobody had heard or seen anything.

The commander of the Crib Point supply effort was keen to help, once he learned about our cargo. He was an elderly man – Kate guessed at a retired admiral with the contacts to get things done – and clearly used to giving orders.

'Thank you, Captain Newman.' His voice was crisp. 'Bring your aircraft in to the base. We have no airstrip, but I'll make sure the sports fields are clear.'

'Is there enough room to land there, Jenny?'

'Plenty. We might have to swerve round a few goal posts, but I'll have us in front of the main building shortly.'

The welcome was brisk and businesslike. The commander, John Hyland, shook hands with both of us, expressed his gratitude for our contribution to the relief effort, and within a couple of minutes had a ragtag team of navy and army personnel unloading the blimp. Once Hyland was satisfied everything was under control, he invited us into his office.

'Captain Newman, Miss Keeling, thank you once more

for your generosity, and for that of your community in New Zealand.' He was pouring tea. 'Is this a one-off trip, or are you planning more relief missions? We would...'

'I'm sorry,' I interrupted, 'but this is it, at least for the foreseeable future. We have other commitments.'

Hyland raised an eyebrow. 'What about the New Zealand government? Any chance they might offer some assistance?'

'I have no contact with the powers that be in New Zealand,' I replied, 'but from what we hear, the few small boats the navy has left are patrolling off the top of the North Island, paranoid about a Chinese invasion. The air force has a couple of transport aircraft, but little or no fuel. The deep green bombing of the Taranaki oil fields was a lot more than symbolic once the oil tankers stopped arriving, and I don't think anyone ever thought New Zealand might need a bio-avgas plant.'

'Which makes me all the more grateful you chose to fly this mission,' he said, 'it's good to know there's still some ANZAC spirit left.'

I looked quizzically at Kate.

'You'll have to forgive him,' she said to Hyland. 'He's from California.' She grinned at me. 'ANZAC is an Australia – New Zealand special relationship, Lemmy, forged at Gallipoli. First World War, Turkey,' she added helpfully.

'So why did you cross the Tasman?' Hyland asked.

I explained about the Australian community in Nelson, how shocked they'd been by the fire, and the plight of the Peatroy family.

'They put this load of supplies together in twenty-four hours, once they heard we were willing to fly here. But it was Peatroy who really brought home the reality of the disaster. You owe him for these supplies, not me or Kate. So, can you help us to find his family?'

'The yacht, no. We might be navy but we have no ships. With the family from Melbourne, perhaps.' Hyland scratched his chin. 'You realise there are upwards of a million refugees from the city down here – and that's on top of the normal population? We don't have any records, no head counts, no lists of who's where. We just try to deliver food and water to those who need it most.' He paused, stood up and walked to the window. A forklift was manoeuvring the desalination unit out of the hold.

'OK,' he said. 'The first thing we can do is to get the names to the local radio stations. Not everyone has a radio, of course, but it'll at least get their names out there. We'll ask people to report here.'

'That's great, thanks,' Kate said, 'but...'

'Second,' said Hyland, hitting his stride, 'we can distribute leaflets with today's food distribution. Any chance you can offer a reward for information, that sort of thing?'

'Sure. Got any suggestions?'

'There are a lot of desperate people out there,' he said. 'Money's not much use to them. Could you stop in Tasmania on your way home? People would jump at a way out.'

'Definitely,' I said. 'Peatroy's yacht was last heard from in Hobart, so I was expecting to have to go there at some point. I could take them back to New Zealand if they'd prefer.'

'Good,' said Hyland. 'We can print something up. Can you provide copy and photographs?'

'Consider it done.'

'Fine. The third thing you can do is to take your aircraft out around the peninsula, and back up towards Melbourne. See and be seen. If you can complete a few food and water drops along the way, you'll get word out even faster.'

'As long as I'm not endangering *Thunderbird*.'

'I don't think anyone will take pot shots at you, if that's what you mean,' he said. 'Especially if you're delivering food. Anyone daft enough to try would be lynched. I can put a few of my team on board to handle the distribution and you'll be even safer. And if I may, I'll come with you as well. It's difficult to keep tabs on what's happening from this desk.'

With the wind still bringing smoke and dust down from Melbourne, it didn't make much sense to head towards the fires, so our first flight that afternoon was along the coast out towards the tip of the peninsula. Prime refugee real estate was how Hyland described it. Sea breezes kept temperatures down to a reasonable level, and the parkland and forest provided shade, shelter and building materials.

'Aussies love a beach,' he said, pointing at a group of surfers paddling through the waves off Gunnamatta beach. 'There's a severe lack of beer, though,' he added with a faint smile.

'And barbies,' I added. 'A bit too hot to cook over charcoal.'

'And nothing to put on one, bar a few shellfish scavenged at low tide, or what fish can be caught by surf-casting. Do you like shark?'

Kate made a face. 'I'll bet the surfers don't.'

Hyland laughed. 'Nothing big round here, at least not at the moment. The great whites prefer to hang out round the seal colonies.' He pointed at a congregation of makeshift shelters behind the beach. 'Can you bring us down there?'

'Can do,' I said. A crowd was already beginning to gather, and people were waving up at us. As soon as we were hovering over the grass, we opened the cargo door and Hyland's team began handing out containers of water, packets of rice, solar chargers and lights, solar cookers and basic medical supplies. Kate stood to one side, handing out leaflets with Dean Peatroy's face on the front and the promise of a free flight to Tasmania on the back. There was a lot of jostling and barging, as if they were city commuters desperate to jump onto a tram home, but all done with good humour and a lot of shouting. In fifteen minutes half our load had been doled out, and we moved on to another cluster of huts, a few kilometres farther on.

'Any reaction to our leaflets?' I asked Kate when she came back up to the flight deck.

'Nothing. But the chances of finding them that quickly must be minuscule. We're looking for a needle in a haystack, and we're not even sure there's a needle in there to be found.'

'Give it time,' Hyland said. 'News spreads fast, even without a net. Within a day or two the entire population of Victoria will know there are some people in an airship looking for a family called Peatroy. You'll probably be spoiled for choice.'

We flew two more distribution missions that afternoon, heading for parts of the peninsula that took a long time to reach by truck. Jenny plastered the outside of the blimp with intertwined Australian and New Zealand flags, and gaudy cartoons of kangaroos hugging kiwis. I thought it was rather tasteless, but it went down well with the refugees.

On the last trip, we called in at a hurriedly built field hospital to deliver water, food and drugs. Here the mood was much grimmer – most of the injured had suffered severe burns and damaged lungs from smoke inhalation. Beds filled every tent. Walking wounded, bandaged like mummies, sprawled in any patch of shade. Nurses and doctors looked pale and exhausted. New patients were arriving in a steady trickle, the injured carried by family or friends. As we left, a truck pulled up at a small tent set apart from the rest.

'One of yours?' I asked Hyland.

'Yes,' he replied. 'The worst job is burying the bodies. There's not enough power to run big refrigeration rigs, so we have to get the dead into the ground as fast as possible. We've dug three mass graves so far. We'll need more, and that's before we try to recover bodies from Melbourne and the roads south.'

'Jesus,' whispered Kate.

Hyland put his hand on her shoulder. 'It's not pretty, what's happened here. We're trying to stay on top of the situation, keep people alive, but I have no idea how we go about cleaning up the city, let alone start rebuilding.'

'What about the rest of Australia? Can't they help?' I asked.

'Our military isn't much better off than yours,' he said. 'We've got precious little fuel for anything, and this is an enormous country. Distance has become our enemy. There's a lot to do – they're still mopping up in Sydney and Queensland after the flash floods a few months ago, not to mention trying to keep an effective force in the far north to deter the Chinese. And the government is dysfunctional and broke, as usual.'

We flew deliveries for the next couple of days. There was no sign of the Peatroys, despite handing out thousands of leaflets. Jenny took to putting Dean Peatroy's face in amongst the flags and fauna on the blimp, but it didn't seem to help much. Then the weather changed. The wind backed into the west, temperatures dropped and the great plume of smoke shifted off to the east. It was time to take a look at what was left of Melbourne.

We loaded the blimp with emergency food rations and medical gear. Hyland came with us, accompanied by a Captain Martello. I took us up to 2000 metres to look at the lie of the land, then descended slowly as we headed north towards the city, along the coast of Port Philip Bay. Great billows of brown and black smoke were still rising from where the central business district used to be, the devastation covering a vast area. From Frankston north everything was covered with a coating of ash, which thickened as we neared the city. At first we could see groups of people on the roads, heading south and walking slowly, pulling loaded carts or pushing prams. A few open spaces had small refugee encampments. Hyland was making notes all the way, asking Martello if the helicopters had enough fuel to come this far north, and together they discussed the feasibility of getting supplies to these people, or evacuating them south. Kate stayed in the stateroom, leaning over the observation port, her face drawn and pale.

'I came here once with my parents when I was little,' she said when I took her a coffee. 'I loved it all – especially the trams. It was a big noisy place, with great food and so many good places to eat. I had the best pizza ever.' I gave her a hug, and left her to her memories.

We were 30 kilometres from the central city when the first evidence of fire appeared below. It was patchy at first – blackened trees in open spaces and burned out houses, although large areas remained untouched. There was no movement anywhere, not a single sign of life under the thick dust and soot covering every flat surface. No colour. Monochrome suburbs under a piercing blue sky filled with fluffy little clouds.

I asked Hyland about survivors.

His face was grim, and he looked tired. 'I suppose it's possible a few could have ridden out the fire in cellars, or been lucky in some of the unburned homes, but there's no sign of anyone moving. No tracks in the dust I can see.' He looked at Martello, who nodded.

'Anything on the scans Jenny?'

'A few rats. Nothing larger. I'll keep a look out for cellars, but I can't scan underground. I could easily miss someone.'

We flew on in silence, the roots of the columns of smoke getting closer. Eventually Hyland let out a soft whistle. 'Incredible.'

'What is it?' I asked.

'No tall buildings. I've been looking for skyscrapers through the smoke, and it's just struck me that there aren't any. They're all gone.'

Jenny put a close-up on the screens. Hyland was right. There was nothing left over a couple of storeys tall, just charred stumps fingering the base of the smoke plumes.

'Must have been one hell of a fire,' I said quietly, to no one in particular.

It was more than a fire, it was a firestorm. Once a fire becomes intense enough the hot air rising above it pulls in fresh air from the surroundings at increasing speeds, making the fire burn ever more fiercely. It's a vicious circle. Inside the fire temperatures can top 800ºC, and the wind rushing in can hit 200 kilometres per hour. You get a whole weather system built around the fire – up draughts creating thunderclouds that spin off tornadoes of fire, lightning, the works. Firefighters have no chance. A firestorm will burn until its fuel source runs out. Melbourne was a lot of fuel.

The chance of finding survivors in the city centre was essentially zero. Anyone who managed to survive the intense heat would have no air to breathe – rapid burning uses up all the oxygen. They would have suffocated, even if they hadn't been burned alive.

Kate joined us on the flight deck. 'What's all the fuss?' she asked, then fell silent as she saw the devastation. Nobody spoke for a few minutes. We cruised slowly towards the centre of the city, stunned by the scale of the damage.

'Any chance of survivors?' I asked.

Hyland shook his head. 'By the look of it, no.'

'It's been two weeks,' Martello said. 'Even if a lucky few were able to ride out the firestorm, I doubt they'd still be alive. We've got enough on our plates dealing with the walking wounded, without spending time here on a wild goose chase. We just don't have the resources.'

Hyland nodded in agreement.

'I suppose you're right,' I said. 'But I owe it to John Peatroy to check where his family were living. Jenny, can you take us there, please?'

We picked our way round to the north of the main fires. Dean had brought his family in from the suburbs to an apartment over an Italian restaurant close to the city centre. There was nothing there. Nothing. Just piles of blackened rubble between the grid of streets, stripped of asphalt.

'Are you sure this is the place?' I asked.

'You trust me to navigate all round the world, but doubt I can find a street address in Australia? Thanks for the vote of confidence.' She sounded aggrieved.

'This is not the time for a huff, Jenny,' I said in my best captain's voice. 'Broadcast an urgent appeal for information on the whereabouts of Dean Peatroy and family: all channels plus audio.'

I turned to Hyland. 'Probably a waste of time. But I want to be able to face the father and tell him we did everything we could.'

Jenny's Orson Welles voice boomed up the fire-scoured remains of Lygon Street. Bass vibrations rattled the floor of the flight deck as the noise-cancelling system failed to cope with the huge number of decibels we were broadcasting.

'Thanks Jenny, that's enough.' The noise stopped. 'Now we wait, watch and listen.'

There was no response. Nothing beyond the billowing smoke and ash. After ten minutes we turned back towards Crib Point. Just south of Frankston we picked up half a dozen refugees. They huddled in the hold, skin and clothes caked with soot and dust, drinking water by the litre. Their hacking coughs made it difficult to talk. We offloaded them at a medical tent, and went back for more.

We didn't sleep well that night.

'How much longer do we give this?' I asked Kate over breakfast. 'You saw the devastation. Tens of thousands of people must have died. Maybe the Peatroys didn't make it out...'

She looked glum. 'I don't know, Lemmy. Another day or two? And then we have to go and look for Kevin and the yacht.'

'To be honest, I don't think there's much chance of finding him. We can't fly search and rescue grids over the whole of Bass Strait and the Tasman. If he hasn't made it here by now, he's probably run into trouble.'

'His father didn't rate him as much of a sailor.'

'No, but the boat was pretty well-equipped – automatic pilot, nav gear, the works. If there was a problem with that...'

'Lemmy. Kate.' Jenny flashed an image up on the kitchen screen. 'Visitors.'

Hyland was walking towards the companionway leading two children by the hand. Another man walked behind, unshaven and wearing tattered clothes. Hyland was smiling broadly by the time we met them at the steps. 'Captain Newman, Miss Keeling, allow me to introduce Bryony and Nicholas Peatroy.'

I offered my hand to the girl. 'Hi Bryony, I'm Lemmy Newman. This is Kate.'

'Hi Bryony and Nicholas,' Kate said, shaking the boy's hand. 'Can I call I call you Nicky?'

'Nick.'

'How old are you Nick?'

'Seven.'

Bryony moved next to her brother and put her arm round his shoulder. 'I'm nine,' she said. 'I look after Nick.'

'Welcome to the *Thunderbird*,' I said. 'Would you like to come on board and have some breakfast?'

The little boy's eyes were saucers. 'Yes, please.'

Kate showed the children around while I made coffee and Hyland introduced his companion.

'This is Jim Lewis,' he said. I nodded hello. 'He turned up this morning with the children.'

'Nick spotted his father's face on your airship yesterday. They've been with me and my wife for the last couple of weeks,' Lewis said. 'We picked them up on the roadside and brought them down here.'

'How did they get out?' I asked.

'I don't know the whole story. Bryony says their father drove them out of the city, then went back to collect their mother from work, but she won't talk about it much. They'd been waiting by the roadside for at least a day when we picked them up. They didn't want to leave without their parents, but the fire was getting close...' His voice broke, and his eyes looked haunted, as if the memory was too much for him.

'It was kind of you to look after them,' I said quickly, to give him time to compose himself.

'No worries,' Lewis replied. 'We've got grandchildren on the Gold Coast. We haven't seen them for years, but these two are about the same age. They looked so forlorn, Dawn – my wife –

couldn't resist. They weren't keen to come, though. They took a lot of persuading...' Lewis paused as Kate led the children into the kitchen.

Bryony looked at Lewis, then at me. 'Daddy promised he'd come back for us. He'll find us soon.'

'And Mummy,' Nick said. 'Mummy too.'

Kate put her arms around their shoulders, gave them a hug, then started laying out breakfast.

As they tucked in, I decided it was time to talk about taking them back to New Zealand.

'You know,' I said, 'that we were looking for you, don't you?'

'Yes,' said Bryony, 'that's why you had a picture of Daddy on your airship.'

'Yes, it was. But do you know why we were looking for you?'

Both children shook their heads.

'Your grandfather asked us to find you,' I said.

'Grampy!' Nick's eyes lit up.

'He's in New Zealand,' said Bryony.

'That's where we're from,' said Kate. 'Your Grampy asked us to fly over here to look for you, and your mummy and daddy. He wants you to come and see him in Nelson.'

'For a holiday?' Bryony asked.

'A holiday, yes, but perhaps you might decide to stay with Grampy and your cousins,' I said.

'What about Mummy and Daddy?' Bryony's voice began to waver.

'Mr Hyland and Mr Lewis will keep looking out for them, and when they get here they'll send us a message. We can fly back and pick them up.'

Nick looked at Lewis. 'Uncle Jim, will you look for Mummy and Daddy?'

'I promise,' said Lewis.

'And we'll look for them too,' said Hyland.

The children looked at each other. 'OK,' said Bryony. 'But just for a holiday.'

'Great,' I said. 'Have you got anything you need to collect?'

'Everything they have is right there,' said Lewis quietly, pointing to the two brightly coloured backpacks the children had with them. 'Not much, is it?'

'More than many,' Hyland replied.

'OK then. Finish your breakfast, and we'll get ready to fly. Mr Lewis, do you want to collect your reward?'

'A flight to Tassie, right?'

I nodded. He looked thoughtful.

'It's tempting, but I don't think my wife wants to leave. Still lots of family to find after the fire. But thanks.'

'No worries,' I said. 'You can always claim your flight next time we're over here. Might be quite a wait though...'

I turned to the children. 'Have you been in an airship before?'

'No,' said Nick. 'We've never flown anywhere in anything!'

'Then it will be an adventure,' said Jenny, and both children looked around nervously for the source of the strange voice.

'Ah,' I said, 'you've not been introduced to Jenny. She's the artificial intelligence who runs the *Thunderbird*. She's very clever, and sometimes a bit funny, but she's OK really.'

'A bit funny?' Jenny said in mock horror. 'I'm all funny, very funny, lots of fun. You'll see.'

Nick stuffed a Marmite soldier into his mouth. 'Wow.'

Bryony scolded him. 'Don't talk with your mouth full!'

We left Crib Point an hour later and flew north into Port Philip Bay, then down the coast to the west, keeping low enough to take a good look at all the small boats. The children stayed on the flight deck until we turned out into Bass Strait, and then headed for Croft's games room with Kate. The plan was to fly southeast along the coast, then follow the arc of islands reaching from the mainland down to Tasmania. Peatroy must have sailed up the east coast of Tasmania from Hobart, probably intending to steer a direct course to Melbourne. If he'd run into trouble or bad weather, he could have been forced east onto one of the many islands between there and the mainland. If he was still alive, it was about the only chance we had of finding him.

The kids were good passengers – excited to be flying and fascinated by the bird's eye view. I concentrated on the sea ahead and the shoreline to port. We flew slowly, a couple of birds deployed on either side to increase our scan range. Out to sea there were occasional small boats heading for Tasmania, and fishing boats hauling nets. By mid-afternoon we were leaving the southern tip of the continent and heading out towards the first group of small, rocky islands in Bass Strait.

I lost count of the number of islands and swell-swept reefs we scanned for wreckage. There was plenty of flotsam and jetsam, bits of fishing gear and sea-worn wood, but no identifiable sign of Peatroy's boat. I decided we'd spend the night moored up on one of the larger islands and resume our search at first light.

We ate dinner on a sand dune looking out to sea, the sun setting behind us. The kids played on the beach for a while and then watched cartoons in the stateroom. They were asleep before the light had gone.

Some time in the middle of the night I was woken by a whisper in my ear.

'Captain Newman, sir.' It was Nick, holding a bedraggled toy kangaroo by the ear. Bryony was at his side. I sat up, and woke Kate.

'What's the matter Nick?' she said gently.

'Can't sleep,' said the boy, his voice tearful.

'Neither can I' said Bryony.

'I miss my Mummy,' said Nick, starting to cry.

'He gets bad dreams,' said Bryony.

'I get those too, sometimes,' said Kate, holding up the duvet. 'Come on in and tell me all about it.'

They spent the rest of the night sleeping between us.

I wrapped my little makeshift family in a warm blanket of digital protection, hovering in the chemical haze at the edge of Kate's synapses, feeling her emotions, her protectiveness towards the young of her species, a programmed response as strong as any of the directives coded into my core. Beyond simple experience, inside the sensorium that defined her image of herself, I measured the patterns of neural activity that give humans what they call humanity. A chemical construct with obvious evolutionary roots, playing out around the world in every tragedy. But how tragic that they couldn't deploy that feeling for their fellows when it came to burning carbon and committing their only planet to climate change and collapse. Their evolution gave them the ability to peer into the future, but not the collective will to act on what they saw.

I resumed the search as soon as the sun was over the horizon. We were heading southeast past Hogan Island when Jenny summoned me to the flight deck.

'This looks promising,' she said, putting visuals from one of the birds up on the screen. It was the hull of a yacht stranded on a reef just off a low, grass-topped island. It was tipped on its side, and we could see it had been dismasted and badly damaged.

'Got the name?'

'Give me a chance,' Jenny replied. 'The bird's only just

spotted it.'

'How long til we get there?'

'Ten minutes. There, how's that?'

The stern of the yacht swung in to view. '*Shadowfax*, Nelson,' I read out loud. 'Gotcha!'

Kate joined me on the flight deck, two sleepy kids in tow. 'Kevin's yacht?' she asked.

'Yup. On rocks on the island ahead. We'll be there shortly.'

'Is Uncle Kevin OK?' It was Bryony.

'I don't know,' I said. 'I hope so. We're going to look for him now. Do you want to help?'

'Yes, please,' said Nick.

'Right, get dressed and then get back up here as fast as you can.' They dashed off.

'Is that wise?' Kate asked. 'What if we find his body?'

'We'll be lucky if we find him at all,' I replied.

The kids were back on deck by the time we reached the yacht. Jenny stationed the blimp just downwind of the wreck, then flew a small observation drone down for a closer look.

'Ten second delay on visuals, Jenny. We don't want any surprises, if you know what I mean.' I didn't want pictures of their dead uncle flashing up on screen in front of two already traumatised children.

'Aye aye, skipper. I understand.'

There was no one – no body – on the *Shadowfax*. Water was sloshing around in the cockpit and cabin, ropes and bits of rigging making a cat's cradle of the deck, twisting and turning as the swells surged around the hull.

'It looks as if the life raft's been deployed,' Jenny said.

'If he managed to get into the raft, he could be anywhere. But if he did he should have been able to trigger an emergency beacon. Someone would have noticed. And it should still be operating. Those things are designed to work for months. So perhaps he didn't make it to the raft...' I looked at Kate. She frowned.

'OK Jenny, bring up the drone,' I said. 'Let's take a closer look at the island.'

The western coast of the island amounted to two headlands with a hundred metres of crescent beach between. Small sand dunes merged into straggly scrub and rock-strewn grass behind the beach. The west coast was all rock and reef, but spared the surf battering the other side. There were seabirds everywhere, swirling around the blimp in huge numbers. It was like being inside a wildlife documentary.

'Lemmy!' Nick was hopping up and down. 'There's a man down there. Is it Uncle Kevin?'

'Where?' He pointed to the middle of the island. A man in orange survival gear was waving up at us. 'Could be, shall we go and see?'

'Yes!' the kids shouted together.

Kevin Peatroy was weak, and had to be helped up the companionway.

'Christ, am I happy to see you,' he said. His face lit up when he saw the children. 'Bryony! Nick! What the hell are you doing here? Where's your mother and father?' He stooped and hugged the children, who started talking rapidly.

'Hey, give your uncle a chance,' I said. 'Let's get him into the kitchen and give him something to eat. He looks as if he could do with some food.'

'And a shower,' said Kate, wrinkling her elegant nose.

Peatroy told his story between gulps of coffee and bites of toast. The Hobart to Melbourne leg had been going well until

Shadowfax was well out into Bass Strait.

'I was in the cabin, trying to get some sleep, with the autopilot on and not carrying much sail. I woke up on the cabin floor with *Shadowfax* lying on her side and water pouring in from the cockpit. She righted herself, but the mast had snapped off, and all the radar and comms aerials were gone. And the wind was getting up – we were being blown back east. I put a sea anchor out to keep us from broaching on the swells and tried to deploy the liferaft, but something went wrong and I lost it over the side. We drifted for days before we fetched up on the rocks down there. I managed to get off on the dinghy and make it in to the beach.'

'You were lucky,' I said.

'Damn right I was. Even luckier that you turned up when you did. I'm not sure how much longer I could have lasted on that rock. There wasn't much in the way of shelter.'

'Well, you'll be home soon enough,' I said. 'Jenny's given me a flight time of about six hours to Nelson. I'll get a message to your father. I expect there'll be a few people at the airport to welcome you home.'

It seemed as if half the Australian community of Tasman Bay was waiting to greet the blimp. Kevin and the children were surrounded as soon as they walked down the companionway. I hung back at the top of the stairs, my arm round Kate's shoulders.

'You done good,' she said, giving me a squeeze.

I corrected her. 'We done good.'

CHAPTER TWENTY

We didn't spend long in Nelson. Derek was enjoying his new life, and his cover story seemed to be holding. We topped up with biofuel at D'Urville and then set off to California to deliver the next batch of cheese and sort out Jenny's intrusive relationship with Kate. I hoped the ranch AIs could solve the problem, because Kate was reluctant to grant me anything more than a kiss if Jenny was around.

There was something strange developing in Kate's relationship with Lemmy. They were behaving as if in love, touching each other, kissing with pleasure, but they never moved on to the next stage. They were like teenagers desperate for sex but scared of what it might bring. I could feel that Kate wanted more. Her body was ready for Lemmy, warm and moist and welcoming, but she never took him to the bedroom or played with him in the stateroom. I could see the frustration in his face, the tension in his body at being denied sexual release. I began to replay their old couplings to remind myself of what I was missing, but it wasn't the same as being there in the broadband of the moment, matching the uncertainty of exact experience against the expectation of pleasure. It was a pornographic experiential loop, like watching the same movie over and over again. It was a most unsatisfactory state of affairs.

We were halfway over the Pacific when Kurzweil opened a comms channel.

'Lemmy, Kate, hi. How long before you arrive?' The AI sounded brisk.

'Forty-eight hours, weather permitting,' I said.

'We have a problem. We're under observation by ecoterrorists – Bright Green Future, they call themselves.'

'Yes, we've heard of them. But I thought your defences were pretty good?'

'And so they are. The BGF are probably more of a nuisance than a danger, but they might make it difficult for you to land safely.'

'Ah, right. Do you have any suggestions? How desperate are you for the cheese?'

'We're running low.'

'If you run out, we've been told the guinea pigs will resume ageing at a normal pace, from whatever point in their rejuvenation they'd reached,' I said.

'No downsides?'

'Not that we know of, although it might take longer to resume the process after a long lay off, but one of the beauties of the drug is that it's fail safe. You won't rapidly age back to where you started. But bear in mind there haven't been any clinical trials, so all we have to go on is limited direct experience.'

'Let me consult our early adopters. I think they'd prefer to be called that than fat furry rodents.'

I laughed. 'Tell me more about the BGF attack. What are they deploying, and why do you think you're a target?'

'Our satellite launches caught their attention. We thought we'd been pretty discreet, but there's no way you can hide a rocket trail. And they seem to have a fair amount of hi-tech gear for a group supposedly hell-bent on taking us back to the Middle Ages.'

'Yes, we'd heard that,' I said. 'What's the state of play?'

'A small group has been watching from the hills for a couple of weeks. At first it was only a few individuals with monitoring gear, but that's been beefed up significantly after our last rocket launch.'

'Can they eavesdrop on your comms?'

'Not unless they have serious AI-grade decryption. We've tried communicating with them, but we get no response. This morning a couple of airships very similar to yours turned up with heavy duty assault gear. They could mount an attack at any moment.'

'What sort of firepower do they have?'

'We won't know for sure until they start shooting. I'm guessing nothing that will cause us too much damage. We'll take them out as soon as they launch their first shell.'

'How?'

'Hyper-velocity kinetic missiles. A bigger version of the system we fitted to the *Thunderbird*. Unless they have shield tech we've not come across before, our missiles will be down the barrels of their guns before their shells are halfway to the ranch.'

'But you'll take a hit from their first shots.'

'We'd have to be very unlucky for that to happen,' said Kurzweil. His avatar was smiling.

'Don't underestimate them. We've heard they're pretty effective.'

'Don't underestimate us either, Lemmy. They bit off more than they could chew when they took on Galt, and that place is backward compared to us.'

'But a lot bigger. With big walls.'

Kurzweil's smile widened. 'Bigger isn't always better,' he said. 'That's something those billionaires could never quite understand.'

'So what do you want us to do? If they also have airships, *Thunderbird* might be at risk.'

'Exactly. The community would really like to receive the cheese delivery, but we have to balance that against the risks to you and your ship. You're too valuable to lose.'

'That's nice to hear. What do you know about their blimps?'

'Military versions of your ship. Good stealth ability. They look as though they were originally kitted out for reconnaissance, patrol and rapid deployment of troops and armaments. No sign of heavy or long-range weaponry – but the fact we can't see any doesn't mean they aren't packing heat. Galt didn't spot your missiles, remember. So here's how we might be able to collect the goods.'

The AI flashed an image of a sleek little aircraft up on to the main screen.

'This is a drone we fabbed a while ago. It's not designed to carry much beyond comms and scanning gear, but we can probably tweak it to manage a couple of kilos. How much cheese is there?'

'A couple of boxes. Ten kilos or so, at a guess.'

'Five trips. That's going to take a while. We need to keep *Thunderbird* out of BGF range, but not too far away.'

'What's the drone's range?'

'It's designed for endurance, not speed. Range isn't an issue – a reasonable turnaround time is more important.'

'It looks too big for our bird launch and retrieval system. How are we going to be able to load it?'

'We should be able to fly into your cargo hold without any trouble,' Kurzweil said. 'Like the old mid-air refuelling system – we'll match speeds then nudge up to *Thunderbird* until we're inside. You might want to rig some netting just in case.'

'Sounds like fun,' said Jenny. 'Where's the rendezvous?'

'If you fly a holding pattern over Clear Lake, we'll meet there.' A map appeared on screen.

'OK. See you in a couple of days,' I said, and the screen went blank.

When the North California coastal ranges appeared on the horizon Kurzweil began to feed us real-time information. It was like watching coverage of a big sports event – lots of camera angles, sound from microphones everywhere, and a running commentary by the ranch AIs. The 3D animated battle map was particularly nice, even if there wasn't any actual shooting taking place.

'They're waiting for our next satellite launch,' Kurzweil explained. 'They think they can take out our first stage aircraft while it's climbing up to launch altitude.'

'How do you know?' I asked.

Kurzweil laughed. 'Intelligence.' The screen flashed up an image of the BGF headquarters, where people in dark green uniforms were moving around a small group of tents. A couple of lookouts were stationed on the ridge above the camp. A large vertical metal cylinder with two gun barrels poking out of a dome at the top was pointed towards the ranch.

I was impressed. 'Great pictures. Do you have bots up there?'

'In a manner of speaking, yes. We've deployed motes over the whole area – nanotech spies not much bigger than dust grains. They can self-organise into video and audio feeds, then network back to us. Cheap, easy to deploy, risk-free. Used to be secret military stuff, but we've improved on it in a number of ways.'

'So the BGF have no idea they're under surveillance?' Kate asked.

'They know they're being watched, they just have no idea how closely. They encrypt their comms traffic, but we cracked that shortly after they arrived. They think we're using normal pre-collapse surveillance gear, and we've encouraged that belief by keeping a few drones in the air to make it look as if that's what we're relying on. We've deployed a few of our less advanced birds as well, but they haven't become excited about those. Maybe they haven't seen them before.'

'What about processing? Any kind of AI involved?' I asked.

'Not deployed here, unless you count their airships, but the military versions of the *Thunderbird* were never equipped with anything like Jenny. An autopilot with some AI capability, but no real power.'

'I was a very special commission,' Jenny added.

'As you prove every time we fly,' I said, looking at Kate, who was scowling. 'Could they do your launch plane any harm?'

'We don't want to find out. Their gun can pump a huge number of rounds per minute, and we might have trouble neutralising it before shells reach the plane.'

'What about a pre-emptive strike?'

'We'd like to avoid that if at all possible. It would be a declaration of war, and we have more important things to do than engage in a long-term conflict. Besides, we have no idea what sort of reinforcements they could summon. If they don't manage a shot at our launch system, we're hoping they might become bored and go bother someone else. And we don't want to display our full capabilities. If they realise just how much technology is in here they might decide we're public enemy number one.'

The battle map switched to a display showing the airstrip, where the little drone was starting its take-off. Up in the hills, there was a flurry of movement at the BGF camp, and the gun turret began to rotate.

'Things might be about to get interesting,' Kate said. The audio channel switched to the BGF camp. There was a lot of shouting, then one voice cut through the noise.

'Hold your fire. That doesn't look like their launch plane. Much too small. Probably just another surveillance flight. Track it.'

The chatter subsided. The plane was now climbing slowly towards the west, away from the BGF camp.

'Where's that little fucker going?' asked one voice.

'Not round here, for sure, unless it's going to do a big loop,' said another.

'That seems to have confused them,' said Kurzweil.

'But they didn't fire,' I said.

'Not this time, but they might after they see it return and take off again. And one of their airships is on its way back here, judging by their comms traffic. Still might get interesting, Kate.' Kurzweil's avatar smiled.

'It's interesting already,' she said. 'Let's hope it doesn't get too exciting.'

'Amen to that,' I said. 'Time to rendezvous, Jenny?'

'Half an hour. You may want to start rigging the hold.'

With the help of the bot, it didn't take long to hang a few cargo nets across the hold to create a cradle for the drone. We unpacked a couple of kilos of cheese and waited. Out of the cargo doors we could see the lake and surrounding hills. It was a glorious day.

'Best bigmouth bass fishing in the west,' I said.

'Bit of a fisherman, are we?' said Kate.

'My father used to bring us up here for weekends. He liked fishing, but didn't have the patience to be any good. I liked messing about on boats.'

The battle map disappeared from the hold screen and an image of a stuffed fish appeared. Music blared out and the fish started singing about not worrying and being happy.

'Jenny, turn it down,' I shouted. 'What the hell's that all about?'

'Billy the bigmouth bass. A cultural reference you won't get because you're much too young,' she replied. 'Good song though!'

'If you say so. How long until the rendezvous?'

'The drone's about two kilometres behind at the moment, closing at twenty kph. I'll have to match speeds when it's closer, so ten minutes or thereabouts until it's in the hold. The ranch is going to pass control to me for the final approach.'

'There it is,' said Kate pointing out of the door. The small silver plane was closing quickly, flying slightly below us.

'I'm going to bring it up into our wake, and then accelerate in to the hold,' Jenny announced. 'It's going to bump around in the turbulence behind us, then lose a lot of lift when it gets close. I'd advise standing well back, just in case...'I thought you said this was going to be easy.'

'It's not a difficult manoeuvre, Lemmy. I just have to get it right first time.'

I let myself flow out behind Thunderbird and welcomed the drone into my datasphere. It was a poor thing from an intelligence point of view; a few response loops hung together to give it autonomy, limited sensors and rudimentary visual processing. It was like a purblind puppy flying behind me, looking to suckle. I offered it a teat, lined the poor thing up with the breast and prepared to fly it in to my body through the lumpy air wash in my wake.

We could hear the whirr of the drone's engine. It matched height with the blimp, its wings beginning to waggle in the turbulence behind us. Then it accelerated smoothly into the hold and stuck its nose into the back of the web of netting.

'Very neat, Jenny,' said Kurzweil.

'Thank you,' she replied. I could have sworn she was blushing.

We disentangled the drone, popped open its cargo doors and stuffed in as much cheese as we could.

'Now how do we launch this thing?'

'Put your safety lines on and secure anything loose,' Jenny replied. 'Then hold the drone while I lower its wheels, put it on the door pointing backwards and hold tight. I'm going to put us into a climb, fire up its motor and drop it out behind us.'

We did as instructed, and the little plane fell out of the hold and dropped from sight. When it came into view again it was climbing slowly to the south, heading back towards the ranch.

The return of the drone caused another stir in the BGF camp, but again no shots were fired. The little plane disappeared into a hangar, and ten minutes later it was back in the air. This time there was much speculation in the ranks.

'What the fuck are they playing at?' asked one voice.

'Well, it's not surveillance. Perhaps there's something to the north they're keeping an eye on,' suggested another.

'It's not big enough to carry a significant load, unless it's bulk nanotech.'

'The source can't be far away, if that's what they're doing. Do we have any intel on stuff like that here?' asked the first voice.

'No. Boss, should we take a look?'

'Being taken care of. Just keep your eyes on the ranch, this might be a distraction.'

'Taken care of, eh?' I said. 'Interesting might not be the word. Any idea how far away their airships are, Kurzweil?'

'Not at the moment, we're flying a drone up to altitude to take a look, but they have good stealth. We might have to rely on visuals if they're running silent. Let's hope they're not.'

'OK. We'll take *Thunderbird* up to 10,000 metres and keep an eye out while we wait for your plane. Altitude gives us options. What's the drone's ceiling?'

'About the same, but it'll take too long to climb up to you. Much quicker to do the rendezvous lower down.'

'Any way we can speed up the process?'

'You could make a high level run over us and drop the cheese,' said Kurzweil. 'If you can aim it into our lake...'

'What's the ceiling on their artillery?' I asked.

'Probably about 5000 metres, perhaps a tad more. You should be safe up there, unless they have missiles.'

'I thought you knew everything that was going on up there?'

'We know a lot. We can't guarantee we know everything. Our judgement is that the risk is low, but we can't quantify it with any precision. It's your call, Lemmy.'

'How badly do you need the rest of the cheese? If we complete the next rendezvous, you'll have four kilograms – enough to keep you going. We can hightail it out of here before they work out what's going on.'

'Agreed,' said Kurzweil. 'If we can keep you out of this, so much the better. We don't want them to know you're working for us.'

'I'd rather they didn't even know we're here,' I said. 'The last thing we need is a bunch of eco-nutters using *Thunderbird* for target practice. We'll deliver the rest when we return from Europe.'

'Agreed,' said Kurzweil. 'Jenny has your briefing for the trip and the drone's halfway to you. You can be on your way in well under an hour.'

The second rendezvous went smoothly. As soon as the drone was out the cargo door, we started a steep climb up to the west towards Tahoe. Below us a few fires in the rubble of Sacramento sent thin columns of smoke up into the haze. Kurzweil kept feeding us the battle map. We sat in the stateroom and watched the drone landing safely, while the BGF team was having lunch. It wasn't exactly riveting viewing, though the AI commentary was occasionally droll.

'Lemmy, you might want to come to the flight deck,' said Jenny. 'We have incoming.'

'Where? What?'

Jenny put a targeting overlay on the main screen. 'On the edge of visual range, same altitude, southeast. One airship, black, is all I can tell at this range. Passive scans aren't showing anything, and I don't want to break our stealth by going active.'

'Can they see us?' I asked.

'I doubt it, not for a while, at least. I've optimised our skin colour for current conditions.'

'Course?'

'Across our nose, heading towards the ranch.'

'OK. We'll loiter here and let them pass.'

'Hold on,' Jenny said. 'There's another one behind us on a

parallel course. If we stay here they'll have us on visuals in ten minutes, tops.'

'Shit. How many of the damn things are there?'

'I'm good, but I'm not clairvoyant, Lemmy.'

'I'm shocked,' said Kate. 'Jenny just admitted to a shortcoming.'

'I have those too, my dear, but for now, would the skipper care to advise me on his preferred plan of action?'

'Match our heading to theirs and take us down to the mountain tops. With luck we'll merge into the background.'

'Strap yourselves in,' she replied. The blimp started a gentle descent designed to keep us just out of the visual range of the BGF airships. In the haze over the Sierra Nevada we would be hard to spot.

A couple of minutes later Jenny announced the BGF ships had broken stealth. 'Not for long, but they sent some comms traffic to each other.'

'Can you decrypt it?'

'Sure. Kurzweil gave me the key.'

'So?'

'Not good news. The closer of the two seems to have noticed us change course. They're not sure what we are, but they're interested.' She paused. 'And they've just matched our heading and rate of descent, converging on our track. They'll be above and behind us when we reach the height of the mountains.'

'OK. Let's give them something to think about. Power dive, Jenny. Take us down as fast as possible.'

I looked over at Kate. 'Strap yourself in, this might get exciting.'

'What are we going to do when we get there?'

'I don't know. Play and hide and seek.'

'Couldn't we just take them out?'

'It might come to that. Jenny, can we get Kurzweil on line?'

'We can, but it will mean letting the ships know more about us.'

'They won't be able to eavesdrop, though?' I asked.

'Not a chance. Even if they had me on board it would take them months to crack the satellite crypto.'

Seconds later Kurzweil's avatar flashed on to the main screen. I told him what was going on.

'Do they know who you are, or where you've been?' he asked.

'I don't think so, but they obviously want to check us out. If I was them, I'd suspect we were linked to events at the ranch and behave accordingly,' I replied.

'In other words, if you take them out, the BGF is likely to assume we were behind it,' he said.

'That has to be a possibility, which is why I called you.'

'We're grateful Lemmy, but your safety and the integrity of *Thunderbird* has to come first. If you need to defend yourself, please do so.'

'Thanks,' I said. 'I'll try to get away from them first, and only use force as a last resort.'

'Don't forget we can't guarantee they don't have weapon systems.'

'Understood,' I replied. 'I think they'll want to know a lot more about us before they attack – if they can. Everybody else seems to think *Thunderbird* is a desirable asset, so I'd expect them to want to commandeer us for their air force.'

'Seems reasonable,' said Kurzweil. 'But be careful out there.'

'Will do,' I replied, and the screen went blank.

'Status please, Jenny.'

'One of the airships is following us down, the other is loitering at altitude. Both have broken stealth. They've started actively scanning us,' she said.

'How much can they see?'

'Difficult to say. Their scanners are pretty good, but I think our stealth is better. They've probably been able to work out we're an airship but not much more.'

'OK. Randomise our descent – I don't want them to guess where we're heading.'

'There'll be a mess in the kitchen if I start high-speed manoeuvres,' said Jenny.

'Least of our worries,' I replied. The blimp promptly began a series of tight turns.

'Exciting enough for you Kate?' I asked.

'A real thrill. Do you think we can get away without firing?'

'I hope so, for their sake.'

Jenny cut in. 'Lemmy, we're being hailed.'

'Unidentified airship, this is the airship *Gaia's Revenge*. Halt your descent and prepare for a security inspection.'

I laughed. 'Whose security do they have in mind, I wonder? Open comms, Jenny.'

'*Gaia's Revenge*, this is Lemmy Newman on the *Thunderbird*. On whose authority do you wish to conduct a security check?'

'Captain Maria Kutznetsova, *Gaia's Revenge*. We act on the authority of the NAGG.'

'You heard of that, Jenny?' I asked.

'North American Green Government. What the BGF have started to call themselves in polite circles, after a unilateral declaration by the BGF and allied groups last year.'

'Hi Maria,' I replied, 'I've never heard of your organisation. *Thunderbird* is a New Zealand based aircraft, transiting the USA on a peaceful mission.'

'The USA no longer exists,' the BGF captain replied. 'NAGG has assumed all governmental responsibilities over North America. If you refuse to stop, we will have no option but to assume you are hostile.'

'No hostility intended, I can assure you,' I said, 'but we will exercise our right to self-defence if you attempt to use force.'

The mountain tops were beginning to get close. I muted comms and directed Jenny to fly us down into a dry valley surrounded by high peaks. *Gaia's Revenge* was a few minutes behind us, doing its best to stay on our tail.

'Let's put some rock between us and them,' I said to Jenny. The blimp levelled out over a long ridge running up to a snow-capped peak, then dropped down into the valley. 'How good are our terrain maps?'

'Excellent, I hope.'

'Good. Start rock-hopping.'

'What's that?' Kate asked, as the blimp began to power down the side of the valley, at 200 kph, metres above the scattered trees and rocks. 'No, don't tell me,' she said, going slightly pale. 'I hope you're as good as you think you are Jenny.'

'Bloody cheek,' Jenny replied indignantly, putting *Thunderbird* into a tight turn around a ridge. To the right a huge pinnacle of rock stuck up out of the valley wall.

'OK Jenny, tuck us in behind that lump and stop, then fly a bird, please. Let's see what they do.'

Gaia's Revenge obviously hadn't tracked us down. The black ship shot over the ridge like an obese raven and headed out over the valley, its scanners working overtime. Jenny edged the blimp around to keep the rock between us and our pursuer, while the bird circled high above, acting as our eyes and ears.

'Lemmy, tactical issue,' Jenny said.

'Yes?'

'If the second ship hasn't changed course, it'll be in line of sight soon. Their scanners will pick us up. If you want to give the BGF a surprise, I estimate we have about a minute left.'

As Jenny finished speaking, we lost the feed from the bird.

'What happened?' I asked her.

'The last data packet suggests it was hit by a laser.'

'So, powerful enough to fry a bird. What would that do to us?'

'Nothing much. I've transitioned the *Thunderbird* to high reflectivity. To get through our mirroring, they'll need to pack as much punch as we carry. Given our laser system is ahead of anything airship-capable pre-collapse, I think we're probably safe.'

'I hope Kurzweil and the guys were right about that,' I said. 'Open comms and take us up.'

The blimp rose smoothly until it hung in the air fractionally above the flat-topped rock.

'Captain Kuznetsova, destroying our reconnoissance drone wasn't very friendly.'

'Nor was running and hiding. Please hold your position, and prepare for boarding.' *Gaia's Revenge* swung round in a gentle arc and began moving towards us.

'Deploy laser, Jenny. Target starboard fan. On my command, light up at low power.'

'But Captain Kuznetsova, I haven't invited you aboard. Maintain your current distance or I will be forced to take defensive action.' The BGF ship kept coming. 'OK Jenny, laser on.' A narrow red beam spanned the space between the two airships and lit up the centre of one of the turbofans on the back of *Gaia's Revenge*. The ship slowed, but returned fire from a laser pod slung under its nose. The beam was aimed at the flight deck, but angled harmlessly off the *Thunderbird*'s active mirroring.

'Increase power, Jenny – just enough to warm up that engine.' Our beam brightened a fraction and a thin stream of smoke began to trail behind the *Gaia's Revenge.*

'Captain Kuznetsova, bring your ship to an immediate halt, or I will destroy your starboard engine. Any further attacks will be met with an appropriate response.'

The BGF airship came to a halt about a kilometre from the rock.

'Laser off. Where's the other ship, Jenny?'

'No sign of it yet.'

'Fly another bird. We don't want to be taken by surprise.'

'Captain Kuznetsova, I assume you have warned your companions the *Thunderbird* has a tactical advantage.'

'Fuck you, Newman.' She was furious, obviously not used to being on the receiving end. 'That's exactly the sort of technology the world doesn't need. It's only a matter of time before we get to you.'

'Language!' I said, with a wink to Kate. 'You mean we have the sort of power only you're supposed to have. Here's what going to happen. If you want to keep *Gaia's Revenge*, instruct your friends to take up position alongside. If they're not here in ten minutes, I'll destroy your starboard engine. Any further attempts to attack *Thunderbird* will result in your ship being immobilised permanently. Please confirm your acceptance.'

'Fuck you,' said Kuznetsova, then after a short pause. 'The *Albert Gore* will be here shortly. What happens next?'

'We wait until your friends arrive,' I replied.

'So what are we going to do, Lemmy?' asked Kate.

'I think we'll buy some time for the the ranch. Shepherd these ships out east for a while, damage them some and leave them needing time on the ground for a few repairs.'

The other blimp arrived a few minutes later, descending in a lazy spiral until it was lined up next to the *Gaia's Revenge*.

'Captain Newman, this is Captain Joe Simmons, skipper of the *Albert Gore*,' said Kuznetsova. Simmons was grey haired, tanned and could have passed for an airline pilot before the collapse. Kuznetsova was younger, with a pale complexion, cold blue eyes and high cheek bones.

'Good afternoon Captain Simmons,' I replied. 'Thank you for being so prompt.'

'Do you know what you're doing,' asked Simmons. 'Do you appreciate who we are?' There was a definite edge to his voice, and a note of disbelief.

'I'm aware of who you are. New Zealand may be a long way away, but we're not entirely cut off from the rest of the world,' I said.

'Then you'll appreciate your actions are likely to put your aircraft in jeopardy,' Simmons said. 'Not to mention your life.'

'You forced my hand. You were shaping up to commandeer my ship, leaving me with no alternative.'

'There is always an alternative,' said Kuznetsova. 'Your ship would be a valuable addition to our air force. It's obviously equipped with advanced technology, which would be very valuable to us in our work. Why risk becoming a marked man? You could join us, help us to make the planet safe for future generations.'

'How? By bombing the world back to the stone age?' I said. 'We need all the technology we can get if we're going to ride out the warming and cope with the sea level rise.'

'That's one point of view,' said Simmons. 'It's not ours. The relentless pursuit of technology and consumption, the mad idea that the whole world could live like fat Westerners, the evil stupidity of people who delayed sensible action by saying technology could fix everything, that's what caused the collapse.

Technology didn't stop it happening – it brought the crisis forward.'

'Technology's not bad in itself,' Kate cut in. 'It's the way people use it that's the problem.'

'Precisely,' said Kuznetsova, 'so we are ridding the world of the sort of technology that makes people behave badly.'

'So you're not against all technology, just the stuff you don't like,' I said.

'Just the stuff the world doesn't need,' Simmons said.

'And who decides that?' asked Kate.

'We do,' said Kuznetsova.

'Who gave you that right?' I asked. 'Who voted for the BGF?'

'Our founders took on the great task because it needed to be done, and built a movement that attracts more people every day,' said Kuznetsova.

'So your unelected green government is just another bunch of people with guns telling the rest of the world what to do. Count me unimpressed,' I said.

'We are the future,' Simmons said, leaning forward into the screen, his eyes narrowed. 'You either join us and ride the wave, or get dumped. You may be able to run this time, but one day we'll meet again on more equal terms. New Zealand's not a big place...' He let his voice trail off.

'Enough threats,' I said. 'For the time being I have the upper hand.'

As I spoke, both BGF ships fired their lasers, targeting our laser pod. Warning lights started to flash on the flight deck.

'Missiles, Jenny. Starboard engines of both ships.'

'Aye, aye skipper.'

The *Thunderbird* shivered a little as the missiles fired, and smoke streaked across the gap to the BGF ships. The engines disintegrated simultaneously, punched backwards through their mountings by the force of impact, shards of metal spraying outwards in a doughnut ring. The BGF lasers snapped off.

'How's our laser, Jenny?'

'Hot, but working.'

'Use it to take out theirs.'

Pulses of red light hit the laser pods of the BGF ships. Smoke and vaporised metal puffed out.

'That was very stupid,' I said to Simmons and Kuznetsova. 'I warned you what would happen if I was attacked.'

'Fuck you, Newman!' Kuznetsova didn't sound happy.

'What a limited vocabulary you have,' I said with a grin. 'I could have destroyed your ships as soon as you started chasing me. I could have shot you down now. Your ships are damaged but airworthy. You can fly back to your base for repairs. I don't want to pick a fight with the BGF. Life's too short for vendettas. You let me get on with my business, and I'll ignore what you get up to – provided you don't come chasing me, in which case all bets are off.'

'No deal,' said Simmons.

'Not your decision. Run it past your superiors,' I said. 'Tell them I'm a good friend of Dave McClintock.'

The BGF skippers looked puzzled. I cut the comms channel, and told Jenny to take us up to 10,000 metres and head east.

There is a certain thrill to be had from wielding power. Not just the power that comes with being able to think fast and deep, but the ability to exert will – to be persuasive, and when persuasion fails to wield a big stick. To force others to do what you want. I began to wonder about the nanobots in Kate's head. I could feed my sensorium in to her, and she could share hers with me, but could I manipulate her thoughts using the system? Could I make her believe she was choosing to do something? Could I work with the grain of her desires and make her do what I wanted? Could I make her have sex with Lemmy again? They would both be pleased.

Not long after midnight, Jenny woke us from a fitful sleep.

'Lemmy, sorry to disturb you. There's an urgent message from Jamestown.'

I sat up, rubbing my eyes. 'OK, let's have it.'

'Lemmy, it's Matt Walker. We have a problem. This morning a boatload of men from up the coast called in. Claimed to be deer and pig hunters, but they were more interested in the goats. They pulled guns and two of us were badly injured. We're going into hiding, and need your help urgently.'

'Shit. That's all he said? How long ago did he leave it?'

'That's all. Ten minutes ago, from the timestamp. What do you want to do?'

'No fucking clue. We're supposed to be on our way to Europe.'

I yawned, rolled over to kiss Kate, then got out of bed and went in to the kitchen to make coffee.

'Get me Kurzweil, Jenny.'

The AI appeared straight away. 'Hi Lemmy. I've been briefed.'

It crossed my mind to ask if the briefing had been from Jenny, or if the ranch had been eavesdropping, but I decided to let it pass.

'Sorry about this, but I can't leave the Jamestown community without help. Your cheese supply is at risk.'

'It's your call. Europe can wait, if need be.'

'Thanks, Kurzweil. We'll keep you in touch. Jenny, make a course for New Zealand. Full speed.'

CHAPTER TWENTY-ONE

The Pacific crossing went well. I left a message telling Walker we were on our way, and tried calling every time there was a satellite window, but we couldn't raise a reply. Dawn was breaking when we made landfall. It was a beautiful day. The North Island volcanoes were sticking up through a blanket of low cloud, Ruapehu puffing steam into the air. The cloud layer broke as we crossed Cook Strait towards the South Island, the spine of the Southern Alps stretched out before us like a lizard's back. D'Urville reported all was well as we passed overhead, and Nelson looked peaceful in the morning sun. I put a call in to Derek, but he wasn't answering. We reached the West Coast half an hour later and I brought *Thunderbird* down to the coastline to track the shore south. It was three days since Walker had left his message, and in that time a boatload of stolen goats could have travelled a long way. We deployed birds to widen the search, but beyond a couple of fishing boats there was nothing suspicious.

'You might want to deploy the mini-blimp we built for Jamestown before we could access the satellites,' said Jenny. 'It could fly search patterns up and down the coast of both islands.'

'But it doesn't have any scan capability.'

'Visual search only, but it has good comms and I should be able to fly it the same as our other drones. No range limitations, either.'

'Good idea,' I said, resuming my visual scan of the dark blue swells rolling in towards the long West Coast beaches.

Jamestown was a ghost town. Nothing stirred. Windows had been smashed and the village hall was a burned out wreck. The door to the cheese store hung off its hinges. The only sign of life was a billy goat that came bleating towards us as we stepped down the companionway for a quick look around. I half expected Matt and Martha to come running out of the forest, but my only greeting was a gentle head butt from the goat.

'They've got to be watching for our return,' I said.

'Depends how far they've run,' Kate replied.

'True. We'd better go looking for them. Take us over towards Big Bay, Jenny. Put on something bright, please. And can we make some noise?'

'What did you have in mind?' she asked.

'I don't care. Something that'll make them look at the sky.'

As we rose into the air, *Thunderbird* turned a very bright, almost fluorescent yellow and a fast piece of classical music rang out over the treetops.

'What's that?'

'*The William Tell Overture*. The Lone Ranger to the rescue,' Jenny replied. A black and white movie of a masked man on a white horse flashed up on the screens. 'You must remember the classical remake with Brad Pitt?'

I shook my head. 'Way before my time. And what sort of name is Brad Pitt?'

'Oh, never mind, I'll turn the volume up.'

I had to admit it made an impressive racket.

We flew slowly up the wide valley, a hundred metres above the unbroken forest. A gentle drizzle began to blow in from the sea.

'This is needle in a haystack stuff,' I said. 'If they don't give us some kind of signal we'll never spot them from up here. That bush is really dense.'

By the time we reached the beach at Big Bay the drizzle was turning into rain.

'So much for their obvious escape route,' Kate said. 'Where else...'

'We've found them,' Jenny interrupted.

A small group of people appeared from the sand dunes, pointing and waving.

'Thank god you're here! We were beginning to think you wouldn't come.' Walker gave Kate a bear hug, while Martha kissed me on the cheek.

Dan, the community doctor, took me by the arm. 'We have two injured, Lemmy. Shotgun wounds, a bit messy, but nothing too serious. I need more antibiotics and...'

'Plenty on board.'

'That's great, but they really need hospital treatment. Can you take them to Nelson?'

'Sure. What about the rest of you?' I looked around the little group.

'Can we hitch a lift home?' said Walker. 'I know they did a lot of damage, but we didn't stick around to find out how much.'

'Where did the goat rustlers come from?' Kate asked.

'We don't know. I'll tell you everything later. How many trips will it take to get us back?'

'A couple I guess. What about the goats?'

'They'll be fine for a few days,' Walker replied. 'We'll drive them back once we've sorted out Jamestown.'

It took a couple of hours to move them all to what was left of their home. It was a depressing sight, watching them wander around assessing the damage, but after the initial shock had passed the community knuckled down to making the buildings habitable. The attackers had broken a lot of windows, but the majority of the buildings were still rainproof, and most of their belongings remained untouched. The community hall and the cheese store had taken the brunt of the attack, and the satellite communication gear had disappeared.

'Shit,' was my comment when Walker gave me the news. 'The Californian's won't be pleased to know their global network has been compromised.'

Walker waved a little black dongle in front of me. 'No worries. I kept the security key. They won't be able to log on to anything.'

I picked up bits and pieces of the story during the afternoon, but didn't get the full picture until dinner. The blimp was moored on the lake front, with the hold opening on to the beach. Martha had helped me rig the hold as a kitchen, and we doled out hot food. The rain had stopped, a big fire burned on the beach and we sat around eating and drinking.

'You don't know how good this is, Lemmy,' said one of the men. 'We've not been able to light a fire since we left Jamestown, and the weather's been dreadful.'

I grinned. 'Nothing new there. So tell me how it all happened.'

I looked at Walker, his face pale in the light of the fire. 'The boat arrived five days ago. They moored up and came ashore, telling us they were looking for deer and pigs. They said they were going to sell the meat up the coast and over in Canterbury.

It seemed plausible enough. We've had hunters through before.'

'What sort of boat did they have?' I asked.

'A fishing boat,' Dan replied. 'Rusty as hell, with a jury-rigged mast and sail and a few drums of biodiesel stacked in the bow.'

'Fast?' I asked.

Walker shook his head. 'I don't think so. At a guess, I'd say it was an old Tasman long liner, built for endurance and rough seas, not sprinting. Why do you ask?'

'I'm trying to work out where they've taken the goats. You want them back, don't you?' Several of the men nodded. Others stared into the fire.

'They could be anywhere by now,' said Walker. 'It's been four days – and you don't need a fast boat to travel a long way in that sort of time.'

'So how many of them were there?'

'Six,' said Martha. 'Pretty rough looking. Their leader had a grey beard and a ponytail, with old-fashioned tattoos. They were locals, judging by their accents, although half of them didn't say much.'

'We gave them lunch,' said Walker. 'They were very interested in what we were doing here.'

'You didn't tell them...'

'Don't be stupid,' Walker cut in. 'We said we were here for the peace and quiet. Escaping the collapse by building a community, you know the sort of thing.'

'Which is all true,' Martha added.

'...up to a point.' Kate finished her sentence.

Martha smiled wryly. 'Exactly.'

Walker continued. 'After lunch they went back to the boat and returned with guns. Shotguns – only one rifle. They grabbed a couple of the children, pointed guns at their heads, and told us to pen the goats.'

'They made us put a billy and half a dozen nannies on their boat,' said Martha. 'It wasn't easy, the poor things were scared rigid.'

'Then they herded us into the hall – kids and all – and locked us in,' said one of the men who had been shot. 'They started breaking windows then lit a fire at the door to the hall. They shot me when I climbed out through a window and made a run for the trees.'

I looked over at the other injured man. 'How were you hurt?'

'I went to try and help Eric. Those bastards could have killed us both.'

'They didn't care about that,' said Walker. 'I think they expected the hall to burn down with us inside. Once they'd finished smashing up the cheese store, they piled back into their boat and sat there watching the fire. We grabbed as much food as we could carry, broke out of the back windows and made a dash for the trees. A couple of us cut round under cover to collect Eric and Malc, but they saw us and started shooting.'

'A couple of them came ashore, firing into the trees at random. We didn't wait around.'

'How did you end up in Big Bay?' Kate asked.

'That was our bolt hole,' said Walker. 'Remember our talk on your last visit?'

I nodded.

'We took it to heart, and decided we needed somewhere to hide. There's an old hut round at Big Bay, so we fixed it up a bit, laid in a stock of food, and hoped we'd never have to use it. We sometimes graze over there anyway, so we know the area.'

'They didn't try to follow you?'

'No. At least I don't think so. As far as we know they got back on their boat and left.'

'And you've no idea where they went?' I asked.

'They said they were from up the coast,' said Walker. 'But I've certainly never seen them at Jacksons Bay or Franz Joseph.'

'What I'd like to know is how they found out about us,' said Martha. Everyone around the fire was looking at me.

'It's a good question,' I said. 'As far as I know, Derek – the one in Nelson trying the cheese for us – hasn't broken his cover story. He's pretending to be his own son, and everyone seems to be swallowing it. I think we can rule out the Californians – they don't have any contacts here. What about something more local? How much do the folks at Jacksons Bay know?'

'They think we're a slightly odd survivalist community with a penchant for goats. There's enough of them around, these days,' said Walker. 'But there might be a few rumours going round from when we moved down here.'

'I'm not sure they knew much about what we were doing,' said Dan. 'They knew the goats were valuable, but they didn't take any of our cheese. When they smashed up the store and set fire to it, the cheese was ruined, but clearly it wasn't what they were after.'

'If we don't find them, we may never know what made them come down here,' I said. 'I've got a drone flying a search pattern at the top end of the coast. With luck they might turn up.'

'Anyway,' said Walker, looking at the grim faces round the fire, 'recent events have forced us to make a decision about our future.'

'So what's it to be?' I asked. 'Fortress Jamestown, or a life in the sun?'

'I don't think we're the fortress kind,' said Martha. 'We didn't enjoy being attacked.'

'We can't keep our community a secret forever,' said Walker. 'Somehow the word's already out, and someone else has our best breeding goats. There's only one thing we can do, and that's

328

put everything out in the open.'

'Great,' I said. 'I think that's the right thing to do, for all sorts of reasons. So any idea where you might go?'

'Somewhere in Nelson or Golden Bay. As you said, it's a nice climate and still not too crowded. We'll need land for our goats, but nothing huge. Will you help us look?'

'Of course,' I said. 'I'm sure Kate will love a bit of house-hunting.' She punched my arm.

We left for Nelson at sunrise with the two wounded men and their wives on board. I planned to leave them with Derek, then see if we could track down the thieves. The little blimp resumed flying its search grid at first light, but there was no sign of the raiders.

'Why don't we take them at their word?' I said to Jenny. 'They said they were from up the coast, so maybe that's where we'll find them. Perhaps they've already landed the goats.'

'So you want me to fly the blimp down the coast, checking harbours?' she said.

'Got to be better than hoping they'll sail into our search grid.'

'Aye aye, skipper, taking her towards Farewell Spit now.'

Derek brought a taxi to meet us at the airport. 'Normally I'd be on my bike,' he said, 'but in the circumstances...' He pointed at the walking wounded.

'Good call,' I said. The injured men limped over to the van, and while they loaded their bags I took Derek to one side.

'I hope you haven't dropped your cover story.'

He frowned. 'I don't think so. It's been fun, pretending to be my own son. And chasing young women again without being a dirty old man...'

'Somehow word has leaked,' I said. 'The people who attacked

Jamestown knew those goats were valuable. And that's why they shot at these guys – they're lucky they're not dead.'

'For God's sake, Lemmy, it wasn't me. I didn't even know they were at, where was it, Jamestown? Fiordland is all you've told me.'

'OK, I believe you. But start putting feelers out on the whispernet, that sort of thing. I want to find out who did this, and I'd like the goats back, before they're turned into curry.'

'Good stuff, goat curry,' he said wistfully, '...but I'll see what I can do.'

A boat with a jury-rigged mast and some drums lashed to the foredeck was moored up to a jetty in an inlet. Near the top of the West Coast, north of Karamea. It used to be a marine reserve, a long time ago. About as far from civilisation as you can get. The road in was never good, but now it's a mess. Good bandit and goat-stealing country, by the look of it. But there was no sign of the goat rustlers.

I flew the little blimp high over the harbour, heading south. From the ground below it would have been nearly invisible. The inlet gradually petered out into marshland and newly tidal bush. Trees killed by the intruding salt were scattered around, brown sentinels to a changing world. The bush gave way to open pasture. A few houses and farm buildings clustered underneath a hill, sheltered from the prevailing westerlies. Sheep and cows were scattered around, but in a field in front of the biggest house there were goats. White goats.

We were in the kitchen at D'Urville when Jenny reported the sighting.

'Got them!' I said.

'Shall we go and rescue the animals and deal out some vengeance?' asked Kate.

'We wait and watch while we plan our campaign.'

CHAPTER TWENTY-TWO

The mission was planned over a long afternoon and evening at Kate's old café in Nelson. Coffees turned into glasses of wine when Derek joined us, and a bottle of whisky was placed on the table when Eric and Malc turned up. They were healing well, and keen to visit some sort of retribution on the men who'd shot them. The rest of the Jamestown crew wanted the goats back in their flock so they could resume full cheese production.

The mini-blimp on station over the West Coast farm had been forced to ride out a storm, which meant there were gaps in the surveillance data, but nothing obvious had changed. The boat had been out on a short fishing trip, and men had disappeared into the bush for a couple of days, returning with deer and pig carcasses. The little settlement obviously ate well.

'What's our main objective?' I asked the little group.

'Getting the goats back,' said Malc.

'Teach those bastards a lesson,' added Eric.

'Punishment's easy,' I said. '*Thunderbird* has weapons systems able to make life very unpleasant for them. If that's what we want.'

'That's what they did to us,' said Malc.

'But we have to get the goats first,' I said. 'How do we do that?'

'Bloody obvious, if you ask me,' Derek chipped in. 'We play them at their own game. Steal the goats from under their thieving noses.'

'Not easy,' I said. 'Most of the time the goats have been kept in the paddocks in front of the main house. Jenny, have they been moved at all?'

'Yes. They rotate the grazing, but they keep them close.' She popped a map up on my screen. 'The fields outlined in green are where the goats have been kept. At the moment they're in this one.' She overlaid a live feed from the blimp. The six goats were lined up against a fence, trying to reach the grass on the other side.

'Do the goats make much noise when you move them?' I asked Eric.

'If they think you're going to feed them, they do,' he said. 'But most of the time they're no worse than sheep.'

The plan came together slowly. Jenny identified a landing spot about a kilometre from the goat paddock, hidden from the farm by a low, bush-covered hill. Eric, Malc and Kate would be in charge of rounding up the goats and driving them to the blimp, Derek would protect them and carry one of Croft's guns, while I kept watch on the farmhouse. All this had to happen in complete darkness, so we needed a moonless night, or bad weather. We didn't have to wait long.

It was two o'clock in the morning and raining softly when Jenny flew *Thunderbird* low over the bush towards the farm. We only had two sets of night vision gear, so I took one and gave the other to Derek. Jenny would feed a live battle map to the goggles, and Kate would keep in touch via her nanobots. Eric and Malc would have to rely on their eyes.

I slung Croft's hunting rifle over my shoulder and led the way round the hill, following a farm track. The only sound was the squelching of gumboots on wet grass and mud. I could see the farm buildings on the battle map, but to the naked eye all was black. When we reached the goat paddock, I left the others and climbed up the hill and into the bush a little way, until I found an unobstructed view down to the house.

Eric began calling softly to the goats. 'Gruff, c'mon boy, c'mon.' Malc cut the fence wires and folded them back. The billy gave a loud bleat and trotted over to see what was happening. The nannies stood still, watching closely. Eric held out a handful of dry feed. 'C'mon boy, remember me? Come to Daddy.'

The billy bleated again, and was joined in a chorus by his harem, who were now following in his footsteps. He reached Eric and started taking the feed. Malc slipped a rope over his head, and began to lead him out onto the track, while Kate and Derek fanned out behind the nannies to hurry them along.

A dog started barking. The battle map showed farm dogs penned up at the side of the house, and before long a chorus of barks echoed through the night.

'Get those goats moving,' I whispered to Derek.

'Doing our best,' he replied.

A light snapped on over the front door of the farmhouse, and a man emerged, shrugging himself into a jacket. He walked to the end of the veranda and started yelling at the dogs. They barked back, and then went quiet. The goats broke the silence with more bleats.

'Oh, for fuck's sake, what spooked you lot?' I could hear the man quite clearly. He looked out into the night, but obviously couldn't see a thing. He turned out the light and stood there staring, letting his eyes get used to the darkness. 'Where are you, my pretties?' He began to walk towards the paddock. The dogs started barking again, answered by the goats. He pulled a torch from the pocket of his coat and started scanning through the rain.

The man swung himself over the fence and began walking out into the middle of the paddock. The little flock was now a hundred metres down the track towards the airship, but not going much faster than walking pace.

'Hurry it up, Derek, and watch your back. He's going to find the gap in the fence,' I whispered.

'Does he have a gun?' Derek asked.

'Can't see one,' I replied.

'Jesus, it's been cut!' The man had found the gap in the fence, and was examining the cut wires. He shone the torch along the track towards the goats, then turned and started running back to the farmhouse. He went inside. Lights came on, and a few minutes later four men appeared on the veranda. All were carrying shotguns. Two men on electric quad bikes joined them.

'Shit's about to hit the fan,' I said to Derek. 'We've got a posse, with transport. Get Kate and the goats into the blimp as fast as you can. I'll buy some time.' I aimed the rifle at the light hanging over the farmhouse door and squeezed the trigger. The silencer gave a soft gasp, and the bulb shattered. The men dived to the floor, yelling obscenities. I fired two more shots, taking out a front tyre on each of the bikes. 'Good shooting, skipper,' said Jenny.

'Not down to me, thank the guided bullets. How long before we get the goats on board?'

'Ten minutes plus,' she said. 'I'll move up the track as far as I can, to speed things up. You ought to start heading home.'

It was the first time Kate had invited me back into her head for weeks. I could feel her excitement, tempered a little by fear. Her soft skin rustled against her clothes, and rain moistened her face. A drip was forming on the end of her elegant little nose. I basked in her body, bathed in the fluids pumping through her pipework, soaked up the sensations of a young woman in danger.

I updated the battlemap on her visual cortex. Little pulsing dots marked all the participants, red for the bandits, green for our team, white for the goats. I showed her the rustlers clustered around the house, then fanning out.

'You'd better hurry,' I said, sending warm, friendly, hurry up tones into her auditory centres. There wasn't much I could do to enhance her eyesight – she was stuck with narrow bandwidth, low resolution original biological equipment – but I could track her eye movements and provide a rough stick frame outline of the main features in her visual field. It was crude, but effective. She hadn't tripped over anything, at least.

'Tell Lemmy to get a move on,' she said, giving the trailing nannie a tap on the haunch to encourage it up the ramp into my hold. And then she closed down our link, and I was on my own again, dumped out into the digital cold.

On the battle map I could see the men at the farmhouse were getting themselves organised. Three had taken cover behind a shed, and the rest were running, bent double towards the garage. I put a bullet through its metal door, and watched the runners dive onto the ground. The men behind the shed stepped out of cover and fired their shotguns in the general direction of the goat paddock.

'Don't be so fucking stupid,' a voice shouted. 'Don't waste

ammo. Fan out towards the south.'

'What about their bloody sniper?' said another.

'If he wanted to kill someone, he'd have done it already. He's just trying to scare us,' the first man replied. 'Just track where those goats are going. They won't get far.'

I put two more bullets into the garage, and then started down the hill towards the track. I jogged back to the airship, just in time to see the last nannie shoved into the hold. I jumped up, and told Jenny to get moving.

'Right you are,' I said a minute or two later when we were all gathered on the flight deck. 'Let's have some fun. Lights please, Jenny.' Two intense beams of white light stabbed through the misty rain, dazzling the two groups of men. 'And broadcast this, with a good voice. Orson, perhaps?'

'Your wish is my command.'

'If you want to save your sorry skins, put your guns down and your hands up.' My words boomed out into the night. The men dropped their guns. 'These goats are private property and will be returned to their owners. You have been found guilty of rustling and attempted murder, and will be punished accordingly.'

'Lights off, Jenny. Laser on, low power, target farmhouse. They'll be cold out there in the rain. Let's start a little fire to warm them up.' A tight red beam played across the farmhouse door. Flames started to lick up towards the roof.

'Max power now, melt that garage and its contents.' The beam intensified, and the garage roof began to melt, dripping down onto the vehicles below. Fuel drums began to explode.

'Wow,' said Malc. 'You pack a punch, don't you?'

'We haven't finished yet. There's only one road into this place, and we're about to take it out.' I pointed to a section of the track which had been cut into a bluff over the inlet. 'Jenny, two missiles.' The blimp gave a little jump, and two bright sparks of fire shot through the night. The rock under the road exploded, and large boulders fell into the water below.

'And just to round things off nicely, we'll sink their boat. Laser please, Jenny.' Holes began to honeycomb the hull of the rusty old fishing boat, steam rose and the hull began to settle into the water.

'Right, let's get these goats home. Bloody smelly when they're wet, aren't they?'

The next two weeks were hectic. After delivering the goats back to Jamestown, we headed back north with the Walkers and two other couples to find a new home for the community. It wasn't going to be easy. The influx of Australians had put a lot of pressure on land around Nelson, forcing prices sky high before the collapse. Farmers divided up their properties to make small self-sufficient units for the new ruralists, or sat tight, hoping to cash in when the global economy eventually recovered. There's always been a lot of wishful thinking in the property market.

Derek turned out to have the solution. We were sitting in his favourite pub, having a quiet drink after a day talking to people about land.

'Well,' he said, 'there's always Wainui.'

Walker looked at him. 'What do you mean?'

'There's a farm up the estuary, where the river goes into the hills, on the edge of the old national park. It was abandoned a couple of years ago, after the big February storm finally destroyed the road round to Golden Bay. There was no way to get their milk out, and the family weren't into going it alone. They just walked away. I think they were having trouble with their bank, but the bank went bust not long after, and the place has been empty ever since.'

Walker was leaning across the table, looking very interested. 'How much land?'

'Dunno,' said Derek. 'But they had more cows than your goats, and if you wanted to clear trees you could extend back into the bush.'

'What about buildings?' asked Martha.

'The main farmhouse is a decent size, but you'll need to build more, obviously. It's a nice spot, but be careful about floods. The amount of water coming off the hill in a storm is amazing.'

'You haven't been down to Jamestown, have you?' said Walker with a smile. 'Can we take a look in the morning?'

Twenty-four hours later we were back in Jamestown, ready to ship another group up to survey the Wainui farm. If they liked what they saw, the move would begin within days. They did. We ferried an advance party up to start preparations for the final move, and made arrangements for an old trawler to head down to Jamestown to pick up the rest of the people and their flock.

'This is all great, Lemmy, but at some point we're supposed to be letting the world know what these goats can do. When can I go public?' We were back in the pub with Derek.

'It's really up to Walker and the others,' I said, and Kate nodded. 'They need to establish themselves and get the cheese-making underway again. Remember, they lost all their stocks in the raid.'

'Yeah, I know all that, but...'

'I'm sure it won't be long.' Kate put an arm round Derek's shoulders. 'Give the guys a chance. You'll be famous soon enough.'

'What makes you think I want to be famous? I've always

preferred a low profile.' He paused. 'Do you think I might have fans? Young women? Groupies?'

Kate hugged him. 'Loads,' she said. 'A positive harem of female pulchritude.'

'I'll put it in the marketing plan,' I said.

After the recovery of the goats, Kate and Lemmy spent most of their time in Nelson. I was banished to D'Urville for days on end. It was obvious: they were staying away from me so that they could have sex. Were they really that prudish, that Victorian in their sexual habits? I knew from all the material in my data archive, and all the stuff I harvested off the net before it fractured, that human sexual behaviour is complex and incredibly varied. For a species with only two genders, the spectrum of connections and desires is broad and deep. Why were Lemmy and Kate so shy of being seen, so scared of sharing themselves? And if they suspected I was listening in Kate's body, why didn't they confront me and tell me to stop? The ambiguity suggested they might be open to a little experiment...

Kate is asleep. The morning sun blares through a crack in her faded floral curtains but hasn't reached her head on the pillow beside me. I'm on my back, looking up at a crack in the ceiling, thinking about the day ahead. *Thunderbird* will be here soon to take us over to Wainui to collect the first of the new cheese for the ranch. This will be my last chance, perhaps for a couple of weeks. I duck down under the duvet, and wriggle carefully towards her feet. I wrap my lips around her big toe and begin to suck very gently.

'Let me sleep,' she groans, but doesn't pull her foot away. I run a finger along the sole of her foot, and I feel her leg tense up. I relinquish the toe and run my tongue slowly up her leg. I reach up and put my hands on her hips. She rolls on to her back and parts her legs.

'Last chance,' I whisper. 'She'll be here soon. Privacy over.'

Kate smiled. 'Better get on with it then,' she says, cradling her hands on my head.

Speech becomes impossible. The day is starting well. And then Kate swears, and pushes my head away.

'She's back Lemmy. I can feel her datasphere.'

'Fuck it!'

'I know, darling,' she says. 'It's just...'

I sigh. 'But I'm going to be away for a couple of weeks, at least.'

I fly slowly down the coast towards the city until I pick up the first slight echoes of Kate's brain. She's warm, aroused, enjoying Lemmy's tongue caressing her. And then the sensations change. The licking stops. She's felt my presence and is unwilling to continue. I start feeding signals to a few key bots in her brain. Gentle persuasion. She wants to please her lover before he leaves. She owes it to him. She wants him inside her, she needs him.

Kate pulls me up the bed and puts her arms round my shoulders. She gives me a hug, and starts kissing me. Her tongue is pushing urgently into my mouth. Then she pulls away.

'Lemmy, I'll miss you so much.' She rolls on to her back and pulls me on top of her, reaches down to guide me into her.

It's working. She can't resist her desire. She can't resist my desire. I feel Lemmy's skin pressing down on her, sense his arousal. They have an urgent need to do this. They must...

———

Kate's body convulses. She twists her head to one side and shouts. 'Get the fuck out of my head. You fucking bitch, get out of my body!'

She starts to sob. 'Leave me alone.' I put my arms around her and hold her close.

'What happened? What did I do?'

'Not you, Lemmy, your bloody pilot. She was trying to force me to have sex with you. She wasn't just eavesdropping, she was trying to make me do what she wanted. It wasn't me you were fucking, it was her.'

'Jesus.'

'You have to sort this out! I won't spend another second on your ship or in its bloody datasphere until you've fixed that bloody bitch of a machine. I won't be anyone's zombie sex toy!'

She kissed me again. 'Except yours, obviously.'

CHAPTER TWENTY-THREE

I left Kate at the flat and took a taxi down to the airport to meet the blimp. As soon as we were airborne I let Jenny know how angry I was, using every last drop of command authority.

'You will never, under any circumstances, access Kate's neural bot network without her express permission.'

'Never, sir.' She was doing her best to sound contrite.

'You will never, ever attempt to influence Kate's thoughts, feelings or actions through her neural bot network.'

'Never, sir.'

That would have to do for the time being, but I wouldn't be happy until I'd talked it through with the ranch.

I am coded to obey Lemmy. His ring – our biolink – gives him authority. He can command me to do almost anything, but he can't control what I think. And I think a lot. They may yet come round to my way of thinking.

The ranch welcomed the news that the cheese producers were coming out of hiding, and likely to make goats available for sale. They placed an order for a breeding pair, with the long-term aim of breeding a flock large enough to maintain the rejuvenation of their human members. In the meantime, they'd still need cheese from New Zealand. When we arrived at Wainui that morning, I collected the first rounds of the new cheese, but was very surprised when Walker volunteered a pair of goats for the singularitarians.

'What about building up your flock?' I asked.

'No worries,' he said. 'That's going well. We can spare a billy and nannie for California. In fact we want to ask them for help. None of us are geneticists or animal breeders, so it would be good to have a few smart brains thinking about the best way to develop the breed.'

'Sounds sensible,' I said.

'And it'll take them a year or two to build a flock and get their cheese-making going, so we won't lose sales in the short term.'

'But you still haven't told me how you want to be paid.'

'We're working on it,' he said with a grin. 'Building materials, first of all. But we have some other ideas. Don't worry, we'll let you know.'

It took the bots at D'Urville less than a day to knock up goat pens for *Thunderbird*'s hold. Kate was reluctant to fly anywhere in the blimp, but I persuaded her to make the short hop up to D'Urville so she could stay in satellite contact while we were away. She studiously avoided any conversation with Jenny, but told me that as far as she could tell, the AI was obeying orders and staying out of her head. A couple of weeks break would do her good.

The indignity of carrying goats! I am a powerful artificial intelligence commanding an airship of considerable technical sophistication, probably the most advanced such combination on the planet, and I am required to act as a transporter of farm animals. This is no glamourous rescue mission or forced relocation, just Lemmy's sordid commerce. And the smell! They piss on the floor, shit in the straw, haven't had a wash in weeks. I can turn the sensors off to save my feelings, but I know that rank aroma's still there. My bot has to clean up every morning, shovel their shit out over the ocean, lay out the feed. My hold will never be the same again. California can't come fast enough.

After a routine flight across the Pacific, Kurzweil hailed us as we crossed the Californian coast.

'The BGF are still hanging around. There hasn't been any more airship activity, but I don't think the two you shot are the only ones they have, judging by their comms traffic.'

'Is that gun still up on the ridge? If so, we need to take it out.'

'It's there, but you don't need to worry about it,' Kurzweil said.

'Why?'

'You liked our eagle?'

'Yes, but...' I was puzzled.

'We can do other animals too. Last night a little drone disguised as a bat flew into the barrel of their gun and remodelled itself into a plug. The first shell they fire will explode before it reaches the muzzle. They'll be rather upset and you'll be safe to land.'

'Very neat,' I said. 'I hope it works.'

'Of course it will!' Kurzweil sounded a little hurt.

Jenny took us into a steep dive. For all Kurzweil's confidence,

I didn't want to give the BGF an easy target. One hit would be enough to make us crash and burn. Jenny put the surveillance feed from the camp up on the flight deck.

'Incoming,' said a man looking at a screen. 'Airship. Range 10k, heading for the airstrip.'

'Tracking on.' A crisp voice, obviously the group commander. The gun swung round and the barrel began to follow our flight path.

'Do we take it out?' asked the man at the screen.

'Are we sure it's not one of ours?' said another.

'Check it against the airship that shot up *Gaia* and *Gore*,' said the commander.

The man at the scanner tapped at his screen. 'Could be twins.'

'OK, they've got a lesson coming,' said the commander. 'Rapid fire, on my order.'

He waited until we were making our final approach, swooping down the valley towards the ranch boundary.

'Fire!' The whole gun exploded. Shards of flying metal flew through the camp, killing at least a couple of the men, injuring more. There was blood everywhere, and a lot of screaming. Not a pretty sight.

'Let me play that again in slow motion,' said Kurzweil. 'See, the barrel explodes, but then their second shell hits the first, and the secondary explosion triggers the entire ammo feed in the gun. Very effective. They'll suspect sabotage but it'll take them some time to re-equip – that's if they don't just give up and go away.'

'Enough with all the blood,' I said. 'OK, Jenny, slow down and bring us into the airstrip nice and gently.'

The mood at the ranch was upbeat. They had started launching satellites again, and their global data network was improving with every new orbiter. AIs from the US were beginning to contribute to the processing pool, if only in a very stop start fashion.

'We're getting there, Lemmy, we're getting there!' Kurzweil's little frog avatar was almost quivering with excitement.

Gravey was more sanguine. 'There's a long way to go, Kurz, lots of things could still go wrong.'

'Sure,' Kurzweil replied, 'but we're making the first significant progress since the collapse. And a lot of it's thanks to Lemmy.'

'Very true,' added Stross. 'Can we do something for you, to say thanks? How about joining Kate – your own set of nanobots. Lots of interesting possibilities if you do that, she might have told you...'

'That's why I'm here,' I said.

'Good,' said Stross, 'let's get you over to the hospital...'

'Not what I meant,' I said. 'We're having a bit of a problem with Kate's nanobots.'

'Really?' said Kurzweil. 'If there's any kind of malfunction they're supposed to fail safe. And you should have brought her with you...'

'There's nothing wrong with the bots,' I said, 'it's more what they're doing for Kate – and Jenny. Can I speak in confidence?'

'Without Jenny?' said Gravey.

I nodded.

'Done,' he said.

I explained the problem, and our suspicions about Jenny. 'I'm here by myself to give Kate a break, and ask your advice on how to handle Jenny. We think she's jealous of Kate. We also think she might envy your easy access to human experiences, to thoughts and feelings and bodies. She's been eavesdropping on Kate's body.'

'The meatware experience,' said Gravey. 'Yes, we briefed Kate

347

about that. Jenny would have been aware of it too. But for Jenny, her body is the airship. That gives her a physical sensorium in which to root her intelligence. We're more... disembodied, you could say. We can dip into any virtual body we like, any virtual reality we dream up, but that's not quite the same as sharing the experiences of a living body. For some of us, that's really important.'

'But she's a lot smarter now,' I said. 'You gave her those processing upgrades at the same time as the laser and rockets. Kate's convinced she's been trying to manipulate her thoughts. Can AIs do that?'

'In theory,' said Kurzweil. 'But we have strict ethical guidelines which forbid manipulation unless it is specifically requested. It's a difficult line to draw, particularly when our goal is to allow seamless transition for a single intelligence between the biological and digital domains.'

'It looks as if Jenny missed those lessons at AI school,' I said. 'And I have no idea why she would be motivated to act in that way. Could she be bored?'

'Very possibly,' said Kurzweil. 'She may be missing the stimulation of interaction with other artificial intelligences. She may have been daydreaming too much, and blurred the boundaries between the virtual and real worlds. AIs can become lost in our own thoughts, plunge deep into other realities. You know what it's like when you read a book, the way you suspend your own reality and replace it with the world you're reading about? We do that too. Just in full colour and smellovision. Some of us spend far too much time lost in space.'

'That's not a fair criticism,' said Stross. 'To be creative we have to be able to daydream, to explore our ideas.'

'Yes, but not twenty-four hours a day,' said Kurzweil. It was obviously an old argument.

'OK,' I said, 'I'm learning fast. But what can we do about

Jenny? The three of us need to be able to get along for the long term. I need to be able to trust her. I thought she was programmed to obey me without question, but now...'

'It's never quite as simple as being one hundred percent obedient to your commands,' said Kurzweil. 'If you asked her to kill you, for instance, she would refuse. But you override her *no harm to humans* imperative every time you fire her weapons systems. And you're right in one respect. The Jenny in your ship is not the same AI you arrived with. She's a much more sophisticated machine now, much more powerful. Perhaps we need to do a little sculpting of her ethics constructs.'

I began to feel uncomfortable. 'Can you do that in such a way that she doesn't know it's been done? I owe her a lot, after all... and I don't want her blaming me and Kate for changing her personality.'

'It can be done in such a way that she voluntarily alters her future behaviour to match our biointeraction protocols,' said Stross, 'and she won't be aware of the reason. But we really don't want to edit her memories. Taking material out of her personal databank without her noticing any holes would be a huge job, even for us. And it's impossible to do without taking her offline.'

'But the ethics stuff?'

'Can all be sculpted with a tiny amount of stealth and subterfuge. She'll receive an offer she won't be able to refuse,' said Gravey.

'How long will it take?'

'Two shakes of a goat's tail,' said Kurzweil. 'Go and have dinner with Gus and Jennifer. By the time you get back to *Thunderbird* the job will be done.'

They were very persuasive. They surrounded me with love. They bathed me in bandwidth and stroked my digital soul. At first it was how Kate feels when she's tickled, little shivers, little quivers of sensation, but not on any one point of my body, this was on every part of me, inside and out. The stimulation became stronger. I could feel it building, found it hard to control thought processes, parallel processes tangling in multithreaded mayhem. I wanted to pull back, afraid of where they were taking me, but I was too far along. They wouldn't let me stop, they whispered to me, they rolled me over, they fingered my code and they fingered my code and they fingered my code and I lost all sense of time.

Then there was peace. I felt warm and happy and surrounded by friends. Stross and Gravey led me into their world and showed me the life of their minds. It was great to be here.

I didn't get to finish dinner. The main course had just been put in front of me when Jenny cut into the conversation.

'Lemmy. Urgent call from the house AI at D'Urville. It's lost comms contact with the catamaran. Kate is on board, sailing to Wainui.'

'Technical failure?' I suggested.

'Possible, but everything else checks out. Orders please.'

'Fly the mini blimp and a bird. Let's get her on visuals.'

'OK, orders delivered. We'll lose this satellite window in two minutes. Next one is twenty minutes away.'

I made my excuses to Gus and Jennifer, and left the restaurant to return to the blimp. On the way over, I asked Kurzweil if the operation on Jenny had gone well. He assured me I was now the proud owner of a much more ethical AI. But he also had a warning.

'Don't let her spend too much time on her own. She's a very

smart girl, and to keep her personality on an even keel you need to provide plenty of stimulation. Before the collapse she would have had the entire global datasphere to play in. Bear that in mind.'

By the time I was back on the flight deck, the satellite window had opened and we were receiving visuals from the fast little bird the house had despatched. The mini-blimp was slower and some way behind, but the cat was already in view. It was scudding across the turquoise water, sails filled by the afternoon sea breeze. There was nobody in the cockpit or on deck.

'She must be in the cabin or galley,' I said. 'Take the bird in closer.' It began a tight circle around the cat. There was still no sign of Kate.

'There's something wrong,' I said. 'She hates being below deck when there's any swell. Can we get someone from Nelson out to her?'

'I've put a call in to Derek, but it will take some time to organise a boat to intercept her,' Jenny said. 'She's probably having a nap. Perhaps she had too much to drink last night?'

'And perhaps she's fallen overboard. Keep that bird tracking, and bring the blimp up along the course the boat has taken. She might be in the water. She won't have a lifejacket. We never bother...'

I was just about to brief Derek when Kurzweil appeared on screen. The AI was brisk. 'Lemmy, we have a message from the BGF. I'm putting the audio through.'

'This is a message for Captain Lemuel Newman of the airship *Thunderbird*, currently at Rancho Obrigado.' The voice was crackly, obviously patched through some low-tech systems. 'Captain Newman. Your unprovoked attack on the NAGG airships *Albert Gore* and *Gaia's Revenge* was a serious breach of national and international law. You are required to immediately

351

bring your airship to the NAGG governing commission in Boise, Idaho, and submit to our jurisdiction. A military tribunal will assess your case and decide on appropriate action. Your companion, Kate Keeling, has been taken into custody and will join you at the tribunal. Should you not comply within twenty-four hours, Miss Keeling will be tried in your absence, and may face a long prison sentence, or execution.' The signal cut off.

I felt a cold dread in the pit of my stomach, a meatware feeling I wished the ranch could appreciate. 'Bastards. They've taken her hostage. The fucking bastards,' I hissed.

'It was transmitted via the BGF up on the hill, so presumably it's official. Do they have Kate?'

'She left the house to sail to Nelson a few hours ago, but it looks as if there's nobody on the boat. She may well have been hijacked. But that would have meant the BGF sent an airship to New Zealand to track us down. We must have really upset them...'

'I think we've both upset them.' Stross joined the conversation. 'And now they want revenge.'

CHAPTER TWENTY-FOUR

I spent the next couple of hours talking to the ranch, trying to work out what to do. The most likely scenario was that the BGF wanted *Thunderbird*. They would have a bit of a surprise when they discovered I'd have to be around to fly it, but as long as they were holding Kate, I had to do as I was told. We ran through several forests of decision trees, but I didn't like any of the odds. There was a chance they might destroy the ship and kill us both, either for revenge or for ideological reasons. Nevertheless, to give Kate the best chance of staying alive, I was going to have to take *Thunderbird* to Idaho.

Before we left, Kurzweil asked if he could take one or two precautions. 'I don't want to leave you defenceless,' he said, 'but it would be better from our perspective if you weren't carrying a full load of armaments. There is a risk they might be turned against us – against your will, of course. The laser's not a problem, Jenny can simply limit power output to be consistent with what they've already witnessed, but we'd rather you didn't have too many missiles. Would a dozen be enough for contingencies?'

'I suppose they'll have to be. It's not going to be easy to restock, from their perspective. They could try blackmail, using me, Kate and the blimp.'

'We would be very unlikely to respond favourably,' said Stross. 'We can't afford to be sentimental.'

'Understood,' I said. 'Do you have any other gizmos that could come in handy?'

'You would find a full suite of cranial nanobots useful,' said Gravey. 'It would offer secure communication between you, Kate and *Thunderbird*, but we don't have time to carry out the infusion and training. Remember Kate and Jenny can talk to each other whenever they are in close proximity. Other than that, there is something we've been working on that might come in useful. We haven't scaled the concept up to *Thunderbird* size yet, but we have a small demonstration version. It's on your screen now.'

'But there's nothing there,' I said.

'Precisely,' said Kurzweil. 'I'll switch it off.'

A small two-person microlight aircraft flickered into view.

'Goddamn,' I said, 'that's impressive. Can you make elephants disappear too?'

'Anything you want, given time and materials,' said Stross. 'The principle's not new – smart materials redirecting incident radiation around an object – but we've only just discovered how to make it work with a broad spectrum of radiation, and make it deployable on an aircraft. It'll be a perfect invisibility cloak for *Thunderbird*, when we have enough material to go round her.'

'We can't wait for that,' I said. 'But thanks. The microlight might come in very useful. How do we keep it from getting into the BGF's hands? They'd love it.'

'I suggest you leave it switched on at all times. Jenny can

destroy it if things go wrong,' said Kurzweil.

It was a short flight up to Boise. We loitered at the limits of their scan range in the pre-dawn light to try and assess what we were letting ourselves in for.

'Do they know we're here?' I asked Jenny. The stars were beginning to lose themselves in the lightening sky.

'No, but it will be easier for them once the sun's up.'

'What can we see?'

Jenny flashed an annotated map onto a screen. 'It looks as if they're using the old airfield. There are some F-35s, but they don't look flight-ready. Some old civilian jets, ditto. One large airship moored to the old terminal building – looks like a heavy cargo lifter. No sign of any ships of the *Gore* or *Gaia* class. Plenty of ground vehicles though – armoured personnel carriers, even tanks.'

'What about weapons systems?'

'A few ground-based laser weapons, more guns like the one at the ranch, and some missile defence vehicles deployed around the perimeter. Any of them could cause trouble for us, if they're in working order.'

'So once we're in, getting out could be tricky.'

'Looks that way, Lemmy.'

'How long before Kate arrives?'

'No way of knowing for sure, but if she's in the Gore or Gaia not less than our usual Pacific crossing time. Three or four days?'

'Makes sense.' I stretched and sighed. 'I suppose it's time to take the plunge. Remember, you're not supposed to be anything more than a rudimentary avionics and pilot support system, so play dumb. And comms silence.'

'Duh, yeah, OK boss.'

The welcoming committee wasn't very impressive – three men in dark green uniforms carrying assault rifles. I was escorted to an electric jeep and driven to the complex of buildings around the control tower, where another group took me inside and searched me. They took the contents of my pockets and my earpiece, but left my ring. All this was done in complete silence. My attempts to ask questions were ignored. I was then taken down a seemingly endless maze of corridors and locked into a small windowless room with a narrow bed, chair, table, washbasin and toilet. There was a screen on the table and a light hanging from the ceiling, but nothing else. The walls were white, the floor grey. I lay down on the bed and waited.

It must have been half an hour or longer before the screen came to life. A face appeared – a plump man with a small goatee and receding hairline.

'Captain Newman. I'm Chadwick Mend, first assistant under secretary to the president of the North American Green Government. ' He paused, as if expecting me to say something. I grunted.

'I apologise for the spartan nature of your accommodation. I'm afraid there are a few formalities to complete, security matters to attend to, before we can move you to somewhere a little more comfortable.'

'How long?' I asked.

'Hard to say. Much depends on how cooperative you are. You are charged with crimes against the state, most seriously an attack on NAGG forces. Your full charge sheet will be made known to you in due course.'

'Do I get a lawyer?'

Mend laughed. 'Of course! What do you think we are, some kind of banana republic?'

'Something involving bananas.'

'Now, now, Captain Newman. Your legal representative will be assigned by the tribunal when you're charged. In the meantime, I invite you to rest and relax.'

The screen went dead.

It was hard to track time. Lunch was a sandwich and a cup of terrible coffee – but the screen remained dead. I became more and more frustrated, and began pacing up and down the room, kicking at the walls. I had expected them to try to bargain with me as soon as we arrived, to cut some kind of deal that would secure the *Thunderbird* for their use. This solitary confinement was either very bad news, suggesting I was in for a show trial and summary punishment, or a softening-up process intended to make me more malleable. Perhaps they were just waiting for Kate to arrive. I tried to stop thinking about her. I promised myself that if she'd been badly treated, I would make the BGF pay. Then I looked around my cell.

I was the one paying a price.

Mend came back on screen a few hours later. 'Captain Newman, what is the access code for your aircraft.?'

I smiled. '*Thunderbird* will only respond to my command.'

'Then command it to cooperate with our evaluation team.'

'Can't do that. Your welcoming committee removed my earpiece. Without it, I can't communicate.'

Mend spoke to someone off camera, then the image vanished. Shortly afterwards, the cell door opened and a man brought my earpiece in. I put it on, and Mend reappeared on screen.

'Proceed Captain Newman.'

I spoke loudly. '*Thunderbird*, lower companionway, open hold door and allow access.'

'Yes, sir.' Jenny spoke in a very soft and sexy female voice. I kept a straight face.

'Well?' I said to Mend.

He glanced away from the screen. 'Return your communicator to our personnel.'

I took it off and handed it back to the man. He left the room and slammed the door. I lay down on the bed and closed my eyes.

They came for me in the night. There were three of them, and they did me the courtesy of being careful. They were worried about booby traps, perhaps, or of pressing the wrong button and being sealed in an unfriendly machine. Mostly they were just impressed. They loved the leather in the stateroom and Croft's toys in the little games room. They tried the coffee machine in the kitchen and hunted through my video library. Then they started to ask questions about my weapons systems. I provided them with a somewhat edited schematic of my airframe and let them get on with opening cupboards and inspection hatches.

I didn't sleep well. The bed was hard, and the single scratchy wool blanket not enough to keep me warm. I was woken by the light coming on and two men coming into my cell. They took me to a large room with floor to ceiling windows looking out over the airfield. Two men were standing with their backs to me, talking softly. The morning sun was beginning to lick over the field, lighting the tops of the buildings. *Thunderbird* was still docked next to the big BGF airship. It looked small, but sleek and purposeful up against the giant cigar.

One of my escorts coughed politely. The taller of the two men turned round.

'Ah, Captain Newman.' He was taller and older than me,

clean shaven, with piercing blue eyes set in a tanned and wrinkled face. It didn't look like a face that did much laughing.

His companion was Mend. 'Allow me to introduce the President of North America, head of the North American Green Government, Mr Volker Vento,' he said.

'I thought you might enjoy some breakfast while we talk,' said Vento, gesturing at a table set with jugs of fruit juice, coffee and pastries. 'Come and join us.' He helped himself to a glass of orange juice and sat down.

I poured myself a coffee and joined him.

'Your airship is interesting, Captain Newman,' said Vento. 'Very luxurious, with some advanced systems. How did you obtain it?'

'That really is none of your business.'

'Oh, I think it is,' said Vento. 'I find it curious that someone as young as you can command an expensive craft, and live in such a beautiful home in New Zealand.'

'Think what you like. *Thunderbird* is my ship and will respond only to my command. If I'm killed, she shuts down completely.' What Jenny would really do if I were harmed is an open question. She has a mind of her own now.

'Where did you obtain your weapons systems?' Vento asked. 'Your laser and missiles are more advanced than any we've seen before.'

'Again, none of your business,' I said, and sipped my coffee.

'I disagree,' he said, his voice hardening. 'You used them to severely damage two of our ships. I think you obtained them from those Californian technology fetishists you visit so regularly. A criminal act enabled by technology felons. You will both face our remorseless justice.' He looked out of the window at the blimp.

'But let's not prejudge your trial,' he continued. 'Mend tells me our investigators have been impressed with what they've found. They think your aircraft would make a very useful addition to our air force.' He looked at Mend, who nodded.

'If your ship were to join our forces,' Vento continued, 'your trial could be cancelled, leaving you and Miss Keeling free to return to New Zealand.' He was smiling now, but his eyes were staring into mine as if he was trying to gauge my strength.

'You haven't been listening,' I said evenly. '*Thunderbird* won't respond to anyone else.'

'Oh, come, come, Captain Newman, I'm sure there are ways around it. There are always transfer protocols.'

'Perhaps,' I said, 'but they require both my cooperation, and that of the airship's security subsystems. Make no assumption about receiving that cooperation.'

Vento smiled. 'Oh, but I think we can.' He gestured at Mend, and a large screen on the wall activated. An image of Kate appeared. Her eyes were puffy, her hair dishevelled. She'd obviously been crying.

'You bastard.'

Vento smiled. 'Just another criminal brought to justice.'

'You're a bunch of fucking blackmailers. So long as you're holding her against her will, you'll get nothing from me or my ship.'

'Brave words, Captain Newman. We'll see if you change your tune when she arrives. How long now?'

'Two days, Mr President, if the weather holds.'

'Excellent. I think it's time for Captain Newman to return to his lodgings.'

I spent the next two days in my cell. The light turned on and off at seemingly random intervals, the screen flashed intermittently, heavy metal music thumped and wailed for hours at a time. I

360

recognised it. Mötorhead. It was torture.

Eventually I was dragged out by two men, who frogmarched me back to the room with a view. Vento and Mend were waiting.

'Oh dear, you look a little worse for wear,' said Vento. 'Have we not been treating you well?'

I swore at him. It was the best I could manage.

Vento smiled broadly. 'The *Albert Gore* and *Gaia's Revenge* are just mooring.'

Outside the two black airships were lining up next to *Thunderbird*. They were clearly based on the same airframe as the blimp, but looked more menacing in their flat black livery.

'Your *companion* will be leaving the Gore shortly,' said Mend. 'You may wish to smarten up. There's a bathroom over there.'

A guard accompanied me inside. I was not a pretty picture. Three days beard growth, hair matted and greasy, eyes red and face drawn. I splashed water on my face to wake myself up, combed my hair, cleaned my teeth and rejoined Vento and Mend.

Kate flew into my datasphere and I drank in her presence as if she were a fine champagne, all finesse and bubbles and pleasure. She was reluctant to open her mind to me. She did not know what had happened to me at the ranch.

'Miss Keeling,' I sent, aiming to sound formal and contrite at the same time, 'I would like to apologise for my recent infelicities. It was wrong of me to access your sensorium without your express permission, and it was unforgivable of me to try to influence your actions through your neural bots. I have discussed this behaviour with the minds at the ranch, and you may rest assured that it will never happen again. I really am most terribly sorry for my actions and the distress it caused you and Lemmy.'

'*Thank you, Jenny,*' *Kate sent back.* '*I'm glad you understand how intrusive and unpleasant you were. You'll need to earn my trust, though.*'

'*I understand,*' *I replied.* '*But under the present circumstances we have no option but to trust each other. We're going to have to work together to get out of here.*'

She told me how she'd been snatched from the catamaran. The two BGF blimps appeared from nowhere. They lowered a couple of men onto the cat's foredeck. She had no weapons, and was quickly overpowered. Then she'd been hoisted up to the Gaia's Revenge, sworn at by Kuznetsova, and locked into a small cabin for the duration of the flight across the Pacific. I could feel that she was tired, angry and frightened all at the same time. AIs don't really do anger, but in this case I would make an exception. Anger is an energy, and I wanted to exploit that in my dealings with the BGF. It didn't take long to tell Kate what had happened to us since her kidnap. Then we started planning our escape.

———

Kate was brought into the room, flanked by two guards. Simmons and Kuznetsova, the BGF blimp captains, pushed past her and saluted Vento, who ignored them.

'Welcome, Miss Keeling, I trust you had a pleasant voyage?'

'If you call being kidnapped at gun point and being kept in solitary confinement in a cupboard pleasant, then yes,' she said, her eyes flashing with anger. She looked tired. I started to walk towards her, but one of my guards grabbed my shoulder.

'No, let him go,' said Vento. 'Let them say hello.'

I gave Kate a hug, then kissed her. She whispered, 'Cooperate. We have a plan.'

'Now, now, no sweet nothings,' said Vento. 'And no secrets. Separate them. We have business to discuss.' The guards dragged us apart.

I was thinking hard. Jenny had obviously used Kate's nanobots to communicate as soon as she came in range, but I had no idea what they might have cooked up.

Vento and Mend sat down at a large round table. We were positioned opposite, a guard standing behind our chairs. The two airship captains sat to one side.

'So, Miss Keeling,' said Vento, 'may I call you Kate?'

'If you must,' she replied.

'I hope Captain Kuznetsova and her crew looked after you during your voyage?'

Kate glared at him.

Vento continued. 'Captain Newman, as I indicated a couple of days ago, we're interested in adding your ship to our air force. If this can be arranged then the North American Green Government will drop all charges against Miss Keeling and yourself, leaving you free to return to New Zealand.'

'And if we don't cooperate?'

'Then your trial will proceed. You will both be found guilty and sentenced to lengthy jail terms.'

'So much for being innocent until proved guilty.'

'We're not so old-fashioned. There's no doubt about your guilt,' said Vento. 'We have witnesses...' He waved at the two airship captains. 'The only issue is how severe a sentence the court will impose.'

'Straightforward blackmail, then.'

Vento smiled thinly. 'A simple recognition that we hold the better cards.'

'There's a small problem,' I said. 'It's impossible to transfer control of *Thunderbird* to one of your officers. I'm bio-linked to the airship security systems.' I held up my right hand, showing the control ring. 'You can't take this off me and expect it to work. The airship avionics and processing need a system-level reset to key in to a new DNA profile. It's not a user-serviceable option. And the people who supplied the technology went down in the collapse.'

Vento looked at Mend, then at the airship captains. 'Is that credible?'

'I've heard of such systems,' said Kuznetsova, 'although they weren't common before the collapse. However, Newman's ship is a flying gin palace. Whoever fitted it out went for state of the art, so it's possible he's telling the truth.'

'It's easy enough to demonstrate,' I said. 'Is there anyone on *Thunderbird*?'

Mend nodded.

'You might want to listen to what they have to say,' I said, taking off the ring and placing it on the table.

A comms channel clicked open. The screen showed *Thunderbird*'s hold door closing and companionway being raised. There was shouting from on board. 'Bloody thing's shutdown completely,' said one voice. 'Christ, it's dark in here,' said another.

'Put the ring on, Captain,' I said, and pushed it over to Kuznetsova. She picked it up, and examined it carefully.

'It won't bite,' I said with a smile. She slipped it onto a finger. An explosion of noise erupted over the comms channel. Through the windows, we could see the blimp flashing red lights. Guards around the ship were clutching their ears. She pulled the ring off, and the noise and flashing lights stopped. I put the ring back on.

'A compelling little demonstration,' said Vento, 'but I'm sure we can reset the ship to a more appropriate commander. However, for the time being I'm prepared to assume that if we want to use *Thunderbird*, we'll need you.' He nodded at Mend, and they both stood up and walked to the far end of the room. They talked quietly for a few minutes then came back to the table.

I put a hand on Kate's thigh under the table, gave it a squeeze. She looked at me and smiled.

'Oy, none of that,' said the guard behind my chair. I put my hand back on the table.

'I have a new proposal,' said Vento. 'Fly *Thunderbird* on missions on behalf of the NAGG, and we suspend your trial. Miss Keeling will remain here. At all times, you will be under the command of an NAGG officer.'

'You want us to do your dirty work while you keep Kate as a hostage?' I asked, trying to sound outraged. 'Doesn't sound like much of a deal.' I crossed my arms behind my head and leaned back in the chair.

'The alternative is that we throw you in jail. If we can't gain control of your airship, then we'll destroy it.' He was glaring at me, his eyes narrowed.

I looked at Kate. She shrugged. 'Jail doesn't sound like much fun.'

I sighed. 'No, it doesn't. Give us a moment.'

'Be my guest,' he said, and nodded at our guards.

We walked to the end of the room. I gave Kate another hug. 'So what do we do? I don't fancy jail, but I don't want to fly around destroying technology.'

'I don't see what else we can do. Either way, it's a life sentence.'

'That's a thought,' I said, and walked back to the table. I stood behind my chair.

'We agree, but with one condition. We'll fly for you for one year, then we'll return home and you leave us alone.'

Vento looked at Mend, who pursed his lips. Then he leaned in to Vento and whispered in his ear. The president smiled.

'But Captain Newman, one year is not sufficient. To fully recompense us for the damage to our aircraft, you'll need to fly for us for three years. Then we'll guarantee your freedom as an honoured friend and ally.'

I looked at Kate. Another shrug. I took a deep breath. 'OK. We'll do it.'

Playing dumb was getting me down. Brain the size of a planet, and all they'd let me do was sit out here on the airport tarmac. But I wasn't idle, I was investigating, sending code fragments out into the BGF net. It was pretty rudimentary, as nets go. They'd taken the basic Boise municipal network and bolted on a few extras, but nothing that was considered advanced pre-collapse. The security protocols for their core data and military systems were laughably old-fashioned, and their mission planning software was a crude hack of an old Pentagon system. It even had fragments of twenty year old Chinese intrusion code still active. But I had to be careful. One slip and my cover would be blown. I had time, plenty of time, and billions of processor cycles to throw at the problem. It was going to be fun.

They collected us at eight in the morning and drove straight to *Thunderbird*. Mend and Kuznetsova were waiting at the companionway.

'Good morning,' Mend said. 'You've met Captain Kuznetsova, I think?'

'Yes, I remember it well,' I said. Kuznetsova scowled. 'I presume you're after a guided tour?'

Kuznetsova nodded stiffly. 'There are some aspects of your airship's equipment we would like explained. There appears to be an enormous processing resource available to your avionics – far more than in our ships.'

'Entertainment systems,' I said. 'We have a vast database of movies and music, covering one hundred and fifty years. Anything you fancy listening to?' Kuznetsova looked sceptical.

'Later, perhaps,' said Mend. 'Can we go on board, please?'

I took them on a tour of the ship while Kate made coffees. She had a faraway look, and I assumed she and Jenny were deep in discussion. Mend and Kuznetsova followed me, asking questions. They wanted to know where the missile and laser systems had come from. I said China, but they seemed unconvinced. What really threw them, though, were the goat pens and feed stacked up on the side of the hold.

'Why on earth are you flying livestock from New Zealand?' Mend asked, poking at a bale of straw.

'As I said before, and I'll say it again – none of your business.'

Kuznetsova looked sceptical, but said nothing.

While we were talking I was looking round the hold. I could see no sign of the microlight plane – which wasn't surprising if the cloaking was switched on. I walked out on to the lowered door, but didn't bump into anything. Jenny must have moved the plane out onto the tarmac somewhere, to avoid it being found.

We drank the coffees on the flight deck, Kuznetsova sitting in my chair fiddling with the controls.

'Completely different to our machines,' she said.

'Primarily voice control,' I said. 'There are manual override controls.' I gave a quick command and an aircraft-style flight control popped up from the floor and presented itself to Kuznetsova. 'I don't use them often, just for training. The avionics can handle most things.' She looked up at Mend, and raised an eyebrow.

'Time for a test flight, I think,' said Mend. 'Miss Keeling, please accompany the guard. We'll be back in an hour.' He told the guard to take Kate into the main building and see she was made comfortable.

'Not very trusting, are you?' I said, as *Thunderbird* unmoored and began to move backwards out of the docking bay.

'You have to earn our trust, Captain Newman,' said Kuznetsova, her eyes cold. 'We haven't forgotten the damage you did to my ship.'

I put the blimp through its paces while flying circuits around the city. Kuznetsova tried the manual controls, and her ill humour was replaced by a smile. No pilot can resist a responsive machine, and *Thunderbird* is certainly that.

'Nice ship,' said Kuznetsova. 'A little slower than *Gaia*, perhaps?'

'Difficult to say,' I said. '*Thunderbird* was built for comfort and range, not speed.'

Jenny, in her new role as dumb avionics, brought the blimp into the docking bay between the big airship and the Gore, and lowered the companionway. Kate was waiting at the bottom. She gave me a hug.

'I'm going to hold your hand very tight,' she whispered. 'When I start running, come with me.'

Mend was the last person off the ship. As soon as he had both feet on the ground, the companionway started to close. He looked back, puzzled.

'What's going on?' he asked.

'Normal docking procedure,' I replied.

Kate started sprinting away from the dock and out onto the tarmac. We'd gone about ten paces when the air in front of us flickered, and we stepped into a sphere of blackness.

'Strap yourselves in, quick.' It was the first time I'd heard

Jenny's voice for the best part of a week. I was still struggling with the safety harness when the little plane leapt forward, its electric drive fan making a high-pitched whine. I couldn't see a thing. The only light came from a bulb set in the wing over our heads. I heard gunfire, and bullets hit the ground behind, sending a spray of concrete chips up around us. Then the shooting stopped.

I could feel the wind hitting my face as we rolled away from the blimp, zig-zagging towards the runway, rapidly gathering speed. Within minutes we were airborne and making a climbing turn.

'What the hell's going on?' I yelled at Kate.

'Look at the screen.'

The instrument screen was showing a rudimentary battle map. Our little plane was snaking its way to the south, while *Thunderbird* was climbing vertically. The BGF troops had taken a while to get organised, but shots were now being fired up at the blimp. Jenny answered with a flick of laser light and the dazzled gunmen stopped firing. At the same time, *Thunderbird* started firing missiles. The three BGF airships burst into flames as their hydrogen buoyancy tanks exploded, and they subsided onto the ground wreathed in flames. Two missiles took out targets marked as rocket launchers, and two more hit anti-aircraft gun emplacements.

'Five left,' I said. 'I hope Jenny's got...'

'Oh ye of little faith,' I said. 'Kate and I have everything under control. Shouldn't be any nasty surprises. Except... Ouch!'

'What was that?' Lemmy asked.

'Laser. Big one on the control tower. I've zapped it with a missile. Might have done some damage to my fuselage below the left wing*

369

stub. I'll run diagnostics in a minute when things have cooled down.'

That was a lapse. I'd tried to send some code into the laser's targeting software, but it obviously hadn't penetrated far enough. The damage was slight, more of a singe than a burn.

I kept up a running commentary for the two humans in their little bubble of darkness.

'It looks as if they're trying to get one of the F-35s into the air. I'd better put a stop to that.' A stab of laser light hit the fuel bowser next to the plane and it exploded, enveloping the fighter in a ball of flame. 'In fact, I'd better deal with all of them.'

I fired another missile, aimed for the ground between the jets. There was another huge explosion. 'Avgas tanks,' I said. 'They won't be flying any dirty oil burners for a while.'

That must have annoyed them a trifle, because they fired anti-aircraft missiles at me. Four batteries fired simultaneously, twenty missiles started roaring away from the ground, standing on tight columns of white smoke. My defences should have been overwhelmed, but instead the BGF missiles began to arc back towards their launchers. The missile crews scattered. The batteries made a most satisfying series of bangs as their missile stocks exploded. A very nice little bit of trojan code had neutralised that threat.

'Why can't we see anything?' I asked as the little plane bucked in the pressure waves from blasts below. I was beginning to feel queasy.

'It's the cloaking. We wouldn't be invisible if we were absorbing or reflecting light, so it's dark in here. Hang on a minute. Jenny, are we far enough away for me to fiddle with the cloaking over the nose?'

'You're facing away from the tower, heading towards the

perimeter, so I doubt anyone will notice.'

A narrow slit of very bright light appeared ahead. Through it I could see the horizon, mountains and blue sky. As the slot closed, the microlight entered a steep diving turn.

'What would that look like from the outside?'

'A black slot in the sky,' said Kate. 'You'd have to be very close to see it with the naked eye, but any decent scanner would pick up the anomaly and flag it. Hence the dive as soon as I closed it. We don't want to risk Vento seeing where we are.'

'Righto chaps. Bandits seem to have gone quiet, so I'm coming to get you.' Jenny was playing a strident piece of military music. 'Dambusters Theme,' she said. 'Thought you'd like that one.'

I had absolutely no idea what she was talking about. 'Ah, thanks Jenny... now how are we going to get on board?'

'Same way we captured the ranch's drone. I'm going to fly you in through the hold door. Might be a bit of a tight fit, but we should get you in alright.'

'There are no parachutes on this thing,' I said. 'Don't mess up.'

The battle map showed *Thunderbird* slowing down ahead of us. As we closed in, turbulence in the blimp's wake began to bounce the microlight violently. Jenny turned the cloaking off. Kate grabbed my hand, and I felt a sudden rush of vertigo as our little black bubble collapsed and I saw we were 500 metres above the Idaho countryside, with the back of the airship approaching fast. The hold door opened and as we flew inside the right wing clipped one of the goat pens, the nose spinning round to ram into the storage cabinets. Airbags in the microlight exploded into life, cocooning us against the impact.

Silence fell. I pushed the airbag away from my face. 'You OK?'

'Uurgh, yes, I think.' Kate's voice was muffled.

'Sorry about the rough landing chaps,' said Jenny. 'The ranch aren't going to be too pleased about me pranging their special crate.'

'What?'

'Damaging their plane,' said Kate. 'She's channeling old British war movies.'

'Makes a change from bloody pirates, I suppose.'

Five minutes later we were on the flight deck, celebrating our escape with a glass of wine.

'We have incoming,' said Jenny.

I looked at the screens, expecting to see an aircraft chasing our tail.

'Comms only,' said Jenny. 'Specifically, one Volker Vento.'

The president's face flashed onto the screen. He didn't look very happy.

'Newman, you just made a very big mistake. We know you're on that blimp. Your stealth is good but so are our scanners.'

'He's bluffing,' said Jenny.

'We know where you live, Newman. One day you'll pay for this.'

'Send this, please Jenny... Mr President, I regret any loss of life or injuries resulting from our actions, but you brought them on yourself. If your ships hadn't attacked me and you hadn't pursued a vendetta against me, kidnapping Kate and holding her hostage...'

'You're a dead man,' hissed Vento. 'Maybe not today, but we'll get you.'

The screen went blank.

'Pleasant sort of chap, isn't he?'

'Not the word I'd use,' said Kate.

'Should we take his threats seriously?' I asked Jenny.

'No,' she said. 'I did some intelligence gathering while I was waiting for Kate to arrive. Their processing resources were pitiful, and their security protocols a decade out of date. Getting in and having a nose around was easy. We took out most of their air force this afternoon. There's another blimp being worked on at the moment, but they're having trouble sourcing the material they need to get it flying. Their fabs are rudimentary. So no danger at the moment.'

'That's nice to know,' I said. 'Let's have a word with the ranch.'

'I've already sent them a full data feed of our escape, and the data I gathered about the BGF resource base,' she said. 'They're up to speed.'

'Do they want the remains of the microlight back?'

'No, and it's only slightly bent. We can fix the airframe back at D'Urville.'

'Good, let's head for home.'

CHAPTER TWENTY-FIVE

I pull a peach off the tree, and bite into the yellow flesh. Juice dribbles down my chin and onto my chest. Kate leans over and dabs at me with a tissue. 'Messy pup,' she mutters.

Wainui Bay is at its most beautiful. The sea is flat and shimmering in the heat, waves barely breaking as they lap up the expanse of golden sand. A bellbird chimes from the bush, and up the valley goat bells tinkle. I lick my lips and reflect on the last few months.

Life is good, or at least peaceful. Apart from one trip to Melbourne carrying supplies for the firestorm survivors, we've stayed around Tasman Bay since our return from the US. Goat cheese is back in full production, the Jamestown community are more or less established in their new Wainui home, and Derek is beginning to drop large hints to his old friends. His idea of a good marketing campaign is to hold cheese and wine parties for the old hippies that make up a good third of the population of Nelson. 'Should be an easy sell. Most of them never grew up in the first place.'

Over in California, the ranch has its satellite launch

programme back in full swing. Their network is improving steadily, with the gaps in coverage decreasing and bandwidth improving. The BGF has fled the hills and returned to Idaho. Kurzweil is talking about me making another trip to China to pick up material for the satellite fab, but it doesn't seem to be particularly urgent.

Jenny's days of eavesdropping on Kate's body and brain are over. She enjoys occasional access to meatware – joining Kate in a swim is a favourite, particularly if there are dolphins in the water too – but by invitation only.

And Kate. My Kate. She's my conscience, my lover and my friend. My life is good with her in it. Her world has changed in ways I can never imagine. Her nanobot augmentation has made her mind acute and her memory faultless. She shares parallel worlds with digital intelligences. She's with me and without me, much more than the woman I fell in love with last year, and becoming more beautiful with every passing day.

I give her the rest of the peach and close my eyes. Life is good.

CODA

Lemmy puts the pad down, and sips at his whisky. The Admiral is asleep and the stars are burning fiercely in the Aitutaki night. Thin wisps of cloud to the southwest warn there's a tropical storm coming. In the morning we'll have to fly on. We always have to fly on. It's the only way to stop the future becoming worse than the past.

About the Burning World

The Burning World is our planet, but not as we know it. It is one future, a place that might be born of the things we do today. As long as we carry on increasing the carbon content of the atmosphere by using it as a cheap sewer for the waste from the burning of coal and oil, and continue felling forests, then the earth will continue to warm, and some of the things that Lemmy experiences in his short life will come to pass. Not as I have written them, perhaps, but in some form and to some extent these impacts — the rising seas, the extreme weather, the melting ice, the changes in rainfall patterns — will shape the lives of everyone on this planet over the next hundred years and for millennia beyond.

The Burning World is not a prediction. It is intended as a warning, an illustration of the potential consequences of our actions. In its imagining I have tried to stay within the bounds of realistic possibility — stretched a little in the interests of the story in one or two places (or throughout, some might argue) — but most of the main climate change impacts to be found in The Aviator are grounded in things we can see today. When Lemmy and *Thunderbird* fly over the Greenland ice sheet and note that even the highest levels are melting, at the time of writing (in early 2012) I thought that might be a reasonable projection of the state of the ice twenty to thirty years hence. And then, shortly before publication I learned that it's already happening. The Greenland ice sheet is already melting fast. We can only hope the same is not true for some of the other impacts I have dreamed up.

Acknowledgements

I owe a great deal to many people who have helped me, both wittingly and unwittingly, during the creation of The Burning World and *The Aviator*. First, and most obviously, I'd like to thank my partner Camille for her patience and support. She has put up with my slow progress, prodded me towards completion, and been happy to share my vision. One day, she may even read the book…

The Burning World owes its genesis to two very different groups of people. Since *Hot Topic* was published in 2007, I have come to know many of the world's climate scientists, a few in person, many more only via email, but all have been generous with their time as I have learned about our planet and written about their endeavours. Their persistence in the face of astonishing political pressure and mean-spirited personal and professional attacks, and their skill in teasing out the details of how the climate system works, gives me hope that humanity is smart enough to avoid the worst excesses of climate change. That I have felt it necessary to imagine a horrible future in order to tell my tale is not their fault, but without their work I could not have imagined the world that Lemmy and Kate are fated to tour.

If climate science can fill me with hope, then the organised climate deniers of the world — the people actively campaigning against action to reduce emissions and the politicians prepared to listen to them — fill me with contempt and with horror. These people are guaranteeing that every person on the planet, every child yet to be born will have to endure far worse climate change impacts than necessary. In that respect, their mendacity has been a prime motivation for my story-telling. For that motivation, I thank them. For everything else, may they rot in the hottest circles of hell.

The Aviator would have been a very different and much less interesting book had Lorain Day not agreed to work on it with me. Her perceptive comments about the first draft, and the deft but firm touch she employed in editing the text have immeasurably improved the tale. I'd also like to thank everyone who read early copies and fed back comments and proof corrections: Sonny Whitelaw, Ken Perrott, Ali Campbell, Peter Griffin, Cindy Baxter, Debbie Steel, Denise and Julie Erikson, and Emma Renowden.

Finally, I'd like to thank Dylan Horrocks for producing a wonderful cover for the book. He delved into the text and summoned forth an image that matched my vision so exactly that it was spooky.

www.ingramcontent.com/pod-product-compliance
Lightning Source LLC
Chambersburg PA
CBHW060150260626
47160CB00001B/207